STAGE WOMEN, 1900–50

Manchester University Press

WOMEN, THEATRE AND PERFORMANCE

Series editors
Maggie B. Gale and Kate Dorney

Already published:

Treading the bawds: actresses and playwrights on the late Stuart stage
Gilli Bush-Bailey

Performing herself: Autobiography and Fanny Kelly's Dramatic Recollections
Gilli Bush-Bailey

Plays and performance texts by women 1880–1930: An anthology of plays by British and American women from the Modernist Period
eds Maggie B. Gale and Gilli Bush-Bailey

Auto/biography and identity: women, theatre and performance
eds Maggie B. Gale and Viv Gardner

Women, theatre and performance: new histories, new historiographies
eds Maggie B. Gale and Viv Gardner

Kitty Marion: Actor and activist
eds Viv Gardner and Diane Atkinson

Female performance practice on the fin-de-siècle popular stages of London and Paris: Experiment and advertisement
Catherine Hindson

Stage rights! The Actresses' Franchise League, activism and politics 1908–58
Naomi Paxton

STAGE WOMEN, 1900–50

Female theatre workers and professional practice

EDITED BY MAGGIE B. GALE AND KATE DORNEY

Manchester University Press

Copyright © Manchester University Press 2019

While copyright in the volume as a whole is vested in Manchester University Press, copyright in individual chapters belongs to their respective authors, and no chapter may be reproduced wholly or in part without the express permission in writing of both author and publisher.

Published by Manchester University Press
Altrincham Street, Manchester M1 7JA

www.manchesteruniversitypress.co.uk

British Library Cataloguing-in-Publication Data
A catalogue record for this book is available from the British Library

ISBN 978 1 5261 0070 2 hardback

First published 2019

The publisher has no responsibility for the persistence or accuracy of URLs for any external or third-party internet websites referred to in this book, and does not guarantee that any content on such websites is, or will remain, accurate or appropriate.

Typeset by
Servis Filmsetting Ltd, Stockport, Cheshire

Contents

List of figures	vii
Notes on contributors	x
Series editors' foreword	xiv
Acknowledgements	xv
Introduction Maggie B. Gale and Kate Dorney	1

Part I: Female theatre workers in the social and theatrical realm

1. 'Believe me or not': Actresses, female performers, autobiography and the scripting of professional practice 17
   Maggie B. Gale
2. Female networks: Collecting contacts with Gabrielle Enthoven 42
   Kate Dorney
3. Past the memoir: Winifred Dolan beyond the West End 69
   Lucie Sutherland
4. Offstage labour: Actresses, charity work and the early twentieth-century theatre profession 94
   Catherine Hindson
5. 'Very much alive and kicking': The Actresses' Franchise League from 1914 to 1928 118
   Naomi Paxton
6. Defending the body, defending the self: Women performers and the law in the 'long' Edwardian period 138
   Viv Gardner

Part II: Women and popular performance

7. Emotional and natural: The Australian and New Zealand repertoires and fortunes of North American performers Margaret Anglin, Katherine Grey and Muriel Starr 163
   Veronica Kelly

8	Lily Brayton: A theatre maker in every sense Brian Singleton	191
9	Aerial star: Lillian Leitzel's celebrity, agency and her performed femininity Kate Holmes	216
10	Ellen Terry: The art of performance and her work in film Katharine Cockin	242
11	Mabel Constanduros: Different voices, voicing difference Gilli Bush-Bailey	262
12	The odd woman: Margaret Rutherford John Stokes	286

Index 307

Figures

1. Lillah McCarthy in Izrael Zangwill's *God of War*, 1911. Author's collection. — 27
2. Gladys Cooper in the laboratory finding time to develop a line of beauty products, *The Sketch*, 13 October 1926. Author's collection. — 35
3. Gabrielle Enthoven in fancy dress, date unknown. © Victoria and Albert Museum, London. — 44
4. Gabrielle Enthoven cataloguing playbills, date unknown. © Victoria and Albert Museum, London. — 50
5. The St James's Company at Balmoral, 16 September 1895. © Victoria and Albert Museum, London. — 75
6. An example of the set designs developed by Winifred Dolan, taken from the 'Scene Plots Diagrams' section of the Winifred Dolan Collection. © Victoria and Albert Museum, London. — 85
7. Publicity photograph for the 'Salon of Fragrance and Fair Women', 1911, Luce Company Archive. Courtesy of Jersey Heritage Collections. — 97
8. Photograph of Gertrude Robins, Robins File, Mander and Mitchenson Reference Boxes. Courtesy of University of Bristol Theatre Collection. — 99
9. 'Variety is the Soul of Life: Actress, Playwright, Aviator, Farmer', *Tatler*, January 1915, p. 117. Courtesy of University of Bristol Theatre Collection. — 105
10. 'Haven', poster for the Star and Garter Home and British Women's Hospital Fund, 1915. Author's collection. — 127
11. Marie Studholme and her bewitching smile. Author's collection. — 145
12. Gertie Millar in three pirated postcards by Ralph Dunn. Author's collection. — 146
13. Jane Wood in an advertisement for Sandow Corsets, and arriving at court, 1914. Author's collection. — 150
14. Seymour Hicks and 'his nice wife', Ellaline Terris, in *The Catch of the Season*, 1905; Phyllis Dare in *Cinderella*, 1905. Author's collection. — 153

15 Maud Allan as Salome in the 'Dance of the Seven Veils', and outside the Old Bailey, 1918. Author's collection. 156
16 Margaret Anglin in 1930, at the time of her NBC broadcast of *Iphigenia in Aulis*. Author's collection. 165
17 Katherine Grey, commercial postcard. Author's collection. 169
18 Muriel Starr seeks work in the USA, *Standing Cast Directory*, Hollywood, July 1931. Author's collection. 171
19 Katherine Grey in costume drama, *c.* 1894. Author's collection. 174
20 Grey as Louka in *Arms and the Man* in Chicago, *The Stage*, July 1895. Author's collection. 177
21 A publicity postcard of Muriel Starr as Mary Turner in 'the great American Drama', *Within the Law*. Author's collection. 179
22 Hal Gye sketch of Muriel Starr in *The Chorus Lady*, *Bulletin* [Sydney], 24 December 1914. Author's collection. 181
23 Harry Julius sketch of the cast of *Sweeney Todd* at the Sydney Savoy, *Sydney Mail*, 17 July 1929. Author's collection. 184
24 Lily Brayton and Oscar Asche offstage. Author's collection. 192
25 Lily Brayton in profile, date unknown. Author's collection. 195
26 Lily Brayton and Oscar Asche in *Hannibal*, 1910. Author's collection. 203
27 Lily Brayton in *Kismet*, 1911. Author's collection. 204
28 Photograph of Lillian Leitzel hanging from Roman rings, 1925, edit of CWi 873 glass plate negative. Circus World Museum, Baraboo, WI, Harry Atwell. 221
29 Lillian Leitzel's pink circus costume, *c.* 1925, Codona Family Collection. From the collection of Timothy Noel Tegge/Tegge Circus Archives, Baraboo, WI, Timothy Tegge. 230
30 Lillian Leitzel's vaudeville costume, late 1920s, Codona Family Collection. From the collection of Timothy Noel Tegge/Tegge Circus Archives, Baraboo, WI, Timothy Tegge. 232
31 Ellen Terry in costume as Buda, surrounded by cast in costume on the set of *The Bohemian Girl*, 1922. © Victoria and Albert Museum, London. 250
32 Ellen Terry as Buda with Gladys Cooper as Arlene Arnheim and Henry Vibart as Count Arnheim, in costume on the set of *The Bohemian Girl*, 1922. © Victoria and Albert Museum, London. Funding made available by the University of Essex. 255
33 Unattributed sketch of Mabel Constanduros as Grandma Buggins, 1937. © Victoria and Albert Museum, London. 267

FIGURES ix

34 *Mr & Mrs Sparkes: Six One Act Plays*, 1941, by Mabel
    Constaduros and Howard Agg, published by Samuel French
    Ltd. Reprinted by permission of Samuel French Ltd.   277
35 Margaret Rutherford as Aunt Dolly in *I'm All Right Jack*,
    1959. © Victoria and Albert Museum, London.   287
36 Margaret Rutherford in *Spring Meeting*, 1938, Angus McBean
    photograph (MS Thr 581). © Houghton Library, Harvard
    University.   293
37a–d Sequence of photographs taken in 1935: the costume in
    which Margaret Rutherford gave her audition for first West
    End appearance in *Hervey House*, 1935, at Her Majesty's
    Theatre. © Victoria and Albert Museum, London. Photo: Olga
    Baswitz.   297
38 A montage of images from *The Happiest Days of Your Life*,
    1948, Angus McBean photograph (MS Thr 581). © Houghton
    Library, Harvard University.   299

Contributors

Gilli Bush-Bailey is Professor Emerita of Women's Performance History at Royal Central School of Speech and Drama. She has published widely on the history of writing and performing women; her monograph *Performing Herself: Autobiography and Fanny Kelly's Dramatic Recollections* (Manchester University Press, 2011) led to her growing interest in women making and performing comedy. Relatively brief references to Constanduros's work appear in 'Women Like Us', *Comedy Studies* 3.2 (2012) and Maggie B. Gale and Gilli Bush-Bailey (eds), *Plays and Performance Texts by Women 1880–1930* (Manchester University Press, 2012). 'Shifting Scenes: The Child Performer and her Audience Revisited in the Digital Age', in Gillian Arrighi and Victor Emeljanow (eds), *Entertaining Children* (Palgrave, 2014), is part of her ongoing work with women and autobiographical performance, which also connects with her participation in UK company Tonic Theatre's 'Advance', a theatre programme working towards gender equality in the industry.

Katharine Cockin is Professor of English Literature in the Department of Literature, Film and Theatre Studies, University of Essex, and has published widely on Ellen Terry and her daughter, Edith Craig, theatre director and suffrage activist. Cockin's most recent monograph is *Edith Craig and the Theatres of Art* (Bloomsbury Methuen, 2017). Her publications also include articles and essays on women's suffrage drama and two volumes (one on women's suffrage drama) in the Women's Suffrage Literature series (Routledge, 2007). She is principal Investigator of the AHRC Ellen Terry and Edith Craig Database (2006–08), the AHRC Searching for Theatrical Ancestors (2015–17), www.ellenterryarchive.hull.ac.uk, and editor of the *Collected Letters of Ellen Terry* (8 vols, Pickering and Chatto). She is also editor of Routledge's Dramatic Lives book series.

Kate Dorney is Senior Lecturer in the Department of Drama at the University of Manchester, having formerly been senior curator of Modern and Contemporary Performance at the Victoria and Albert Museum. She is co-editor of the journal *Studies in Theatre and*

Performance and of the series Women, Theatre and Performance with Maggie B. Gale (Manchester University Press). She has published widely in the area of modern and contemporary theatre and performance curation and documentation. Publications include *Played in Britain: Modern Theatre in 100 Plays*, co-written with Frances Gray (Bloomsbury, 2012); *The Changing Language of Modern English Drama 1945–2005* (Palgrave Macmillan, 2009); *The Glory of the Garden: English Regional Theatre and the Arts Council 1980 to 2009*, co-edited with Ros Merkin (Cambridge Scholars Press, 2010); and *Vivien Leigh: Actress and Icon*, co-edited with Maggie B. Gale (Manchester University Press, 2018).

Maggie B. Gale is Chair in Drama at the University of Manchester. She is a co-editor of the journal *Contemporary Theatre Review*, and of the series Theatre – Theory – Performance with Maria Delgado and Peter Lichtenfels, and Women, Theatre and Performance with Kate Dorney (both Manchester University Press). Recent publications include *Vivien Leigh: Actress and Icon* (Manchester University Press, 2018, ed. with Kate Dorney), *Fifty Modern and Contemporary Dramatists* (Routledge, 2014, ed. with John F. Deeney), *The Routledge Drama Anthology: Modernism to Contemporary Performance* (2nd edn, 2016, ed. with John F. Deeney), *Plays and Performance Texts by Women 1880–1930* (Manchester University Press, 2012, ed. with Gilli Bush-Bailey) and *The Cambridge Companion to the Actress* (Cambridge University Press, 2007, ed. with John Stokes). She was awarded a Leverhulme Trust Major Research Fellowship grant to complete *A Social History of British Performance Cultures 1900–1939: Citizenship, Surveillance and the Body* (Routledge, 2019).

Viv Gardner is Professor Emerita at the University of Manchester. A theatre and performance historian, her work focuses on gender and sexuality at the *fin de siècle*, particularly the exchange between the radical and popular. Recent publications include 'The Image of a Well-ordered City: Nineteenth-century Manchester Theatre Architecture and the Urban Spectator', in Janet Woolf and Mike Savage (eds), *Culture in Manchester: Institutions and Urban Change since 1850* (Manchester University Press, 2013); 'The Sandow Girl and her Sisters: Edwardian Musical Comedy, Cultural Transfer and the Staging of the Healthy Female Body', in Len Platt, Tobias Becker and David Linton (eds), *Popular Musical Theatre in London and Berlin: 1890 to 1939* (Cambridge University Press, 2014); and 'The Theatre of the Flappers? Gender, Spectatorship and Musical Theatre 1914–1918', in Andrew Maunder (ed.), *British Theatre and the Great War*

1914–1919: New Perspectives (Palgrave Macmillan, 2015). Her annotated edition of the autobiography of actress, suffragette and birth control reformer Kitty Marion is being published by Manchester University Press in 2019.

Catherine Hindson is Reader in Theatre and Performance Studies at the University of Bristol. Her work focuses on popular stage entertainments and offstage elements of the theatre industry between 1830 and 1920. She has also written on the role of historic theatres within the contemporary cultural industries. Publications include *Female Performance Practice on the Fin-de-siècle Popular Stages of London and Paris: Experiment and Advertisement* (Manchester University Press, 2007) and *The Stand and Deliver Business: Charity, London Theatre and the Actress, 1880–1920* (University of Iowa Press, 2016).

Kate Holmes is an independent researcher who has recently completed a PhD in Drama at the University of Exeter entitled 'Aerial Stars: Femininity, Celebrity and Glamour in the Representations of Female Aerialists in the UK and USA in the 1920s and Early 1930s'. This research drew on her experience as an amateur aerialist and explored the celebrity of aerial stars in circus and American vaudeville/British variety. It was supported by an AHRC scholarship and the Society for Theatre Research's 2015 Anthony Denning Award. Her research on aerialists and circus glamour has been published in a special circus edition of *Early Popular Visual Culture*.

Veronica Kelly is Professor Emerita of the School of Communication and the Arts at the University of Queensland. She researches touring actors of the early twentieth century, and is a specialist in nineteenth-century Australian theatre history. She collaborates with the Popular Entertainments research group of IFTR, and is working with Jim Davis on a co-authored book on the social and cultural presence of British stage, radio and film entertainers in Australia. Her study *The Empire Actors: Australasian Stars of Costume Drama 1880s–1920s* (2009) was published by Currency House.

Naomi Paxton is a researcher, writer and performer. Her research interests include the performative propaganda of the suffrage movement, and networks and cultural histories of feminist theatre. She frequently speaks about her research at public events and on radio and TV, and is a BBC Radio 3/AHRC New Generation Thinker. She recently curated an exhibition in the UK's Parliament (2018) entitled *What Difference Did the War Make? World War One and Votes for Women*. She is the editor of *The Methuen Drama Book of Suffrage Plays* (Bloomsbury, 2013), *The Methuen Drama Book of Suffrage Plays: Taking the Stage* (Bloomsbury, 2018), and author of *Stage Rights! The Actresses' Franchise League, Activism and Politics 1908–1958* (Manchester University Press, 2018).

Brian Singleton is Samuel Beckett Professor Drama & Theatre, and Academic Director of The Lir – National Academy of Dramatic Art at Trinity College Dublin. He is former editor of *Theatre Research International* (Cambridge University Press, 2001–03) and former president of the International Federation for Theatre Research (2007–11). In 2012 he and Janelle Reinelt won the ATHE Excellence in Editing Award for their book series Studies in International Performance published by Palgrave Macmillan. He is currently editing a new book series (with co-editor Elaine Aston) entitled Contemporary Performance InterActions for Palgrave Macmillan. He has published widely on theatre and performance practice in Irish and European contexts with a particular interest in interculturalism, orientalism, gender and memory.

John Stokes is Emeritus Professor of Modern British Literature at King's College London and Honorary Professor of English and Drama at the University of Nottingham. He is author of numerous essays and chapters on contemporary theatre, co-editor of *The Cambridge Companion to the Actress* (2007), author of *The French Actress and Her Audience* (2005), *Oscar Wilde: Myths, Miracles and Imitations* (2006) (all for Cambridge University Press), and editor with Mark Turner of *The Complete Works of Oscar Wilde, Vols VI and VII: Journalism I & II* (Oxford University Press, 2013).

Lucie Sutherland is Assistant Professor in Drama at the University of Nottingham. She has written on aspects of nineteenth- and twentieth-century British theatre, including the impact of formalised training upon commercial practice, regional performance cultures, and managerial autonomy in West End theatre. Her work has been published in journals including *New Theatre Quarterly* and *Nineteenth Century Theatre and Film*. Current work includes *Peter Pan* for the Routledge Fourth Wall series, and a critical biography of actor-manager George Alexander for Palgrave Macmillan.

Series editors' foreword

The *Women, Theatre and Performance* series was born out of a desire to bring together research on the many aspects of women's contributions to theatre and performance histories. Historically the 'Second Wave' women's movement in the 1980s produced research on women in the theatre industry, and their work as playwrights, performers, designers, theatre makers and consumers of theatre and performance. Feminist performance analysis and women's theatre history has now become an established part of performance practice and theatre studies at both a university and a more popular level, although work made by women frequently remains marginal to many educational curricula and within the mainstream repertoire.

In the 1990s, the journal *Women and Theatre Occasional Papers*, from which this series arose, placed an emphasis on history and historiography. Founding series editors Maggie B. Gale and Viv Gardner were concerned to open out women's theatre histories beyond those considered within feminist praxis. Work made by women seen as more mainstream or more commercial was explored alongside more innovative and politically oriented practices. This came from a desire to find a consistent outlet for the retrieval project of women's theatre and performance histories. The emphasis on history does not preclude engagement with contemporary practice, as our edited volumes evidence. *Women, Theatre and Performance* seeks to make research and debate on women's performance practices available on a more than 'occasional' basis and has so far included edited volumes and single themed monographs as well as reprints of performance texts by women, all of which share in common the consideration of women's theatre and performance as part of a wider nexus of theatre histories and of social and cultural practices.

Maggie B. Gale and Kate Dorney,
The University of Manchester
Editorial Board: Gilli Bush-Bailey, Emeritus Professor
of Women's Theatre History at the Royal Central School
for Speech and Drama, London; Viv Gardner, Emeritus
Professor of Drama, the University of Manchester.

Acknowledgements

This volume has been inspired by the work of theatre historians and historiographers who have invested in making women's work visible. It would not have been possible without the enthusiasm and support of friends and colleagues. Particular thanks are due to Matthew Frost at Manchester University Press who has supported the series, *Women, Theatre and Performance*, from its inception. The editors would also like to thank our institutions for their research support, both in terms of time and finance, during the project, and our colleagues at the Victoria and Albert Museum and at the University of Manchester. We would also like to thank the curators and librarians whose knowledge and labour were given willingly and with enthusiasm. Individual archives are acknowledged for their support with permissions, but again we are extremely grateful to the numerous organisations that have allowed us to reprint images. Thanks as ever are due to our patient and supportive partners Jenny and Richard, and to our team of contributors.

Introduction

Maggie B. Gale and Kate Dorney

Stage Women, 1900–50: Female Theatre Workers and Professional Practice brings together recent research exploring women's participation in the theatre and entertainment industries during the first half of the twentieth century. Its chapters variously explore their professional practice and partnerships, their careers, celebrity and cultural status, and the intersections between the social, the historical and the professional that shaped their working lives.

The decades covered in this collection are more usually divided or periodised as 'Edwardian', 'First World War', 'interwar' and then 'Second World War', with specific decades described as 'the roaring twenties' and 'the hungry thirties'. Recent years have seen a renewed focus on the period around the First World War (1914–18), marking the centenary since its beginning and end, and on the anniversary of the Representation of the People Act (1918) which bought with it enfranchisement for a wider demographic of the population than ever before, and specifically for many women over 30.[1] Media coverage and popular and scholarly literature have recently reviewed the role of women more generally in this moment. As editors our aim has been to add to and extend this reappraisal, through curating a volume of essays that focuses specifically on women, theatre and performance. The collection provides broad-based coverage and analyses of women's professional practice in theatre as actresses, activists, teachers, administrators, writers and popular performers over a period bookended by the death of Queen Victoria and the decade of major social reforms epitomised by the establishment of the welfare state and the beginnings of organised state funding through CEMA and the Arts Council of Great Britain.

The women whose working lives are discussed here lived through the struggle for enfranchisement, the First World War and the transformation of the arts bought about by technology. Some, such as Ellen Terry and Ada Reeve, had careers that found momentum in the late Victorian and Edwardian periods; others, such as Gladys Cooper and Margaret Rutherford, worked up to and beyond the mid-century. Some, such as Winifred Dolan and Mabel Constanduros, radically shifted professional roles: in Dolan's case from working with George Alexander in the West End to teaching drama at a convent school; in Constanduros's from middle-class housewife to radio performer and writer. All of them lived through a range of legislative changes that impacted on their work and personal lives as women, as well as a series of profound changes to their industry including, but not limited to, the invention and rise of stage photography, radio drama and film. Many of the women featured here found themselves working across media – Ellen Terry experimenting with film late in life; Gladys Cooper moving into film in her forties and back to theatre in her seventies. Others, such as Lily Brayton and Lilian Leitzel, continued to work in more singularly defined practices and performance contexts. The transformation of visual cultures during the period enabled an enhanced circulation and commodification of women's presence in the industry.

Many of the chapters included here explore and contextualise how this impacted on women's sense of professional agency, both as individuals and in terms of public understandings of their status. Access to professional status was still relatively new to women at the beginning of the period covered here. Women's work was largely presumed to be connected to domestic duty, and in practice various marriage bars prohibited women from having equal employment status to men. Prejudice about women's capacity for the sustained accumulation and application of professional skills added to existing inequities in terms of social status and citizenship: assumptions that women were unsuitable for traditionally male professions such as medicine and law prevailed. The few women with access to university study could not officially be awarded degrees until the late 1870s: in the case of Oxford University not until 1920 and Cambridge, 1948. While small numbers of women were qualified in medicine by the last decades of the nineteenth century, women could not, for example, practise law or accountancy until the Sex Disqualification (Removal) Act of 1919. Jane Lewis notes that both direct and indirect discriminatory practices sustained the inequities in women's professional status in occupations from teaching, through medicine and law, to the civil service (Lewis, 1984: 220).

Harold Perkin's assertion that these decades saw the continuation of the 'rise of professional society' is of interest here, as it resonates with developments in the theatre and performance industries in particular (Perkin, 1989). Various associations and formal professional affiliations began to dominate by the early decades of the twentieth century, as part of a continuing move to specifically professionalise the industry and raise its social status. While not 'equal', women had much more access to professional status within the theatre and performance industry than elsewhere (Davis, 1991), and indeed, they understood how professional associations could improve their security of employment and range of professional choices (Gale, 2019; Paxton, 2018). Nevertheless, heightened levels of professional status offered in the industry existed within, and were shaped by, wider social frames of inequality. This is the context within which the women whose working practices are explored in this volume negotiated their own, often extensive and prolific, professional lives.

As a group, those born at, or working from, the latter end of the nineteenth century were the first generation of women in the performance industries for whom there are substantial amounts of visual memorabilia and, in some cases, films of their work. In reading and assessing their professional lives we have the benefit of a proliferation of photographs, postcards, memorabilia and audio and audio-visual records of performances. Increasingly through the networked space of the internet, discussed in more detail later in this introductory chapter, we have faster, more connected access to such materials which were once only available in archives with limited access. Similarly, fans and enthusiasts have created their own free-to-access archives where, for example, one might find extraordinary collections of postcards or lovingly digitised magazines, born of the dedicated free labour of fandom and an obsessional drive to collect and collate materials on performance.

Theatre is possibly one of the most networked of professions. It relies on tacit knowledge of layered networks in terms of their function, membership and the cross-currents between them. Several of the women discussed here were friends and colleagues, advising, assisting and supporting each other, and were knowledgeable about each other's work. One of our concerns in bringing this collection together has been to draw attention to the variety of ways in which women worked over the period, both on- and offstage, and how they used their personal connections and experiences to further their professional aspirations and secure economic stability. Their networks were not always as formally constituted as the Actresses' Franchise League discussed by Naomi Paxton, or the Theatrical Ladies' Guild discussed by Catherine Hindson. Some were characterised more by shifting affiliations and practices and, as a result, can be more challenging to map. In response to such a challenge Catherine Clay, in her study of British women writers between 1914 and 1945, selected three *foci* to reveal the personal and professional networks of writers including Vera Brittain, Winifred Holtby and Stella Benson. These *foci* are geography – based on different areas of London; publishing – specifically *Time and Tide* magazine; and critical frameworks for understanding the changing nature of female friendship (Clay, 2006).[2] Clay mapped a web of connections emanating from *Time and Tide* that reveals a number of women who also make recurrent appearances in this volume: Cicely Hamilton, Christopher St John and Elizabeth Robins. St John, who contributed a weekly music column to the magazine, was the partner of producer and director Edith Craig, the daughter of Ellen Terry (see Katharine Cockin's chapter). St John, Craig and Terry were friends of Gabrielle Enthoven, the focus of Kate Dorney's chapter. Robins and Hamilton were prominent members of the Actresses' Franchise League, the focus of Naomi Paxton's chapter. The phrase 'small world' seems both an entirely appropriate response to this shared network of creative, politically motivated women working in and around London, but also entirely inappropriate in that it belies the still circumscribed area in which women were operating.

Clay reconstructs and analyses these networks through a range of 'unpublished material, notably letters and diaries, supplemented by such published writing as fiction, poetry and autobiographical memoir' (Clay, 2006: 2). She acknowledges an additional 'recuperative dimension to this study to make "forgotten" lives and writings newly visible' (2006: 2). In many ways our collection shares her approach to a similar range of sources, but rather than merely 'recuperating' forgotten lives, we seek to ask, and explore the complexities of, why these lives or works might be 'forgotten' and what the processes of their forgetting can tell us about historiographical practices in relation to theatre and performance histories more generally. The theatre workers examined here can be mapped through professional associations (working in the same shows), through personal connections, through their work in particular forms of performance and through the public presentation of their autobiographical selves or their legal status as professional citizens, as Maggie B. Gale and

Viv Gardner demonstrate in their chapters. There are of course different levels of forgetting, and as we go on to explore, this is not just to do with a 'gender agenda'. It is as much to do with the ways in which certain kinds of theatre and performance histories are written: women's labour often falls victim to processes of historical forgetting, but it is not the only victim.

Stage Women is divided into two sections, 'Female theatre workers in the social and theatrical realm' and 'Women and popular performance'. While coverage is largely focused on British case studies, Veronica Kelly, Kate Holmes, Brian Singleton and John Stokes are concerned with performers whose work was also circulating outside Britain, demonstrating transnational networks in action. Equally, and notwithstanding their individual focus, the issues raised by our contributors have a global resonance, especially in terms of Anglo-American theatre and performance histories. The scope of coverage allows for the interweaving of onstage and offstage lives both in terms of professional practice and of the materials used in the construction of narratives around the personal and private. Tracy C. Davis's oft-quoted proposal that we need to connect the woman and the work 'and the work with the world at large' (Davis, 1989: 66) remains as pertinent now as it was in the late 1980s. Almost three decades have passed since this invitation, during a cultural moment that saw the beginnings of a substantial production of research on women and performance histories from second-generation feminists. These revisionist histories may not have yet permanently altered the dominant narrative (Bennett, 2010), but they have challenged that narrative by complicating a conveniently over-simplified picture. The documentation and reading of the complexities of women's labour have troubled and thickened traditional historical narratives more generally, both broadening the repertoire of the workers whose labours are explored and assessed, and re-focusing the methodologies through which such scrutiny is processed. This revisionist approach has provided new perspectives on women's vital and productive roles in the theatre and performance industries. Writing in the late 2010s, it is still crucial to maintain the momentum of unearthing and repositioning the materials that such an approach facilitates.

The research represented in this collection of essays by established and early career researchers reveals a range of recent work that sets out to counterbalance the still discernible limitations of studies of women's careers. Influential work has been done to retrieve key figures from relative obscurity, but these accounts often exist within a frame where the successful professional woman is perceived as an outlier among a field of men. It is interesting to note here the gendered tension between a revisionist history that expands the field of enquiry, and one that deepens the field. So for example, a publisher might be far more open to *another* book that offers a *different* perspective on the same (male) practitioner, than it would to another study of a female practitioner who has already been 'researched'. Playwright Susan Glaspell and producer/director Edith Craig are perhaps two notable exceptions here. The series Women, Theatre and Performance was set up in the 2000s precisely to deal with this tension, and has the support of a publisher that is genuinely interested in both expanding and deepening histories of women in the arts. Moreover, there is now a new generation of research on women's theatre. Naomi Paxton's *Stage Rights! The Actresses' Franchise League, Activism and Politics 1908–58* (2018) goes back to the history of the AFL and moves research on its extensive activity forward from the work of Holledge (1981), Kelly (1994) and Hirschfield (1987). As well as enriching the documentation and analysis of the AFL's work in the 1910s, Paxton focuses on its continuities beyond the initial campaign for suffrage, and assesses its stronger connection to work within the theatre industry of the day.

Like many of the practitioners explored in this volume, while the work of the AFL has been marginalised, it was not marginal in its time but both prolific and highly publicised. Those names that have made the journey forward in time and remain in our consciousnesses are not necessarily the names that gained significant public attention in their day, as Hindson reiterates when reporting back from her explorations of the biographical files of individual actresses which are part of the Mander and Mitchenson Collection.[3] This is not just the case with women's labour of course, but the work of women is more likely to be discarded, to be dislodged from the contexts in which is was made, or to be embraced by a revisionist history and then 're-forgotten'. Our bookshelves now contain multiple studies of female theatre and performance professionals – playwrights, directors, performers – and anthologies of plays and performance texts by women, none of which were available thirty years ago. While our curiosity can be sustained, only a limited number of these works have become embedded in the kinds of theatre and performance histories taught to students for example, or those written for the general public. The complex task of both undoing and revising history is ongoing.

It may be that to use new histories to 're-vise' history we have to re-embed them in that process of revision, to make them *work* by embracing them and applying them as part of a more generic discourse on theatre and performance histories. So, for example, we have written elsewhere (Dorney and Gale, 2018) that it is surely time for a new volume with a similar historiographic approach to Tracy C. Davis's landmark study *Actresses as Working Women: Their Social Identity in Victorian Culture* (1991). Published almost thirty years ago, this remains a major reference point. What if, however, it became a point of departure for a new study that takes a similar frame for investigation, and makes use of newly available research materials and methods to connect and explore changing patterns of employment, labour and productivity through the early part of the twentieth century, during a time of expansion, and beyond? Why is there only one such study currently? There are multiple studies of the director, so why not the actress?

Theatre and performance histories, 1900–50: historiographic approaches

Contemporary histories of the period covered in this volume remain somewhat beholden to the 'modernist project': a project in which the text dominates, and most frequently the male-authored text. Critical histories are often built around plays or groups of connected playwrights, rather than other types of theatrical material or events. Thus we find more treatments of relatively obscure modernist plays than we do of popular or commercial workers or their work. The theatre industry of the period is often viewed as conservative, commercialised and positively middlebrow. This was in fact an era in which new forms operated alongside or even developed from established ones, when there was a consistent sense of emergent cultures functioning productively alongside, and moving between, both dominant and residual cultures, to use Raymond Williams's terminology. In the UK, we have very few academic histories of the period from the 1900s that focus predominantly on what the majority of audiences went to see, on commercial or even popular stages (Savran, 2004). Such histories would open out all kinds of avenues for exploration in terms of the social and of histories of leisure cultures. While there may have been ideological reasons for their exclusion in the past, their exclusion now creates limitations to our understandings of how theatre and performance cultures function in social, relational and historical terms. It is also, incidentally, in the commercial sector that women's labour has had a more discernible and consistent presence, building substantially from the nineteenth century (Bratton, 2011).

As noted earlier, the period covered in this volume might well be characterised by the sense of significant social as well as technical transformations: political activism around issues of class, labour and gender equality, social care and citizenship also shaped the arts. In her work on early cinema Christine Gledhill noted that 'opposition between art and commerce tapped into unresolved class issues under pressure of democratisation', and that these gave shape to debates on the relation of the cinema, and we would suggest the performing arts more generally, to the 'social landscape' (Gledhill, 2008: 20). It is this division between art and commerce, and sometimes the conversations between the two, that shapes many of our theatre and performance histories of the period. This division, false as it is in practical terms, has also historically been one of the roots of exclusion in terms of assessments of women's labour in the industry of the early to mid-twentieth century. Just as practitioners and critics from the era debated the logistics of, and business case for, 'art versus commerce', so too theatre workers more generally reflected on their sense of 'the professional' and on their own professional practice. Women have a particular place in such reflections, in part because of their unequal social status and in part because of their own particular and complex position in the professional hierarchy of the fast-developing industry itself. As we have previously noted (Dorney and Gale, 2018), the sterling work of nineteenth-century theatre historiographers in the process of unpacking and rethinking fabricated silos of theatrical activity has not always been taken up by those working in the early twentieth century. Here a hierarchy of literary or hagiographic approaches still predominates, a factor that this volume attempts to challenge in its inclusion of diverse practices and people.

Our attitude in *Stage Women* has been to prioritise the need for a more holistic approach to understanding both the theatre and performance industries of the period, and the roles played by women in the development of those industries. This requires us to open up the historiographic aperture as it were, to try and read the period as composed of contrasting forms and registers of work by women rather than focusing on individual elements. Rethinking the historiographic approach to the period involves applying more nuanced understandings of the complex and dynamic interplay between different areas of the industry and the workers within it, as well as more nuanced understandings of the interrelationship between a social culture and the arts cultures it produces. Here, then, work carried out for the commercial sector is not left as sediment while the non-commercial rises to the top. In the US,

INTRODUCTION   9

scholars have produced more multi-dimensional readings of the industry of the period, offering historiographic and compositional strategies that embrace and connect commercial, popular, modernist, literary and visual performance cultures. In so doing, their analysis of women's labour overall has been more successful in creating gender-inclusive histories (see Glenn, 2000; Marra, 2006; Schweitzer, 2009). This volume applauds such a strategy, and intentionally participates in an agenda that embraces the idea of looking at what connects female performance workers, rather than what separates them or indeed makes them atypical. In putting together the volume our objective has been to refresh and extend a continuous history.

The theatre and performance industries over the period operated as social and cultural domains, as places of employment, as well as being the location for the production of art and entertainment works. In the absence of state funding, theatres were largely places of business, and the business of art held a fascination for those both within and beyond the mainstream. Female professionals belonged to *both* the commercial *and* the independent sectors, working in theatre and film. A fluidity of employment between one form of theatre, performance and arts practice and another was not uncommon. Equally, as a number of the chapters in this collection evidence, the necessity and ability to shift between different professional roles – writer, performer, manager, producer, public servant and philanthropist – was not uncommon.

The business of women in theatre and performance

Katharine Cockin's chapter locates Ellen Terry as a performer interested in film as a new medium late in her career, an interest with a significant economic imperative driving it. Like Lily Brayton – in her day as well known and loved as Terry – fame and celebrity did not necessarily equate to financial liquidity. Brian Singleton's and Veronica Kelly's chapters demonstrate how carefully even successful artists and shrewd businesswomen, such as Brayton or Muriel Starr, had to negotiate the precarious tensions between fashion, touring and financial viability in their response to the market. Actresses and theatre workers also responded to social need; thus Naomi Paxton's chapter looks at how an association of politicised women theatre workers developed practices of networking, organising and producing that brought achievements beyond their theatrical endeavours into the social world, despite extant prejudice against women's labour that prevailed even in a time of need such as the 1914–18 war and its aftermath. Catherine Hindson has published on actresses and charity in the theatrical sphere elsewhere (Hindson, 2016); here she turns her attention to one event where a number of actresses, networked through being in the same theatre production, engaged in charity fundraising, also for the war, by 'retailing' their considerable charms in Harrods. They displayed a growing awareness of their cultural commodity value, where their appearance was offset by public exposure and an opportunity to engage with and extend their fanbase.

Here, equally, it is difficult to discuss labour without reference to exploitation, and Viv Gardner's chapter explores the interstices between willing exposure and collaboration in self-commodification, and the appropriation of image or reputation as cultural cachet by opportunists. This is achieved through delineating contemporary law cases, some of which had surprising outcomes. Thus, when one actress was sacked as a 'dispensable' chorus girl, the courts agreed with her self-definition as an actress against the industry's interpretation of the contractual framework of her employment. Maggie B. Gale also explores the ability of actresses to exploit their own professional achievements and sense of agency through the autobiographical form. John Stokes thinks through how we might read the career of an actress who grew into her performance persona late in her professional life and through film: Margaret Rutherford's career was sustained by her ability to create herself as the 'odd woman out', the exception to the rule as an actress who marketed herself through *precisely* her lack of glamour. While these chapters tell very different stories, they connect in their attention to the dynamic complexities of women's professional lives and their ownership of their own professionalism in practice.

Negotiating the tyranny of plenty: theatre and performance historiography in the digital age

The generation of research is dependent on funding, on the politics of publishing, on the appeal of historical research in theatre and performance more generally – an appeal that is in a fairly constant state of flux. Historical research is expensive and labour-intensive. Even with the enhanced levels of accessibility to archives created by the internet, it requires heightened levels of curiosity, time and patience. While we are perhaps in a moment of renewed interest in all things historical, in putting together this volume we are pleased to be offering alternatives

INTRODUCTION

to dominant histories, to facilitate an undoing of the 'facts' of history as we receive them. Our hope is that this volume contributes to the creation of more fluid histories, more multi-purpose narratives that not only question the place of gender in history, but the formation of historical narratives themselves.

Our ability to add more lives and practices to the existing historical repertoire has been eased immeasurably by the digitisation efforts of various libraries, archives and commercial organisations over the last two decades and by Web 2.0. The digitisation of newspapers, of census records, of plays, biographies and autobiographies, of manuscripts and of photographs, designs and prints has reduced the amount of time it takes to find at least some 'facts' about a person, regardless of their ongoing visibility or whether they ever made it into *Who's Who in the Theatre*. The challenge for us as historians is not simply to assemble the facts, but to read them, and the absences that the internet cannot resolve, in a critical and, after Jacky Bratton, 'intertheatrical' manner. In *New Readings in Theatre History* (2003), Bratton advanced the idea of intertheatricality as way of re-interrogating dominant ideas of early nineteenth-century theatre as a period of decline, by looking again at the available evidence and reading it 'intertheatrically', the theatrical analogue of intertextuality. Thus, an 'intertheatrical reading goes beyond the written. It seeks to articulate the mesh of connections between all kinds of theatre texts, and between texts and their users', it requires us to be aware of the 'elements and interactions that make up the whole web of mutual understanding between potential audiences and their players' (Bratton, 2003: 37). Bratton demonstrated this through her readings of histories, anecdotes and playbills, showing that rather than just abstracting the 'facts' of the playbill (who, what, when, where, for how much?) in order to create a new document or verify an existing one, it could be approached as a text that offers clues as to what its first readers already knew, not only by what is written, but by what is not written – the audience's knowledge of theatrical conventions, of other shows, and of the ways in which they and the performers are expected to behave.

Contributors to this volume have similarly sought to articulate the mesh of connections between early twentieth-century theatre practitioners and their audiences on- and offstage, ever mindful of the dilemma of the challenge of proliferating evidence (Bratton and Peterson, 2012). Bratton and Peterson discuss the extent to which Web 2.0 creates plenitude and democratises access to information, but also leads to the proliferation of inaccuracies, dubious readings and a disregard for authentication. As a result Peterson sees a space for academics as

> the ones who help solve the abundance issue. We can develop the critical acumen to discern, navigate and critique these new forms of information. We can expand our cognitive maps of our subject to include, accommodate and filter a multitude of sources that engage with our subject and also to possibly address new and larger audiences. (Bratton and Peterson, 2012: 311)

Bratton, who has stated that there is no such thing as 'too much' as far as she is concerned, articulates a different concern, one that we have shared as editors of this volume, a concern to provide a 'platform on which we may climb in order to challenge the incumbents and hope to be heard' (Bratton and Peterson, 2012: 311). We are at pains in this volume to challenge both incumbent histories and the tyranny of plenty, and to pay attention to the particular. Thus the chapters by Lucie Sutherland, Kate Dorney, Veronica Kelly and Gilli Bush-Bailey are concerned with thickening the sparsely documented professional lives of their subjects and using them as examples of what these 'untypical' women's lives might tell us about the history of the industry more generally. Similarly, the chapters by Catherine Hindson, Maggie B. Gale and Kate Holmes articulate the tension between a researcher's expectations on approaching archival material and the realities of what the archive contains. Some of our authors have relied more than others on reading the materials available in archives – whether digital or not. All, however, attempt to enhance and deepen our processes of archiving women's theatre and performance labour as historians.

In conclusion then, *Stage Women, 1900–50: Female Theatre Workers and Professional Practice* offers an exploration of theatre as a networked world, the dynamics of which reflect our own age much more than current histories might allow. It explores the work of women theatre and performance professionals within the context of a diverse, multifaceted and complex industry that was constantly developing and changing, alongside its audiences, in relation to market forces. Critiquing and celebrating careers that converge and cross over the broad and various employment opportunities offered by the theatre and performance industries, the contributors to this volume take an interdisciplinary approach to reading and celebrating women's professional lives as central and integral to the shaping of the theatre and performance industries of the first half of the twentieth century.

Notes

1 All men over the age of 21 were granted the vote, along with women over 30 who met a property qualification, which meant that only 40 per cent of the UK female population were eligible to vote until an amendment in 1928. While the Representation of the People Act in 1918 increased the male voting population from 8 million to 21 million, it gave only 8.5 million women the vote, and even then not on equal terms. See https://www.parliament.uk/about/living-heritage/transformingsociety/electionsvoting/womenvote/overview/thevote/ (accessed 24 August 2018).
2 *Time and Tide* was a weekly magazine founded by Lady Margaret Rhondda. Originally connected to the feminist Six Point Group, it focused on politics, literature and the arts and was published from 1920 to 1986. See Spender (1984).
3 This is now part of the University of Bristol Theatre Collection.

References

Bennett, Susan (2010), 'The Making of Theatre History', in Charlotte Canning and Thomas Postlewait, eds, *Representing the Past: Essays in Performance Historiography*, Iowa City: Iowa University Press.

Bratton, Jacky (2003), *New Readings in Theatre History*, Cambridge: Cambridge University Press.

Bratton, Jacky (2011), *The Making of the West End Stage: Marriage, Management and the Mapping of Gender in London 1830–1870*, Cambridge: Cambridge University Press.

Bratton, Jacky, and Grant Tyler Peterson (2012), 'The Internet: History 2.0?', in David Wiles and Christine Dymkowski, eds, *The Cambridge Companion to Theatre History*, Cambridge: Cambridge University Press, pp. 299–313.

Clay, Catherine (2006), *British Women Writers 1914–1945: Professional Work and Friendship*, Aldershot: Ashgate.

Davis, Tracy C. (1989), 'Questions for a Feminist Methodology in Theatre History', in Thomas Postlewait and Bruce McConachie, eds, *Interpreting the Theatrical Past*, Iowa City: University of Iowa Press, pp. 59–81.

Davis, Tracy C. (1991), *Actresses as Working Women: Their Social Identity in Victorian Culture*, London: Routledge.

Dorney, Kate, and Maggie B. Gale, eds (2018), *Vivien Leigh: Actress and Icon*, Manchester: Manchester University Press.

Gale, Maggie B. (2019), *A Social History of British Performance Cultures 1900–1939: Citizenship, Surveillance and the Body*, London: Routledge.

Gale, Maggie B., and Gilli Bush-Bailey, eds (2012), *Plays and Performance Texts by Women 1880–1930: An Anthology of Plays by British and American Women from the Modernist Period*, Manchester: Manchester University Press.

Gledhill, Christine (2008), 'Play as Experiment in 1920s Cinema', *Film History*, 20, pp. 14–34.

Glenn, Susan (2000), *Female Spectacle: The Theatrical Roots of Modern Feminism*, Cambridge, MA: Harvard University Press.

Hindson, Catherine (2016), *London's West End Actresses and the Origins of Celebrity Charity, 1880–1920*, Iowa City: University of Iowa Press.

Hirschfield, Claire (1987), 'The Suffragist Playwright in Edwardian England', *FRONTIERS*, IX.2, pp. 1–6.

Holledge, Julie (1981), *Innocent Flowers: Women in Edwardian Theatre*, London: Virago.

Kelly, Katherine (1994), 'The Actresses' Franchise League Prepare for War: Feminist Theatre in Camouflage', *Theater Survey*, 35.1, pp. 121–37.

Lewis, Jane (1984), *Women in England 1870–1950: Sexual Divisions and Social Change*, Sussex: Wheatsheaf Books.

Marra, Kim (2006), *Strange Duets: Impresarios and Actresses in the American Theater 1865–1914*, Iowa City: University of Iowa Press.

Paxton, Naomi (2018), *Stage Rights! The Actresses' Franchise League, Activism and Politics, 1908–58*, Manchester: Manchester University Press.

Perkin, Harold (1989), *The Rise of Professional Society: England since 1880*, London: Routledge.

Savran, David (2004), 'Towards a Historiography of the Popular', *Theatre Survey*, 45.2, pp. 211–17.

Schweitzer, Marlis (2009), *When Broadway Was the Runway: Theatre, Fashion and American Culture*, Philadelphia, PA: University of Pennsylvania Press.

Spender, Dale (1984), *Time and Tide Wait for No Man*, London: Pandora.

Part I
FEMALE THEATRE WORKERS IN THE SOCIAL AND THEATRICAL REALM

1

'BELIEVE ME OR NOT'

Actresses, female performers, autobiography and the scripting of professional practice

Maggie B. Gale

Confessing the professional

Borrowed for the title of my chapter, *Believe Me or Not!* was the first of two autobiographies written by the Gaiety Girl, stage and screen performer, writer and celebrity raconteur Ruby Miller (1889–1976). Published in 1933, after the early death of her husband, the pianist Max Darewski, the book takes the reader on a chronological journey through Miller's career, from objectified 'stage beauty' to silent film star and society celebrity – with an uncanny onscreen resemblance to the film 'vamp' Pola Negri (Darewski [Miller], 1933: 178; Miller, 1962: 111–12). Miller's intense authorial voice shifts in register between a woman concerned to assert her professional achievements and one still grieving for a love lost too soon. Her second autobiography, *Champagne from My Slipper* (Miller, 1962), repeats numerous anecdotes from the 1933 autobiography, but covers an additional thirty years of professional activity: it speaks to an altered market and an ageing, differently nuanced readership. Both autobiographies articulate a professional presence in an industry transformed from one end of the century to another – by war, the emancipation of women, the development of the film industry and its impact on live theatre, by class conflict and shifts in the relationship between class and leisure, and by changed understandings of the social and cultural function of theatre. Miller challenges us to 'believe her or not' – and questions, up front, the precarious and fluid relationship between fact and fiction, through time and within the frame of autobiographical writing.

Fifteen years her senior, Ada Reeve (1874–1966), who had also spent a substantial proportion of her career working as a Gaiety Girl and in musical comedy, titled her late autobiography *Take It for a Fact* (Reeve, 1954), with a similar pointed reference to her sense of agency and authority in the writing of her own professional life story. Reeve, with a characteristic lack of charm, orders us to read her reminiscences as a 'record' of fact, even though they were written in a moment of almost desperate nostalgia, late in her career, after numerous disasters with financial investments and professional disappointments (Lipton, 2013: 136). Reeve was a collector and avid custodian of theatre ephemera and documents relating to her own career: articles, reviews, letters, bills, bookings for shows, documents about purchases, sales and legal disagreements, contracts and invoices. Her archive was given to UK theatre collectors Raymond Mander and Joe Mitchenson, who added to it from their own collection, as well as helping Reeve to piece her autobiography together and secure a publisher in the 1950s.[1]

Reeve's autobiographical 'facts', many of which can be evidenced by the materials in her archive, are woven into the fabric of a detailed and orderly recapitulation of a career spanning three-quarters of a century. This history tells us much more about professional practices than it does about Reeve's private life as a celebrity – her private 'self' is only implied or delineated in passing. We learn next to nothing about her disastrous marriages to men who clearly exploited her, or about her children, who she did not see from the mid-1930s to the end of her life in 1966. Nor indeed does she rely on 'telling tales' about her celebrity associates to maintain the rhythm and focus of attention from her reader. Reeve's main interest is to draw our attention to her role in shaping a successful career as the professional persona, Ada Reeve. She offers brittle but insightful criticisms of her colleagues, of unscrupulous or inadequate producers and performers, and is forthright in her assertions about her own unique talent and achievements over time. One ends up admiring her honesty and the detail with which she recalls working as a child performer in London's East End in the 1880s, in music hall, in musical comedy, as a producer; touring through the 'Dominions' – South Africa, the Antipodes and so on. She details how she supported a family; her prolific charitable war work – for which she was given the name 'Anzac Ada'[2] – and how she 'retrained' herself to work in 'straight theatre' and in film in her late sixties. While its author is intent on expressing her own unique individuality, *Take It for a Fact* offers the historian much by way of material about patterns of labour and the professional experiences of performers from the period. Equally, both Reeve's and Miller's autobiographies, as is the case with those of many other women working in the early half of the twentieth century, offer essential materials about theatre and performance practices more generally, as well as helping us to shape historiographic questions about the autobiographic scripting of women's professional lives.

Many female performers of Reeve's and Miller's generation autobiographically locate their labour within a public culture of self-affirmation and reflection. Catering to a mass, fan-based market, they evidence an awareness of the growing interest in their activities as public figures and practitioners, in a labour market largely owned and run by men. Yet this is also, as Tracy C. Davis has suggested, a market where women were able to operate as self-defined professionals in ways less generally available to them as a gendered group in other spheres of work. From the late nineteenth century, 'the social stigma of acting, singing, or posturing in public was less distasteful than the rigours of manufacturing, distributive, or domestic trades' and 'the stage could provide a higher wage than any other legitimate occupation freely accessible to women' (Davis, 1987: 115). Female performers were still, however, obliged, in Sos Eltis's terms, to embrace 'carefully staging a private, domestic self to counterbalance their public stage persona' (Eltis, 2005: 171). This is reflected in the processes and productivity of what I call here the 'autobiographic scripting' of professional practice, which allows description and analysis of professional practice by the practitioners themselves. These cultural interventions make explicit contributions to our historiographic constructions and readings of women's professional theatre practice, allowing both a horizontal and vertical expansion of the analysis and field of enquiry, taking us beyond existing received and revisionist narratives. While recent work on nineteenth- and early twentieth-century actresses' autobiographies has shifted the emphasis from analysis of their involvement in the 'new drama' or in suffrage politics towards investigations of celebrity, philanthropic enterprise and professional practice (Eltis, 2005; 2013; Hindson, 2011; 2016; Paxton, 2018), overall there remains a significant body of autobiographical work by performers operating largely outside the 'legitimate' or literary theatre that is still untapped by feminist theatre historians.

The autobiographic script, revisionism and the (feminist) historian

There are two key challenges associated with an analysis of these autobiographies, which are both performative acts of writing and material objects. One challenge relates to 'how' we read them – hinted at by Miller and her request for us to 'Believe me or not' – and the other relates to how we process these readings. I have argued elsewhere for a 'spectrum' of reading approaches to actresses' autobiographies (Gale, 2006), in order to interpret their contribution to an understanding of 'business practices, the careers of women, the nature of audiences and the cultural status of theatre' (Postlewait, 2000: 159). Here Jacky Bratton's warning against the 'masculinist assumption ... that men ... have a sense of their unique importance in the public life of the day' (Bratton, 2003: 102), while women don't, resonates for the historian. Autobiographies by female performers often share similar characteristics – written at speed, frequently without editing, containing glossy photographs from childhood, professional stardom and back to domestic scenes of the 'actress at home'. They might include correspondence with other artists and fans, or bear witness to the fame and infamy, rise and fall of fellow performers. Absorbing in and of themselves, they are part of a wider accessible auto/biographic scripting process that might include interviews, reviews, scrapbooks, letters, lectures and reminiscences (Gale, 2018).

Questions of authenticity are frequently applied to critiques of actresses' autobiographies as repositories of data. For Thomas Postlewait they are 'historical records but ... epistolary fictions' (Postlewait, 1989: 254) or 'records of consciousness' (Postlewait, 2000: 160). However, Bratton's insistence that the autobiography has to be read 'in its own terms, accepting the picture it paints as the intended activity of its authors' as 'actors, those who do, not objects' is key here (Bratton, 2003: 101). Female performers' autobiographies are markers of their authority as both professional and social actors, as well as being 'manufactured' for 'publicity and profit' (Postlewait, 2000: 164).

'Autobiographic scripting' is embedded in both public and private processes of self-formation and self-fashioning. Theories of selfhood and identity generally accept that the 'performance of self' is 'already entangled amongst a complex web of relations' (Holmes, 2009: 400), the articulation of which is as valuable as any narrative of singular identity provided in a theatrical autobiography. For the feminist theatre historian, any search for a 'coherent and stable identity' (Smith and Watson, 2002: 11) is overridden by the desire to find confluences between different generations of performers, and the ways in which they do or do not express their collective identity as professional workers. An integral component of any process of revisionist history formation, autobiographies are reflective of a process of self-evaluation, written by workers who spent their professional lives *performing and inventing* fictional characters and personae, and mixing socially and professionally with people who did the same. Authors sometimes explicitly and quite deliberately play with notions of the authentic and the inauthentic, as Bratton notes, deflecting 'us from themselves even as they describe who they are' (Bratton, 2003: 101).

Revisionist histories are resource-consuming and labour-intensive: for Susan Bennett, such histories have not reversed the fact that 'new knowledge remains collectively marginal, still in the shadow of theatre history's customary archives' (Bennett, 2010: 66). Her analysis is based on the suggestion that revisionist histories have included 'both people and places that had heretofore been ignored' (2010: 63), facilitating a kind of salvaging of loss. Revisionist practice might be better expressed, however, as facilitating the undermining of the more pro-active historical process of *intentional dismissal* and *deliberate misplacement*. The greater proportion of the autobiographies examined in this chapter, for example, have been largely dismissed, and this mirrors the generic exclusion of women's cultural labour from histories, exclusions that feminist revisionist processes have sought to override. A largely masculinist ownership of theatre history persists, as does, of course, gender inequality. The rationale for the continuing marginalisation of revisionist histories, therefore, is the same as that which has driven the need for such histories in the first place: the marginalisation of women's creative labour continues and, as the following case studies evidence, you don't have to work in the margins to become marginalised. The 'dynamics of disavowal and forgetting' so eloquently identified by David Savran (2004: 211) remain dominant in our historiographic practices: revisionist histories, involving a *continual process of renewal and challenge*, act as a means of interrogation, and a mode of continually unsettling entrenched and received narratives. They disrupt the authority of what Bennett sees as the immovable 'customary archives' of theatre history.

For Postlewait, female performers' 'own ambitions and contributions are seldom acknowledged' (Postlewait, 1989: 260) in their autobiographies, but a nuanced spectrum of reading practices suggests that this is more of an exception than a rule. Any kind of 'writing-out of self' will be dependent on the social and cultural frame for gender at any given historical moment, and autobiographic scripting represents, 'not the revelation, but the *construction*, of identity' (Bratton, 2003: 104, my emphasis). Autobiographic authors intentionally operate an *undoing* of a constructed or mythologised 'self', explicitly reconstructing the divided relationship between the public and private as part of the process of writing autobiography. Following George Herbert Mead's definition, the division between the 'I', the veridical or 'true' self, and the 'me', the public self as 'seen by others', is inevitable (Rojek, 2001: 11). This divide, particularly nuanced for celebrities, is constructed anew in autobiographic writing, and many actresses' autobiographies play creatively with this so-called fissure between the self, as scripted by others, and the self-scripted 'I'.

When critiquing the autobiographic intercession of layers of 'self' over time on stage or film, with 'selves' as developed through familial, educational and social contexts, we have to question our impulse to make absolute divisions, as Erving Goffman suggests, between the 'false' and the 'authentic' (Lawler, 2008: 109), or the public and the private. We need to understand articulated selves as relational interactions of all these aspects. A central impulse behind many women's theatre autobiographies from the first half of the twentieth century, contrary to Postlewait's suggestion above, appears to be precisely the need to discuss work and the experience of labour – alongside taking the opportunity to capitalise on the momentary currency and market value of celebrity status. The impulse to script autobiography is also entangled with formations of private or domestic life and with the complex dynamics of autobiography as 'a popular form of communication' more generally (Postlewait, 2000: 166). The autobiographic self arguably then reflects the 'modern attempt to comprehend the relation of self to society' (Gagnier, 1991: 221). For female performers, this 'society' is determined by issues of professional practice and legacy, as well as by their social and cultural position as women: they offer what Gagnier, following Beatrice Webb, sees as a subjective view of a 'philosophy of life or work' (Gagnier, 1991: 266).

Performing women employed in London's commercial West End theatres and in early and mid twentieth-century film were working with the 'kinds of theatrical practice ... that have held millions spellbound but have been routinely dismissed by scholars' (Savran, 2004: 212). Many of these workers fall outside definitions of 'feminist', 'political' or to a large extent 'experimental' or modernist: their careers sit outside an academic analysis which, in David Savran's words, 'valorize[s] the transgressive over the normative, theory over practice' (Savran, 2004: 217). Rather, they epitomise the impact of 'industrialisation, urbanization and the emergence of commodity culture' (Savran, 2004: 215) on the making and selling of theatre in the first half of the twentieth century.

The autobiography of a career not yet 'lived': Phyllis Dare

The musical comedy star Phyllis Dare (1890–1975) wrote her autobiography in her mid-teens, less than ten years into her career. It is lively, confessional, wistful and replete with acute observations about theatrical life and the experience of fandom. Presumably encouraged to write this work by her, largely parental, professional support team, *From School to Stage* was serialised in *The Penny Illustrated Paper and Illustrated Times* from July 1907, then published in book form in the same year. Having had some success in children's roles and in the musical comedy *The Catch of the Season* in 1905, a short UK tour ended with Dare's sudden withdrawal from the London theatre scene to a boarding school in Belgium: a surprising career move by a performer with a rising professional profile. Dare was one of the most popular of the postcard beauties whose images were reproduced on dozens of postcards for mass circulation in the early 1910s. Her sudden professional exit is perhaps explained by a high-profile libel case in 1906 that linked Dare's name to Seymour Hicks, who brought the case against a Liverpool man caught spreading libellous rumours (see also Viv Gardner's chapter in this volume). The accused had tried to impress his fiancé by claiming to have insider information on Dare and Hicks's 'forbidden' sexual assignations (she would have been underage, and Hicks was married to the popular musical comedy performer Ellaline Terriss [1871–1971]). The libel case ran through the latter months of 1906: the accused was sentenced to eight months with hard labour, having 'exposed Mr. Seymour Hicks and Miss Dare to the contumely of their fellow-men'.[3] The press gave little credence to the accused, who had posed as Dare's brother. He had given misleading information to his fiancé, a barmaid in a public house in Lime Street, Liverpool, well used by the theatrical profession. By the time of sentencing, Dare had already returned to England and successfully taken over the lead in *The Belle of Mayfair* at very short notice from Edna May in October 1906, ahead of May's understudy. Dare was just 16 at this point. The market value of her autobiography was no doubt generated in part by the publicity value of the libel case. *From School to Stage* also marked an important moment in her professional transition from child star and postcard beauty to leading lady.

Dare had barely lived a life at the time of writing *From School to Stage*, and yet the life she describes is shaped by the never-ending pressures of employment. Written very self-consciously for an adoring audience, her 'sketch of a schoolgirl actress's life' (Dare, 1907: 84) details her experiences of stage fright and anxiety about performing, and makes frequent reference to the poor employment conditions of children in the theatre industry, many of whom 'have kept their parents from starvation' (14) and 'have lots of responsibilities' (18). There are hints of her distaste for 'the trials of publicity' (114), or for the potential personal damage caused by gossip (96–8). She is also keen, however, to show her public that she appreciates their devotion, reprinting letters from admirers and fans. Hers is the autobiography of both an ingénue and a canny professionalised celebrity.

After 1907 Dare continued to work in high-profile productions such as the revival of *The Dairymaids* (Queens Theatre, 1908) and *The Sunshine Girl* (Gaiety, 1912), but she didn't quite achieve the difficult transition in performance register that other musical comedy women – for example, Cicely Courtneidge or Gladys Cooper – did by the time the form had lost favour in the 1920s (see Courtneidge, 1953). Although there were numerous rumours of courtship, Dare never married. In later interviews she also stressed that she had wanted to be a dancer, not an actress.[4]

Many of her obituaries fail to acknowledge Dare's achievements outside musical comedy; a number even comment that she was essentially a child star who faded along with the popularity of the performance form that had made her famous.[5] Nevertheless Dare worked successfully through the First World War and beyond, touring and performing in the commercial theatre, finally appearing with her sister Zena Dare in Ivor Novello's last production, *King's Rhapsody*, in 1949. But in later life she gave clues as to why she did not enjoy the work as much as she had appeared to when young:

> Looking back on my early career [...] I had practically no say in it. My mother arranged everything and I was put on the stage without being stagestruck or really enjoying it. One engagement led to another [...] it was rather terrifying to shoulder that immense responsibility when I was so young and had so little experience.[6]

The scripting, over time, of her professional selves – one from the hectic and prolific beginnings of her career, and the other expressed in interviews post-retirement – mirror each other in interesting ways. Her formal autobiography played with iterations of her professional self repeated and circulated in the press, capitalising on the marketability of the teenage performer as pre-sexualised beauty. On the other hand, Dare is at pains to write about the endless training, rehearsing and sheer workload of professional life, learning parts in record time, having to move from successful roles because of pre-contract agreements for other engagements, touring through illness and exhaustion, being overwhelmed by crowds of fans and so on.[7] In later life, a series of interviews reveal a professional self with a different balance in terms of what Smith and Watson identify as a knowledge/self-knowledge binary (Smith and Watson, 2010: 244). Here, Dare is critical of the ways in which she was exploited by her parents, and of her lack of choice and control over her early career. She acknowledges that sitting for hours on a regular basis in the photographers' studios of Edwardian London, having photos taken in all sorts of costumes 'as skaters in the snow, under a tree in blossom or as dairy maids in a meadow', brought her income, but she is critical about these postcard poses having nothing to do with her stage work.[8] She was critiqued later in the century as one of a number of 'young women with little or no acting talent'.[9]

Such so-called 'talentless' women dominated the London stages of the first decades of the twentieth century, and earned both themselves and their producers a more than significant income. The link between business, talent and the production of art or entertainment is not a coincidence, nor is the link between Dare's sense of a lack of control over her career and the growing technological framing of celebrity culture, in which the circulation of, particularly, the visual-professional self is beyond the control of the individual. Charles Taylor's suggestion that the turn to the self which has been so much a part of modernity is not necessarily framed by an idea of a unitary self, but rather a fragmented one, is useful here (Taylor, 1989: 462). Even as a teenager, able to capitalise on the selling power of the innocent voice of childhood, Dare understood the impact of the disintegration and loss of that childhood. The young Dare uses the autobiographic moment to formulate a subjective public self. She also begins the process of deconstructing this professional self, and regulates her use of the markers of child-turned-celebrity: the hardworking innocent, the surprise at success, her faithfulness to adoring fans from whom she nevertheless feels alienated.

Lillah McCarthy: resistance to the diminution of a professional life

Turning now to an actress who was central to the establishment of the 'new drama' which had infiltrated the British industry by the 1910s, Smith and Watson's notion of a serial autobiography (Smith and

Watson, 2010: 280) is appropriate in the case of the actress and manager Lillah McCarthy (1875–1960). *Myself and My Friends* (1933) was written at what she assumed to be the end of her theatrical career, rather than at a moment of heightened celebrity status like Phyllis Dare's. In her late fifties and married to an Oxford don, McCarthy's autobiography was rewritten after her first husband, Harley Granville-Barker, placed sanctions on her mentioning his name in it. Granville-Barker had been a central figure in a significant proportion of her working life, as both domestic and professional partner. A serial autobiography might be published in many parts, as '"chapters" in an ongoing life story' (Smith and Watson, 2010: 280), and here I suggest that having been banned from writing out her life in a manner fully reflective of her achievements and professional associations, McCarthy employed other autobiographic strategies over the years in order to do so. She kept the working papers that Granville-Barker had 'abandoned at the time of their divorce' (Kennedy, 1985: 215) and passed these on to his first biographer, offering substantial advice and assuming agency in the shaping of *his* biographic life, when denied the agency to shape her own. She also donated her own archive, containing correspondence and exquisite photographic evidence of her extraordinary career from the 1890s through to the early 1930s, to the British Theatre Museum Association, a body dedicated to preserving and celebrating the greats of the British stage.[10] Three of the extant file boxes consist of A3-size scrapbooks that document the famous McCarthy–Granville-Barker tour of the US in 1915. Two are identical – she had perhaps created one for herself and one for him, but he must have left this behind along with his own working papers when they divorced. Both were, however, placed in her archive, an archive which in turn builds a picture of her life almost entirely through documentation of her work with Granville-Barker. One can only imagine what it must have been like to be told that she could not write about such an important period of her career with reference to the key person with whom it was designed and developed. McCarthy arguably got her revenge in small ways, however, by leaving certain documents in the archive that open up a more complex picture of her marital and professional relationship with Granville-Barker: her serial autobiography can be read like clues laid out in a detective novel.

Lillah McCarthy's partnership with the actor, playwright, director, sometime British spy and lecturer Harley Granville-Barker had been both public and private, professional and domestic: she was married to him from 1906 until their acrimonious divorce in 1918.[11] In *Myself and My Friends*, McCarthy notes every role that she played prior to her professional and private relationship with Granville-Barker: she details training with Herman Vezin (McCarthy, 1933: 10), touring with Ben Greet and Wilson Barrett, and in Australasia and Africa. By the time of coming to work with G. B. Shaw in *Man and Superman* (1905), she felt that she had already 'learned her business under many managers' and had moved from an apprentice 'to an improver' to 'full craftsman' (McCarthy, 1933: 53–5). McCarthy intentionally scripts her professional self as having learned her trade through hard graft and determination, before becoming entangled with Granville-Barker: 'Actresses have often written about what they feel, but there are few books which show by what cold, laborious methods they learn their business [...] the business of feeling to order' (McCarthy, 1933: 68). She documents her excitement at moving into theatre management, and the strange discomfort

1   Lillah McCarthy in Izrael Zangwill's *God of War*, 1911.

of resigning herself 'to that curious monotony of a long run' when Shaw's *Fanny's First Play* (1911), written for her and which she produced, proved so popular with audiences. The production brought McCarthy and Granville-Barker temporary financial security, with its run of some twenty months in the West End, as the 'shop-girl, the storekeeper, the suburban mother […] all came to see the wicked Mr. Shaw' (McCarthy, 1933: 136).

Both McCarthy and Dare stress the collective dynamics of their craft as well as constructing themselves as individual and professionally distinctive workers in their autobiographic writing. But McCarthy, crucially obliged to omit her vital collaborator through a process of 'censoring by Barker' (Gardner, 2007: 185), is forced into a particular mode of obfuscation in the creation of her autobiographic script.

As an actress associated with a number of key twentieth-century practitioners, McCarthy has come in for much criticism. Oddly assuming her autobiographically 'invisible husband' to be Desmond MacCarthy,[12] Christine Etherington-Wright critiques McCarthy's 'adamant avoidance of any reference to personal relationships during her re-telling of her very public career', suggesting that she 'gave only perfunctory trivia' and that 'McCarthy herself is subsumed' (Etherington-Wright, 2009: 77). Ironically, in misreading McCarthy's omission of materials on Granville-Barker, Etherington-Wright fails to understand the significance of either the abundant other, non-marital professional relationships explored in the autobiography, or McCarthy's narrative emphasis on her own labour, and erroneously claims that McCarthy's is a text where 'discourse about […] public experiences evokes a forbidden and dangerous area', that it is 'an insecure and diffident text' (Etherington-Wright, 2009: 84).

Despite McCarthy's activity within the suffrage movement, there is little in the autobiography about her friendships with women. McCarthy's recognition that in its reflections on the men with whom she worked, her book might bear the title 'Let us now praise famous men in general and Shaw in particular' (McCarthy, 1933: 177) is perhaps less a slight on women than a pointed snub of Granville-Barker. She reclaims agency in actually defining him through his overt exclusion – he is precisely *not* one of the famous men included. This may in part explain the level of homosocial vitriol aimed at McCarthy in a number of Granville-Barker's biographies. Dennis Kennedy portrays her as obstructive to the man of genius and claims her 'aggrieved view' of Granville-Barker's second marriage was left unchallenged, unduly influencing the biography written by C. B. Purdom in 1955 (Kennedy, 1985: 4). She is framed as 'willful, headstrong, a bit silly' (Salmon, 1983: 298) or as a 'princess of promoters', with a 'wondrous ability to extract funds from the rich' (Kennedy, 1985: 194, 158). In fact Kennedy's sneering at her ability to find investors for their theatrical experiments belies the fact that both she and Shaw bankrolled a great deal of Granville-Barker's work. In view of her securing the rental of the Little Theatre for him to direct a series of productions, and her performances as the leading lady of the famous Vedrenne-Barker season at the Court Theatre between 1904 and 1907, and of Granville-Barker's Shakespeare seasons at the Savoy Theatre between 1912 and 1914, one wonders just what his career would have been without McCarthy's collaborative energies, her drawing power as a popular actress and, of course, her labour.[13]

While the marketable aspects of McCarthy's autobiography were bound up with her numerous professional relationships, especially with Shaw, *Myself and My Friends* also drew on the currency of numerous other actresses' autobiographies published in the late 1920s and early 1930s. She was a well-loved figure from an era of theatre about which there was already a feeling of nostalgia. Despite her enforced omissions, McCarthy negotiated well the 'ambiguous tension between entertaining her readers, and the authenticity of the events she is recording' (Gardner, 2007: 176). The serial nature of her autobiographic endeavours extends beyond the autobiography, however, to the creation of an accessible spectrum of professional selves as documented in her archive, where she locates her work as part of a legacy of important innovatory practices.

Her archive of papers and photographs includes a preface and two chapters of an unfinished, unedited biography, along with photographs clearly marked with the biographer's name suggesting them for 'the book'. A number of Granville-Barker's biographers suggest that McCarthy's professional life ended after her divorce, and that she made frequent unsuccessful attempts to revive it, but the serial narrative available from her archive includes references to her professional life after re-marriage in 1922, her roles in productions, poetry recitals, lecture tours, recitations, her work for various social and philanthopic organisations and her travels abroad.

How, though, do you develop an autobiographic script of your life if the person with whom you created your major body of work refuses to be acknowledged in your story? Numerous references to Granville-Barker's extraction of himself from McCarthy's autobiography combine to suggest that Shaw originally wrote a preface that included his version of the story of their divorce, given to Granville-Barker's solicitor by Shaw's publisher. On reading it, Granville-Barker returned to England and insisted that all references to him must be removed. Purdom notes that McCarthy wanted to abandon the project at this juncture as there seemed no point in continuing, but that her second husband 're-wrote' it for her (Purdom, 1955: 190–1). The archival evidence suggests that in fact they rewrote it together. This was the act of a husband proud of his wife's achievements, as Harald Melvill writes in the unpublished biography:

> [Granville Barker] took out an injunction of restraint against her to this effect. Whether or not in point of British law he was legally in a position to enforce it, his action so upset Lillah that in desperation she was ready to throw her manuscript upon the fire. Fortunately Sir Frederick Keeble was able to dissuade her, and between them they entirely re-wrote her story, so that when 'Myself and My Friends' (Thornton Butterworth) appeared, they had managed to cut out all reference to Harley and Helen Granville-Barker.[14]

Michael Holroyd's version of the story differs slightly: Granville-Barker wanted the book withdrawn, 'he wished to forget Lillah whose very name' disturbed his new wife. Holroyd suggests that Granville-Barker was apparently surprised at the eventual publication of the book without 'any reference to him' (Holroyd, 1997: 478). While John Gielgud, many years later, suggested that 'The second Mrs Barker strongly disapproved of his former triumphs in the theatre',[15] Holroyd's proposition that Granville-Barker's 'past had been obliterated' is rather odd – as clearly it was *he* who had tried to obliterate the private and professional past of his former wife (Holroyd, 1997: 478).

The inclusion of the unfinished biography in her archive reveals some of the oddities of her marital relationship with Granville-Barker:

> any frigidity in their marital relations was entirely on the side of Granville-Barker who was not the sort of man who should have married any girl.
> At the time of their wedding, Lillah was not completely ignorant of the facts of life but she was entirely innocent in experience. Granville Barker, on the other hand, though technically still a virgin, enjoyed a moral code of his own devising.
> To Lillah, coming from a large and happy family, her fondest hope had always been one day to hold a child of her own to her breast, so that the sterility of her wedding night both shocked and frightened her.
> Some time later, in an effort to fulfil her hopes, she reversed the usual course of procedure by herself undertaking the lover's function. At

first it seemed it she had succeeded, but one day during rehearsals she was taken so desperately and tragically ill that an operation had to be performed – after which all future hopes became useless and barren [...].[16]

The notion that Granville-Barker 'was not the sort of man who should have married any girl' paints a picture of a somewhat tense and sexless marriage. While the archive undermines Granville-Barker's desire for an intimate marriage, it corroborates the credibility of McCarthy's career as having its own successes and cultural resonances. Her work in the US during the early years of the 1914–18 war, for example, was almost entirely framed by the media as productions by McCarthy and Granville-Barker and not the other way around. Negotiations for a proposed Scandinavian tour during the First World War were marred by Granville-Barker's inability to participate, but hopes for this 'propaganda' tour – the Germans were sending Reinhardt productions on tour for the same purpose – were kept alive by the belief that McCarthy could be persuaded to reprise key roles and put together a decent company – she was producer and manager as well as leading lady.[17]

Again, contrary to Postlewait's assumption that women do not reveal their own ambitions in their autobiographic writing, the assured tone of McCarthy's exposes secure knowledge and understanding of the significance of her own career, her ambitious undertakings as an actress-manager and her insights into the working practices of a particular aspect of the theatre industry of the era. The exclusion of her long-term professional collaborator and husband from the narrative somehow makes it more imperative that we read the autobiography as one component of a serial autobiographic scripting process. McCarthy celebrates the discoveries about herself created through her work as an actress, noting that while 'others [...] could paint my portrait far better than I [...] no one except myself could discover the portrait that was to be painted' (McCarthy, 1933: 10).

Gladys Cooper, postcard beauty and actress-manager: writing her self at an 'unlined forty'

I *might* have [...] gone in for car racing [...] but I went on the stage. I run my own theatre, and that is really a sufficiently large-sized job to satisfy even my capacity for hard work [...] I was offered plays without seeking them, and I was not rich enough to refuse to act until someone saw fit to produce Shakespeare [...] (Cooper, 1931: 31–2)

I now turn to the auto/biography of Gladys Cooper (1888–1971), who shared with Phyllis Dare an early career as a postcard beauty and musical comedy performer, as well as sharing the professional shift to actress-manager with Lillah McCarthy, although in the commercial sector and over a far longer period.

Various biographical studies of actresses and performers of the era under discussion 'oscillate between dreary, encyclopedic catalogs and wildly impressionistic flights of the imagination' (Savran, 2004: 213).[18] They often also share an unhealthy focus on the actress as significant professional and domestic '*other*', on emotional and domestic failings, or on either the celebrated or prohibitive nature of her physical appearance and range of skills. Gladys Cooper is no exception, introduced in the following manner by Eric Johns:

> Gladys Cooper was only fifty when I met her, but I was astonished to discover the face of this celebrated beauty more wrinkled than I had ever seen. It could only be compared to the traditionally shriveled apple [...] Until her last appearance [...] she retained her slender figure and boundless energy. Even the short distance between the footlights and the front row of the stalls was sufficient to lend enchantment and with the right flattering shade of pink in the stage lighting she could pass for an unlined forty. (Johns, 1974: 133)

Two further biographies of Cooper, one by her grandson Sheridan Morley (1979), and the other by the journalist, playwright and biographer Sewell Stokes (1953) – a professional colleague of her son-in-law, the actor Robert Morley – attest to the failing of biography in its capacity to provide objective analyses. Each of these is layered upon and repeats varying anecdotes and personal statements made by Cooper in her own autobiography, entitled simply *Gladys Cooper*,[19] and published in 1931 when she was in her early forties.

Reportedly said by Dirk Bogarde to have 'all the charm of an electric carving knife' (Morley, 1979: xvi), Cooper began her career before her teens. A hugely popular postcard beauty, like Phyllis Dare, and later a Gaiety Girl like Ruby Miller, Cooper was frequently photographed as a child for sales and for publicity shots with Marie Studholme, by, among others, celebrity photographers W. and D. Downey. Her photographic image was one of a number which drove the postcard craze in the 1890s and early 1900s.[20] Her stage work in her teens gave material presence to her existing celebrity status. After a series of theatre successes, Cooper went into management with Frank Curzon in 1917 and ran the

Playhouse Theatre until 1933, when a number of less successful shows left her unable to take any financial risks on future productions. The rest of her career – she carried on performing until her early eighties – was spent between the UK and the US in stage and screen roles – with *Rebecca* (1939), *Now Voyager* (1942) and *My Fair Lady* (1964) among her better-known films.

With its sketch of an idyllic middle-class childhood in south London, *Gladys Cooper* shares with other autobiographic work of the era a detailing of various early professional engagements, letters from and portraits of other notable performers, and well-composed photographs of herself at work and at play. One whole section is dedicated to her letters to her first husband written during the 1914–18 war (Cooper, 1931: 103–46), from which he returned to a woman with an 'entirely different mentality and outlook on life', who 'when war broke out […] was earning £20 a week [… and] when it ended […] was earning £200' (Morley, 1979: 75). She clearly saw herself by this point as 'a free and independent woman' (Cooper, 1931: 273). By no means a dedicated feminist in her affiliations, Cooper laughingly describes 'being thrilled by the sight of struggling women [suffragettes] being thrown out of the theatre by perspiring policemen' at a charity performance attended by royalty at the St James's Theatre in the early 1910s: 'One woman was so firmly chained to her seat that they had to take out her seat and all' (255). Cooper does not perceive herself as part of a network of politicised women theatre workers, but she was nevertheless aware of the impact of gender bias in the industry. Known in the 'theatre world' as 'a woman with a certain amount of business' (17), she returns again and again in her autobiography to the difference between working with men and women.

> Well I prefer to do business with women than with men. Men are usually very conservative; they are inclined to argue that because a thing has 'never been done', or has always been done with certain success in a particular way, that there is no point in changing. Women are more alert to new ideas in business – perhaps because they are newer to business. Also, they make up their mind more quickly. Men are far too fond of going out to lunch to talk business. (161)

Voted most popular actress in the *Bystander* poll of 1923, with Phyllis Dare coming in at number 8 (Cooper, 1931: 219), Cooper refuses to be drawn into more than passing discussion of her reputation as a 'beauty', noting that it 'will not take one very far unless there is brain and the determination to work and struggle behind it' (32). Her autobiographic script frequently returns to issues of work and labour, the *business* of making theatre and the *business* of selling it, in a professional life represented by 'one contract after another' (165). Having fallen into the profession, she was self-taught and stresses that she had no kind of natural 'calling' to the stage. She does, however, express a belief that her own creativity grew with her understanding of the mechanisms of its productivity, through absolute graft, as she notes: 'I can say of myself most truthfully that I have *slaved* at times at my work. I do not believe that real success ever comes without hard work' (33). Similarly, as the autobiography progresses, Cooper's own sense of her industry knowledge becomes more apparent as she reflects on what she might usefully offer by way of anecdotal insider information to her reader:

> I suppose an audience never realises the tremendous organisation that is called into being with the rise of the curtain, before, during and after the time they have seen the finished product! After all, why should they? We are only selling them something they cannot buy elsewhere, and we never think of how, why, where or by whom our goods are obtained [...] it all *looks* so easy. (211–12)

Cooper's grandson Sheridan Morley is perhaps remembered as being far more successful at critiquing other people's theatrical careers than managing to sustain his own. His biography of his grandmother thus frames her achievements in rather doubtful terms: for him, Cooper's career appeared to be all so easy. Morley suggests, for example, that Cooper was never secure with her lines until convinced a production was going to run (Morley, 1979: 144), that she was a poor manager of finances and often in debt to the tax man, and that many of her Hollywood films were 'distinctly B' movies (1979: 204). He also claims that her 'gossipy and oddly uninformative though lengthy volume of memoirs' (1979: 138) was ghost-written during her spare time between parts or even during a production. The lively tone of *Gladys Cooper*, however, suggests that it was in fact dictated – a ghost writer would have surely edited the many repetitions so characteristic of a dictated text. It is equally interesting in the light of Morley's critique that Sewell Stokes's earlier biography in 1953 is based almost exclusively on the repetition of content from Cooper's autobiography. Neither man, however, accords much faith to Cooper's ability to script her own biographical self.

2 Gladys Cooper in the laboratory finding time to develop a line of beauty products, from *The Sketch*, 13 October 1926.

Scripting professional histories

While for Postlewait, actresses often 'fail to articulate fully the social significance and personal consciousness of a professional woman in theatre' (Postlewait, 1989: 268), the evidence in fact suggests that female performers engaged in autobiographic scripting had a far stronger sense of their cultural locale. They often use autobiographic scripting to define their career trajectories, explaining how they put together touring companies, or shifted the emphasis of their professional identity as performers, offering advice on careers in the industry and so on. Such autobiographies undermine received histories of the operational construction of the industry; Hesketh Pearson's *The Last Actor-Managers* (Pearson, 1950) excludes women altogether. This is somewhat surprising in light of the significant numbers of actresses and female performers whose careers made it possible for them to 'dictate the policy of their theatres', and who were engaged in management activities (Pearson, 1950: v). Tracy C. Davis's identification of some 330 female 'managers, lessees and proprietors' operating until 1914 suggests that there was in fact a tradition of women 'setting up in business to exploit their own popularity' in the late nineteenth and early twentieth centuries (Davis, 2000: 115), and here we can see the tradition extending and developing further up towards the Second World War.

The process of autobiographic scripting explored here through works by women with such contrasting careers as Miller, Reeve, Dare, McCarthy and Cooper reveals perhaps an awareness on their part that their historical significance as professional theatre workers might become displaced in future histories of British theatre. This is certainly the sense one has with Ada Reeve: *Take It for a Fact*, with its dense chronological detailing, is indeed a history of her professional practice, written as a means of correcting the history in which she might be constructed as an absent or diminished player. Working in the dominant sector of the theatre industry that has suffered in terms of historicisation through what Savran calls 'long-standing, class-based prejudices about the superiority of art to entertainment' (Savran, 2004: 211), female theatre workers such as these perhaps understood that, as Gladys Cooper put it, when 'a woman begins to get on and make a name on the stage, there are always people ready to throw mud at her' (Cooper, 1931: 166), or that they might only ever really be historically framed as a significant other – as in the case of Lillah McCarthy.

Some scholars have drawn a firm distinction between autobiographies that are introspective and those that are more of a 'chronological catalogue of professional activities, interspersed with business documents, press clippings and selections from letters and journals' (Postlewait, 2000: 163). In fact, introspection is not at the other end of the spectrum from the process of professional cataloguing or life scripting.

Many autobiographies were written at transitional career points, or during what were ostensibly the closing years of a career, but all are introspective in terms of subject formation through processes of reflection. Irene Vanbrugh talks of the double life of an actress (Vanbrugh, 1948: 101–2), but other female performers are less willing to engage with the psychodynamic connection they feel at any given point between the characters they play on stage and the life they live off it. Cooper's own recapitulation of her past veridical self and her present self is not untypical of the ways in which other female performers reflect upon identity:

> When I look back on the Gladys Cooper that was between sixteen and twenty-five and the Gladys Cooper that is now, I see almost a complete stranger. My outlook is different, my mind works differently, my whole idea of life is different. (Cooper, 1931: 168)

The process of autobiographic scripting is one that facilitates a lively flow and interaction of different historical selves and forms of documentation. Of the women focused on here, only Ada Reeve and Lillah McCarthy appear to have left a formal archive of their work. Gladys Cooper's grandson-biographer claims she was 'not a lady who believed in the past and [...] kept very little of it' (Morley, 1979: xiii), but Cooper's autobiography and those of others of her generation attest to the complex matrix of professional selves created by performing women, and invite us to capitalise more imaginatively perhaps on the ways in which these autobiographically archived selves facilitate a shaping of more inclusive, dynamic and, yes, feminist/revisionist histories of women's professional theatre practice in future.

Notes

1 The Ada Reeve papers are housed at the University of Bristol Theatre Collection as part of the Raymond Mander and Joe Mitchenson Theatre Collection. In the file on her autobiography Reeve kept a collection of the rejection letters from various publishers who thought her autobiography would have no audience in the 1950s, that the generation for whom she had been significant as a celebrity and public figure was not part of their key market. She also kept the list of those invited to the book launch, with the publishers who had rejected her work strategically crossed off it. See Mander and Mitchenson Collection at the University of Bristol, MM/REF/PE/AC/1531.
2 See Lipton (2012). For an interesting reading of the mediation of Ada Reeve's 'afterlife', see Lipton (2013).
3 *Citizen* [Gloucester], 28 November 1906.

4   Phyllis Dare made instructional films with George Grossmith on new 'craze' dances such as the Turkey Trot and the Argentine Tango in the 1910s (*Evening Telegraph and Post* [Scotland], 30 December 1913).
5   See, for example, *Daily Telegraph*, 29 April 1975.
6   *Stage and Television Today*, 17 January 1963.
7   *Manchester Courier and Lancashire General Advertiser*, 1 October 1907.
8   *Theatre World*, December 1961, n.p. Phyllis Dare: Biographical File, V&A Theatre and Performance Collection.
9   *Daily Telegraph*, 29 April 1975.
10 Lillah McCarthy Archive, THM/182, V&A Theatre & Performance Collection. For information on Granville-Barker's work for the Secret Intelligence Services during the First World War, see Gale (2019).
11 George Bernard Shaw, who had written numerous parts for her, reportedly negotiated the settlement for the divorce, after which his professional relationship and friendship with Granville-Barker came to an abrupt end.
12 A literary critic and journalist, Desmond MacCarthy was drama critic for the *New Statesman* from 1917 to 1920.
13 Sharing the belief that theatre should be available as a civic experience, and not simply produced as a commodity, was pivotal to many key developments in early twentieth-century British theatre – we should note that while Granville-Barker and William Archer were theorising about a 'National Theatre', McCarthy went out and raised the first substantial donation of £70,000 towards its foundation from Carl Meyer in 1908 (Kennedy, 1985: 194) – worth £6–7.5 million in today's money.
14 Lillah McCarthy Archive, THM/182/1, V&A Theatre and Performance Collection.
15 John Gielgud, 'Lillah McCarthy 1875–1960', *Sunday Times*, 19 August 1978.
16 Lillah McCarthy Archive, THM/182/1, V&A Theatre and Performance Collection.
17 Correspondence in the file suggests that even though the organisers wanted Granville-Barker for his production innovations, he was perceived by many as 'undesirable from an English point of view. There have been some scandals about his relations to his wife and his actions towards men in his employment. He is also said to be pro-German.' He was in fact employed by the Secret Intelligence Services for the latter part of the war, and in the US on a mission during the period of correspondence in 1917 (see Gale, 2019). See the Lillah McCarthy Archive, THM/182/3, V&A Theatre and Performance Collection. Letters A, B and C from Mr Edwin Bjorkman at Stockholm to Mr Vansittart, January/February 1917: in fact the letters run to late March along with the ultimately unsuccessful negotiations around the possible tour.
18 More recent biographies, such as Helen Grime's critical study of the actress Gwen Ffrangcon-Davies, model a more analytical approach to biographical study (Grime, 2013).

19 Although the book is publicised as *My Life* in the back page adverts within the first edition.
20 An online collectors' fan site has lovingly catalogued and digitised more than 1800 postcards of her early career – see http://www.gladyscooper.com (accessed 24 August 2018).

References

Bennett, Susan (2010), 'The Making of Theatre History', in Charlotte Canning and Thomas Postlewait, eds, *Representing the Past: Essays in Performance Historiography*, Iowa City: Iowa University Press, pp. 63–83.
Bratton, Jacky (2003), *New Readings in Theatre History*, Cambridge: Cambridge University Press.
Cooper, Gladys (1931), *Gladys Cooper*, London: Hutchinson.
Courtneidge, Cicely (1953), *Cicely*, London: Hutchinson.
Dare, Phyllis (1907), *From School to Stage*, London: Collier.
Darewski, Madame Max [Ruby Miller] (1933), *Believe Me or Not!*, London: John Long.
Davis, Tracy C. (1987), 'Victorian Charity and Self-help for Women Performers', *Theatre Notebook*, 41.3, pp. 114–28.
Davis, Tracy C. (2000), 'Female Managers, Lessees, and Proprietors of the British Stage (to 1914)', *Nineteenth Century Theatre*, 28.2, pp. 114–44.
Eltis, Sos (2005), 'Private Lives and Public Spaces: Reputation, Celebrity and the Late Victorian Actress', in Mary Luckhurst and Jane Moody, eds, *Theatre and Celebrity in Britain 1660–2000*, Basingstoke: Palgrave Macmillan, pp. 169–88.
Eltis, Sos (2013), *Acts of Desire: Women and Sex on Stage 1800–1930*, Oxford: Oxford University Press.
Etherington-Wright, Christina (2009), *Gender, Professions and Discourse: Early Twentieth-Century Women's Autobiography*, Basingstoke: Palgrave Macmillan.
Gagnier, Regina (1991), *Subjectivities: A History of Self-representation in Britain 1832–1920*, Oxford: Oxford University Press.
Gale, Maggie B. (2004), 'Lena Ashwell and Auto/biographical Negotiations of the Professional Self', in Maggie B. Gale and Viv Gardner, eds, *Autobiography and Performance: Women, Theatre and Performance*, Manchester: Manchester University Press, pp. 91–125.
Gale, Maggie B. (2005), 'The Many Masks of Clemence Dane', in Mary Luckhurst and Jane Moody, eds, *Theatre and Celebrity in Britain 1660–2000*, Basingstoke: Palgrave Macmillan, pp. 48–61.
Gale, Maggie B. (2006), 'Autobiography, Gender and Theatre Histories: Spectrums of Reading British Actresses' Autobiographies from the 1920s and 1930s', in Sherrill Grace and Jerry Wasserman, eds, *Theatre and Autobiography:*

Writing and Performing Lives in Theory and Practice, Toronto, Talon Books, pp. 185–201.

Gale, Maggie B. (2018), 'Making Vivien Leigh Mad', in Kate Dorney and Maggie B. Gale, eds, *Vivien Leigh: Actress and Icon*, Manchester: Manchester University Press, pp. 43–66.

Gale, Maggie B. (2019), *A Social History of British Performance Cultures 1900–1939: Citizenship, Surveillance and the Body*, London: Routledge.

Gardner, Viv (2007), 'By Herself: The Actress and Autobiography, 1755–1939', in Maggie B. Gale and John Stokes, eds, *The Cambridge Companion to the Actress*, Cambridge: Cambridge University Press, pp. 173–92.

Goffman, Erving (1960 [1959]), *The Presentation of Self in Everyday Life*, London: Penguin.

Grime, Helen (2013), *Gwen Ffrangcon Davies: Twentieth-Century Actress*, London: Pickering and Chatto.

Hindson, Catherine (2011), '"Mrs Langtry seems to be on the way to a fortune": The Jersey Lily and Models of Nineteenth-century Fame', in Su Holmes and Diane Negra, eds, *In the Limelight and Under the Microscope: Forms and Functions of Female Celebrity*, London: Continuum, pp. 17–36.

Hindson, Catherine (2016), *London's West End Actresses and the Origins of Celebrity Charity 1880–1920*, Iowa City: Iowa University Press.

Holmes, Rachel (2009), 'Theatre of the Self: Autobiography as Performance', *International Journal of Qualitative Studies in Education*, 22.4, pp. 399–416.

Holroyd, Michael (1997), *Bernard Shaw: The One-Volume Definitive Edition*, London: Chatto and Windus.

Johns, Eric (1974), *Dames of the Theatre*, London: W. H. Allen.

Kennedy, Dennis (1985), *Granville Barker and the Dream of Theatre*, Cambridge: Cambridge University Press.

Lawler, Stephanie (2008), *Identity: Sociological Perspectives*, Cambridge: Polity Press.

Lipton, Martina (2012), 'Tactical Agency in War Work: "Anzac Ada" Reeve, "the Soldiers' Friend"', *Popular Entertainment Studies*, 3.1, pp. 7–23.

Lipton, Martina (2013), 'Memorialization, Memorabilia, and the Mediated Afterlife of Ada Reeve', *New Theatre Quarterly*, 29.2, pp. 132–45.

McCarthy, Lillah (1933), *Myself and My Friends*, London: Thornton Butterworth.

Mead, George Herbert (1934), *Mind, Self and Society*, Chicago: University of Chicago Press.

Miller, Ruby (1962), *Champagne from My Slipper*, London: Herbert Jenkins.

Morley, Sheridan (1979), *Gladys Cooper: A Biography*, London: Heinemann.

Paxton, Naomi (2018), *Stage Rights! Actresses, Activism and Politics: 1908–1958*, Manchester: Manchester University Press.

Pearson, Hesketh (1950), *The Last Actor-Managers*, London: Methuen.

Postlewait, Thomas (1989), 'Autobiography and Theatre History', in Thomas

Postlewait and Bruce McConachie, eds, *Representing the Theatrical Past*, Iowa City: Iowa University Press.

Postlewait, Thomas (2000), 'Theatre Autobiographies: Some Preliminary Concerns for the Historian', *Assaph*, 16, pp. 157–72.

Purdom, C. B. (1955), *Harley Granville Barker: Man of the Theatre, Dramatist and Scholar*, London: Rockcliff.

Reeve, Ada (1954), *Take it for a Fact: A Record of My Seventy-five Years on the Stage*, London: William Heinemann.

Rojek, Chris (2001), *Celebrity*, London: Reaktion.

Salmon, Eric (1983), *Granville Barker: A Secret Life*, London: Heinemann.

Savran, David (2004), 'Towards a Historiography of the Popular', *Theatre Survey*, 45.2, pp. 211–17.

Smith, Sidonie, and Julia Watson (2002), *Interfaces: Women, Autobiography, Image, Performance*, Ann Arbor, MI: University of Michigan Press.

Smith, Sidonie, and Julia Watson (2010), *Reading Autobiography: A Guide for Reading Life Narratives*, Minneapolis, MN: University of Minnesota Press.

Stokes, Sewell (1953), *Without Veils: The Intimate Biography of Gladys Cooper*, London: Peter Davies.

Taylor, Charles (1989), *Sources of the Self: The Making of the Modern Identity*, Cambridge, MA: Harvard University Press.

Vanbrugh, Irene (1948), *To Tell My Story*, London: Hutchinson.

Vanbrugh, Violet (1925), *Dare to Be Wise*, London: Hodder and Stoughton.

2

Female networks

Collecting contacts with Gabrielle Enthoven

Kate Dorney

In her *Times* obituary Gabrielle Enthoven (née Romaine)¹ (1868–1950) was described as an 'archivist of the theatre' and an amateur actor who had 'some success as a dramatic author'.² For *Who's Who in the Theatre* she described herself as a

> theatre historian and dramatic author [...] for many years a prominent amateur actress appearing with the Old Stagers, Windsor Strollers etc. and author of *Montmartre*, Alhambra 1912; *Ellen Young* (with Edmund Goulding), Savoy 1916; *The Honeysuckle* (from D'Annunzio's play), Lyceum, New York in 1921. (Parker, 1930: 318–19)

More colloquially, she was described as 'the theatrical encyclopedia' – initially a one-woman, one-stop shop for information on the where, when and how of theatre; by the time she died, the instigator and overseer of the Victoria and Albert Museum's (V&A) theatre collection.³ Persuading the museum to accept the collection was no easy task, despite Enthoven's social and professional connections to a range of influential figures, and this chapter examines the ways in which she used her connections to further her work as a practitioner, collector and spokesperson and what this can tell us about women's influence in the theatrical sphere and in public life. It also reflects further on my motivation for excavating Enthoven from the obscurity she apparently sought.

As I have discussed elsewhere, despite, or perhaps because of, her evident talents as a preserver of theatre history and as a worker for the British Red Cross's missing persons units in the First and Second World Wars, Gabrielle Enthoven is an elusive biographical subject (Dorney, 2014a; 2014b). She appears in passing in biographies and autobiographies of other, more famous people, notably Ellen Terry, Oscar Wilde, Noël

Coward, Edmund Goulding, Radclyffe Hall and Lillah McCarthy, but these reveal little about her. Shortly after Enthoven's death, Muriel St Clare Byrne wrote a short tribute for *Theatre Notebook*, the journal of the recently formed Society for Theatre Research.[4] She noted

> her important Red Cross records work during both wars was described in *The Times*'s notice of her death, which also mentioned her work as a dramatic author. It is to be hoped that presently someone more nearly of her own generation may give us a more personal sketch, telling us, perhaps, of the young amateur actress who was coached by Henry Irving for her part in *Twelfth Night* only to find her carefully rehearsed rendering of a crucial passage disapproved of by her producer, William Poel [...] She was a born raconteuse and would keep any company enthralled by her theatre reminiscences, but glimpses of herself were all too rare. (Byrne, 1950: 2–3)

St Clare Byrne hoped in vain: such a personal sketch never appeared. Enthoven's museum colleagues James Laver and George Nash both provided reminiscences of her that reproduced many of her favourite anecdotes, but few personal details (Laver, 1952; Nash, 1956). Michael Holroyd once considered writing a biography of her, but early on in his research at the V&A he was drawn to a Rodin bust of Eve Fairfax and ended up writing about her instead (Holroyd, 2004: 62). He called it *The Book of Secrets*, which would have been an equally appropriate name for a book on Enthoven, who so effectively covered the traces of her own personal life. Even the 'facts' that the theatrical encyclopaedia provided for her *Who's Who in the Theatre* entry are difficult to verify. She is not listed in the Windsor Strollers or Old Stagers membership records and she seems to have appeared with them only once.[5] She did work for the Red Cross, but never seems to have discussed how she came to work there or what she did. The vignettes and passing mentions in biographies and autobiographies add little flesh to the bare bones: she certainly knew Noël Coward and Radclyffe Hall, although it's hard to work out how well.

Fleshing her out has become an exercise in mirroring her own practice of collecting, compiling and verifying 'facts' and anecdotes from newspapers and from the collection she initiated and others, now housed in the V&A and elsewhere:[6] an exercise in sifting through accumulated layers of documents, reports and footnotes of work on other more famous figures in order to build a fuller picture of her life and work, for information that will corroborate (or not) the anecdotes that circulated

3 Gabrielle Enthoven in fancy dress, date unknown.

from her 'inexhaustible fund of stories about personalities' ranging from Queen Victoria and General Gordon, to Sarah Bernhardt, Noël Coward and Mrs Patrick Campbell (Laver, 1952: 8). Her 'personal' collection in the V&A consists of a small number of boxes of scrapbooks, letters, photographs and notebooks that contain little personal information.[7] Letters to and from her in the archives of her wider circle of acquaintance are often either short and business-like, or long and revealing about the writer, but not the receiver. Reading some of the letters, I often suspected that she wrote them only in order to receive a response which she could file and so increase her collection, the growth, organisation and custodianship of which obsessed her.

Like the collection, the version of herself that Enthoven bequeathed to posterity was carefully arranged. Her will instructs that her solicitor, to the exclusion of all other persons whatsoever shall go through the whole of my papers and deal with the same as to him, in his uncontrolled discretion shall seem best [...] and to see that all Paper matters and things relating to Theatre go to my collection at the Victoria and Albert Museum.[8]

'Uncontrolled discretion' suggests scandal, but is actually a legal term allowing trustees to act without prior permission from the court. The 'personal papers' at the museum contain no information about her parents, her brother or her husband other than photographs of them. They do contain a short history of the Romaine family and a history of her childhood home, but nothing about her education, her involvement in amateur theatricals or the Red Cross other than her certificate of membership, badges, OBE and photographs. The chief source of information about her is anecdotes she related in interviews, which are then, in turn, related by others in remembrances and obituaries. What I have learned has come from those interviews, public records, reviews and the few personal letters that, for reasons unknown, escaped the solicitor's discretion. She had seen at first-hand how compromising letters could be, through the trial of Wilde and through the public disagreement of her friends Edith Craig and Edward Gordon Craig over how their mother, Ellen Terry, should be remembered. As well as establishing a museum at Smallhythe dedicated to Terry's memory, Craig placed an announcement in the national press asking for letters written by her mother to be returned to her for publication. According to Katharine Cockin, the subsequent publication, including letters from George Bernard Shaw, was regarded by Gordon Craig as 'as an act of indecent exposure, misrepresentation and betrayal' and he retaliated by publishing *Ellen Terry and her Secret Self* (1932) in which he 'claims for himself the authorised portrait of his mother, privileged access to her "secret self" not available to his sister' (Cockin, 2010: xx). In her introduction to the recently published volumes of Terry's correspondence, Cockin notes that the 'collection has been subjected to censorship in later years by means of selective destruction ... since many of Ellen Terry's letters, especially those to significant male intimates and to others in certain periods of her life, appear to have been destroyed there are gaps in her life story' (Cockin, 2010: xvi–xvii).

In Enthoven's case, there is more gap than story. In her walk-on role in other people's biographies, she is usually described as a lesbian and as part of the London lesbian *haut monde* of the 1920s. She appears most frequently in biographies of Radclyffe Hall, where she is variously identified as being introduced to Hall by Hall's partner Mabel Batten (Cline, 1997: 67, 73–4, 80) or by the tennis player and former ambulance squadron founder Toupie Lowther (Baker, 1985: 134). According to a third biographer, Diana Souhami, Enthoven's relationship with Hall and Una Troubridge foundered because she urged 'discretion and camouflage' in the wake of *The Well of Loneliness* libel trial of 1928. They criticised her for 'repudiating her own kind when opportune to do so' and Troubridge declared, 'she's a rat and we have no use for her' (Souhami, 2013: 328). Researching Enthoven further through Troubridge's diaries, Eve Smith found further evidence of Troubridge and Hall's belief that Enthoven hid her sexuality.[9] Given Enthoven's proximity to Wilde and Hall and the vantage point it offered her on the vilification of 'inverts', it is not surprising that she favoured discretion.[10] Nor is it surprising that there are no letters from Hall or Troubridge among Enthoven's correspondence, nor any other frank discussions of relationships, lesbian or otherwise. As Laura Doan points out in her account of women's experience of work and relationships during the First World War, frankness over such matters is uncommon:

> Rumours and accusations of a sexual nature put some of the women in my case studies in the national spotlight, but I found no private papers disclosing their innermost thoughts about their romantic entanglements or their sexual desires, preferences, or inclinations; and during the war and into the interwar period, none ever spoke of themselves or others in reference to modern categories of sexual identity. (Doan, 2013: 5)

Enthoven's sexuality may well account for the absence of many personal documents, and it was never my purpose to 'discover' evidence of it. However, it would have been nice to discover something about her journey from adolescence to adulthood: how she met people like Wilde and Ellen Terry; how she came to the Red Cross; what she thought about the suffrage movement, cinema, or any of the changes and innovations she lived through.[11] But Enthoven's correspondence reveals little about her personal relationships, health and happiness – although it's clear that she was often unwell, and in old age, unhappy. There are few signs of affection, ease or humour in her dealings with people with whom she is supposed to have been friends, such as Noël Coward – the correspondence I have seen from Coward to Enthoven is polite rather than friendly, yet she left him 'my Chinese statuette of a warrior on a horse' in her will[12] – or Oscar Wilde – there are no letters from Wilde in Enthoven's correspondence. The exception to this are letters from Ellen Terry, Terry's daughter Edith Craig and her partners Christopher St John and Tony Attwood, the actress and dancer Letty Lind, Nancy Price and Charles Maude.[13] These offer a glimpse of the generous, larger-than-life personality alluded to in Enthoven's obituaries and tributes. The letters kept in the collection are illuminating about how she used her contacts to get advice on her writing, her acting and as a means of expanding and effectively serving her collection. They reveal a network in which the public and private, the professional and personal, the petitioner and the patron shift in relation to herself, her acquaintances and each other.

Jacky Bratton has shown how women's role in management and business in the West End theatre of the mid-nineteenth century was previously obscured by academic accounts of Victorian business that focused on 'the urgent demands of masculine identity formation' from which women were excluded by social restrictions on where they could go and who they could visit (Bratton, 2011: 105). She also points to the fact that the 'theatrical/Bohemian public sphere' continued to rely on patronesses, and that the 'gatherings they facilitated were still important in the artistic world, after the patronage culture had ostensibly given way to market relations, and it is in accounts of the salon that theatrical women can most easily be seen' (Bratton, 2011: 107). Born in 1868, Enthoven benefited from the social changes that saw women of her class move beyond the salon. She was raised in a tradition of privilege and public service: her father, William Govett Romaine (1815–93), was a colonial administrator and highly valued public servant who served Lord Raglan in the Crimean War, earning the soubriquet 'the eye of the army' (Williams, 2004: n.p.). He then served in India before becoming Advocate General in Egypt. Her mother, Frances Tennant, was the daughter of Henry Tennant, a lawyer, and Elizabeth Roupell, daughter of a Master in Chancery. Enthoven was born in Spring Gardens in London, a street that borders both the West End theatres she chronicled so obsessively and the government ministries that her father represented during his various postings. She and her mother travelled with him, and she claims that by the age of three she could speak several languages, but that she didn't learn to read until she was eleven when the family returned to England on her father's retirement (Nash, 1956: n.p.). They settled at the Priory in Old Windsor, described in 1826 as 'delightfully situated in full command of most beautiful reach of the River Thames', and enjoying 'convenient offices, a capital large garden with a neat cottage and hot house, stabling for six or seven horses, double coach house, farm buildings and about 47 acres of rich land'.[14]

The photographic albums, commonplace books and one diary of Enthoven's in the V&A suggest that her adolescence was typical of her class and era: a life of regattas, amateur theatricals, balls and dinner parties. It was a period in which the proportion of actresses increased and women occupied important roles on stage and behind the scenes as managers, writers and patrons as well as performers.[15] She met Oscar Wilde as a young woman and in 1889 he dedicated 'Remorse (a study)' to her 'in exchange for an autograph sonnet of Paul Verlaine' (Fong, 1979: 13).[16] This is the first evidence we have of Enthoven as a collector, trading one piece of desirable memorabilia for another. Sometime between 1890 and 1893 she had a limited edition of stories told to her by Wilde privately printed under the title *Echoes*. Enthoven sent a copy to the British Museum's Library (now the British Library), ensuring that at least one copy remained in public hands.[17] Her photo albums show her mingling with soldiers from the nearby garrison and newspaper reports confirm that she attended performances of the amateur theatre company, the Windsor Strollers, at the Theatre Royal in Windsor with her mother.

Enthoven's father died in May 1893, and in December that year she married Captain Charles Henfrey Enthoven of the Royal Engineers at St George's, Hanover Square, London: a smart, fashionable church. Sometime after their marriage the Enthovens moved from Windsor to Cadogan Gardens, a fashionable and wealthy area of London. They also spent time in Chatham, Kent, the regimental headquarters of the Royal Engineers. According to George Nash, her successor at the V&A:

> When Mrs Enthoven came to London as a young bride at the end of the last century, she began to mix with the same sort of people she had known at Windsor. With the newly found respectability of the Theatre it was possible for her – a woman whose personality was always on the grand size – to count among her friends such lions of the theatrical world as Sir Beerbohm Tree, Sir George Alexander and Forbes Robertson, Ellen Terry, Sarah Bernhardt and Eleanor [sic] Duse […] Also numbered among Mrs Enthoven's friends were several important writers – she knew Oscar Wilde very well and bitterly condemned George Alexander and others for their treatment of Wilde. (Nash, 1956: n.p.)

'The newfound respectability of the Theatre' that Nash alludes to here was signalled by the knighthood given to Henry Irving in 1895, which, as Tracy C. Davis suggests, provided performers with 'public acknowledgment of their long struggle for recognition as respectable, responsible citizens on a par with what the census designated as "Class A" professionals – barristers, physicians, the military and the clergy' (Davis, 1991: 4). Irving's knighthood was not the only indication of the relaxation of social hierarchy. Christopher Kent notes that 'the years 1884 to 1914 saw nineteen marriages between actresses and members of the English nobility, 14 of whom were peers' (Kent, 1977: 115).

Now that the theatre was respectable, women of Enthoven's class were able to enlarge their acquaintance and shift roles from patron to petitioner: and in the same period an increasing number of women from 'good' backgrounds appeared on the professional stage. Enthoven seems to have wanted to join them: in 1894 she was presented to the Queen at Buckingham Palace,[18] and in 1896 she was in correspondence with the actress-manager Sarah Thorne – who ran a School of Acting from the Theatre Royal in Margate – and was asking to attend rehearsals. Her request was refused, but in 1899 she had a small part as Mrs Coleman's maid in a production of *The Passport* staged at the Theatre Royal Haymarket in aid of the Deptford Fund. The *Lady's Pictorial* reported that 'Mrs Charles Enthoven, if at moments unduly emphatic, proved completely at home as Markham the censorious'.[19] By 1901 Enthoven counted opera singer David Bispham, actresses Mrs Patrick Campbell, Letty Lind, Marion Terry and Violet Vanbrugh and actor-designers Edith Craig and Edward Gordon Craig among her friends. She was now firmly established among the newly respectable theatre folk (Alexander and Forbes Robertson) as well as the bohemians (Wilde and the Craigs). Alongside acting, she also had a new hobby: collecting theatre memorabilia:

> soon after my marriage [I] began pasting up in scrapbooks various press cuttings dealing with the theatre. The idea of starting a collection of playbills came into my head when I purchased a quantity of them, two hundred I think, from a naval officer which was the foundation of my collection as it stands today.[20]

Collecting gave Enthoven another path into the theatre world that she evidently craved admission to. In this early period it is difficult to get a sense of how much time she spent on collecting and how much on performing. Her correspondence reveals that she performed a whistling solo for Helen Mar in 1900, that Edward Gordon Craig wanted her to play the Virgin Mary for him, and that by 1907 she was renting

Ellen Terry's country home Smallhythe and inviting her to come to the play she was appearing in at the Peckham Crown Theatre.[21] It is hard to discern any sense of the conduct of her marriage, and references to Charles are few and far between, until his untimely death in 1910. We might expect a woman who lost her mother and husband in the same twelve-month period to reel somewhat in the aftermath; Enthoven's focus on all things theatrical intensified. In 1911 she began a campaign to establish 'a theatrical section in a national museum', became a founding member of the Pioneer Players alongside Edith Craig, and appeared in Cicely Hamilton's *A Pageant of Great Women*, produced by Craig for the Actresses' Franchise League (AFL; see Naomi Paxton's chapter in this volume), as 'a graduate' (Enthoven, 1911a: n.p.). Her roles as a theatre collector, 'theatrical encyclopedia' and theatre worker begin to

4 Gabrielle Enthoven cataloguing playbills, date unknown.

merge, and the links made in one domain are exploited in the other. If the producers, actors and writers of her acquaintance cannot help her get parts, or get her plays read or produced (though she continued to ask them until the late 1930s), they can at least support her campaign for a theatre museum and provide material for it. Reading through the correspondence Enthoven saved, there are few extended exchanges with theatre workers that do not make reference to an agreement to send programmes, or provide information.[22]

Enthoven's plays and short stories tend towards the melodramatic, and if she was writing this narrative, her campaign would be precipitated by the death of her husband and mother, which had left her with nothing else to live for. My own more prosaic interpretation is that their deaths meant she was no longer bound by their ideas of decorum, was now independently wealthy,[23] and benefited from the public appetite for all things theatrical in terms of press coverage of her museum scheme and support for it.[24] I would further suggest that her peripheral involvement in the suffrage movement and the model it offered for networking and campaigning provided her with both a useful example of practice and an enlarged set of contacts.[25] The suffrage movement is one example of how associations, clubs and organisations enabled women of Enthoven's age, class and aspiration to network. In Beatrice Harraden's *Lady Geraldine's Speech*, the suffragist portrait painter Gertrude Silberthwaite[26] describes how

> the Suffrage Movement has brought all us professional women out of our libraries and studios and all our other hiding places. We had to take our share in it, or else be ashamed of ourselves [...] And quite apart from anything to do with the vote itself, it is so splendid coming in intimate contact with a lot of fine women all following different professions or businesses. (Harraden, 2013: 37)

Enthoven is not listed as a member of the AFL, but she was associated with suffrage activities through the Pioneer Players, a subscription society in which members could be both actor and audience. The organisation

> was funded by its membership and drew its actors as required from them for each production, honouring them with a reduced fee [...] it was designed to produce only a small number of annual productions for an audience of its membership and was therefore not engaging with the commercial context of public performances for a profit. (Cockin, 2017: 24)

Enthoven also counted many AFL members and suffragists among her correspondents, including Lena Ashwell, Adeline Bourne, Cicely Hamilton, Gertrude Kingston, Lillah McCarthy, Nancy Price and Irene and Violet Vanbrugh. With them and through them she was involved with a number of charities: the Theatrical Ladies' Guild, the Society of New Players, the Three Arts Club Ball Committee, the Actors' Benevolent Fund and the Stage Society.[27] They asked her for support, financial and practical; she asked them for introductions, programmes and other items for her collections and advice on getting her work produced. Thus a pattern was established in trading acquaintances, commodities and knowledge.

On at least one occasion it seems that Enthoven was able to use her theatrical heft to assist her friends. Radclyffe Hall's biographer Michael Baker describes her using her influence as member of the Stage Society's council to 'push through' a production of Una Troubridge's translation of Colette's *Cheri* (1930). There was also an argument over the Baroness's costume which led Troubridge to write in her diary that 'Gabrielle Enthoven behaved disgracefully' (Baker, 1985: 266). The production's poor reviews apparently hastened the end of the Enthoven–Troubridge–Hall friendship and did nothing to further any of their theatrical aspirations, but it does show that Enthoven was able to act as patron as well as petitioner (Souhami, 2013: 167).

The campaigner

In her campaign for a theatre museum, Enthoven worked assiduously to generate publicity. She wrote a number of letters to the press outlining the kind of institution she had in mind, while making personal approaches to a number of museums including the V&A, the London Museum and the British Museum, and gathering support from the theatre sector. She proposed

> a comprehensive theatrical section in an existing museum to comprise specimens of all the different branches necessary to the workings of a play from the construction of the theatre, the designing of the scenery and costumes, to the smallest workings necessary in the house. Also a library and a collection of playbills, prints, pictures and relics etc. I want the section to be the place where the producer, actor, author and critic will naturally go for information, both on what is being done in this and other countries at present, and what has been done before. (Enthoven, 1911a: n.p.)

In a letter to the *Referee* she also proposed that

> [t]he Copyright Act should be extended to the printing of playbills, to the intent that a copy of the bill of every first performance or revival should be deposited at the museum and duly filed, so as to ensure the keeping of a complete record. (Enthoven, 1911b: n.p.)

She was not simply collecting as a hobby; this was a serious and focused attempt to benefit the theatre profession and theatre scholars.

Her proposals were supported by a number of theatre managers and writers, including George Alexander and Herbert Beerbohm Tree, but were met less enthusiastically by the museum profession. Despite the expansion in museums that took place during her lifetime and the existence of theatre museums and collections in Europe and the US, the idea of theatrical history being documented and studied in a museum context was not a priority for the British establishment. Enthoven offered her collection as a means of creating a national centre and was rebuffed and discouraged for more than a decade. The Keeper of Printed Books at the British Museum thought it 'a very interesting thing', but 'hopeless to think of establishing a theatrical section which should embrace miscellaneous exhibits as theatrical literature here' because of the way the museum was rigidly split into departments.[28] He suggested that such a section would be more suitable for the V&A or the 'London Museum that is in the air'. The V&A's director Cecil Harcourt Smith described the 'difficulties of our undertaking such a scheme' as 'insuperable. I should have thought that it ought to form naturally part of the proposal for a National Theatre', which was supposed to be being built opposite the museum.[29]

Enthoven, however, continued to collect and to campaign undaunted. For a while it looked as if the London Museum would take the collection once the move to a bigger site had been effected, and Keeper Guy Francis Laking had the difficult task of managing Enthoven's expectations, explaining the lack of space in his existing premises, lack of resources in the new ones and, at one point, trying to dissuade her from selling the collection to America.[30] Enthoven was in frequent correspondence with American collections and in 1922 spent two weeks working

> at Harvard each day for a fortnight and gave two lantern talks on the London stage to some society I forget which – I worked in the Library as they wanted my advice about cataloguing the London ones they had – but at that time they did not mount them – and they were getting very badly handled – and if not mounted I should think they would all be

destroyed by now. They thought mounting would do away with their value. My point was that they would have no value if they were all in Ribbons – also I thought they made a mistake in separating things so much, as you know I put the playbill, the cuttings, engravings, letter all together, which I think is easier to the student to take in at once.[31]

She stressed the calls on her expertise from other collections as part of establishing the credentials of her collection and herself as its curator.

After more than a decade of petitioning, the V&A finally agreed in March 1924 to accept her collection of more than 80,000 playbills, prints, books and engravings in order to establish a national collection of the performing arts. The collection was based in the Department of Engravings, Illustrations and Drawings, and Enthoven was allowed a budget of £200 a year for expenses including postage and packing; everything else, acquisitions, wages and storage, had to be met from her own pocket. After a year of packing, the collection, its founder and workers arrived at the museum and the great task of cataloguing and cadging materials resumed. Enthoven, her volunteers and paid assistants were not only cataloguing the playbills, prints and other material that formed her gift, they were also continuously soliciting contemporary material from venues, managements and performers. Her connections with London's and New York's theatre scene ensured a steady stream of material, enquiries and opportunities for her to enlarge her acquaintance base. The collection enabled her to write to people with whom she wasn't already acquainted, and their replies gave her material for the collection. Until the middle of the 1930s she was also continuing to look for opportunities to write and perform, alongside her curatorial activities.

The theatre 'professional'

Enthoven's desire to perform seems rarely to have been fulfilled in any public contexts. Aside from the review quoted above of her performance as 'Markham the censorious', other comments on her acting prowess come from the anecdotes related by St Clare Byrne and others – the source of which always seems to have been Enthoven herself. She appears to have set her mind instead on being what she called 'a dramatic author', and her style and choice of subject matter seem to reflect her large personality and taste for the tall story. In 1912 her sketch 'Montmartre' appeared in the long-running revue *Kill That Fly!* at the Alhambra, described in the *Sketch* 'as a Grand Guignol playlet':

The scene is laid in an evil-looking and ill-lighted slum in a Quartier in Paris. Hither stealthily comes an Apache who has successfully brought off a robbery, and brings with him his booty in his bag. But his footsteps are dogged by another of the same kidney, who falls upon him and stabs him. There is a long and fiercely fought combat with knives, which results in the defeat of the original thief who is finally killed. But this does not mean triumph for his assailant, for all the while events have been quietly and closely watched from an open window by a third ruffian, who leaps down upon the exhausted victor and stabs him to the heart, disappearing into the darkness of the night with the 'swag'.[32]

The writer goes on to praise how effective the wordless struggle is and how the grunts of the fight linger and add to the mounting sense of horror. The actors were Charles Maude (also the producer, and married to Enthoven's friend Nancy Price), Victor Maude, Edmund Goulding and 'Mr Hill'.[33]

In 1914 Enthoven was working with Cecile Sartoris on a translation of the Italian poet and Fascist politician Gabriele d'Annunzio's play *The Honeysuckle*. Like Enthoven, Sartoris was a well-connected widow, and like other women of their acquaintance (Romaine Brooks, Elenora Duse, Hall and Troubridge), they seem to have been fascinated by d'Annunzio.[34] Among Enthoven's papers is a letter to Sartoris from their publisher warning them that 'I cannot anticipate for this play more than a succèss d'estime and I shall be very much surprised if it sold to any extent, so that neither you nor the author must anticipate any substantial return.'[35] The translation was published in Britain by Heinemann in 1915 and in the US by Frederick A. Stokes and Company in 1916. A generous interpretation might see it as a 'succèss d'estime': the *Sketch* listed it as one of the best books of the week[36] but the *Times Literary Supplement* was rather less complimentary: 'the version before us is written in the tongue best described as translation-English. It would be unfair to select the worst examples, because the whole play (though it improved in the third act) is an example.'[37] It was produced in New York in 1921 and in London in 1937.

Ellen Young, the only other full-length play of Enthoven's to be performed, was co-credited to Edmund Goulding, one of the actors from 'Montmartre'. Produced by the Pioneer Players at the Savoy Theatre in 1916, the play is a meditation on theatre, the art of living and the role of women. Ellen Young, the heroine of the title, is a young woman from Peckham who works as a typist and whose bluff, working-class parents cannot understand her and her brother's desire for a life beyond seeing

George Robey at the music hall. On learning that she has tuberculosis and has only a year to live, Ellen accepts an offer from a theatre designer to attend an Arabian Nights ball at Covent Garden and abandons her family: 'I'll go away from here. I <u>will</u> live – for <u>this</u> year.'[38] In Act 2 she is a highly paid dancer performing as Madame Ziobie, worshipped by fans and visited by admirers who are struck by her 'don't care' attitude. When one of them, Stanley Bretton, accuses her of being unnatural she snaps:

> My dear boy, how could I make a living if I was natural? I tried to once – 30 bob a week – being natural – and typing from nine to six; and a hundred pounds a week for letting my voice and legs go at the theatre. The two letters, U N, which separate the difference between natural and unnatural mean a princely 98 pounds and ten shillings a week to me – and to any girl who, either by force of circumstance or natural tendency, becomes hysterical – which is what you really call personality. And then, Stanley, the strength of mind or the strength of circumstances to hold that hysteria with you keep you unnatural.[39]

She later confesses to him that she is dying, but in the nick of time a doctor turns up and says that he can cure her if she will only come and live quietly in his sanatorium.

Act 3 begins with Ellen restored to health, newly 'kind and thoughtful to everyone' and determined to become 'a great artist' by learning her craft. She takes to the stage that evening and it becomes clear to her and her admirers that the hysteria that drove her was the key to her success. After the show she refuses Lord Maperley's offer to keep her as his mistress and is about to shoot herself, but Bretton turns up, again in the nick of time, and challenges her to try a new art, 'the art of living'. She agrees. Curtain.

In 1914 Christopher St John provided a critique of a draft praising the idea, characterisation and dialogue but advising Enthoven to develop theme and pacing, particularly in the final scene in which Ellen struggles between Bretton and Maperley.[40] St John's letter makes it clear that Enthoven had sent it to her with a view to having it produced by the Pioneer Players, and that she is happy to send it out to the reading committee. She suggests Hilda Moore for the lead role and that Enthoven should invite all the commercial managements along to see it. There is no mention of Goulding's involvement at this stage, so it is possible that Enthoven began it alone and later invited Goulding to co-author with her. Goulding's biographer Matthew Kennedy describes Enthoven as 'a generous, well-read "lady of the world", and Edmund found her the most captivating and outsized personality he had ever encountered', not that you would know this from the one letter in Enthoven's papers. Kennedy is rather less enthusiastic about their play.

> The plot of *Ellen Young* serves as a precedent for the many over-heated movie melodramas that would soon consume Edmund's working life. It begins with Ellen predicted to die within a year. She's temperamental and full of fight, and so becomes a wild music-hall dancer. By the final act, a happy marriage has cured her of consumption, morphine addiction, and chronic irritability. 'I wanted to smack the heroine', wrote one first-nighter. 'She was a conceited spitfire of a woman, who was rude to her Peckham parents, but I couldn't help being interested in Hilda Moore's performance.' (Kennedy, 2004: 18)

The production was reasonably well received, with reviewers singling out Hilda Moore's performance as Ellen. A letter from St John in 1916 speaks of an American production being almost 'a *fait accompli*'; however, it doesn't seem to have come off, nor did a commercial production in Britain. It did, however, become a film, *The Quest of Life* (1916), directed by Ashley Miller and distributed in the US by Paramount Pictures. It's not clear if Enthoven and Goulding were credited at the time, or paid for their work, though they are now credited on IMDB and in the Library of Congress record for the film.

Although silent on many other subjects, Enthoven's personal papers are revealing about her custodianship of her work and payment for it. Her energetic pursuit of royalties for *The Honeysuckle*, and her co-writer's credit and royalties for the one-act play *The Confederates*, written with established playwright and theatre manager H. M. Harwood and performed at the Ambassadors Theatre in 1930, are well documented in her correspondence.[41] We can interpret this in several ways: first as determination to be paid for her theatrical work and to be able to claim professional status for herself in that regard: authorship is clearly not within the realms of the reciprocal work with her theatrical networks described above. Second, the determination of a wealthy woman not to be taken advantage of, particularly when working in partnership with men. As discussed earlier, at this stage in her life Enthoven was constantly petitioning male directors of museums and libraries to secure her vision for a theatrical section in an institution, and male theatre managers and producers to support her proposal. I like to imagine that she refused to play second fiddle to them in any other sphere of activity, preferring instead to be a version of Lady Bountiful, sending money and gifts to Edward Gordon Craig, Edith Craig and others and, on one occasion at least, helping out Noël Coward.

In 1921 Enthoven was in New York for a production of *The Honeysuckle* at the Lyceum Theatre. She and Cecile Sartoris lived in a small apartment in Washington Square and made space for the young Noël Coward,[42] then trying to make his name in America. No one had told him that New York theatres closed during the summer months because of the oppressive heat, and he was unable to earn any money, let alone make his fortune. He recalls that the three of them were very poor and often 'dined quietly in pyjamas' (Coward, 2004: 122). Enthoven was never poor, as far as I can make out, although she worried constantly about money (Nash, 1956: n.p.), so it's unclear whether she was pleading poverty at this point, or performing it.[43] Neither she nor Coward got their lucky break in New York that year, and in fact Enthoven's lucky break as an author never came, despite her describing her work as an author on equal terms with her work as a theatre archivist in *Who's Who in the Theatre*. *The Honeysuckle* got a London production at Playroom 6, a small theatre on the first floor of 6 Old Compton Street in 1937. One reviewer commented:

> I am not one of the admirers of D'Annunzio the dramatist [...] However, I disliked *The Honeysuckle* a good deal less than I have disliked other plays I have seen by him, and I thought that not only the makers but also the interpreters of this English version [Hilda Maude, Jean Forbes Robertson, Terence O'Brien] had done their work very well. As I looked round during the interval I caught sight of several people well-known in the world of arts and letters, and I came away feeling that 'Playroom Six' had made a very promising beginning. How far it will go remains to be seen.[44]

Enthoven's dramatic work here, ostensibly the primary focus of the review, has become secondary to her theatrical network in the audience who have turned out to support her. From this point on she seems to have concentrated full-time on collecting, apart from during the Second World War when she returned to the Red Cross.

War worker

According to her obituary, Enthoven's first role as a war worker was as Chief of Records for the War Refugees Committee 'before the Red Cross claimed her'.[45] Then she became Chief of the Records Department for Central Prisoners of War and Missing Persons (1915–20). As is often the case with Enthoven, this is not quite what the official records suggest. According to her British Red Cross record, Enthoven was at the London Office for the Wounded and Missing of the Central Prisoner of War Committee at Carlton House Terrace from December 1915, 'six months before enrolling'. She then became Head of Section in the Records Department between April 1917 and June 1918 before retiring due to ill-health at the age of 50 (British Red Cross, n.d.: n.p.). It should come as no surprise that Enthoven left no written record of her war work, so one can only speculate about her duties based on accounts from other Red Cross workers and from official documents.

In 1921 the government published the 823-page *Notes from Reports by the Joint War Committee and the Joint War Finance Committee of the British Red Cross and the Order of St John of Jerusalem in England on Voluntary Aid rendered to the Sick and Wounded at Home and Abroad and to British Prisoners of War 1914–19*, which set out the development and eventual standardisation of services provided by the Red Cross and Order of St John. It is clear is that it took time for a centralised system for dealing with prisoners of war and missing persons to be established, and in the earliest period of the war care packages and letters to service-men were organised regiment by regiment, while enquiries for missing persons were dealt with by the Red Cross. At the suggestion of the War Office, the packing and distribution of parcels, managing of contacts for PoWs and searching for the wounded and missing was centralised. The Central Prisoners of War Committee was established in 1916, bringing together the activities of the Prisoners of War Help Committee (formed in March 1915) alongside the British Prisoners of War Fund, which was 'financially assisted by the Red Cross as well as by private generosity' (HMSO, 1921: 544).

Enthoven is described in the official report as a Superintendent in the Records Department of the Central Prisoners of War Committee. The job of the Records Department was to gather information on PoWs and wounded and missing men on a card index containing name, number, rank, regiment, battalion, company, date and front. They also kept the War Office and next of kin updated on the health and location of PoWs and cross-checked names against lists of those wounded, killed or taken prisoner, received through Frankfurt Red Cross (HMSO, 1921: 533). The Superintendent and her assistant

> were responsible for the issue and carrying out of all orders; for the sorting and despatch of incoming post to the various groups; for the

checking of all outgoing correspondence; for the entry in all the appropriate books of all particulars regarding lists sent out of the department; also for answering any questions and giving any assistance necessary for the efficient maintenance of the work of the department on receipt of information from one of the sources described above, the Superintendent would stamp the date thereon, and place the document in the pigeonhole appropriated to the group of Regiments to which it pertained. If the document contained the names of men belonging to various groups, it was first dealt with by the senior group and then returned to the Super, to be passed on to the next group. (HMSO: 1921, 548)

In the V&A, Enthoven managed her own collection in much the same way, but whether she went to the Red Cross because she already had these organisational skills, or used what she learned from the Red Cross to organise her collection afterwards, is, like many other things about her, a matter of speculation. *The Report of the Joint War Committee of the Red Cross and Order of St John* records that it was 'Mrs Barnadistone, who organised the work [of the Records Department] and laid the foundations of the system, carrying it on until Oct 1917', but that to Enthoven's 'organising capacity and devotion to duty, often in the face of bad health, we owe no small part of the success of the work' (HMSO, 1921: 550).

Women and work

There are parallels to be drawn between Enthoven's work at the Red Cross and her subsequent work in the theatre and at the V&A, and the work of another Red Cross worker, Velona Pilcher, particularly her play *The Searcher*, published in 1929. The play is a highly poeticised account of the work of a Red Cross worker at an evacuation hospital whose job it is to update lists of missing and wounded men and send them back to the Red Cross. Pilcher based the play on her experiences as part of the Stanford University Women's Unit of the American Red Cross in an American hospital in France. After the war she became a producer at the Gate Theatre, London, a venue that became renowned for staging experimental and controversial work (Purkis, 2016: 505). *The Searcher* was produced in Stanford in 1929 and at the Grafton Theatre in London in 1930, and has rarely been performed since. There is no evidence that Pilcher and Enthoven knew each other, but the questions that the Searcher asks in her efforts to trace the missing are not dissimilar to those Enthoven used to organise her own collection, or indeed to the questions I have asked of records and archives up and down the country in an effort to track down the missing collector:

> Name of missing man?
> Number?
> When last seen?
> Where last seen?
> Under what circumstances?
> Eye-witness?
> Name of informant?
> Number?
> Remarks? (Pilcher, 1929: 4)

Like the Searcher, Enthoven's system is predicated on gathering information about persons and events based on the evidence of eyewitnesses and official reports. Like her Red Cross colleagues, she compiled relational indexes of people and places (venues) and titles of works to allow researchers to trace people and works. Unlike her Red Cross colleagues, she worked from first appearance rather than last, underlining the first appearance of an actor, writer, designer or producer in order to create a cross-reference on index cards. She organised the physical material around the information provided on the playbill, filing them by venue in chronological order, supplemented by press cuttings, engravings and any other evidence she could acquire: for example, tally sheets, tokens, letters and designs. Enthoven believed that this made it 'easier for the student to take in at once'.[46] So, for example, the file for the first production of Sheridan's *The School for Scandal* at Drury Lane in 1777 contains all the bills she was able to collect for the run, along with any newspaper announcements, prints of Sheridan or members of the cast, and any other 'extra' material she was able to collect. Her belief that this made it easier for readers was probably influenced by the popularity of 'Graingerized' or 'extra-illustrated' volumes during her youth. Extra-illustration is the process by in which the owners of printed books unbound them, inserted extra material relevant to the subject, usually prints, photographs and perhaps autographs, mounted on paper or card, and then rebound the whole to create an 'extra-illustrated' edition, sometimes running to multiple volumes. As Robert R. Wark notes:

> the words and the pictures are created separately and brought together by a third party who functions neither as a publisher nor a printer but as an interested collector who has the opportunity to create a new artifact out of materials furnished by writers and artists. (Wark, 1993: 152)

Enthoven found her creative role as such a collector, creating new artefacts out of the materials she acquired through her network of collectors, dealers and theatre workers. As the collection grew, theatre workers came to her for advice and information on historical staging, costuming and on the behaviour of audiences, actresses and everything else.[47] The collection she began is now the largest of its kind in the world, and renowned among theatre and performance scholars, but, unusually, the person who created it is not: the collection no longer bears her name and many of the elements of it that she acquired are no longer distinguishable because of the way in which she organised the filing system. It is common for collectors to request that the items they have collected remain discrete and/or that the collection bears their name, as with the Mander and Mitchenson Collection now housed at Bristol University, or the collection in the Folger Library in Washington. Enthoven bequeathed her collection to posterity, but obliterated her own story, leaving us with an incomplete context for the establishment and organisation of the collection.

For the duration of my career working with the collection that she founded, I have tried to build a fuller picture to bring context to her collection and to win the same recognition for her as her male contemporaries in theatre and other art forms enjoy.[48] I resented the lack of attention she had received from theatre scholars and also, historically, from museums and those who wrote about their histories and the histories of collecting. My aim has been to make a place for her in a feminist theatre history by enlarging the connections between the woman and her work 'and the work with the world at large' (Davis, 1989: 66). I had hoped to find more evidence of the spirited raconteur with a fondness for fancy dress hinted at in early interviews, letters and photographs, as well as in the appreciations of those who knew her at the end of her life. But that woman seems to have been too aware of how the judgements of the world at large could impact on a life's work, so what has emerged instead is a picture of a woman who was determined to be judged on her work rather than her life, and who arranged the evidence of her own life as the slimmest of extra-illustrated volumes.

Notes

1 She is referred to throughout this chapter as Enthoven, even when I am discussing her life before her marriage.
2 'Mrs Gabrielle Enthoven', *The Times*, 18 August 1950.

3 She is referred to as 'the theatrical encyclopedia' in a cutting from the *Daily Graphic* entitled 'Government Theatricals' pasted into an unnumbered scrapbook, Personal Papers of Gabrielle Enthoven, V&A, THM/114.
4 Enthoven was the first president of the Society for Theatre Research.
5 The Windsor Strollers and Old Stagers archives (U449) are housed at Canterbury Cathedral archives.
6 Archives and collections consulted include the Barry Jackson archive at Birmingham Central Library; the Windsor Strollers and Old Stagers archives at Canterbury Cathedral; the archives of Gwen Ffrangcon Davies and Lillah McCarthy at the V&A; and the archive of John Gielgud at the British Library.
7 The papers are known as the 'Personal Papers of Gabrielle Enthoven', archive reference THM/114.
8 Copy of the will of Mrs Augusta Gabrielle Eden Enthoven, Nominal File: Enthoven, Gabrielle Part 2, V&A.
9 See 'The Private Life of Gabrielle Enthoven', http://www.vam.ac.uk/blog/theatre-and-performance-2/the-private-life-of-gabrielle-enthoven (accessed 24 August 2018), and Smith (2016).
10 Following Havelock Ellis, Hall described herself as a 'congenital invert' (quoted in Souhami, 2013: 245).
11 Wilde and Terry were friends and both were also friends with Aimee Lowther, as was Enthoven, so it is possible that Enthoven, or Romaine as she was then, met one through the other. The earliest verifiable acquaintance seems to be Wilde, who dedicated 'Remorse' to her in 1889. In 1893 Enthoven's papers show she was staying with Aimee Lowther and by 1902 was in correspondence with Ellen Terry.
12 Copy of the will of Mrs Augusta Gabrielle Eden Enthoven, Nominal File: Enthoven, Gabrielle Part 2, V&A.
13 Nancy Price provides a pen portrait of Enthoven in her autobiography *Into an Hour-Glass* (1953), which reproduces many of the familiar facts about Enthoven's relationship with Duse, first-night attendance and fierce dedication to her collection, but also adds a hitherto unreported dimension to her character: 'though not what I would call a religious woman, she had an unassailable faith which many might envy' (Price, 1953: 84).
14 *Reading Mercury*, 27 March 1826.
15 Census data between 1841 and 1911 shows a steady increase in the number of women reporting as actresses and authors. See Kent (1977) and Davis (1991) for further details.
16 'The poem is written on a card embossed with the address 2 Ryder Street, St James, with the words, 'Written for me by Oscar Wilde in exchange for an autograph sonnet of Paul Verlaine. 10 November, 1889. GE' (Fong, 1979: 13).
17 The stories, and variations on them, subsequently appeared in *The Mask*, the magazine published by Gordon Craig, and Aimee Lowther was credited

as the source (see Fitzsimons, 2015: n.p.). They subsequently appeared in Vyvyan Holland's *Son of Oscar Wilde* (1954).

18 According to Enthoven this wasn't her first encounter with royalty. George Nash recalls that in old age she sometimes reminisced about being invited to Windsor Castle to play with Princess Mary of Teck and of once having slapped the young princess (Nash, 1956: n.p.).
19 Windsor Strollers album 1895–1928, Canterbury Cathedral archives. U499/7/2.
20 Enthoven biographical file, V&A.
21 The transaction is documented in letters between Terry and Enthoven (Cockin, 2014: 81–3, 84–5, 97).
22 Letters from Arthur Bouchier, Alfred Butt, Harley Granville-Barker, Lewis Casson, Charles Hawtrey, Barry Jackson, Edward Knoblock, Charles Maude, Nigel Playfair, Fred Terry and Herbert Beerbohm Tree all make such an undertaking, as do letters from actors and actresses such as Lilian Braithwaite, Hayden Coffin and Ellen Terry.
23 The probate register shows Charles's estate totalling £2,891 on his death in 1910, equivalent to more than £200,000 today.
24 See Kent (1977: 110–11) for a succinct summary of this.
25 See also Clay (2006) for another example of the elaborated professional/personal network, in this case, writers for *Time and Tide* magazine.
26 Silberthwaite goes on to elaborate on her current activities, which include painting all the prominent suffragists including Christabel Pankhurst. Pankhurst was in fact painted by Ethel Wright and the painting was exhibited the same year as the play was produced, 1909. Enthoven was also painted by Wright sometime between 1880 and 1900 and mentions the portrait in her will. Its current whereabouts are unknown. It was last recorded as being sold at Bonhams in 2002, titled 'Lady with the White Carnation'.
27 See Hindson (2016) for a detailed discussion of actresses and theatrical charities in late nineteenth and early twentieth centuries.
28 Farqharsson Sharp, letter to Gabrielle Enthoven, no date, Enthoven scrapbook, V&A, PN1620.L7.
29 Cecil Harcourt Smith, letter to Gabrielle Enthoven, no date, Enthoven scrapbook, V&A, PN1620.L7.
30 Guy Francis Laking, letters to Gabrielle Enthoven, Enthoven scrapbook, V&A, PN1620.L7. The London Museum moved from Kensington Palace to the West End of London in 1914.
31 Gabrielle Enthoven, letter to Constance Kyrle Fletcher, 22 May 1945, Gabrielle Enthoven Collection, V&A, THM/114/6.
32 'About the Halls', *The Sketch*, 15 January 1913, p. 60.
33 No first name is given for Mr Hill in the programme.
34 James Laver, Enthoven's friend and colleague at the V&A, noted that Duse was 'infatuated' with d'Annunzio. 'Sphere of Books', *The Sphere*, 12 April 1930, p. 82.

35 Letter to Enthoven, 16 July 1914, Personal Papers of Gabrielle Enthoven, V&A, THM/114/6.
36 *The Sketch*, 20 October 1915.
37 *Times Literary Supplement*, 14 October 1915.
38 Gabrielle Enthoven, unpublished typescript for *Ellen Young*, p. 16, Personal Papers of Gabrielle Enthoven, V&A, THM/114.
39 Ibid., p. 12.
40 Christopher St John, letter to Gabrielle Enthoven, 10 July 1914, Gabrielle Enthoven Collection, V&A, THM/114/6.
41 Personal Papers of Gabrielle Enthoven, V&A, THM/114.
42 Coward's friend and secretary Cole Lesley describes Enthoven as one of 'four friends' Coward had in New York; the other three were Lord Alington, Teddie Gerard and Cecile Sartoris (Lesley, 1976: 67). His biographer Sheridan Morley describes her as 'a vague acquaintance' (Morley, 1974: 74).
43 Nash refers to her worry about 'living on her capital', but the probate value of her estate was £20,727 (around £480,000 today).
44 H. M. Wallbrook, '*The Honeysuckle*', *Play Pictorial*, June 1937, p. xiii.
45 'Mrs Gabrielle Enthoven', *The Times*, 18 August 1950.
46 Enthoven to Contance Kyrle Fletcher, 22 May 1946, Personal Papers of Gabrielle Enthoven, V&A, THM/114/6.
47 During her lifetime Enthoven submitted an annual report to the V&A outlining her acquisitions and also who had used the collection and for what purpose.
48 As Eve Smith notes, collecting theatrical memorabilia, with the exception of Shakespeareana, has never had the same cultural capital as collecting books, fine and decorative arts, and their collectors are rarely written about or discussed (Smith, 2016). Furthermore, even in fine and decorative art studies, women collectors, as opposed to patrons, are rarely discussed. Charlotte Gere and Marina Vaizey's *Great Women Collectors* (1999) is a rare exception. Enthoven now has an entry in the *Oxford Dictionary of National Biography* because I was invited to contribute an entry on a subsequent curator of the collection, and pointed out that it seemed odd for the founder of the collection not to be included.

References

Baker, Michael (1985), *Our Three Selves: The Life of Radclyffe Hall*, London: Hamish Hamilton.
Bratton, Jacky (2011), *The Making of the West End Stage: Marriage, Management and the Mapping of Gender in London, 1830–1870*, Cambridge: Cambridge University Press.
British Red Cross (n.d.), 'First World War Volunteers', http://www.red

cross.org.uk/en/About-us/Who-we-are/History-and-origin/First-World-War (accessed 24 August 2018).
Byrne, Muriel St Clare (1950), 'Gabrielle Enthoven O.B.E', *Theatre Notebook*, 5, pp. 1–3.
Clay, Catherine (2006), *British Women Writers 1914–1945: Professional Work and Friendship*, Aldershot: Ashgate.
Cline, Sally (1997), *Radclyffe Hall: A Woman Called John*, London: John Murray.
Cockin, Katharine (2010), 'General Introduction', in *The Collected Letters of Ellen Terry, Volume 1 (1865–1888)*, ed. Katherine Cockin, London: Pickering and Chatto, pp. xiii–xxii
Cockin, Katharine, ed. (2014), *The Collected Letters of Ellen Terry, Volume 5 (1905–1913)*, London: Pickering and Chatto.
Cockin, Katharine (2017), *Edith Craig and the Theatres of Art*, London: Bloomsbury.
Coward, Noël (2004), *Present Indicative*, London: Bloomsbury.
Davis, Tracy C. (1989), 'Questions for a Feminist Methodology in Theatre History', in Thomas Postlewait and Bruce McConachie, eds, *Interpreting the Theatrical Past*, Iowa City: University of Iowa Press, pp. 59–81.
Davis, Tracy C. (1991), *Actresses as Working Women*, London: Routledge.
Doan, Laura (2013), *Disturbing Practices: History, Sexuality and Women's Experience of Modern War*, Chicago: University of Chicago Press.
Dorney, Kate (2014a), 'Excavating Enthoven: Investigating a Life of Stuff', *Studies in Theatre & Performance*, 32.2, pp. 115–25.
Dorney, Kate (2014b), 'Augusta Gabrielle Eden Enthoven', *Oxford Dictionary of National Biography*, Oxford: Oxford University Press, https://doi.org/10.1093/ref:odnb/57054 (accessed 11 September 2018).
Enthoven, Gabrielle (1911a), letter to the *Observer*, 12 November, Enthoven scrapbook, V&A, PN1620.L7.
Enthoven, Gabrielle (1911b), letter to the *Referee*, 12 November, Enthoven scrapbook, V&A, PN1620.L7.
Fitzsimons, Eleanor (2015), *Wilde's Women: How Oscar Wilde Was Shaped by the Women he Knew*, London: Duckworth.
Fong, Bobby (1979), 'Oscar Wilde: Five Fugitive Pieces', *English Literature in Transition, 1880–1920*, 22.1, pp. 7–16.
Gale, Maggie B. (1996), *West End Women: Women and the London Stage 1918–1962*, London: Routledge.
Gere, Charlotte, and Marina Vaizey (1999), *Great Women Collectors*, London: Philip Wilson.
Harraden, Beatrice (2013), *Lady Geraldine's Speech*, in Naomi Paxton, ed., *The Methuen Drama Book of Suffrage Plays*, London: Bloomsbury.
Hindson, Catherine (2016), *London's West End Actresses and the Origins of Celebrity Charity, 1880–1920*, Iowa City: Iowa University Press.

HMSO (1921), *Notes from Reports by the Joint War Committee and the Joint War Finance Committee of the British Red Cross and the Order of St John of Jerusalem in England on Voluntary Aid rendered to the Sick and Wounded at Home and Abroad and to British Prisoners of War 1914–19 with Appendices*, London: HMSO.
Holroyd, Michael (2004), 'Finding a Good Woman', in Mark Bostridge, ed., *Lives for Sale: Biographers' Tales*, London: Continuum.
Kennedy, Matthew (2004), *Edmund Goulding's Dark Victory: Hollywood's Genius Bad Boy*, Madison, WI: University of Wisconsin Press.
Kent, Christopher (1977), 'Image and Reality: The Actress and Society', in Martha Vicinus, ed., *A Widening Sphere: Changing Roles of Victorian Women*, London: Routledge, pp. 94–116.
Laver, James (1930), 'Sphere of Books', *The Sphere*, 12 April 1930, p. 82.
Laver, James (1952), 'Gabrielle Enthoven', in *Studies in English Theatre History: In Memory of Gabrielle Enthoven, O.B.E., First President of the Society for Theatre Research, 1948–1950*, London: Society for Theatre Research, pp. 1–9.
Lesley, Cole (1976), *The Life of Noël Coward*, London: Penguin.
Morley, Sheridan (1974), *A Talent to Amuse: A Biography of Noël Coward*, London: Penguin.
Nash, George (1956), 'Talk on the Gabrielle Enthoven Theatre Collection with introductory descriptive note about Mrs Enthoven for the Green Room Dramatic Club', unpublished typescript, V&A Enthoven biographical file.
Parker, John, ed. (1930), *Who's Who in the Theatre*, London: Pitman.
Pilcher, Verlona (1929), *The Searcher*, London: Heinemann.
Price, Nancy (1953), *Into an Hour-Glass*, London: Museum Press.
Purkis, Charlotte (2016), 'The Mediation of Constructions of Pacifism in *Journey's End* and *The Searcher*, Two Contrasting Dramatic Memorials from the Late 1920s', *Journalism Studies*, 17.4, pp. 502–16.
Smith, Eve (2016), 'Private Passions, Public Archives: Approaches to the Private Collector and Collection of Theatrical Ephemera in the Context of the Public Theatre Archive', unpublished PhD thesis, University of London.
Souhami, Diana (2013), *The Trials of Radclyffe Hall*, London: Quercus.
Wark, Robert (1993), 'The Gentle Pastime of Extra-Illustrating Books', *Huntington Library Quarterly*, 56.2, pp. 151–65.
Williams, W. R. (2004), 'Romaine, William Govett (1815–1893)', rev. Lynn Milne, *Oxford Dictionary of National Biography*, Oxford: Oxford University Press, online edition.

Archives

Victoria and Albert Museum

Gabrielle Enthoven, unpublished typescript for *Ellen Young*, Personal Papers of Gabrielle Enthoven, V&A, THM/114.

Gabrielle Enthoven, letter to Constance Kyrle Fletcher, 22 May 1945, Gabrielle Enthoven Collection, V&A, THM/114/6.
Gabrielle Enthoven, Last Will and Testament of Augusta Gabrielle Enthoven, 1951, Nominal File: Enthoven, Gabrielle, V&A.
Guy Francis Laking, letters to Gabrielle Enthoven, Enthoven scrapbook, V&A, PN1620.L7.
Farqharsson Sharp, letter to Gabrielle Enthoven, no date, Enthoven scrapbook, V&A, PN1620.L7.
Cecil Harcourt Smith, letter to Gabrielle Enthoven, no date, Enthoven scrapbook, V&A, PN1620.L7.
Christopher St John, letter to Gabrielle Enthoven, 10 July 1914, Gabrielle Enthoven Collection, V&A, THM/114/6.

3

Past the memoir

Winifred Dolan beyond the West End

Lucie Sutherland

As an actress, producer and teacher, Winifred Dolan (1867–1958) had a long and varied working life. Leaving professional theatre in 1904, Dolan later called her time as an actress 'years of rich experience and testing endeavour'.[1] These words appear in her memoir, *A Chronicle of Small Beer*, written in 1949 for private circulation within the school where Dolan had been employed as a drama teacher and amateur theatre producer for almost three decades. Here an initial career in professional theatre is positioned as a constructive contribution to subsequent work in education; 'experience' and 'testing' imply the formative significance of time spent working in the West End. That time is not the epitome of a professional life; rather, it informs theatre production by Dolan in a different professional realm, later in the twentieth century.

Dolan did not achieve any form of celebrity status as a professional actress. Born in Leeds in 1867, she was a student and then a student teacher at Leeds Girls' High School by the late 1880s, where as an amateur actor and producer she founded a drama society. In April 1891 she joined Sarah Thorne at Margate to receive some training, and by October she was employed as an understudy by actor-manager George Alexander, at the St James's Theatre in London; her first credited role was the following year as the maid, Rosalie, in the premiere of *Lady Windermere's Fan*. From this point she worked for Alexander and other West End and touring managers for just over a decade. However, employment was erratic, as was the alternative work sometimes offered by Alexander, to assist with play selection and theatre management. Early in 1904 Dolan moved on to a post as London Secretary for the Women's Unionist Association (an adjunct of the Conservative Party), and when the organisation was disbanded in 1917 she became a teacher at the Catholic New Hall School (then with an all-female student body), in Chelmsford. She was responsible for the introduction of regular drama work for the students, a feature that continues to be cited as characteristic of the school.[2] Dolan was offered a home there, even into retirement, and she developed a range of materials on theatre production for teaching purposes, as well as *Small Beer*. These materials have been housed at the Victoria and Albert Museum since 2004, and an edited version of the memoir was published in 2010, signalling recognition, more than half a century after her death, of specific contributions to the professional theatre industry and to the evolution of drama teaching.

Alongside production manuals, prompt books, set designs and *Small Beer*, there are included a number of plays written by Dolan, many for young actors; for example, an adaptation of *Toad of Toad Hall*. A very small number of letters – those directly quoted in the memoir – and some pictures are also present.[3] Looking across the collection, the majority of the material is there as a guide to future theatre makers, and the ephemera – letters and photographs – serve to consolidate the account of professional work outlined in *Small Beer*. This kind of evidence is rare; while it is possible to examine the published and unpublished autobiographical accounts and personal papers of many prominent theatre workers, a range of practice-focused manuals alongside a memoir, rearticulating the use of theatre in a pedagogic context, is a unique resource. Dolan's working life might not seem characteristic for an actress of the period, but in fact it points to the dexterity required of those actresses who did not achieve celebrity or consistent employment in theatre. Her life and collection are evidence of the range of skills that could be acquired in the West End to be redeployed in other sectors.

Surveying the Winifred Dolan Collection allows for analysis of the individual female subject, without her working practices becoming obscured by attention to more prominent West End workers. While *Small Beer* refers to the celebrities whom Dolan encountered, the collection is predominantly concerned with the way in which its author translated early work into theatre making at New Hall, promoting her aptitude as an independent producer and teacher. The school environment provided space for Dolan to construct a distinct form of professional identity that was not contingent upon what Christine de Bellaigue has described as 'an ideal-type model that simply reproduces the ways in which late-nineteenth century professional men sought to define themselves', querying 'the idea of women storming, or slipping in to, the professional citadel' (de Bellaigue, 2001: 965).

The production manuals she created display a reliance upon skills honed through West End work, but clearly represent Dolan as a producer who had established her own 'citadel' and who sought through her writing to pass on, and so to sustain, the practices she developed for New Hall so that students and staff of that school would, beyond the point of her retirement in the 1940s, continue the drama work she had instituted. In comparison, *Small Beer* is presented as having a less explicit relationship to her work there, describing the development of skills in acting and production, but not their application within the school environment. This creates a form of distance between her later working life and early professional experience, a distance that is explicitly insisted upon in the Foreword to *Small Beer*: '[n]ow that I am a very old woman I find that I can look back across the chasm of 60 years with a curious degree of detachment as though the story was that of another person I once knew' (Dolan, 2010: Foreword, n.p.).

This effort to separate an earlier self historicises professional work in the theatre, allowing the idea of perspective and authority over past experience and its subsequent influence to come to the fore. As recent work on the actress and autobiography has made explicit, the memoir is a form of autobiographical writing that provides space for the writer to present themselves as actor, not an object (Bratton, 2003: 101), and this is exemplified by the perspective Dolan takes upon her former career. Dolan was not alone in portraying her experience of the theatre industry at the end of the nineteenth century in this way.[4] An actress employing this technique was representing her work on her own terms, rather than solely inhabiting what Maggie B. Gale – in relation to the autobiographical writing of Lena Ashwell – has described as 'a history of English theatre, a history largely written and inhabited by men at the point at which she found herself looking autobiographically back on her own contributions' (Gale, 2004: 99). Mapping the narrative of *Small Beer*, it is evident that the aim is to present a constructive, active portrait of an earlier working life; while the treatment of Dolan by industry leaders is referenced, the structure and focus of the memoir foregrounds her developing expertise. Dolan uses *Small Beer* to advertise, for a New Hall readership – the original volume includes the phrase 'For private circulation only' – her presence in and experience of West End theatre, placing her own endeavour at the centre of the narrative.

The brief summary so far of a working life, and its legacy as the collection, provides an initial sense of both the professional expertise and personal interests we can attribute to Dolan. It also begins to unpick the range of evidence left behind, to assess the skills she developed as an actress, that were of value beyond the theatre industry. At New Hall, control over drama and performance work was far in excess of the professional agency experienced by Dolan in the West End. Therefore, a return to teaching was more than the aftermath of an acting career and recourse to a field which, by the early twentieth century, had long been recognised as a feasible professional sphere for middle-class women in need of regular income. The collection allows us to dig down into creative and pedagogic practice, the precise detail of her work as a teacher, and to examine how her working knowledge of professional theatre was used to mount full-length productions on New Hall's purpose-built stage. This chapter explores the way in which Dolan developed performance at the school in response to her work in the West End. She ceased all work in professional theatre in 1904, unable to secure regular employment as an actress or administrator in the theatrical mainstream. However, she did then use expertise honed within the theatre industry to mount an ambitious repertoire of Shakespeare and drama written by her for young people. Dolan was able to foreground her own expertise and creative ambition, adapting the kind of creative autonomy witnessed within the actor-manager system to work as an independent producer in a school environment.

West End work on and beyond the stage

Space for individual professional development at New Hall contrasted with the limits imposed upon the work Dolan could take on for West End managements. This is exemplified in correspondence from Alexander to Dolan:

> My dear Winifred,
> Candidly my thoughts about the secretary work in the autumn only spring from my wish to put you well on your feet – I am delighted to hear you are on a firmer footing. If you had been a man I should have given you the push this way ages ago with a view to you becoming my acting manager later on, but you see that wouldn't be possible.[5]

Alexander's attitude as actor-manager represents the 'demarcationary closure' (Witz, 1992: 47) that influenced the opportunities afforded to women in white-collar professional spheres, including theatre management, by the final decades of the nineteenth century. This is a useful concept in relation to Dolan's experience, as obvious restrictions were placed upon opportunities for her own professional progress. More specifically, sociologist Anne Witz notes:

> Gendered strategies of demarcationary closure describe processes of inter-occupational control concerned with the creation and control of boundaries between gendered occupations in a division of labour. They turn not upon the exclusion, but upon the encirclement of women within a related but distinct sphere of competence in an occupational division of labour and, in addition, their possible (indeed probable) subordination to male-dominated occupations. (Witz, 1992: 47)

This process may be perceived in practice with Dolan, where progress in the field of theatre management was obstructed on the grounds of gender, while a career in education involving the construction and management of a theatre space was feasible. Dolan could re-apply theatre industry practice in a field where women had an established professional status by the early twentieth century, sometimes in a very direct sense: she hired West End personnel to enhance the level of professionalism associated with New Hall productions, specifically a London-based scenic artist and a retired Drury Lane carpenter to develop and construct sets for annual Shakespeare productions from the mid-1920s into the 1930s (Canonesses, 2012: 41).

Although prominent West End personalities are frequently mentioned in the memoir – Ellen Terry is foregrounded as a friend and inspiration, and Alexander is a sustained presence since she worked mostly for him – personal professional development is the focus. So, it is made clear that while Terry introduced Dolan to the 'card' system – how to use a business card listing the St James's Theatre as her address to gain free entry to other West End productions, to develop her experience of repertoire and performance technique – it was Dolan who chose to capitalise upon this by regular theatregoing.[6] Similarly, while Alexander approved of her desire to watch each performance from the prompt corner as a junior member of the St James's Company, it was her idea to do this in the first place.[7]

She consistently features her pattern of promoting her own constructive practice and individual agency, although the memoir does not discount the informal networks that initially facilitated her acting career. Dolan admits that family relationships ultimately propelled her into employment; she met Henry Irving and Ellen Terry through her uncle, the poet Alfred Austin.[8] This is one example of the particular *habitus* to Dolan's early life, the social processes contributing to middle-class behaviours and social networks that afforded introductions to influential theatre professionals.⁹ Such networks frequently characterised the entrance of middle-class women into the theatre profession by the late nineteenth century. The following letter demonstrates the informal, influential networks that could provide a route from training into professional work:

> Dear Alfred Austin,
> If your niece is doing nothing I will attach her to our staff as an understudy and give her a guinea a week so that she could get an idea of London theatre, and if I found her intelligent I wd. try to give her a small part later on. Telegraph me if you think she would care for this.
> Yours sincerely,
> George Alexander.¹⁰

Small Beer admits personal advantages, but these are combined with details of how Dolan built upon opportunities to support herself; independent action to propel developing experience and employment is emphasised as paramount:

> So I telegraphed "Yes" to my Uncle, and to Mr. Alexander that I was on my way, wrote the news to my mother, packed my cabin trunk and was in London early next morning, presenting myself at the stage door of the St. James's Theatre about midday.¹¹

Dolan makes space to describe with precision her own endeavour in response to the communications between Alexander and Austin.

In their critical edition of *The Importance of Being Earnest* and its 1895 premiere, Joseph Donohue and Ruth Berggren describe the type and level of success experienced by Dolan, citing her career as a particular example of the kind of theatre professional who is almost lost to the historical record (certainly the case before the collection was acquired by the Victoria and Albert Museum). Their focus upon Dolan is prompted by her relationship to the play not as an actress, but as typist for an 1898 copy based upon Alexander's house script and used for the first published version (Donohue and Berggren, 1995: 75–6). They note that the entry for Dolan in the *Dramatic and Musical Directory* of 1893 describes her range as 'juv. ingen. light com.', which expresses her versatility and usefulness for a manager, but also her relative anonymity (Donohue and Berggren, 1995: 76). Between 1891 and 1899 Dolan appeared in a number of St James's productions in minor roles, including Rosalie in *Lady Windermere's Fan* (1892), Lady Orreyed in *The Second Mrs. Tanqueray*

5 The St James's Company at Balmoral, 16 September 1895.
Winifred Dolan is seated, second row, far right. George Alexander
is second row centre.

(at the first cast change, 1893), Miss Hickson in *Liberty Hall* (1895) and Margaret in *Much Ado About Nothing* (1898). However, she did not progress to more prominent roles within the company, and was frequently relegated to understudy work, which was 'only valuable as further practice, not for publicity'.[12] Interestingly, late in 1892 Edith Craig joined the St James's Company and took on the kind of minor roles that Dolan had been given. Most often, therefore, Dolan took over parts first performed by other actresses, or understudied, resulting in a lack of real opportunity for career development as an actress.

The memoir demonstrates that while class and social relationships supported entry to the profession, gender and a kind of outsider status simultaneously limited professional development: 'One of the difficulties I experienced as a lone wolf on the stage was that, not belonging to any theatrical family and, as a woman, unable to drink at bars, I never knew of a coming production till I read of it in the *Daily Telegraph*.'[13] However, when 'resting' between acting roles, Dolan frequently took on work associated with the processes of theatre management and production, and she describes this work in detail. Significantly, the more straightforward administrative work she took on, like the preparation of the *Earnest* script, is not mentioned. Much of the managerial and production work was prompted by the absence of Alexander's private secretary, R. G. Legge, from the St James's Theatre. For example, in 1896 Legge became acting manager at the Royalty Theatre, when Alexander took a short lease on the venue to produce the farcical comedy *His Little Dodge*.[14] Dolan describes the offer that she should take on the role of private secretary for a limited period, Alexander asserting that this was 'on the understanding that if and when I give up The Royalty you have kept his [Legge's] seat warm for him to come back to'.[15] Between 1895 and 1904 Dolan was then asked to undertake a range of production work, for example as Alexander's representative at rehearsals for the national tour of *Dodge*, which had been optioned by Ben Greet.[16] During the 1890s Dolan also travelled to Paris on at least two occasions to watch productions and subsequently to advise Alexander on whether to option plays.[17]

The trajectory of her work at the St James's Theatre suggests a growing reliance by Alexander upon Dolan in the areas of play selection and production development. During this period this was the type of work still undertaken almost exclusively by men within the West End realm, with few exceptions.[18] When covering for Legge, the kind of support offered by Dolan to the ostensibly autonomous actor-manager was integral to management:

> I'll describe a typical timetable as experience evolved it:
> First I had to be at the two theatres for the morning's letters & take them to Pont Street by nine o'clock – this meant my day started about 8am! I only quitted my post for a quick lunch at some restaurant (tea at the office) and left it around 6 or 6.30 p.m Home to dinner. Back at 7.30 p.m. & on duty until close on midnight. <u>Da capo</u> except on Sundays, for six months as it turned out. Pretty strenuous! My duties included: having taken instructions concerning the letters, return to St. James' to answer them; to keep G.A. posted as to his various engagements; writing his speeches when he was called upon to make them; to interview endless people on various matters; &, as his reader of plays, to keep abreast with a tide never less than 2ft high & on my own responsibility reject or, if I were in doubt as to a "possible one", submit a scenario of it upon which he decided to read it, or not! [...] G.A. was certainly giving me chances no <u>woman</u> had had at that time![19]

Dolan does not critique an actor-manager system that required such extensive support from unacknowledged personnel. Rather, she advertises her achievement in fulfilling designated tasks, and the benefits to her of taking on the work. She is an active participant in the evolution of her career, and the memoir indicates the care taken by its author to maintain a sense of her own agency in relation to the authority of the actor-manager. Thus when recounting that in 1896 Alexander asked her to enquire about English-language rights to the Henri Lavedan comedy *Le Prince d'Aurec* while she was in Paris, Dolan explains that she was already in the city to further her understanding of French theatre practice, taking classes with the Comédie Française actress Jenny Thénard.[20] *Small Beer* resists any impression that Dolan was simply a passive subordinate when employed in the actor-manager system.

Alexander did eventually offer her a long-term post as his private secretary in 1904, but this was not secure enough for a woman alert to the need for long-term employment in order to ensure financial security: 'Would it be permanent this time? Would my health stand the strain of those six months I have described, stand it for years? I refused.'[21] Again, Dolan emphasises her own participation in the development (and indeed the termination) of her career in the West End. The way her own initiative is foregrounded in *Small Beer*, alongside the technically specific manuals that make up the rest of the collection, indicates proactive behaviour translated into a career that offered more security and eventually a more senior role as producer:

> If I failed – not altogether, I think? – I am inclined to wonder whether my "line" lay less in acting than in "producing". But, you see, I wasn't a MAN – and in the 90's – ! Could it be that Providence permitted me this training that I might one day be of some little use to New Hall? If so, I deny I failed.[22]

As a woman who had a limited number of options available to her on ceasing to work as a professional actress, Dolan created a collection of resources to demonstrate the manner in which she self-consciously built upon West End practice to create a distinct identity as a teacher and producer at the school.

Drama in schools, drama schools and Dolan at New Hall

Dolan's later work was made possible by a number of factors alongside her experience in the theatre industry; again work was to some extent fostered by informal family networks. A form of 'patronage-based recruitment' (de Bellaigue, 2001: 964) more common in the teaching profession up to the mid-nineteenth century characterised the employment gained by Dolan at New Hall:[23] her sister was Prioress of the community attached to the school and, unlike her predecessor, supported the introduction of regular drama work (Tuckwell, 2006: 153). However, Dolan was a qualified teacher after her time at Leeds Girls' High School, and she was one of a number of lay teachers who joined New Hall on a permanent basis so that it could meet the requirements of the Education Act 1918 (Tuckwell, 2006: 157). In looking beyond family relationships to working practices, it is possible to see a sophisticated form of professional development in evidence, combining teaching experience and West End expertise.

An analysis of the collection defines its author as a dominant producer-teacher figure, so much so that Dolan coordinated the construction of a permanent theatre space at New Hall, the Eaton Theatre, in 1925.[24] As subsequent examples from the collection will make clear, Dolan used her previous professional experience to develop a precise approach to drama in education: practice by amateurs guided by professional standards. Her work at New Hall was not without precedent, however; as a qualified teacher she leveraged the tradition of drama in Catholic school environments and a growing interest in embedding performance practice within formal education to introduce professional standards in her drama teaching and theatre production work at New Hall.

There is evidence of drama work in monastery schools from the tenth century onwards, in Europe. This was not a straightforward and sustained presence, however, and in England it was a practice compromised by the anti-theatrical prejudices of Reformation culture. New Hall School, founded in 1642 and based at Liège until 1799, had its roots in the Augustinian tradition, which in relation to formal, Catholic school education demonstrated features including a focus upon developing and sustaining community – an aim that could potentially be fostered by collaborative performance practice – alongside distinct anti-theatrical prejudice.[25] The long-term (if contested) presence of some drama work in European Catholic schools over a number of centuries, in spite of this historical suspicion around the work of theatres themselves, is therefore one contextual factor that contributed to the kind of work Dolan was able to undertake at New Hall. Also, in the wake of the 1870 and 1902 Education Acts and increased state involvement in all schools – including faith schools – Catholic educational establishments were committed to the preservation of authority to determine curricula, again providing space for Dolan to develop drama work.[26]

These factors allowed an essential flexibility to provision in the early twentieth century so that the priorities of an individual school and an individual teacher-practitioner could be foregrounded. This development of drama work within a girls' school also echoed some characteristics of the new London drama schools, which fostered the idea that training provided women with particular skills applicable beyond the stage. The Academy of Dramatic Art, after its foundation in 1904, and with its majority female intake, was perceived in part to be a kind of finishing school for middle- and upper-class young women in the early decades of the twentieth century; a perception encouraged by some features of the curriculum, such as the teaching of French language alongside classes in acting technique and speech. This risked obscuring the role of the school as a training ground for professional actors and actresses – the stated aim of the industry leaders who were integral to the establishment of each school, including the actor-managers Frank Benson (Central School of Speech and Drama) and Beerbohm Tree ([R]ADA). But it did signal how drama work could play a valuable role within education, tied as it was in these new institutions to other kinds of vocational training and skills development, in a combination that was particularly appealing to female students at the time.[27] The increasing prevalence of drama work in permanent scholastic institutions was representative of a desire to consolidate the idea of theatre as a regulated and a reputable professional arena.

Although Dolan ended her career as an actress just as these drama schools were being established, she had worked with figures who supported their foundation, such as Tree and Alexander, and the collection asserts that she shared with these individuals a desire to promote, in an educational context, the rigour to be found in professional theatre:

> We, at New Hall, have for some years past set up a standard of acting Shakespeare which we humbly hope approximates to the worthiest efforts elsewhere. A gifted amateur is to be preferred to a bad professional, because the weaknesses of the one may be condoned while the vices of the other can not be too strongly condemned.[28]

The concept of the 'worthiest' productions versus the 'bad professional' displays an anxiety about less rigorous sectors of the theatre industry that risked undermining the plausibility of her role as former actress turned independent producer and teacher. While her more prominent West End contemporaries were developing actor training in permanent institutions to enhance the professionalism associated with the theatre industry, Dolan encouraged acting and stage management techniques that aspired to exacting industry standards.

She refers insistently to her particular personal expertise as a qualification for New Hall practice. In the handwritten 'Shakespeare Coach's Manual', for example, the edits to *Macbeth* are intrinsically linked to this expertise:

> I confess I have taken great liberties with the plays I have produced at New Hall – cutting out whole scenes, shortening speeches, even transposing the order of some scenes to simplify scene-shifting and reduce "waits" between the Acts. For instance, in "Macbeth", after the Tea Interval I have transposed Scenes 1 and 2 of Act iv because the interval gives time to set the heavy sleep walking scene and then the two short scenes England, and Birnam Wood follow together without any injury to the sequence of events. This is an expert job if balance, plot, etc. are not to suffer, and needs a very professional measure of experience and technique.[29]

Dolan positions her work as both particular to the precise school environment, and as being built upon her professional knowledge. Her focus upon pre-existing dramatic texts translated to performance, and not on drama as a route to personal expression or well-being as is encountered in many Theatre in Education initiatives later in the twentieth century, also demonstrates a close correlation to a mainstream theatre model. Dolan's method was structured for a precise institutional framework, but that did not mean it was a wholly unique way of working, based as it was upon a range of established factors including personal expertise in professional theatre, and wider, increasing attention to drama as a discrete area for study.

Amateur theatre and professional expertise

The presence and practice of Dolan within a school environment also exemplified frequent links between professional theatre and amateur production in the first decades of the twentieth century. Dolan's work at the school was essentially a branch of amateur theatre based upon the perseverance of established practice rather than innovation, unlike, for example, some of the amateur work that had been integral to the emergence of 'New Drama' earlier in the century. Attention to her work provides an alternative to 'accounts of the twentieth century [which] have tended to focus on tracing the evolution and continuities of the new rather than recognising the parallel continuities of the old' (Cochrane, 2011: 11), a tendency that has, as Claire Cochrane attests, 'contributed to the further disparagement and thus marginalisation of the widely practised "not new"' (2011: 11). Dolan explicitly called upon the authority of previous West End work; as a producer – in the collection that word is frequently employed to designate her role – she asserts the value of her own experience, while making amateur theatre a viable and regular feature of a Catholic school education.

Amateur theatre work was not a new experience for Dolan. She had founded an amateur company in Leeds during the 1880s, and, as a professional actress, accepted work in prominent amateur productions, for example at Shrewsbury in the Yeomanry Centenary Pageant mounted by Lord Kilmorey in 1895.[30] On returning to amateur production in a school Dolan developed a particular kind of small theatre environment for revivals of canonical drama and her own plays for young people. Control over every aspect of a production allowed her to maintain engagement through practice with forms of theatre that were in line with her own ideals for drama, informed by aesthetic and religious beliefs. In comparison, in *Small Beer* she identifies the 'New Drama' movement and syndicated production as developments that were to the detriment of professional theatre repertoire by the final decade of the nineteenth century. The moral imperatives that guided these views are evident in the memoir, and are implicitly linked to the time at which she ended her work in professional theatre in 1904:

> So long as the old Queen lived the trend was hardly noticeable, but with the Edwardian age it burst into full bloom. We see the mature fruit today in our Divorce Court lists, in the sex-appeal, strip-tease nudity of our cabaret entertainments, the hysterical worship of film stars[.][31]

Identifying the first years of the twentieth century as a tipping point further endorses the implementation of expertise beyond what was, to Dolan, a theatre industry changing for the worse.

Her work sat outside the primary amateur theatre organisations of the early twentieth century – notably the British Drama League – but material in the collection designates a similarity to the movement as a whole with the contribution of a (former) professional theatre worker to amateur production. In the Foreword to her 'Guide to Amateur Theatrical Production', Dolan makes this explicit: 'This little guidebook is respectfully and diffidently offered by one whose professional acquaintance with the stage and her whole-hearted love of it are her sole excuses.'[32] Dolan designates New Hall work as quite consciously a kind of 'pro-am' practice. The overt use of her former career as qualification for this also attests to the way in which autobiographical traces are present throughout the collection, signalling the function it performs.

West End work is insistently promoted as one influence upon a complex and developing professional life, but it does not receive extended attention beyond *Small Beer*. In the 'Guide to Stage Management', Dolan describes her integral role in the evolution of drama work at New Hall, before providing technical specifications for the theatre space. When assessing how West End work is used, the final page of the Foreword to this volume is of particular interest. Here, it is made explicit that early experience has been translated into clear lines of practice, to enhance personal authority as a teacher and producer. The Foreword concludes 'Winifred Dolan, Newnham Paddox, Rugby, 1945' (the school having relocated during wartime), accompanied by a list of sites where she had been employed during her time as a professional actress:

St. James's Theatre

Criterion   "
Court   "
Avenue   "   } 1891–1904
Terry's   "
Daly's   "

Underneath this list, Dolan has made handwritten additions, emphasising the authority conferred by a previous career:

Command Performance Balmoral Castle.

Lyceum Theatre } Single 'Benefit' performances[33]
Haymarket

Here Dolan provides endorsement of her experience and aptitude – serial employment in high-calibre theatres – as a stage manager by listing professional work with London companies. Apart from this listing, there are no references to her West End work in this volume; it is not another version of the memoir. This is a formal summary of an earlier working life, positioned in isolation and in brief, confirming to the user that the author is qualified to create the guide.

Like all the materials in the collection, this demonstrates a sense of professional authority. The volumes on stage management and amateur theatre sit alongside the guide to producing Shakespeare and the 'Scene-Shifters' Manual', a number of prompt copies, and set design illustrations. Materials are either handwritten or typed, and most often in bound volumes. In creating these resources, Dolan echoes the growing prevalence of published technical guides for amateur theatre written by industry professionals and educators. Many of these had a particular focus upon appealing to women, and situating practical drama as suitable for female students.[34] Once again Dolan is shown to be operating as a woman within a precise environment, creating her own repertoire but demonstrating awareness of parallel developments in drama and theatre work.

Dolan had ultimate authority over productions, but the nature of that authority was quite different to the type assumed by celebrity actresses of her generation, for example Irene Vanbrugh, who also worked frequently at the St James's Theatre during the 1890s.[35] Vanbrugh achieved a form of control over her career through prominent status and regular work in the mainstream theatre industry:

> To a woman the profession of acting is one which, provided she has talent and is prepared to work hard, is as satisfactory financially as a woman can have, because, although it is precarious and uncertain, it is independent of others, to a great extent, and is one in which a woman has equal chances with a man – in which her own individuality is her chief asset – in fact, she is dependent upon this for the market value she attains. (Vanbrugh, 1951: 98–9)

As a woman working 'behind the scenes' and performing in minor roles by comparison, Dolan's presence was less prized in the West End marketplace, but the skills developed in that arena were translated into distinct authority and professional agency within a subsequent professional context, and bolstered via strategies such as the listing of sites of employment in the 'Guide to Stage Management'.

Another technique used in Dolan's writing is the inclusion of quotes from other sources summarising the working practices of her former colleagues, thus linking her own expertise, as evident in the creation of the technical guides, with a kind of scholarly procedure in developing materials for the school. Actress and teacher are both represented through this process. In her guide to producing amateur theatre, for example, she includes pre-existing accounts by Bram Stoker and Ellen Terry of how Irving staged *Macbeth*. Dolan explains her recourse to other texts thus:

> Dame Ellen Terry's "Story of my Life" and Bram Stoker's "Personal Reminiscences of Henry Irving" are two volumes packed with instructions for the aspiring actor. Neither being written with any such purpose

in view, the knowledge is to be gathered by a process of sifting and gleaning.³⁶

Experience of West End work and the ideas of well-known theatre industry professionals combine in material that advertises Dolan's own technical expertise, epitomised in the typed 'Scene-Shifters' Manual', which provides intricate instruction as to how to construct a set and check sight lines in the theatre space.³⁷ One further example is the detailed sound plot for *Macbeth* reproduced in the 'Guide to Amateur Theatrical Production' to exemplify the kind of aural accompaniment required for a New Hall play in performance. This demonstrates the precise and professional attention to stage management encouraged in her amateur practitioners:

> Orchestra Time Plot
> E.G. "Macbeth"
> Overture: "Finlandia" 8 minutes
> Act I Sc 1: Desert [*sic*] place. Leitmotif to take the curtain up 1¼ mins.
>   Chopin's Prelude in C 1¾ minutes
> Sc 2: Palace of Forres
> Sc 3: Blasted heath. Leitmotif as before.
> Dvorak's New W. Symphony. 1½ minutes³⁸

Here Dolan guided student actors and musicians to realise intricate production practice, adopted from professional theatre work. Further evidence reinforces how focused she was on meeting professional standards as she advertises, in the 'Guide to Stage Management', how she promoted her qualifications when developing drama work at New Hall:

> Reverend Mother told me they would place in my hands, as an expert in theatrical matters, the planning of a Stage in the new Gymnasium, worthy of New Hall's dramatic reputation.
>   Accordingly, I drew up a plan setting forth measurements, rake of Stage, gadgets etc. Etc., with meticulous detail. This I took with me to the architect in the City explaining the source of my authority together with my credentials as an expert.³⁹

In the repeated insistence upon her qualifications and their application, Dolan not only records the development and achievements of her own working life, but also provides evidence of the type and breadth of professional expertise available to women theatre workers by the end of the nineteenth century. Her later career is one example of how this expertise

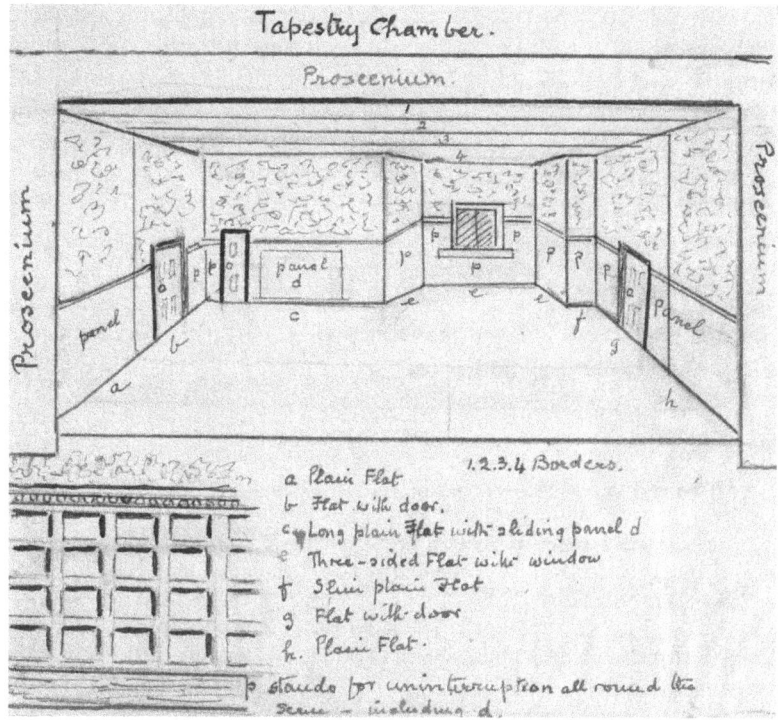

6 An example of the set designs developed by Winifred Dolan, taken from the 'Scene Plots Diagrams' section of the Winifred Dolan Collection.

was influencing subsequent theatre making, here within an educational environment.

Expertise and New Hall repertoire

Consistently, Dolan's focus is on translating texts into performance rather than other forms of activity, such as training exercises. Her interest was clearly in the redeployment of West End production practice, adapted to a specific context. The texts for production were canonical or of her own composition or adaptation, and some plays for young actors, including *Toad of Toad Hall*, are included in the collection, while plays written for production in professional theatre were not retained. Writing under the name Rothwell Haig (adapted from an area in her home city of Leeds), Dolan had written work for the professional theatre, and there is evidence that at least one of her plays was staged. Dolan continued to write after leaving the acting profession, and her play *Kynaston's Wife* was produced by Madge Kendal on tour in 1907, and then in revival for charity performances, as late as 1921 for Lord Haig's Officer's Association on 28 February of that year.[40] The absence of this work from the collection further consolidates the idea that surviving materials were kept to sustain a particular kind of production practice at New Hall, influenced by but distinct from the professional theatre industry.

Both practice and repertoire were shaped by Dolan as producer, director and stage manager. She also performed the role of censor in preparing plays for a Catholic school environment, noting in relation to the production of Shakespeare:

> A producer called upon to produce a classic has a much harder task than if called upon to produce a modern play. She has greater need of proficiency in technique and considerable scholarship [...] Shakespeare's plays have to be ruthlessly "cut" for School performance owing to time limit and because some of the text is unsuited to the lips of children, especially girls.[41]

The prompt books for Shakespeare productions included in the collection reinforce the measure of control exercised by Dolan, and include a number of precise directions for her actors that are categorised under specific headings. In the 'Guide to Amateur Theatrical Production' she emphasises that these are not the only, but rather the primary categories to consider when directing actors:

1. Business
2. Bye-play
3. Movements and positions
4. Exits and entrances
5. Music cues
6. Lighting cues (sometimes).[42]

Using these markers, Dolan was able to designate intricate levels of work. For example, the prompt book for *Macbeth* in the collection includes intricate 'Business' and 'Bye-play'. Business: 'During this scene down at door L. the Servants hand meat on spits to each guest. Then one with a flagon fills the goblets, leaving the flagon on the table: they all exeunt off up stage L.' Bye-play: 'Lady Macbeth has noticed that Macbeth has been called aside on some business and is worried about it.'[43] She also provided guidelines for acting technique, outlining for her amateur student-actors a necessary process from retention of information to articulation of performance:

> Theory, alone, serves fully the purposes of the Critic and the Teacher, but it is inadequate to those of the Artist.
> The critic may – the Artist dare not – part Theory from Practice.
> For the Artist, they must go hand-in-hand, because there is a certain <u>mechanical dexterity</u> to be acquired before the beautiful conceptions he processes can be communicated to others.
> Acting is an ear-directed and a mind-directed art; ear-directed in our study of it, mind-directed in our exercise of it.
> BUT – his preparatory toil over, the actor must <u>forget himself in his subject</u>. He must let his voice henceforth be prompted NOT by the ear (however musical and exact it may be); but by his <u>sympathy</u> with the matter.
> Similarly with his gestures, expression, poses and so on: they, also, must be prompted not by memory but by sympathy too.
> All must come <u>from WITHIN!</u>
> If this natural precept be overlooked the actor must not expect to gain much from his so-called study of elocution, gesture, and the rest!
> The Artist must <u>digest</u> his subject-matter before he can offer it to that <u>successful assimilation</u> by his audience which constitutes <u>success</u>.[44]

This not only suggests the attention to technique embedded in New Hall practice; it also portrays Dolan's work with the students as a producer concerned primarily with intricate and thoroughly rehearsed performance. Her expertise as an actress informs the precision of work presented by amateur cast members, the application of professional standards and the use of processes imported to promote sophisticated amateur theatre work.

An implicit and sustained argument for the necessary relationship between creativity and expertise is characteristic of the collection, as is the drive to argue for one presiding producer figure; authority over a production by one individual. This rearticulates the actor-manager model for use by Dolan in a specific environment; in the 'Guide to Stage Management', Dolan acknowledges the importance of collaboration while arguing that ultimate control should reside with a single individual:

> May I give you a piece of advice? – Establish from the outset a spirit of collaboration. Let them realise the pecuniary value of the stuff they are handling and that, once spoilt, it cannot be replaced. Give your <u>reasons</u>

for certain "insistings" when they obviously think you are just "being pernicketty"!
Make a point of being there, on the spot. Never "leave them to it"![45]

The approach to stage management found in the guide attests to the conviction that regulation and control are integral to theatre making. This was also a characteristic of the kind of West End work Dolan regularly experienced in her earlier professional life, for example under Alexander, who implemented stringent practice – he consistently rehearsed his company for three hours each day in preparing a new production – and was consequently renowned for close management and supervision throughout the production process.[46]

Tracing a link between characteristic West End practice and the work conducted by Dolan does nothing to disrupt or challenge dominant perceptions of mainstream theatre, around the pre-eminence of the West End and the male theatre industry leaders operating there in the late nineteenth and early twentieth centuries: indeed, these are markers used by Dolan to authorise her subsequent work. Instead, material in the collection demonstrates how Dolan appropriated the forms of authority and practice she experienced as a subordinate employee in the West End, and implemented those qualities to work as a creative figurehead in a single location for three decades. Prior to Theatre in Education initiatives later in the twentieth century, the work of Dolan at New Hall demonstrated particular expertise in informing and propelling the introduction of regular and concerted drama work within a school environment. Dolan developed the materials which later formed the collection at a time when training in practice in schools and at the vocational, drama-school level was expanding. Women took prominent roles in this expansion as both teachers and students; as such the collection expresses not only a personal sense of professional authority, but also a desire to create a legacy at New Hall, through resources that would bequeath knowledge and mark her proficiency as a theatre maker in a specific context. Dolan was a producer figure who translated West End work into a subsequent career where professional agency and authority were profound, and this situates her as one kind of inheritor of the actor-manager role. Her work at New Hall exemplifies the expertise and professional dexterity that could be implemented by actresses negotiating the theatre industry and alternative career trajectories by the start of the twentieth century.

Notes

1. Winifred Dolan, 'A Chronicle of Small Beer' [bound manuscript], 1949, V&A Theatre and Performance Collection, The Winifred Dolan Collection, THM/394/1.Throughout this chapter, the Winifred Dolan Collection (hereafter referred to as 'the collection') has been used for all quotations, including *Small Beer*. Although this volume has been published (Dolan, 2010), the original handwritten version is the source for the quotations here. It includes distinctive features of punctuation and expression from Dolan's text, many of which were standardised for the 2010 edition. Archive materials are quoted as accurately as possible, employing features used by Dolan including upper-case letters and underlining for emphasis. This assists in examination of both the content and aims for the collection.
2. Prominent in the 'About Us – History' section of the school website is the following: 'School developments have included, for example, the Eaton Theatre, which was completed in 1925, with a stage and green room at one end and a studio above. The old theatre at New Hall was last used for the performance of "O what a lovely war", in December 1986. The refurbished Eaton Theatre was reopened in September 2008, with new tiered seating' (New Hall School, 2016).
3. There are a few, additional items that do not conform to type: *Whittington of London*, a historical novel, Dolan's handwritten notebook containing the poems she worked with for elocution classes (and there is a note in that book acknowledging that someone else at the school added this to the collection at a later date) and a mid-nineteenth-century collection of writing for children, *The Child's Own Book*, which, according to names inscribed, was a family heirloom.
4. For example, both Lena Ashwell and Elizabeth Robins experienced very different levels of success to Dolan as professional actresses. These three women held diverse personal and political beliefs when operating in West End theatre at the end of the nineteenth century, but there are similarities in how they wrote, later in life, about their experiences, employing a sense of distance as a way to demarcate their current practice and to historicise professional work on their own terms. This point of similarity in life writing by actresses of the era has been examined in Gale (2004) and Gardner (2004).
5. George Alexander, letter to Winifred Dolan [correspondence], no date, V&A Theatre and Performance Collection, The Winifred Dolan Collection, THM/394/7/3.
6. Dolan, 'A Chronicle of Small Beer', p. 26.
7. Ibid., p. 68.
8. Austin (1835–1913) became poet laureate in 1896 after a delay in appointing someone to the role following the death of Tennyson in 1892. A prominent

Conservative, he edited the *National Review* and publicly supported both Disraeli and Salisbury during their terms as prime minister.
9   *Habitus*: the interplay of social structure and individual activity according to class as defined by Bourdieu (1984).
10 George Alexander, letter to Alfred Austin [correspondence], c. 1892, V&A Theatre and Performance Collection, The Winifred Dolan Collection, THM/394/7/3.
11 Dolan, 'A Chronicle of Small Beer', p. 61.
12 Ibid., p. 86.
13 Ibid., p. 215.
14 Producing work at another West End theatre was an unusual venture for Alexander; he staged the play at the Royalty (24 October 1896–16 January 1897) while *The Prisoner of Zenda* was running at the St James's Theatre. Alexander was motivated to mount this second production, at least in part, as a vehicle for the actor Fred Terry, whose wife Julia Neilson had been contracted by Alexander for work at the St James's. The offer of work to Terry was, according to Dolan, integral to Neilson's contract (Dolan, 'A Chronicle of Small Beer', p. 156).
15 Dolan, 'A Chronicle of Small Beer', p. 157.
16 Ibid., pp. 163–4.
17 George Alexander, letter to Winifred Dolan [correspondence], c. 1896, V&A Theatre and Performance Collection, The Winifred Dolan Collection, THM/394/7/3; Dolan, 'A Chronicle of Small Beer', pp. 155, 166.
18 One example of such an exception would be the work of Helen Carte Boulter at the Savoy between 1875 and 1913.
19 Dolan, 'A Chronicle of Small Beer', pp. 156–61. The second theatre referred to here is the Royalty.
20 Ibid., p. 155.
21 Ibid., p. 235.
22 Ibid., p. 236.
23 de Bellaigue (2001) charts the altering professional field of teaching for women, using the personal writings of 83 school teachers working between 1780 and 1860.
24 Winifred Dolan, 'Guide to Stage Management' [bound manuscript], 1945, V&A Theatre and Performance Collection, The Winifred Dolan Collection, THM/394/2/2.
25 This tension between a perceived use for drama and anti-theatrical prejudice is examined by Bolton (2007: 45–62).
26 More fine detail on Catholic school autonomy and education legislation may be found in Tenbus (2008: 432–51).
27 For example, the ratio of female to male students at the Academy by 1909 was estimated at four women to one man (Barnes, 1958: 67).
28 Winifred Dolan, 'Guide to Amateur Theatrical Production' [bound

manuscript], no date, V&A Theatre and Performance Collection, The Winifred Dolan Collection, THM/394/2/1, foreword.
29 Winifred Dolan, 'The Shakespeare Coach's Manual' [manuscript], no date, V&A Theatre and Performance Collection, The Winifred Dolan Collection, THM/394/5/3, p. 2.
30 Dolan, 'A Chronicle of Small Beer', p. 171.
31 Ibid., p. 149.
32 Winifred Dolan, 'Guide to Amateur Theatrical Production' [bound manuscript], no date, V&A Theatre and Performance Collection, The Winifred Dolan Collection, THM/394/2/1.
33 Dolan, 'Guide to Stage Management', foreword.
34 An example of such a work would be Elsie Fogerty's 1907 adaptation of Tennyson's *Princess*, aimed primarily at girls' schools. The emergence of these guides receives more detailed coverage in Newey (1998: 93–111) and Cochrane (2011).
35 Irene Vanbrugh (1872–1949) was promoted within the company during the 1894 and 1895 seasons, and then recruited by Alexander as leading actress for nine productions between February 1906 and December 1915. Initially, she played Charley Wishanger in *The Masqueraders* (1894), Fanny in *Guy Domville* (1895), Gwendolyn in *The Importance of Being Earnest* (1895), Ellean in *The Second Mrs. Tanqueray* (1895) and Kate Merryweather in *The Idler* (1895). She returned to the theatre to play leading roles with the company after this period: Nina in *His House in Order* (1906), Marise in *The Thief* (1907), Dorothy Faringay in *The Builder of Bridges* (1908), Celia Faraday in *Colonel Smith* (1909), *The Thief* revival (1909), Zoe Blundell in *Mid-Channel* (1909), Cynthia Herrick in *Open Windows* (1913), *His House in Order* revival (1914) and Ottoline in *The Big Drum* (1915).
36 Dolan, 'Guide to Amateur Theatrical Production', p. 83.
37 Winifred Dolan, 'Scene-Shifters' Manual' [bound manuscript], no date, V&A Theatre and Performance Collection, The Winifred Dolan Collection, THM/394/2/3.
38 Dolan, 'Guide to Amateur Theatrical Production', p. 227.
39 Dolan, 'Guide to Stage Management', foreword.
40 Dolan, 'A Chronicle of Small Beer', pp. 195–6.
41 Dolan, 'The Shakespeare Coach's Manual', pp. 1–2.
42 Dolan, 'Guide to Amateur Theatrical Production', p. 20.
43 Winifred Dolan, *Macbeth* prompt book [bound volume], no date, V&A Theatre and Performance Collection, The Winifred Dolan Collection, THM/394/3/3.
44 Dolan, 'Guide to Amateur Theatrical Production', pp. 62–3.
45 Dolan, 'Guide to Stage Management', foreword.
46 The practice employed by Alexander of rehearsing from 11 until 2 is

confirmed by Mason (1935: 24–5) and Dolan, 'A Chronicle of Small Beer', p. 66.

References

Barnes, Kenneth (1958), *Welcome, Good Friends*, London: Peter Davies.
Bolton, Gavin (2007), 'A History of Drama Education: A Search for Substance', in Liora Bresler, ed., *International Handbook of Research in Arts Education*, Dordrecht: Springer, pp. 45–62.
Bourdieu, Pierre (1984), *Distinction: A Social Critique of the Judgement of Taste*, trans. Richard Nice, Cambridge, MA: Harvard University Press.
Bratton, Jacky (2003), *New Readings in Theatre History*, Cambridge: Cambridge University Press.
Canonesses of the Holy Sepulchre (2012), *Fishy Tales: Living Memories of New Hall 1930-2012*, Colchester: Canonesses of the Holy Sepulchre.
Cochrane, Claire (2011), *Twentieth Century British Theatre: Industry, Art and Empire*, Cambridge: Cambridge University Press.
De Bellaigue, Christina (2001), 'The Development of Teaching as a Profession for Women before 1870', *The Historical Journal*, 44.4, pp. 963–88.
Dolan, Winifred (2010), *A Chronicle of Small Beer*, ed. Andy Moreton, London: Society for Theatre Research.
Donohue, Joseph, and Ruth Berggren, eds (1995), *Oscar Wilde's 'The Importance of Being Earnest': A Reconstructive Critical Edition of the Text of the First Performance*, Gerrards Cross: Colin Smythe.
Gale, Maggie B. (2004), 'Lena Ashwell and Auto/Biographical Negotiations of the Professional Self', in Maggie B. Gale and Viv Gardner, eds, *Auto/biography and Identity: Women, Theatre and Performance*, Manchester: Manchester University Press, pp. 99–125.
Gardner, Viv (2004), 'The Three Nobodies: Autobiographical Strategies in the Work of Alma Ellerslie, Kitty Marion and Ina Rozant', in Maggie B. Gale and Viv Gardner, eds, *Auto/biography and Identity: Women, Theatre and Performance*, Manchester: Manchester University Press, pp. 10–38.
Mason, A. E. W. (1935), *Sir George Alexander and the St. James's Theatre*, London: Macmillan.
New Hall School (2016), 'About Us, History', http://www.newhallschool.co.uk/History (accessed 4 December 2016).
Newey, Kate (1998), 'Home Plays for Ladies: Women's Work in Home Theatricals', *Nineteenth Century Theatre*, 26, pp. 93–111.
Tenbus, Eric G. (2008), 'Defending the Faith through Education: The Catholic Case for Parental and Civil Rights in Victorian Britain', *History of Education Quarterly*, 48.3, pp. 432–51.
Tuckwell, Tony (2006), *New Hall and its School*, King's Lynn: Free Range Publishing.

Vanbrugh, Irene (1951), *Hints on the Art of Acting*, London: Hutchinson.
Witz, Anne (1992), *Professions and Patriarchy*, London: Routledge.

Archives

Victoria and Albert Museum

George Alexander, letter to Alfred Austin [correspondence], c. 1892, V&A Theatre and Performance Collection, The Winifred Dolan Collection, THM/394/7/3.

George Alexander, letter to Winifred Dolan [correspondence], c. 1896, V&A Theatre and Performance Collection, The Winifred Dolan Collection, THM/394/7/3.

George Alexander, letter to Winifred Dolan [correspondence], no date, V&A Theatre and Performance Collection, The Winifred Dolan Collection, THM/394/7/3.

Winifred Dolan, 'Guide to Stage Management' [bound manuscript], 1945, V&A Theatre and Performance Collection, The Winifred Dolan Collection, THM/394/2/2.

Winifred Dolan, 'A Chronicle of Small Beer' [bound manuscript], 1949, V&A Theatre and Performance Collection, The Winifred Dolan Collection, THM/394/1.

Winifred Dolan, 'Guide to Amateur Theatrical Production' [bound manuscript], no date, V&A Theatre and Performance Collection, The Winifred Dolan Collection, THM/394/2/1.

Winifred Dolan, *Macbeth* prompt book [bound volume], no date, V&A Theatre and Performance Collection, The Winifred Dolan Collection, THM/394/3/3.

Winifred Dolan, 'Scene-Shifters' Manual' [bound manuscript], no date, V&A Theatre and Performance Collection, The Winifred Dolan Collection, THM/394/2/3.

Winifred Dolan, 'Scene Plot Diagrams' [miscellaneous illustrations, unbound], no date, V&A Theatre and Performance Collection, The Winifred Dolan Collection, THM/394/2/4.

Winifred Dolan, 'The Shakespeare Coach's Manual' [manuscript], no date, V&A Theatre and Performance Collection, The Winifred Dolan Collection, THM/394/5/3.

Winifred Dolan, 'Toad of Toad Hall' [manuscript], no date, V&A Theatre and Performance Collection, The Winifred Dolan Collection, THM/394/6/1.

4

Offstage labour

Actresses, charity work and the early twentieth-century theatre profession

Catherine Hindson

Though their stage performances often feature as the subjects of focused attention, early twentieth-century actresses functioned as part of a wider theatre industry that was sustained by the non-theatrical social, material, consumer and economic cultures that surrounded it. In this context, the onstage performances offered by actresses of this period were just one element of more expansive, diverse professional repertoires that also included offstage public appearances and representations. Such offstage work, performed for a range of audience demographics in diverse, non-theatrical metropolitan spaces, was the source of considerable day-to-day labour for actresses and necessitated ongoing attention and responsive action. Nonetheless, the activities involved in offstage work rarely form the subject of scholarly focus and are regularly omitted from histories of the theatre. In this chapter I consider one particular area of early twentieth-century offstage labour: the numerous and demanding public appearances made by actresses in aid of charities. Focusing on a high-profile fundraising event that took place at the London department store Harrods in 1911, I offer such occasions as ways of both extending our holistic understandings of the stage profession of the day and acknowledging the multiple professional roles that actresses performed.

Charity work can be identified as a key feature of the gradual, uneven process of improvement in the theatre industry's social status that marked the nineteenth century. The stage's charitable reputation was firmly rooted in the late eighteenth century, but the 1880s and 1890s brought a paradigm shift in the types of charity activity that theatrical performers led and contributed to. Most notably, there was a clear increase in the expectation that stage performers, a professional body previously known primarily for their industry-based charitable activity and benevolence, would consistently contribute to large-scale public fundraising events in aid of non-theatrical charities (Hindson, 2014; 2016). The end result was a significant change in the public, and publicised, face of theatre's charity work. While leading actors and actresses continued to govern the industry's own charitable bodies – including the Actors' Benevolent Fund, the Theatrical Ladies' Guild and the Actors' Orphanage Fund – and to support other philanthropic endeavours by organising performances or attending meetings, dinners and other networking events (Richards, 2005: 68), accounts indicate that the majority of high-profile charitable public appearance work in the late nineteenth and early twentieth centuries was undertaken by well-known actresses. By the 1880s theatre's leading ladies were organising and participating in year-round, crammed, professional calendars of bazaars, tea parties, garden parties, costume balls and fundraising shows (Hindson, 2016). As the twentieth century arrived, actresses had become an anticipated feature of the fashionable charity event, populating and representing fundraising occasions and modelling Britain's much-lauded charitable spirit.

The consequent increase in time and labour that theatrical performers expended on charitable work did not pass without question within the stage profession: professional appearances that supported non-theatrical charity activities became a site of intra-industry debate. While the mainstream press consistently celebrated the amount of charity work undertaken by stage personalities, theatrical trade publications repeatedly returned to and fuelled ongoing arguments about the professional ethics and practical challenges triggered by such labour. Two key issues were foregrounded: first, that charity work required performers to give a significant amount of their time and professional skills for free, and secondly that theatrical personalities were neglecting industry-based charities in favour of their non-theatrical fundraising work. The focal point of unpaid labour around which these arguments circulated was encapsulated by F. H. Madden's opinion piece 'Charity and the Drama', published by *The Theatre* in 1897, in which he argued that the drama had done 'more than is dreamt of for Charity', yet when the question 'what has charity done for the Drama is asked', the answer is 'nil'.[1] Madden's assertion captured anxieties about the logistical difficulties that charity work created for the industry and the sense of neglect of theatre's own causes that he identified in this shift of support. It also raised a pervasive question about whether giving their time and skills for free might devalue the work of theatrical professionals, and thus potentially impact on the reputation and status of the stage and its personnel. What it failed to account for, however, was the positive, day-to-day reputational and publicity work that charity labour offered both individual performers and the theatre industry as a whole. Non-theatrical charity work was an area of high-profile public activity that promoted and endorsed the theatre industry. While the increased number, scale and spectacle of fundraising events during the 1880s and 1890s and into the early twentieth century reconfigured understandings of the fashionable, commercial stage and placed a new set of expectations on its performers, these occasions also took stage personalities outside of theatre spaces, showcased their polished public personalities to different audiences and widely publicised the stage's generosity and kindness through a different set of interactions between performers and spectators. This arena of public, and heavily publicised, labour, which was represented and dominated by actresses, simultaneously changed and became crucial to the wider theatrical ecology of the day.

The increasing demands that charity work placed on actresses' time and energy were considerably – and deliberately – less visible outside the columns of the trade press. Well-honed promotional strategies drawn from the fashionable consumer culture that theatre formed an active part of were central to the success of large-scale public charity events. Up to the outbreak of the First World War public charity was framed by a language of leisure and pleasure more than one of duty and labour. As competition in the charity events market increased, the promise of fundraising occasions as pleasurable, unique experiences, where participants were offered spectacle and leisure in return for their donations, became of increasing importance. Any focus on the labour of those involved in staging events detracted from this key dynamic and image. Thus, while actresses promoted and celebrated the fundraising occasions they supported, they rarely spoke publicly of the effort involved. Understanding the planning and detail of charity events is challenging: the work was hidden from the public; planning documents were not designed to be kept; evidence of the extent and types of managerial, performance and financial work such occasions incurred is scant.[2]

The consciously hidden nature of this history aligns such offstage activity with the area of enquiry called into focus by Osborne and Woodworth's recent study of backstage and production histories, in which they argue that 'theatre has long been an art form of subterfuge, concealment and illusion, and practicing artists often actively hide the work in the wings in order to foster a sense of theatrical magic' (Osborne and Woodworth, 2015: 2). Actresses' charity contributions drew on a range of roles and identities intrinsically connected to their professional work and skill sets, but they also demanded a separate set of strategies, abilities and gendered practices that were distinct from onstage performance, yet crucial to the ongoing public favour that nourished their professional careers. Such work has consistently taken place offstage and been characterised by a skilfully constructed illusion of effortlessness and beauty: duty disguised as spectacle. Identifying and acknowledging public charity appearances as professional work that took place outside of theatre spaces and was entwined with cognate constructions of leisure and pleasure supplies a different lens through which we can explore the range of work and public roles demanded of actresses in the early twentieth-century theatre industry. It also invites a question about the extent to which offstage work was a fundamental element of successful actresses' professional careers. The remainder of this chapter considers one case study event – the Salon of Fragrance and Fair Women – staged

7 Publicity photograph for the 'Salon of Fragrance and Fair Women', 1911.

at Harrods department store in March 1911, and seeks to foreground the significance of these activities to the wider theatre industry and to actresses' professional identities.

The Harrods Salon, March 1911

> In a large and daintily-decorated apartment, amid a luxurious display of the richest blooms the British gardener can produce, a bevy of beauty offered perfume to the shopping throng.[3]

The Harrods Salon of Fragrance and Fair Women was a week-long fundraising event that ran from 27 March to 1 April 1911, which offered shoppers the opportunity to buy perfume from well-known London actresses. Harrods had loaned a sale-room for the Salon free of charge, the scent had been donated by the Jersey-based company Luce & Co. and the actresses volunteered their time. Collectively, the fashionable London department store, the perfume producer and the theatrical personalities raised one thousand guineas for the Middlesex Hospital Prince Francis of Teck Memorial Fund.[4] The contributions made by Harrods and Luce are more tangible than those made by the actresses. Gifting of space and product can be accounted for. They were also relatively low-resource actions: as we will see later, Harrods and Luce gained a considerable amount of recognition and publicity for their involvement, but the transactional costs remained low. Tracing and accounting for the labour of the actresses who volunteered at the event is less straightforward. Press accounts covering the fifty actresses recorded as being involved present them as both individual celebrities and as part of a collective group. Individual offstage appearances are highlighted in relation to actresses' public identities, and distinctive contributions to the overall 'bevy of beauty' offered in the Salon are described and celebrated. With the exception of the Salon's lead actress-organiser, Gertrude Robins (1886–1917), the labour incurred by the event is, however, almost entirely attributed to the collective group of performers. The work is constructed as a collective professional act. Press advertising and coverage does not offer information about when certain performers would be present. Neither Luce's nor Harrods' archives contain any planning documentation concerning the event, and extant correspondence between the actresses involved does not cover the event's logistics. The spectacle offered by offstage actresses and the possibility of being sold perfume by them is the sole source of the press's focus; the concealment of the work that created the event mirrors the

8 Photograph of Gertrude Robins.

general pattern in press accounts (noted above), demarcating the labour as backstage work that enabled the on-/offstage performance.

The wider context within which the Salon of Fragrance and Fair Women was located further emphasises the concealment of actresses' labour by spectacle. The Salon was presented as a feature of 'All British Shopping Week', a nationwide promotional celebration of British manufacturing and commerce during which London's major West End shopping streets and stores attracted the greatest attention. Bunting and Union Jacks mapped out and decorated the capital's chief shopping thoroughfares, and spectacular window displays at Peter Robinson on Oxford Street, Liberty on Regent Street, Debenham and Freebody on Wigmore Street and John Barker of Kensington (among others) promoted British-made goods. One unidentified London store used its plate glass display windows to showcase the latest styles of straw hats, with several girls seated amidst them demonstrating the art of deftly plaiting straw.[5] Such commercialised craft performances also found a home in Harrods, where lace-making, embroidery and hand weaving were 'executed by pretty Irish colleens in their national costumes', echoing the living displays of national cultures and empire that permeated London's exhibition culture.[6] The promotion of British products provided an overarching theme for a week of commercial activities driven by spectacle, performance, publicity and financial opportunity. Harrods' charity Salon distinguished the store within London's up-market consumer culture by offering a space in which shopping was defined as simultaneously fashionable, patriotic and altruistic.

The Harrods Salon recycled a fundraising format grounded in the high-profile, celebrity-staffed charity bazaars that had dominated the landscape of nineteenth-century fundraising events. West End actresses had acted as saleswomen throughout the Victorian period, with their skills at selling regularly showcased at fundraising bazaars and fetes in concert halls and hotels. From the dramatic fetes staged in aid of the Royal Dramatic College in the late 1860s and 1870s, to spectacular charity bazaars in the Royal Albert Hall between the 1870s and 1890s, actresses including Julia Neilson, Maud Tree and Cora Brown Potter became renowned for being able to extricate exorbitant sums of money from bazaar-goers for simple items including roses, sweets and photographs. The celebrity interaction was presented as a justification for the inflated cost, with actresses enabling an economy of encounter that sustained and salvaged many late nineteenth-century charitable organisations. Though the popularity of bazaars had peaked and troughed, the public appeal of the celebrity encounters they foregrounded remained a secure fundraising formula in 1911, and one that was repeatedly mined for charitable and promotional purposes. The promise that any purchase made at the Salon would be passed to the buyer by 'the hands of some of the most popular and lovely ladies of the British stage' proved a powerful draw.[7] Writing later in the same year, the actress Marie Tempest recalled that five thousand bottles of perfume were sold over the five afternoons, while the *Evening Post*'s coverage of the event recorded that most buyers went away with more bottles than they could comfortably carry.[8] Buyers were not just purchasing for themselves, they were buying to distribute to others, performing their charity identity and participation in this fashionable fundraising event. The Salon was a complex site of cultural activity located at the intersections of theatrical, leisure, charity and consumer cultures and targeted at buyers with ample leisure time and expendable income. In return for their cash, shoppers were offered a fourfold experience: the opportunity to visibly support charity, meaningful participation in All British Shopping Week, the perfume, and the celebrity encounter.

Actresses playing shop girls

Connections between department stores, theatre and charity had been developed and strengthened during the early decades of the twentieth century, with Richard Burbidge and Gordon Selfridge, the managing directors of Harrods and Selfridges, regularly hosting charity events involving theatrical stars, and financing and dressing West End musical comedies as part of their ongoing self-promotional and strategic commercial activities (Rappaport, 2001: 179, 201). The two groups of professional women foregrounded in this hybrid activity – shop girls and actresses – came together in the act of selling as public charity duty in a space that Marlis Schweitzer has identified as the 'Department Store Theater', creating a new representational area that warrants brief consideration here (Schweitzer, 2011: 51–95). While actresses performing as charity saleswomen were a familiar sight at London's fashionable fundraising events, the shift of charity sales from concert halls and hotels to department stores was a relatively recent phenomenon. At the Harrods Salon this change in location was accompanied by a further modification to the conventions of charity sales: the perfume was sold at recommended retail price, making the celebrity experience seemingly free of charge. This decision to remove the anticipated celebrity encounter mark-up was well received, with the *Evening Post* praising the fact that 'fancy prices' were not permitted at the event.[9] The change had a clear impact on the roles played by the women involved. The 'actress/barterer' became the 'actress/shop girl', and the two professions were temporarily conflated on the sales floor in a new configuration of their already well-established connection in London's wider entertainment culture.

The 'shop girl' was a familiar metropolitan figure and a popular character type in the musical comedies of the mid-1890s and the Edwardian period (Bailey, 2003; Gundle and Castelli, 2006: Sanders, 2006; Rappaport, 2001). Harrods Salon, in 1911, was interwoven with this dominant imagery. The hugely successful musical comedy *Our Miss Gibbs*, which told the story of a shop girl, featured scenes at 'Garrods' department store and was part-financed by Richard Burbidge, had been staged at the Gaiety Theatre during the 1909–10 season. Actresses from its cast worked at the Salon. The charity space of the Salon thus simultaneously affirmed recent memories of the production and the women who starred in it, staging a distinct representation of actresses as shop girls in a public charity space. The hybridity of identities and role-playing here needs to be taken into account: like Garrods, the department store charity sale was a temporary, consciously constructed space that fused two sets of professional women in new ways and required that actresses perform. While Katherine Mullin's recognition that the representation of shop girls in media and the arts lays bare 'an understanding of shop-girls taking charge through capitalizing, sensibly, upon their own desirability' (Mullin, 2016: 110) can certainly be transposed on to dominant iconographic models of actresses, the appearance of actresses as shop girls in a charity context conflated, embodied and troubled current ideas about the two commercial leisure industries, as well as their personnel.

The presence of actresses in department stores as volunteer workers conjured a fluid area of visual culture and embodied practices. Women employed in both professions had triggered considerable social and moral anxieties, and as Erika Rappaport has noted, the reputation and meaning of shopping was the site of constant negotiation and remained 'by no means stable' (Rappaport, 2001: 143). Charity prompted further negotiations, as did the wider activities engaged in by both groups of professional women. One useful example can be discovered in the production of *The Suffrage Girl* at the Court Theatre in March 1911, where the cast featured Selfridges shop girls turned actresses. Actresses playing shop girls for charity presents us with a complicated and deeply unstable moment of social display and encounter that was further cemented by the decision taken to begin charging admission to the Salon in the middle of the week in response to the event's popularity. Half way through the Salon, the economy of encounter returned. In line with London's other entertainment providers, charity event organisers had to continually respond to their market, adjusting, adapting and recasting the events they staged in dialogue with changing trends and societal conventions. Each event and individual participant must be considered within these factors.

Indefatigable women: actresses and hard work

While Richard Burbidge and Prince Alexander of Teck were nominally responsible for the Salon of Fragrance and Fair Women, the event was delivered by the 25-year-old, Oxford-educated actress-dramatist Gertrude Robins. Table 1 collates the names of thirty-nine of the estimated fifty actresses whom Robins recruited to support the event, alongside records of their most recent professional stage appearances and their ages (where evidence is available).[10] The names of the remaining eleven or so actresses were not recorded by the press. I offer such detailed data here in the interest of generating a better understanding of the collective body of individual personalities that this – and many other – charity events offered. I will return to these other performers and questions shortly, for it is helpful to start with Robins, who was a well-known figure in the London theatrical world at the time of the Salon. Robins had come to the public's attention with her appearance as Lady Millicent Eggington in the 1907–08 Wyndham's Theatre production of Harriett Jay's comedy *When Knights Were Bold*, a leading role that followed an apprenticeship in Wilson Barrett's company.[11] By 1911 she was also becoming a well-known dramatist; her most recent stage play *Makeshifts* had been produced by Annie Horniman's company at the Coronet Theatre during February. Offstage Robins was a regular paid after-dinner speaker and was closely affiliated with the Actresses' Franchise League.[12] Charity work slotted into actresses' professional, offstage identities, forming part of a range of public and 'publicised-private' behaviours that attracted positive praise and interest from the press in the years around the Harrods event, and Robins supplies a clear example of this. In May 1913 the *Bystander* published a collage of images of Robins under the headline 'The Age of Versatility: One Crowded Hour in the Life of an Author-Actress'; the photographs included were labelled Mother, Airwoman, Author and Feeder of Geese.[13] The text accompanying a full-page image of Robins in the January 1915 edition of *Tatler* was entitled 'Variety is the Soul of Life: Actress, Playwright, Aviator, Farmer' and enthusiastically documented Robins's love of flying, farming and running the village pub that she owned, presenting these interests as evidence of an admirable predisposition for hard work.[14] The image of actress as grafter is a familiar motif in the press of this period and one that was recognised by both actresses and the press as a key means of attracting and sustaining public favour. Hard work was an asset: in an interview with Robins entitled 'A Woman of the Day' published in 1911, the journalist Eleanor Armstrong concluded that the actress was 'indefatigable' and was 'not in the least spoiled by her success for she can never forget the amount of drudgery and hard work that went to make it, and she also knows that only by hard work can a hold be maintained upon the public'.[15] While the specifics of the work actresses undertook at charity events were not the subject of press commentary, a common understanding that they were working hard permeated the public image of the profession created by journalists and social commentators.

Charity work might rarely have been publicly acknowledged as 'work', but it is clear that most actresses balanced regular participation in such events with their current theatrical engagements (see Table 1), and that offstage activities were recognised and treated positively in representations and reports of their professional identities. Versatility and variety were indeed both celebrated and a professional expectation. Robins juggled the coordination of the Salon with her role in a short run in the Little Theatre production of Harley Granville-Barker's dialogue *Ask No Questions and You'll Hear No Stories* (an adaptation of one of Arthur Schnitzler's Anatol series, staged between 11 and 25 March 1911), which closed two days before the Harrods event opened (Carson, 1912: 142). Such ability to multi-task appears to have been an assumed skill for early twentieth-century actresses, yet – unlike the enthusiastic attention paid to her flying and farming – the extent of Robins's charity-based managerial labour was not the subject of press commentary, signalling that this was an area of assumed, not unusual, activity. Such labour was an expectation of actresses, not a celebrity quirk that strengthened and distinguished the offstage public identity of a particular familiar stage performer. Its presence was assumed and unspoken. Nonetheless, Robins's role in organising the Salon was widely acknowledged in other contexts. Her name appears on the frontispiece page of the souvenir publication produced to mark the occasion and the majority of press

9 'Variety is the Soul of Life: Actress, Playwright, Aviator', *Tatler*, January 1915, p. 117.

Table 1 Actresses recorded as having contributed to the 'Salon of Fragrance and Fair Women'

Name	Dates	Where performing around the time of the Salon	Age
Maud Allan	1873–1956	Palace Theatre of Varieties	38
Pearl Aufrere	1894–1940		17
Adrienne Augard	1882–1913		29
Phyliss Bedells	1893–1985	Empire Theatre Company member	18
Chrissie Bell	?	Adelphi Theatre, *Quaker Girl*, 5 November 1910–11 May 1912	
Stephanie Bell	1900–47	Duke of York's Theatre, *Peter Pan*, closed 4 February 1911	11
Lilian Braithwaite	1873–1948	Comedy Theatre, *Preserving Mr Panmure*, 19 January–15 April 1911	38
Nell Carter	1887–1965	Playhouse, *One of the Dukes*, 18–29 March 1911	24
Dolly Castles	1884–1971	Drury Lane Theatre, *Jack and the Beanstalk*, closed 8 March 1911	27
Pauline Chase	1885–1962	Duke of York's Theatre, *Peter Pan*, 26 December 1910–4 February 1911	26
Ivy Lilian Close	1890–1968		21
Laura Cowie	1892–1969	Her Majesty's Theatre Company	19
Cicely Courtneidge	1893–1980	Shaftesbury Theatre, *The Arcadians*	18
Phyllis Dare	1890–1975	Gaiety Theatre, *Peggy*, 4 March–16 December 1911	21
Constance Drever	1880–1948	Lyric Theatre, *A Chocolate Soldier*, 10 September 1910–9 December 1911	31
Clara Evelyn	1886–1980	Vaudeville Theatre, *The Girl in the Train*	25
Madge Fabian	1880–1958	Drury Lane Theatre, *Sins of Society*	31
Audrey Ford	1873–?	Touring, *When Knights Were Old*	37
Gladys Guy	1888–1968	Gaiety Theatre, *Peggy*, 4 March–16 December 1911	23
Gloria Hamilton	?		
Elvira Hardinge	?		
Iris Hoey	1885–1979	Criterion Theatre, *Baby Mine*, 22 February–13 May 1911	26
Ola Humphrey	1884–1948	Strand Theatre, *The Man from Mexico*, closed 21 January 1911	27
Marie Lohr	1890–1975	Comedy Theatre, *Preserving Mr Panmure*, 19 January–15 April 1911	21

Name	Dates	Where performing around the time of the Salon	Age
Mabel Love	1874–1953	Pavilion and Metropolitan Music Hall appearances throughout February	37
Doris Lytton	1893–1953	Prince of Wales's Theatre, *Inconstant George*, 1 October 1910–8 April 1911	18
Olive May	1886–1947	Gaiety Theatre, *Peggy*, 4 March–16 December 1911	25
Lillah McCarthy	1875–1960	Little Theatre, Manager, *A Farewell Supper*, closed 25 March 1911; *A Master Builder*, 28 March 1911	36
Nancy More	1881–1976	Gaiety Theatre, *Peggy*, 4 March–16 December 1911	30
Unity More	1894–1981	Empire Theatre, *Ship Ahoy!* (ballet), had also 'commèred' revue in February (George Grossmith)	17
Gabrielle Ray	1883–1973	Gaiety Theatre, *Peggy*, 4 March–16 December 1911	28
Gertrude Robins	1886–1917	Little Theatre, *Ask No Questions*, closed 25 March 1911	25
Dorothy Selbourne	?	Gaiety Theatre, *Peggy*, 4 March–16 December 1911	
Nina Sevening	1885–1958	Wyndhams, *Passers-by*, opened 29 March 1911	26
Lily Sheppard	?		
Connie Stuart	?	Gaiety Theatre, *Peggy*, 4 March–16 December 1911	
Madge Titherage	1887–1961	Globe, *Bardely the Magnificent* 21 February–8 April 1911	24
Rosalie Toller	1885–1960	Lyceum Theatre, *The Prisoner of Zenda*, 1 March–20 May 1911	26
Jessie Winter	1885–1971	London Hippodrome, *The Right Sort*, 20–27 February 1911	26

reports and accompanying images noted her active involvement in the management of the event (see Figure 8).

Robins did not work alone at the Harrods Salon, but was supported by a group of actresses who embodied current theatrical celebrity.

Collectively, the actresses represented a wide range of performance styles and professional backgrounds, from the fashionable music hall stage and West End musical comedy, to romantic ballet and opera. Robins was one of the few performers present who was not affiliated with musical comedy in some way, along with Lillah McCarthy, who was managing the Little Theatre and had also appeared in the recent run of her husband Harley Granville-Barker's short plays. Some onstage performance networks are clearly visible among the participants in this event. Phyllis Dare, Gladys Guy, Olive May, Nancy More, Gabrielle Ray, Dorothy Selborne and Connie Stuart were all in the cast of the Gaiety Theatre's musical comedy *Peggy*, which ran from 4 March to 16 December 1911. The show had opened just over three weeks before the Salon, but was already proving popular with reviewers and audiences, reflecting and extending the fashionable Gaiety brand and adding to the theatre's familiar programme of long-running productions. All seven actresses would have worked at the Salon on one or several afternoons, making the journey from Knightsbridge to the West End to perform in the evening. The two o'clock opening time selected for the Salon not only responded to current fashionable shopping patterns, it also enabled actresses to secure some rest before a working day that involved two separate jobs. The Salon would also have brought together women who had not performed together onstage, creating and facilitating new professional and social networks, the influence and impact of which remain untraceable and intangible, but are unlikely to have been negligible.

Among the actresses' names listed in Table 1 are some that are instantly familiar to those interested in this period of theatre, while others are far less so. Many of the actresses recorded here have been of little sustained interest to scholars, or are entirely absent from our considerations of the theatre industry of the day. Countering their disappearance from history are the archived biographical files in the Mander and Mitchenson Collection. Here there are some 1,500 archive boxes filled with files of clippings, programmes, photographs, postcards and correspondence connected to eighteenth-, nineteenth- and twentieth-century stage performers, theatres, organisations and performance forms that were collected by Raymond Mander and Joe Mitchenson. Each actress listed here has a file in the collection, though their contents vary considerably – some contain three or four items, others are filled to overflowing with images, clippings and letters. It is not always the case that the performers who are the easiest to trace today are the same performers whose folders are replete with items. Pearl Aufrere is a good example of an actress whose cultural presence has faded with history, but whose familiarity to local, national and international audiences of the day is evidenced by the number of photographic prints and postcards of her that were manufactured – in excess of 150 different images can be found in her Mander and Mitchenson file alone. Mander and Mitchenson's active collecting period began in the mid-twentieth century, three or four decades after the time at which the majority of these images were produced. The availability of this number of postcards and photographs suggests that Pearl Aufrere's reputation had a degree of longevity. Their survival is perhaps the visual equivalent of the nostalgia for the early twentieth-century London stage captured in works by star-struck stage chroniclers who were writing as Mander and Mitchenson were collecting; most prominently that most 'wistful remembrancer' Walter MacQueen Pope. As Jim Davis and Victor Emeljanow have argued, while the narratives offered by MacQueen Pope, including *Gaiety: Theatre of Enchantment* (1949) and *Carriages at Eleven: The Story of the Edwardian Theatre* (1947), present historiographical challenges, they also offer a different way in to understanding the theatre industry, its personnel and its fans (Davis and Emeljanow, 2001). Different narratives concerning the actresses who had currency, familiarity and appeal during the pre-war period are similarly indicated by the Mander and Mitchenson files and events such as the Salon, a position that is further supported by the *Sketch*'s publication of a 'frieze' of forty leading actresses in the month following the Harrods' event.[16] Just over a quarter of those featured by the *Sketch* participated in the Salon.[17] Moreover, sixteen of the actresses involved had entries in the 1912 edition of *Who's Who in the Theatre*, with a further seven gaining an entry by the 1922 edition (Parker, 1912; 1922).

The incremental number of women included in the 1922 *Who's Who* indicates the relatively young average age of the actresses involved in the Harrods Salon. By the second decade of the twentieth century the arena of public charity work was very much the domain of young and beautiful female representatives from the stage, a step change in itself from the late Victorian phase of the theatre industry's wider public charity work, when older actresses including Mrs Keeley and Mrs Bancroft led events, showcasing their more dominant matriarchal personae and managing the group of younger actresses who worked alongside them. The Salon is also notable for the considerable number of recently minted theatrical celebrities involved: many of the performers who contributed had just discovered fame. Constance Drever's vocal performance as Nadina in *The Chocolate Soldier*, which had opened at the Lyceum Theatre in

September 1910 (and closed in December 1911), was the role that her *Bulletin* obituary identified as the one that brought her 'international fame';[18] Doris Lytton had 'sprung to fame' in the Prince of Wales's Theatre production of *Inconstant George* (which had opened in October 1910),[19] and Olive May had stepped up to cover the musical theatre star Gertie Millar's absence from the popular musical comedy *Our Miss Gibbs* at the Gaiety in 1910, the production financed in part by Harrods and set in a department store (Rappaport, 2001: 179). By the time of Millar's return May had become so popular with audiences that instead of returning to her place in the Irish Girl chorus, she was given the role of Lady Elizabeth Thanet, and her own song, which quickly became the hit of the show.[20] Read together, this information indicates that high-profile charity appearances formed a part of the mechanism of pre-war celebrity culture, offering a means through which actresses could consolidate and sustain their fame that reached across a wide range of performance styles and entertainment forms. Involvement in public charity work brought a set of professional and personal returns for actresses that bear consideration within the wider commercial benefits offered by such occasions.

The tangible and intangible benefits of public charity activity and appearances

Harrods' and Luce's material and spatial contributions to the Salon brought a clear set of widely acknowledged returns in relation to publicity and brand awareness. The issue of *Chemist and Druggist* published the week before the Salon dedicated a column to the event, noting that the perfume on sale at Harrods was likely to sell quickly *and* that 'the effect upon the popularity of the perfume should be felt by retailers generally'.[21] The contact details for Luce's London distributors were published at the end of the article, priming suppliers to place their orders and bolstering the Salon's commercial opportunity. Later in the year, the actress Marie Tempest's chatty piece for the *Daily Mail* on what she would be buying her friends and family for Christmas noted, 'I believe Luce's name has been a household synonym for Eau de Cologne for many years, but somehow I did not discover it until last Spring at Harrods's Salon of Fragrance and Fair Women.' Praise for the 'public spirited' firm followed, detailing how the perfumer had also supplied scent free of charge for the perfumed fountains at the 1911 Crystal Palace Festival of Empire and Fair of Fashions.[22] By selecting this product for her Christmas gifts,

Tempest aligned Harrods, Luce, actresses and herself as an actress with charitable activity, quality products and British national identity.

Tempest is not recorded as having participated in the event: she would have been a featured participant had she been there, so it is reasonable to conclude that she was not involved. Nonetheless, through this article she weaves herself into the story of the Salon, using her own professional identity as a renowned actress. The article functions as a rich and skilled piece of celebrity construction that positions the Salon of Fragrance and Fair Women within a wider network of celebrity, fashion and consumer culture. Tempest thus benefits from the charity activity of her professional colleagues. The *Chemist and Druggist*'s confident prediction that sales of Luce's perfume would increase as a result of the Harrods Salon offers a helpful way to consider the more intangible set of benefits such events brought to the theatrical profession, some of which we can trace here in Tempest's piece for the *Daily Mail*. While we cannot track supply and sales as straightforwardly in terms of the benefits charity work brought to the stage profession, the clearly established and acknowledged economics of charity signalled here, coupled with Tempest's article, allows us to conclude that public appearances in aid of charity would have brought a set of positive returns for both the industry and its personnel.

The significance of public appearances to actresses' careers increased as the forces of international mass celebrity accelerated during the early years of the twentieth century. Fuelled by the fast-advancing media industries, the celebrity press coverage that had characterised the late Victorian period increased, and gossip columns thrived, as public interest in, and access to, the period's favourite stars was further fuelled by the more regular use of film newsreels to circulate celebrity stories of the moment (Weiner, 2011). The position of theatre's stars as public figures of interest in their own right expanded. Textual and pictorial reports in newspapers and magazines focused on where celebrities had been, who they had been with and what they were wearing at a level of almost obsessive detail. Socialising in select fashionable circles attracted further press coverage, increasing day-to-day familiarity for their many audiences. Coverage of theatrical celebrities' offstage activities regularly equalled and frequently exceeded the attention given to their onstage professional appearances. Indeed, the amount of newsprint given over to the offstage domestic lives and social engagements of stage celebrities indicates that they were understood to be a site of unceasing interest to many early twentieth-century readers, across a wide range of publications from the *Sketch*, the *Sphere* and the *Illustrated London News* to the *Daily Mail*, the *Penny Illustrated Paper* and the *Daily Telegraph*.

Such fame was recognised and negotiated among the profession. One typed response to a letter from Lilian Braithwaite to an unidentified Mr Jons offers a rare example of actresses' thoughts around such celebrity:

> Popularity is such a desirable and gratifying asset that I think it would be, perhaps ungrateful to quality it [*sic*] by ascribing to it penalties!! Implying, as it does, appreciation, I think one should accept it when it comes! With gratitude. Yours sincerely, Lilian Braithwaite.[23]

There are two areas of interest here. The first is the letter's content and particularly Braithwaite's discursive tone; she responds to a seemingly prevalent tendency to resent the outcomes of fame in her reference to the penalties that it incurs. The second is the materiality of the letter itself – the underlined words here identify Braithwaite's handwritten additions to a typed letter that might well have been produced by the actress's personal assistant, of whom there were a growing number in this period. Braithwaite's annotations stamp the formal, typed response with her own personality, giving the letter a tone and expression that creates the semblance of the personal touch, so key to the construction of celebrity/public interactions (Rojek, 2001). The letter functions as a small example, representative of a larger, more fundamental set of practices that created and nourished celebrity identity, which included actresses' public charity work.

Appearing before the public in strategically chosen offstage roles was a key element of a celebrity career. In a 1911 interview, Salon of Fragrance and Fair Women actress-seller Pauline Chase praised British audiences for their loyal quality of 'never forget[ing] you when you make good' and noted that their American counterparts understood professional success as a 'momentary flash in the pan, unless you keep playing good parts you are soon forgotten'.[24] Chase's carefully constructed response to British readers not only evidences her skill at self-(re)presentation, but indicates a knowledge of the need for continual presence in the public eye that most likely applied to her British career as well. Charity activities were professional acts akin to the processes of self-fashioning and self-publicity that were central to press interviews, to autobiographies and to photographic images, and they were well understood by theatrical celebrities. Looking closely at a range of publications from the first two weeks of March 1911, it is clear that, with the exception of one individual, each of the actresses who worked at the Harrods Salon and were in the cast of *Peggy* at the Gaiety Theatre attracted more press attention for their involvement in the Salon than they did for the show. The exception was Phyllis Dare, the Gaiety's current leading lady. The Salon is representative: working at a bazaar or ball or garden party invariably resulted in a name-drop for an actress, often accompanied by a visual image. For well-known actresses who had not yet reached the ranks of the leading lady, the press coverage received through their work for charity events often exceeded that accorded in theatre reviews in the non-specialist press (Hindson, 2016). Leading ladies' ongoing contribution to such occasions signals the multiple benefits offered by public charity appearances; press coverage was valuable, but the construction and endorsement of public identity remained of significance to those who had reached the pinnacle of public favour and fame.

The offstage charity performances that Pauline Chase and others offered at the Harrods Salon and at other fashionable fundraising events are, without doubt, interwoven with questions related to autobiographical strategies, the significance of anecdotal evidence to historiography and the construction of public selves which have preoccupied feminist theatre historiographers over the past two decades (see Gale and Gardner, 2004). Photographs, interviews and gossip columns allowed theatre's stars to offer tantalising glimpses of their 'offstage' selves at closed social occasions, including dinner parties, house parties and salons, and at public events including gallery openings, bazaars and festivals. Similarly, interviews and autobiographies presented the seemingly 'personal' transmission of knowledge about the celebrity to the reader (see Maggie B. Gale's chapter in this volume). The offstage 'exclusive' moments of access to the 'authentic' performer behind her onstage roles that these celebrity charity events and products appeared to offer were, in practice, carefully choreographed, *staged* events that temporarily enabled controlled moments of interaction between the actress 'herself' and the public. Charity work built on these foundations, but was a distinct area of public appearance that offered access to the embodied star in the same space as the participant; not across the footlights, but in the room. Faye Hammil has argued that the mass-reproduced photographs of female personalities that became available in the late nineteenth and early twentieth centuries fuelled the reader's or viewer's desire for the 'in-person' encounter with the star: the spectre of familiarity created by the ownership or sight of multiple images created an appetite for personal interaction (Hammil, 2009: 107). Public charity appearances offered a temporary space in which the possibility of the 'in-person' encounter was increased, and created and sustained an economics of encounter grounded in the dynamics of wider celebrity culture and its products.

Actresses' offstage appearances replicated, constructed and challenged professional and culturally embedded and embodied modes of public performance. They were delivered to audiences ranging from one to hundreds, and then transmitted to numerous other audiences, including other attendees at the event in question, passers-by observing the event but not participating in it, the press whose role was to document and construct the event and its celebrities for readers and viewers, and those learning of the event through press coverage, conversation with a participant, or anecdote. Managing this area of activity and its immediate and extended reception was a complex professional task that demanded a constant process of skilled negotiation between stars and their various (extra-theatrical) audiences. Such events should caution us to look amid the multiple public roles that actresses were playing in order to understand the professional contexts that they worked within and the range of offstage identities they adopted. Charity work occupied a range of complex, public, professional spaces that required specific working practices and skills. The profile of fundraising events and the centrality of actresses to their operation signal that we need to register and address the entangled, multiple, sometimes simultaneous stagings of professional identities that actresses offered in their day-to-day working lives, and balance our considerations of their on- and offstage work. As the actress-seller at the Harrods Salon Cicely Courtneidge later recounted, when advised by a friend to deal with a public-speaking engagement by telling funny stories and being herself: 'What is myself? The character I'm portraying on stage at the moment – or the me, entertaining you here? I dunno.'[25] Acknowledging the range of characters created and harnessed by actresses enables a fuller understanding of the operation of the theatre industry, the skills that fostered and sustained a successful theatrical career and the multiple roles that women occupied within the profession.

Notes

1 F. Madden, 'Charity and the Drama', *The Theatre*, February 1897, p. 87.
2 Evidence of some events can be discovered in the archives of charitable organisations (see Hindson, 2016). For the event covered in this chapter

there is a small amount of material in the Harrods archives and the Luce and Company archives. Together these items amount to copies of press reports, souvenir publications, photographs and transcripts of correspondence sent to Prince Alexander of Teck that present the final sum raised.
3 'All-British Shopping Week: Successful Opening', *Daily Telegraph*, 28 March 1911, p. 11.
4 'The Increasing Vogue of the Blonde', *The English Illustrated Magazine*, August 1911, p. 480.
5 'All-British Shopping Week: Successful Opening', *Daily Telegraph*, 28 March 1911, p. 11.
6 J. May, 'The All-British Shopping Week: Features of the Display', *Observer*, 26 March 1911, p. 19.
7 'A Salon of Fair Women', *The English Illustrated Magazine*, March 1911, p. 86.
8 M. Tempest, 'My Christmas Presents', *Daily Mail*, 13 December 1911, p. 4, and *Evening Post* press clipping, Luce Company archives.
9 Undated clipping, Luce Company archives.
10 These names have been drawn from different lists of women that appeared in the *English Illustrated Magazine*, *The Times*, the *Mirror*, the *Observer*, the *Sketch* and the *Daily Telegraph*.
11 'The Late Miss Gertrude Robins', *Daily Mail*, 26 December 1917, p. 5.
12 'A Salon of Fair Women', *The English Illustrated Magazine*, March 1911, p. 634. Robins had appeared as an after-dinner speaker at the Caravan Club of Great Britain and Ireland's annual dinner on 15 February 1911; her wit and delivery were well received.
13 'The Age of Versatility: One Crowded Hour in the Life of an Author Actress', *Bystander*, 21 May 1913, p. 400.
14 'Variety is the Soul of Life: Actress, Playwright, Aviator, Farmer', *Tatler*, 23 January 1915, p. 117.
15 Undated clipping, Gertrude Robins File, Mander and Mitchenson (M & M) Reference Box Collection, University of Bristol Theatre Collection, MM/REF/PE/AC/1554.
16 'The Sketch Frieze', *The Sketch*, 10 May 1911: supplement.
17 The Salon contributors who also featured in the *Sketch* frieze were Pauline Chase, Laura Cowie, Phyllis Dare, Iris Hoey, Marie Lohr, Olive May, Nancy More, Gabrielle Ray, Nina Sevening, Madge Titherage and Rosalie Toller.
18 *Bulletin*, undated clipping, Constance Drever File, M & M Reference Box Collection, MM/REF/PE/AC/639.
19 See Doris Lytton File, M & M Reference Box Collection, MM/REF/PE/AC/1238.
20 *New Magazine*, June 1910, p. 12.
21 *Chemist and Druggist*, 18 March 1911, p. 45.
22 M. Tempest, 'My Christmas Presents', *Daily Mail*, 13 December 1911, p. 4.

23 Correspondence, Lilian Braithwaite File, M & M Reference Box Collection, MM/REF/PE/AC/286.
24 Undated clipping, Pauline Chase File, M & M Reference Box Collection, MM/REF/PE/AC/419.
25 Undated clipping, Cicely Courtneidge File, M & M Reference Box Collection, MM/REF/PE/AC/507.

References

Bailey, Peter (2003), *Popular Performance and Culture in the Victorian City*, Cambridge: Cambridge University Press.
Carson, Lionel, ed. (1912), *The Stage Year Book*, London: The Stage.
Carson, Lionel, ed. (1915), *The Stage Year Book*, London: The Stage.
Davis, Jim, and Victor Emeljanow (2001), 'Wistful Remembrancer: The Historiographical Problem of MacQueen-Popery', *New Theatre Quarterly*, 17, pp. 299–309.
Gale, Maggie B., and Viv Gardner, eds (2004), *Auto/Biography and Identity: Women, Theatre, Performance*, Manchester: Manchester University Press.
Gundle, Stephen, and Clino T. Castelli (2006), *The Glamour System*, New York: Springer.
Hammil, Faye (2009), *Women Celebrities and Literary Culture Between the Wars*, Austin, TX: University of Texas Press.
Hindson, Catherine (2014), 'Gratuitous Assistance? The West End Theatre Industry, Late Victorian Charity and Patterns of Theatrical Fundraising', *New Theatre Quarterly*, 30, pp. 17–28.
Hindson, Catherine (2016), *London's West End Actresses and the Origins of Celebrity Charity, 1880–1920*, Iowa City: University of Iowa Press.
MacQueen Pope, Walter (1947), *Carriages at Eleven: The Story of the Edwardian Theatre*, London: Hutchinson.
MacQueen Pope, Walter (1949), *Gaiety: Theatre of Enchantment*, London: W. H. Allen.
Mullin, Katherine (2016), *Working Girls: Fiction, Sexuality and Modernity*, Oxford: Oxford University Press.
Osborne, Elizabeth A., and Christine Woodworth, eds (2015), *Working in the Wings: New Perspectives on Theatre History and Labor*, Carbondale, IL: SIU Press.
Parker, John (1912), *Who's Who in the Theatre: A Biographical Record of the Contemporary Stage*, London: Pitman.
Parker, John (1922), *Who's Who in the Theatre: A Biographical Record of the Contemporary Stage*, Boston: Small, Maynard.
Rappaport, Erika (2001), *Shopping for Pleasure: Women in the Making of London's West End*, Princeton, NJ: Princeton University Press.

Richards, Jeffrey (2005), *Sir Henry Irving: A Victorian Actor and his World*, London: Continuum.
Rojek, Chris (2001), *Celebrity*, London: Reaktion.
Sanders, Lise (2006), *Consuming Fantasies: Labour, Leisure and the London Shop Girl, 1880–1920*, Columbus, OH: Ohio State University Press.
Schweitzer, Marlis (2011), *When Broadway was the Runway*, Philadelphia, PA: University of Pennsylvania Press.
Weber, Brenda R. (2012), *Women and Literary Celebrity in the Nineteenth Century: The Transatlantic Production of Fame and Gender*, London: Routledge.
Weiner, Joel H. (2011), *The Americanization of the British Press, 1830–1914*, Basingstoke: Palgrave Macmillan.

Archives

Luce's Jersey Eau de Cologne Company Ltd Archive, Jersey Heritage Archives

Daily Mirror, press clipping, L/A/12/D1/2
The Evening Post, press clipping, L/A/12/D1/2
Publicity photograph, L/A/12/D1/2
Souvenir publication, L/A/12/E2/1

Mander and Mitchenson Reference Box Collection, University of Bristol Theatre Collection

Lilian Braithwaite File, MM/REF/PE/AC/286
Pauline Chase File, MM/REF/PE/AC/419
Cicely Courtneidge File, MM/REF/PE/AC/507
Constance Drever File, MM/REF/PE/AC/639
Doris Lytton File, MM/REF/PE/AC/1238
Gertrude Robins File, MM/REF/PE/AC/1554

5

'VERY MUCH ALIVE AND KICKING'

The Actresses' Franchise League from 1914 to 1928

Naomi Paxton

During the years between the outbreak of the First World War and the passing of the Equal Franchise Bill, the Actresses' Franchise League (AFL) continued to open up new opportunities for actresses and female theatre professionals to become involved in political and feminist activism by extending its work as an organisation across a diverse portfolio of social, political and philanthropic projects. Although they could not have known it, the commencement of the First World War in August 1914 would change the way the AFL had been operating and campaigning almost beyond recognition. After six successful years of activism within the suffrage movement and the theatre industry, and with over 900 members, an affiliated men's group and over a hundred Patrons, the organisation was confident and capable. Maintaining a strictly neutral stance on militancy despite strong feelings within its membership both for and against violent direct action, the AFL sustained its connections with both militant and constitutional suffrage societies and continued to take part in suffrage meetings, exhibitions and demonstrations after the outbreak of war. Many members were involved in a new society, the United Suffragists, which welcomed female and male members of all other suffrage societies, regardless of militant affiliation. Formed on 6 January 1914,[1] the United Suffragists hoped to be an organisation free from some of the toxic issues around leadership, partiality and violent activism that had plagued other suffrage societies, particularly the Women's Social and Political Union (WSPU). The Actresses' Franchise League provided entertainments at the United Suffragists' Christmas Sale in December 1914,[2] was represented among other suffrage societies at a Women and Army Work Exhibition held in Caxton Hall in May 1915,[3] and had a stall at the United Suffragists' Woman's Christmas Sale in Central Hall, Westminster in November 1915.[4] The AFL also joined established theatrical charities such as the Theatrical Ladies' Guild and the Actors' Benevolent Fund in financially supporting theatre performers and workers suffering wartime hardship, administering many other projects such as the Era War Distress Fund and the Three Arts Employment Fund that gave work to unemployed theatre professionals.

Two of the League's wartime satellite projects are explored in this chapter – the Women's Emergency Corps and the British Women's Hospital Fund. Both ventures moved the League into new areas of campaigning, and utilised the skills, generosity and resourcefulness of its members.

> Aug 4 – All so strange, unreal – wild rumours of naval engagements, ships sunk – the streets as we walked home were full of excited people waving flags … then the tension – the rumours – the hopes the fear … and life went on … the A.F.L. started organizing The Women's Emergency Corps, meetings every day – women came from all over the Country to register for Service, and here the work for Suffrage showed its value – women were organised trained, ready to face dangers.[5]

The foundation of the Women's Emergency Corps (WEC) by members of the AFL just two days after the outbreak of war on 4 August 1914 was 'one of the most remarkable initiatives undertaken during the War by members of the profession' (Sanderson, 1984: 164). Combining their social activism with their production experience, Lena Ashwell, Decima Moore, Eva Moore and the militant suffragette Eve Haverfield capitalised on their celebrity in both the theatrical world and the suffrage movement to start a national organisation that moved far beyond the scope of their previous theatrical activities. The WEC was 'devised to be elastic, unhampered by political or social prejudices, and prepared to undertake any work that should be useful, whatever that work might prove to be'.[6] *Votes for Women*, now the newspaper of the United Suffragists, reported that four days after the WEC's foundation, 2,000 women had volunteered at Gertrude Kingston's Little Theatre (Kingston, 1937: 191) 'to drive motorcars, to ride or drive horses … to take care of crèches, of kindergartens, to cook, to sew, speak several foreign languages, or serve in any other way'.[7] A month later, the WEC headquarters moved to seventy-nine rooms in the Old Bedford College on Baker Street.[8] Freed from any negative association with the suffrage movement in spite of the involvement of prominent militants such as Emmeline Pethick Lawrence on its committee, anti-suffragists were as welcome as suffragists to volunteer their services. The Corps provided a safe space for such collaboration – united as it was around the war effort and the employment of women, rather than political activism. The WEC held regular and free public meetings in theatres and venues in across the UK to appeal for funds and update supporters, with high-profile speakers including Elizabeth Robins, Lilian Braithwaite, Constance Collier and G. K. Chesterton. The schedule often included simultaneous meetings across the country – thus, on 30 October Lena Ashwell spoke in Cardiff's City Hall and Eva Moore in the Theatre Royal, Manchester, and on 9 December Lady Tree and Emily Pertwee spoke in Bournemouth's Theatre Royal while Lena Ashwell and Eva Moore were at the Tyne Theatre, Newcastle.[9]

By January 1915 the Corps had fifteen branches across England and Wales[10] and eighteen departments including Clerical Work, Housecraft, Interpreting, Land Development, Medical and Nursing, National Food Fund, Needlework, Toy Industry and the Women's Volunteer Corps. The Corps organised the teaching of French and German in over forty military centres outside London, and published two booklets of French and German phrases, subtitled 'The Soldiers' "First Aid" to Foreign Languages', for English soldiers abroad.[11] The idea for the phrasebooks had come from H. M. Paull, playwright, novelist, journalist and honorary secretary of the Dramatists Club, whose gently comic suffrage monologue *An Anti-Suffragist or The Other Side* had been published by the AFL in 1910. Together with the Women's Imperial Health Association, the WEC published a wartime directory of societies engaged in war work,[12] and briefly opened a shop at 180 Oxford Street in which to sell the goods made in its workshops alongside 'Work done by Women of the Artistic Professions (Painting, Music and Stage)'.[13] The toy department in particular was a huge success, developing original designs and registering a trademark. The enterprise was widely reported in the press soon after it began:

> At Old Bedford College the Women's Emergency Corps have for the past fortnight opened workrooms for the employment of women in this industry. The results even in that short time have been remarkable, and the big shops like Harrods, the Army and Navy Stores, Peter Robinson's and Selfridge's have given them large orders. One firm has ordered six gross of one toy alone.[14]

Keen to keep the Corps in the public eye, less than a month after the visit by *The Times* reporter, the WEC workrooms had produced the 'Guy-ser', a figure of the Kaiser to be stuffed with straw and burnt on Guy Fawkes night. Attached to each figure was the following verse:

> We all shall remember
> This Fifth of November
> By Wilhelm's infernal plot!
> We see no reason
> Why Germany's treason
> Should ever be forgot![15]

The 'Guy-sers' were on sale at WEC public meetings in aid of another AFL satellite project, the Three Arts Employment Fund, as well as at a special stall in Selfridges on Oxford Street on 4 and 5 November, run by members of the Women Writers' Suffrage League (WWSL). Lena Ashwell told the *Daily Chronicle* that she took a hundred 'Guy-sers' to Cardiff for a WEC meeting and 'could have sold three or four times that number'.[16] Other caricatures of prominent wartime figures were made from designs by artist W. A. Wildman, and the WEC toy-making department also began working with the curator of the Tower of London Armouries, Charles Ffoulkes, to design a wooden model of Henry VII.[17] By February 1915 the number of women working in the toy-making department had grown considerably, with the WEC reporting that there were twenty branches across the UK employing 228 women workers, and that the number of girls making toys at Bedford College had grown from twelve to 111 in less than six months.[18] In March 1915 the WEC exhibited its toys at the British Industries Fair, held at the Agricultural Hall in London. *Games and Toys*, the trade journal of the toy industry, described the diverse range of goods at the WEC stand:

> They are specialising in the manufacture of wooden toys, and are turning out in large quantities such lines as Noah's arks, model ambulances, Belgian dog carts, doll's bedsteads, etc. They are also making dolls ... Alsatian Peasants, Boulogne Fishwives and toy soldier dolls in khaki uniforms. Other lines they are making in wooden toys are bathing machines, doll's houses, engines, elephants, ducks, Boy Scouts, etc.[19]

They were not alone in representing women's labour at the fair, as the newly formed East London Federation of Suffragettes Toy Factory also had a stand, selling dolls and wooden toys.[20]

The WEC drew formal support from thirty different societies,[21] and both national and international support for its work in the press and at public meetings also helped to keep the organisation publicly visible. Actresses were personally involved with the work of the WEC – Eva Moore recalled spending her days at the Little Theatre and her evenings performing at the Vaudeville Theatre (Moore, 1923: 74) in August

1914,[22] and her sister Decima Moore, who had travelled extensively, ran the Interpreting Department, sending female interpreters to meet and assist refugees from the war upon their arrival in London.[23] These WEC interpreters were part of a large network of women's groups and societies helping Belgian refugees arriving at London stations to find accommodation, work, medical treatment and, if necessary, legal advice. These volunteers came from both suffrage and non-suffrage backgrounds, and 'from a portion of society untapped in earlier wars, the vast network of organised women's groups and associations that had been growing for several decades' (Vining and Hacker, 2001: 362).

One such group, the Women Police Service, was founded in September 1914 by anti-vivisection campaigner Margaret Damer Dawson and journalist and Women's Freedom League activist Nina Boyle. Boyle had thought it unfair that female victims of sexual assault had to give evidence to all-male courtrooms, and had been calling for the formation of a women's police unit to take statements and escort witnesses since 1912, centring her argument on questions of 'justice, dignity and legal rights for women and children' (Jackson, 2006: 17). A former rescue worker with the National Vigilance Association, Damer Dawson's initial motivation for setting up her Women Police Service was a concern for the dangers faced by young girls and women upon arriving in London, focused primarily around sex trafficking. Interviewed as part of the Home Office Inquiry into the addition of women to the Metropolitan Police Force in 1919, she said:

> In August 1914 ... I formed a small body of workers to go to the stations to meet the refugees who were coming from the falling Belgian towns ... My work was concerned with the meeting of girls and women ... one night I lost two girls under suspicious circumstances ... a fortnight afterwards I came across a woman who changed her dress and the colour of her hair three times in the same night. I had seen her at the station, and I caught her trying to take from me two girls. I realised that it would be very difficult to do that kind of work, if there were attempts at white slave traffic, without having a body of uniformed and trained women, and I think that gave me the first idea of having women police. (Allen, 1925: 136)

A highly visible presence in London railway stations and outside military venues in the West End, there were at least ten uniformed members of the Women Police patrolling the area around the AFL offices on the Strand, stationed at venues including the Beaver Hut (Canadian YMCA), Eagle Hut (American YMCA) and Savoy Hotel.[24]

The white slave trade, 'one of the most talked about social and political issues in the years before 1914' (Nicholson, 2003: 105), and issues of prostitution and socio-economic realities for women had been of interest to suffragists and suffragist playwrights in the preceding years, although it was a controversial and difficult topic to stage. In July 1914 the AFL had announced that Cicely Hamilton was adapting a novel by Elizabeth Robins about sex trafficking into a play for the second season of the Woman's Theatre, a project Inez Bensusan had set up in 1913 to improve conditions for women theatre professionals, to help women develop skills in administrative and backstage theatre work, and to further both feminist and suffragist agendas through theatre. In Hamilton's stage adaptation of Robins's *Where Are You Going To?*, two teenage sisters, Honor and Bettina, travel to London from the countryside to visit their aunt, who they have never met. Upon their arrival at Victoria Station they are met by a woman who they assume is their aunt and driven in her car to what they think is her address. Over the course of the play it becomes clear that they have been taken to a brothel and have no idea where they are. Originally recommended for licence by the censor, it was due to be performed in December 1914, but the licence was ultimately refused because of the brothel scenes, and also because of the controversy surrounding Bernard Shaw's play, *Mrs Warren's Profession*, which had been refused a licence in 1894.[25] Squire Bancroft, when consulted about *Where Are You Going To?*, wrote to the Lord Chamberlain's Office, 'I fail to see how The Lord Chamberlain can grant his licence to the second act of this play and refuse it to "Mrs. Warren's Profession".'[26] The play had to be dropped from the Woman's Theatre programme, much to Bensusan's disappointment.

Although the 1914 Woman's Theatre week eventually had to be cancelled, Bensusan adapted and diversified the project in response to the changing environment brought about by the war, introducing a spin-off venture, the Woman's Theatre Camps Entertainments, to support the war effort and entertain the troops at home and abroad.[27] The AFL's president, Gertrude Elliott, became president of the Women's Theatre Camps Entertainments and their first performance was at Aldershot on 6 November 1914.[28] 1915 and 1916 saw demand for the AFL's suffrage propaganda fall, but its war work flourished, with the Woman's Theatre Camps Entertainments giving 300 entertainments in 1915,[29] and over 600 the following year in clubs, huts, hospitals and camps. Averaging six to eight concerts per week, the League employed 451 artists over this period.[30] The last performance of the Woman's Theatre

Camps Entertainments appears to have been in July 1917 at the Gables Theatre in Surbiton, and featured storytelling, short plays, songs and music recitals with a cast that included Inez Bensusan, May Whitty and Ben Webster. The programme for the performance proudly stated that over the first six months of 1917, 426 concerts had been given by the organisation.[31]

Katherine E. Kelly's essay on the AFL during the First World War (Kelly, 1994: 121) refers to the organisation as 'feminist theatre in camouflage', and as well as the Woman's Theatre Camps Entertainments, AFL members were involved in organising performances at a number of military venues, including the YMCA Shakespeare Hut on Gower Street and the Endell Street Hospital in Covent Garden. At the Shakespeare Hut, which had Johnston Forbes-Robertson, Gertrude Elliott and Israel Gollancz on its committee for Drama and Music, the entertainments featured a mix of plays, music, songs and recitations.[32] For a night of variety entertainment on 6 January 1917, Gertrude Elliott organised a packed programme of one-act plays, including J. M. Barrie's *The Twelve Pound Look* and Gertrude Jennings's *The Bathroom Door*, alongside songs and recitations from AFL members Irene Vanbrugh and Decima Moore.[33] The entertainment committee for the Military Hospital on Endell Street also included AFL and WWSL members Bensusan, Robins, Beatrice Harraden and Whitty.[34] League members also became involved in war work outside of their theatre-related projects – Cicely Hamilton spent most of the war working for the Scottish Women's Hospitals in France (Whitelaw, 1990: 138); Adeline Bourne served overseas as an officer in Queen Mary's Army Auxiliary Corps and worked as an acting paymaster in the War Office (Law, 2000: 32); while Olga Nethersole joined the Voluntary Aid Detachment and nursed at Hampstead Military Hospital, subsequently founding the People's League of Health in 1917.

What becomes evident in the few accounts of the AFL's work immediately after the outbreak of war written by those who took part is the prejudice they faced as women wanting to assist, rather than challenge, the government. Initially, the voluntary work done by women was barely acknowledged, financially unsupported and undervalued by the very organisations the AFL was trying to help. Lena Ashwell remembered that 'Weekly lists were sent to the War Office, containing full particulars as to the numbers of women we could supply for transport, cooks, interpreters, and so forth; and each week a letter was received in acknowledgement, saying that women "were not needed"' (Ashwell, 1936: 75). The

Women's Emergency Corps saw this as 'ludicrous and shameful', noting that the Home Secretary had refused the offer of the services of women interpreters among others:

> twenty-five women motor-cyclists, able to repair their own and other people's machines, has been similarly neglected. And how about the post-office work, the ticket-selling, the express-message carrying, and other useful and necessary employments that are now suspended or working short? Women could carry them on just as well as men, while men are in the field. But 'No women need apply' has been this narrow-minded Government's rule, whether for votes or anything else.[35]

The many satellite projects that the AFL was supporting meant that fundraising was a constantly pressing issue, and their experiences with the propaganda of the suffrage movement made members unafraid to appeal directly for help to potential supporters on feminist, suffragist, theatrical and patriotic grounds. League member Margaret Webster, daughter of May Whitty and Ben Webster, attributed the success of the AFL in wartime to the skills learnt through its participation in the suffrage movement:

> Actually, the League was performing an educational function of much wider scope, though its members did not know it at the time ... they learned everything there was to know about how to run an organisation or a stage ... they learned how to raise money, how to run a public meeting, how to think on their feet, how to turn hostility or apathy into laughter and enthusiasm. (Webster, 1969: 249)

All too aware of the manipulation of the press and public by government, the AFL used patriotism for its own ends rather than as an ideology that informed its work. The use of patriotic allusions and appeals by the AFL is an example of its adaptability and awareness of the social and financial climate in which it wanted to succeed. This is particularly visible in the work of the British Women's Hospital Fund, another organisation based at the AFL's offices at 2 Robert Street.[36] Initially a sub-committee of the AFL, the first meeting was held on 12 August 1915, a year after the outbreak of war.[37] The advisory committee was made up entirely of AFL members, including Bensusan, Nina Boucicault, Madeleine Lucette Ryley, Decima and Eva Moore, Auriol Lee, Ashwell, Whitty, Bourne and Winifred Mayo, with the AFL's president, Gertrude Elliott, also president of the committee. The initial aim of the committee was to raise funds to start and run a complete hospital unit of 250 beds to be given to the French government 'for their sick and wounded soldiers'.³⁸ The AFL advertised the scheme widely in the national and international press, asking for donations to be sent directly to the offices in Robert Street:

> On behalf of the Actresses' Franchise League, of which she is president, Lady Forbes-Robertson is making an appeal to all parts of the British Empire to help, with their sympathy and their money, in the formation of a British Women's Hospital … The committee have every confidence that the daughters of Britain and of her Overseas Empire will not refuse to come forward at the is supreme hour of need, and aid, to their utmost, a splendid work of mercy.³⁹

A month later, the *Daily Telegraph* reported that the initial scheme had been postponed in favour of another – the refurbishment and conversion of the Star and Garter Hotel in Richmond, Surrey, into a home for permanently disabled soldiers and sailors.⁴⁰ The British Women's Hospital and the AFL organised a procession to advertise the first public meeting of the fund. Women marched with banners, posters and sandwich boards through the West End, accompanied by a number of smaller supporting groups, including an all-female band in uniform from the Church Nursing and Ambulance Brigade,⁴¹ an event that seems to have been inspired by, and directly to reference, pre-war suffrage marches. Ever aware of the power of propaganda, Bourne wrote to Maud Arncliffe Sennett on 27 October 1915 to ask her to speak on behalf of the British Women's Hospital. Bourne was candid about the outcome she wanted: 'It is really a recruiting meeting, the subject to stir them is Edith Cavell.'⁴² Cavell, a nurse stationed in Brussels, had been shot at dawn by the German army on 12 October for assisting the escape of Allied soldiers. International protests had followed her arrest and execution and her story and memory was potent with patriotic and moral power (Daunton, 2004). Bourne reported that the Committee of the British Women's Hospital had decided that to 'associate and perpetuate' the name of Edith Cavell, they should appeal to supporters to raise funds to name a wing of the Star and Garter Home for disabled servicemen after her.⁴³ An appeal was duly made in the press and Bourne publicly sought and gained the approval of Cavell's sister for their campaign.⁴⁴ The Star and Garter Home for disabled servicemen was one of the British Women's Hospital Fund's most successful ventures and they raised £150,000 (over £10 million at 2015 values) – three times the initial target – to restore and rebuild part of the building in Richmond to make it suitable for wounded troops (Figure 10).

10 'Haven', poster for the Star and Garter Home and British Women's Hospital Fund, 1915.

Members of the AFL continued to take part in public fundraising days and performances, demonstrating their patriotic visibility on the streets and in the theatres, much as they had previously demonstrated their suffragist affiliations. Friday 12 May 1916 was appointed 'Lamp Day' to commemorate Florence Nightingale's birthday, and the British Women's Hospital asked for funds to be sent to support its own project, as well as the Women's Service Bureau and the Women's Emergency Corps. *The Times* reported that 6,000 women were on the streets of central London on 'Lamp Day' selling small cardboard lamps at a penny, threepence and a shilling each, and the London County and Westminster Bank in Victoria Street stayed open until midnight to receive collection boxes.[45] Actresses Nina Boucicault, Gertrude Kingston, Janette Steer and May Whitty sold lamps outside the Star and Garter Fund offices in Bond Street, while Lilian Braithwaite, Gladys Cooper and Marie Lohr were stationed in Harrods. The amount raised for the societies was over £5,600.[46]

The British Women's Hospital organised a number of fundraising performances, including a star-studded matinee at the London Coliseum in June 1916. Produced by Lillah McCarthy, the matinee was well supported by the theatre industry, with over sixty performers, including Adeline Genée, Nigel Playfair and Gertrude Kingston, volunteering to sell programmes in the auditorium.[47] The programme featured *The Admirable Crichton*, four topical comic sketches by J. M. Barrie and some musical performances.[48] The sketches were presented together under the heading *Irene Vanbrugh's Pantomime*, and included a monologue performed by Mrs Patrick Campbell and a duologue between Johnston Forbes-Robertson and Gertrude Elliott which referenced their interest in the Endell Street Hospital:

> LADY F: (*to audience*) It is about an extraordinary thing that happened at the hospital to-day. (*troubled*) Forbes, I oughtn't really to tell it before them, it's so frightfully personal!
> SIR F: Well, I wasn't there, so it can't be personal to me.
> LADY F: Oh can't it! It's just the sort of thing dear that might wreck a happy home.
> SIR F: Woman, you are trying to work upon their feelings, like some play-actress. Out with it.
> LADY F: (*to audience*) You see it's *he* who insists, so if anything unpleasant comes of this, you'll take my side won't you? It began two days ago, when a soldier was brought to the Hospital suffering from nerve-shock. It had deprived him of the power of speech, as you know sometimes happens.
> SIR F: Yes.
> LADY F: The doctor was most anxious to make him speak, and he begged me to help – and all day yesterday I sat beside the poor man's bed talking and talking and trying to get a word out of him.
> SIR F: Are you sure you gave him a chance, my love?
> LADY F: Ungenerous! I repeated a 100 times "The one thing I want to know in the world is what regiment you belong to! Oh, if only you would tell me what regiment you belong to" – and one could see he wanted to tell me, but he couldn't do it. This morning I began again. I said "I couldn't sleep all last night for wondering what regiment you belong to, I'll never sleep again if you don't tell me what regiment you belong to!" and, so it went on, and he was obviously frightfully anxious to tell me, he kept opening his mouth but no word would come, I was so sorry for him I began to cry – (*she cries now*) and that did it. He spoke![49]

The duologue continues, and Gertrude Elliott sends her husband offstage in search of her handkerchief, using the opportunity of his absence to confess to the audience that she kissed the invalid soldier because when he did finally speak he said she looked like his mother. The audience is left to decide if the soldier was genuinely confused, or was just taking advantage of her good nature. However, Barrie is careful not to mock the inarticulacy of the shell-shocked soldier, but rather to gently poke fun at the happy marriage of the Forbes-Robertsons.

The British Women's Hospital Fund also held fundraisers for other related projects that involved League members. After a successful charity matinee performance on 23 March 1917 at the Coliseum,[50] *The Passing of the Third Floor Back* transferred to the Playhouse for a three-week run, with the entire proceeds going to the Scottish Women's Hospital Fund. The cast, who all appeared voluntarily for eight shows a week, included Elliott and Whitty. This generosity was matched by Frank Curzon, who lent the Playhouse for free for the run, and Jerome K. Jerome, who waived his author's fee.[51] At the matinee performance on 18 April 1917 'organized by the British Women's Hospital Committee in Aid of Scottish Women's Hospitals Abroad', many performers including Eva Moore and Adeline Genée worked as programme sellers inside the auditorium alongside the daughter of the Prime Minister, Elizabeth Asquith,[52] who was by then on the committee of the British Women's Hospital Fund.

Despite its success, the AFL discovered again that, as with the WEC, even when women were attempting to assist the war effort and gaining national press coverage, the government and established institutions obstructed their participation at every level. May Whitty found that the British Women's Hospital 'encountered enormous difficulties from the British Red Cross who were still very prejudiced against women's work' and would only allow female nurses, not doctors, to travel.[53] The Red Cross benefited from the work of the British Women's Hospital, WEC and other organisations set up by the AFL in spite of its lack of support for them. Without genuine government support for its initiatives, the League's projects relied on sponsorship, gifts in kind, fundraising and appeals to those in positions of power and influence. Unhindered by pre-war debates around the effectiveness or appropriateness of suffragette militancy, it was easier for League members to garner high-profile support, and their many wartime projects, including both the WEC and the British Women's Hospital, had titled ladies as members and patrons – the beginning of formal and overtly publicised connections with the upper classes that would go on to characterise much of their later charitable work. The success of the Star and Garter Fund and the work of the British Women's Hospital prompted an invitation for Whitty and Lady Cowdray, as chair and treasurer of the Fund, to join the previously all-male Red Cross Committee of the Star and Garter, and although reluctant to accept the title from the Lloyd George government, Whitty became the first actress to receive a damehood when the Red Cross recommended her for a DBE in 1918 (Webster, 1969: 255). The Women's Emergency Corps was formally disbanded in November 1919, a year after the First World War ended, having been the foundation organisation for many other groups including the Women's Volunteer Reserve.

Theatre ownership and management structures, particularly in the commercial West End houses, were very different after the war. Actor-managers had largely given way to syndicate ownerships that some argue had 'little or no interest in theatre as an art form' as opposed to a commercial proposition, and the costs of mounting and attending shows had increased due to higher rents and the introduction of the Entertainment Tax in 1916 (Gardner, 2008: 76). Wartime restrictions had also adversely affected provincial theatres and touring theatre companies, and the regional repertory theatres that had been established before 1914 had struggled to remain active and successful. The AFL continued to campaign not only for the equal franchise but for equality for women in all areas of social and political life, using its experiences during the war as well as from the pre-war suffrage campaign to maintain a political presence. As Karen Hunt and June Hannam have noted, 'the interwar era saw new "women's issues" cohere and seek space on the wider political agenda' (Hunt and Hannam, 2013: 133), and the AFL after 1918 had a broader portfolio of connections in industry and politics than before the war and just as fervent a desire to agitate for change. Thus an AFL meeting with the theme 'The Artist's Place in Reconstruction' was held at the St James's Theatre on 20 June of that year. Whitty chaired the meeting, saying:

> On account of the war they had lost touch with members and friends … but they had all been trying to do their bit, and … the League's bit had been pretty extensive … they had not lost sight of the fact that the League was a suffrage society first and foremost. They were very much alive and kicking, as of old, against injustice and inequality, and trying to better conditions.[54]

Maud Arncliffe Sennett reiterated Whitty's comments, suggesting that 'they had not got complete equality of the sexes either in Parliament or out of it, and until they did she could not believe there would be a really settled world'.[55]

The 1920s saw the AFL continuing its constitutional campaigning with suffrage societies and newly formed groups, and although it does not seem to have produced or commissioned suffrage plays after the end of the war, AFL members were able to use their wartime experiences of women's social, political and legal inequality directly in the ongoing campaign. In 1921 a number of AFL members and supporters became part of the Six Point Group, a non-party political organisation founded by Lady Rhondda to establish equality for women. The Six Point Group and the AFL continued to share membership and fundraising opportunities as well as building on the success of the AFL's networks and skill-sharing experience. The executive committee, social committee and vice presidents included Clemence Dane, Eva Moore, Elizabeth Robins, Nina Boucicault, Una Dugdale and Ethel Smyth, with Winifred Mayo as the organising secretary.[56] The Six Point Group was one of the forty-nine societies affiliated to the Consultative Committee of Women's Organisations, first formed in 1916 by the National Union of Women's Suffrage Societies (NUWSS) and then reorganised by Lady Astor in 1921 to promote 'networking ... among women activists and politicians, seeking to draw women into the normal processes of political lobbying' (Thane, 2013: 61). During the fifth annual meeting of the Consultative Committee of Women's Organisations, Winifred Mayo announced that the AFL would be giving half the funds raised by its 1926 December birthday party to the committee.[57] Held at the Hyde Park Hotel, the event's twenty-three hostesses included Madge Kendal, May Whitty, Decima Moore, Ruby Miller, Clara Butt and Gladys Cooper.[58]

Earlier in 1926, the AFL, dressed in its colours of pink and green,[59] marched in London in the Women's Equal Political Rights procession on 3 July.[60] Forty women's societies took part in a procession reminiscent of the pre-war suffrage campaign, walking in formation from Charing Cross to Hyde Park.[61] The press had not forgotten the League's role in demonstrations before 1914:

> The procession took ... a route full of memories for the veterans ... the Actresses' Franchise League ... remembering that since they marched in the last great procession they had set going the schemes of service that led to the wide development and organization of women's war work.[62]

A year later, the AFL was a signatory to a letter from Lady Rhondda – who had first petitioned in 1920[63] for the right to take her place as a hereditary peer in the House of Lords, based on the Sex Disqualification (Removal) Act 1919 – on behalf of the Equal Political Rights Campaign Committee to the government to demand that votes for women at the age of 21 would be included in the King's speech at the opening of

Parliament in 1927.[64] Again the suffrage societies joined to show support for the Equal Franchise Bill, and the Women's Freedom League (WFL) held a mass demonstration in Trafalgar Square in July 1927 calling on the government to pass an Equal Franchise measure 'so as to ensure the inclusion of the new women voters ... in time to vote at the next General Election'.[65] Adeline Bourne represented the AFL and spoke to remind her audience 'that, before the war, people were full of reasons against giving women the vote; after the war, no one could find any reasons against'.[66]

Alongside members of the WFL, the NUWSS and WSPU, May Whitty, Decima and Eva Moore and Edyth Olive represented the AFL at Emmeline Pankhurst's funeral, held in St John's Church, Westminster on 18 June 1928.[67] The Equal Franchise Bill was passed a month later,[68] and the AFL was part of the evening victory reception of the Equal Political Rights Campaign Committee on 24 October 1928 at Caxton Hall. Nearly twenty years after the original production, Winifred Mayo and Kitty Willoughby produced *How The Vote Was Won* at the victory reception, 'with some members of the original cast and in the fashion of 1908'.[69] The first General Election at which women could equally vote with men was held in May 1929.

1914 had begun with the hope of a successful second season of the Woman's Theatre and a commitment to the continuation of suffrage campaigning, but despite the halting of the production and commissioning of suffrage plays later in that year, the AFL, the Woman's Theatre and the Woman's Theatre Camps Entertainments sustained a feminist and suffragist presence, space and visibility onstage and off throughout the war years. Unafraid to try new ventures and to work hard to develop them, the AFL responded to the challenges of the war by utilising and trusting the strengths, instincts and experience of its membership. The Women's Emergency Corps was a project with a significant national reach that sought to practically transform the lives of women and girls left out of work by war, teaching them new skills, harnessing existing ones and encouraging their creativity. Started as it was by actresses used to working at the top of their profession, it is perhaps not surprising that the WEC was a confident, outward-looking organisation – or that the toy-making department, for example, exhibited among well-known makers and competed for sales successfully at a national level just a few months after its formation. Despite the unwillingness of established institutions and systems of government to fully support and recognise the contribution made by the WEC, the Corps became part of a network of women's organisations working at grassroots level to effect positive change in the lives of British subjects as well as refugees from the war. The British Women's Hospital Fund also raised significant sums of money through applying many of the successful elements of the public-facing propaganda of the constitutional suffrage campaign to its own projects, by utilising the AFL's existing networks within the theatrical profession and reacting quickly to changing circumstances.

During the war, suffragist actresses familiar with the intimidation of female campaigners by the government came to see clearly that it was not their specific participation in the suffrage campaign that most antagonised and threatened the male establishment. The vocal presence of women from every class wanting to move freely and equally in society and industry, even the hundreds of thousands of women volunteers who worked both at home and abroad assisting the war effort, was both passively and actively discouraged and resented, highlighting the unequal position and status of women in society. After the war, the presence of female Members of Parliament created opportunities for feminist and suffragist campaigners to access and contribute to committees that were part of the working process of government, welcoming women into physical and political spaces that they had been prevented from entering before 1914. AFL members keen to remain actively involved in feminist campaigns now had greater opportunities for participation and more resources to draw on. While many original AFL members continued to work in the professional theatre industry after 1928, others such as founder member Adeline Bourne devoted all their time to charitable and philanthropic work, using their performance skills and their organisational experience to continue to campaign for equality for women directly and in collaboration with established and newly emerging groups. Having thrived and expanded during the period 1914–28, the Actresses' Franchise League would continue as an active campaign group and network for a further thirty years, through another world war and a new wave of feminist activism.

Notes

1 Lena Ashwell was a committee member and Maud Arncliffe-Sennett, Beatrice Harraden, Charlotte Shaw, Ben Webster, May Whitty and Laurence Housman were all vice presidents. *Votes for Women*, 6 February 1914, p. 281.
2 *Votes for Women*, 11 December 1914, p. 52.
3 *The Times*, 11 May 1915, p. 5.

4 *Votes for Women*, 12 November 1915, p. 50.
5 May Whitty diaries, Library of Congress.
6 Women's Emergency Committee Half Year Report, January 1915, p. 3, British Library.
7 *Votes for Women*, 14 August 1914, p. 692.
8 Women's Emergency Corps Half Yearly Report, 1915, p. 22.
9 Ibid., p. 2.
10 Ibid., p. 18.
11 Ibid., p. 14.
12 *The Lancet*, 24 June 1916, p. 1282.
13 Leaflet advertising the Women's Emergency Corps shop, c. 1914.
14 *The Times*, 3 October 1914, p. 11.
15 *Daily Chronicle*, 3 November 1914.
16 Ibid.
17 *Pall Mall*, 30 October 1914.
18 Women's Emergency Corps Half Yearly Report, 1915, pp. 12–13.
19 *Games and Toys*, 1.9, March 1915, p. 362.
20 Ibid., p. 374.
21 The Women's Emergency Corps Half Yearly Report lists thirty societies including the Young Women's Christian Association, AFL, WWSL, Women's Institute and American Women's War Relief Fund.
22 Moore was performing in her husband's play *Eliza Comes to Stay*, which had transferred from the Criterion Theatre to the Vaudeville on 6 July 1914.
23 *Votes for Women*, 9 October 1914, p. 13.
24 The Women Police Service report, 1919, pp. 14–15, British Library.
25 The play would not be passed for public performance until 1925.
26 Lord Chamberlain's Correspondence, 1914/2, British Library.
27 *Woman's Theatre Mission Statement*, War Relief matinee programme, 1915.
28 *Observer*, 5 November 1914.
29 *Votes for Women*, March 1916, p. 151.
30 *The Times*, 7 January 1915, p. 5.
31 Programme for Woman's Theatre Camps Entertainments, 13 July 1917, Bristol Theatre Collection.
32 For more about Gertrude Elliott and the Shakespeare Hut, see Grant Ferguson (2013).
33 Programme for the Shakespeare Hut, 6 January 1917.
34 Programme for the Military Hospital, Endell Street, 29 December 1916.
35 *Votes for Women*, 4 September 1914, p. 719.
36 Gertrude Elliott was the president of the advisory committee; other members included Lena Ashwell, Inez Bensusan, Gertrude Kingston, Auriol Lee, Winifred Mayo, Decima, Eva and Mary Moore, Madeleine Lucette Ryley, May Whitty, Lilian Braithwaite, Janette Steer and Miss Compton. Ashwell

'VERY MUCH ALIVE AND KICKING' 135

and Edyth Olive were joint honorary treasurers, the honorary secretary was Nina Boucicault and the honorary organising secretary was Adeline Bourne.
37 British Women's Hospital Committee minute book, Wellcome Library.
38 Letter from British Women's Hospital, Wellcome Library.
39 *Daily Telegraph*, 28 August 1915.
40 *Daily Telegraph*, 25 September 1915.
41 *Morning Post*, 27 September 1915.
42 Letter from Adeline Bourne to Maud Arncliffe Sennett, 27 October 1915, Arncliffe Sennett Collection, British Library.
43 Ibid.
44 *Manchester Guardian*, 1 November 1915.
45 *The Times*, 13 May 1916, p. 3.
46 *Evening Standard*, 7 June 1916. This is over £340,000 at 2016 values.
47 Programme for performance in aid of the Star and Garter Building Fund of the British Women's Hospital, 9 June 1916.
48 Ibid.
49 J. M. Barrie, *Irene Vanburgh's Pantomime*, LCP 1916/13, British Library.
50 *Daily Mail*, 24 March 1917, p. 3.
51 *The Times*, 31 March 1917, p. 9.
52 Programme for Playhouse, 18 April 1917, Wellcome Library.
53 May Whitty diaries, p. 75, Library of Congress.
54 *Stage*, 26 June 1919, p. 16.
55 Ibid.
56 *Time and Tide*, 5 January 1928, p. 21.
57 Minutes of Fifth Annual Meeting of the Consultative Committee of Women's Organisations, July 1926, p. 3.
58 Actresses' Franchise League Birthday Party notice card, 1926.
59 *Vote*, 9 July 1926, p. 210.
60 *Stage*, 17 June 1926, p. 12.
61 *The Times*, 17 June 1926, p. 11.
62 *Manchester Guardian*, 5 July 1926.
63 Despite petitions in 1920 and 1948, bills in 1924, 1925, 1926, 1927 and 1928 and a vote in 1930, there was no official acceptance of the principle of admitting women to the Lords until 1949. Lady Rhondda did not live to see the admittance of women to the House of Lords. On the passing of the Life Peerages Act in October 1958, three months after her death, women became eligible to take their places in the Lords.
64 *The Times*, 4 February 1927, p. 10.
65 *Vote*, 22 July 1927, p. 225.
66 Ibid., p. 227.
67 *Manchester Guardian*, 19 June 1928, p. 12.
68 Parliamentary Archives, HL/PO/PU/1/1928/18&19G5c12.
69 *Manchester Guardian*, 13 October 1928, p. 17.

References

Allen, Mary S. (1925), *The Pioneer Policewoman*, London: Chatto and Windus.
Ashwell, Lena (1936), *Myself a Player*, London: Michael Joseph.
Daunton, Claire (2004), 'Edith Cavell', *Oxford Dictionary of National Biography*, Oxford: Oxford University Press, http://www.oxforddnb.com/index/32/101032330/ (accessed 23 November 2014).
Gardner, Viv (2008 [2000]), 'Provincial Stages, 1900–1934: Touring and Early Repertory Theatre', in Baz Kershaw, ed., *The Cambridge History of British Theatre*, Cambridge: Cambridge University Press, pp. 60–85.
Grant Ferguson, Ailsa (2013), 'Lady Forbes-Robertson's War Work: Gertrude Elliott and the Shakespeare Hut Performances, 1916–1919', in G. McMullan, L. Cowen Orlin and V. Mason Vaughan, eds, *Women Making Shakespeare*, London: Bloomsbury, pp. 233–42.
Hunt, Karen, and June Hannam (2013), 'Towards an Archaeology of Interwar Women's Politics: The Local and the Everyday', in Julie Gottlieb and Richard Toye, eds, *The Aftermath of Suffrage*, Basingstoke: Palgrave Macmillan, pp. 124–41.
Jackson, Louise A. (2006), *Women Police: Gender, Welfare and Surveillance in the Twentieth Century*, Manchester: Manchester University Press.
Kelly, Katherine E. (1994), 'The Actresses' Franchise League Prepares for War: Feminist Theatre in Camouflage', *Theatre Survey*, 35.1, pp. 121–37.
Kingston, Gertrude (1937), *Curtsey While You're Thinking*, London: Williams and Norgate.
Law, Cheryl (2000), *Women, A Modern Political Dictionary*, London: I.B. Tauris.
Moore, Eva (1923), *Exits and Entrances*, London: Chapman and Hall.
Nicholson, Steve (2003), *The Censorship of British Drama 1900–1968*, Exeter: Exeter University Press.
Sanderson, Michael (1984), *From Irving to Olivier: A Social History of the Acting Profession in England, 1880–1982*, London: Athlone Press.
Thane, Pat (2013), 'Impact of Mass Democracy on British Political Culture', in Julie Gottlieb and Richard Toye, eds, *The Aftermath of Suffrage*, Basingstoke: Palgrave Macmillan, pp. 54–69.
Thomas, Sue (2005), 'Crying "the horror" of Prostitution: Elizabeth Robins's "Where Are You Going To…?" and the Moral Crusade of the Women's Social and Political Union', *Women: A Cultural Review*, 16.2, pp. 203–21.
Vining, M., and B. Hacker (2001), 'From Camp Follower to Lady in Uniform: Women, Social Class and Military Institutions before 1920', *Contemporary European History*, 10.3, pp. 353–73.
Webster, Margaret (1969), *The Same Only Different*, London: Victor Gollancz.
Whitelaw, Lis (1990), *The Life and Rebellious Times of Cicely Hamilton*, London: The Women's Press.

Archives

British Library

Arncliffe Sennett Collection/General Reference Collection C.121.g.1
Lord Chamberlain's Correspondence
Women's Emergency Corps Half Yearly Report/General Reference Collection 8416.k.17
Women Police Service Report/General Reference Collection YD.2005.a.128

Library of Congress, Washington DC

May Whitty Diaries/Margaret Webster papers, MM 75052142
Military Hospital Endell Street programme
Shakespeare Hut programme
University of Bristol Theatre Collection, Mander and Mitchenson Collection/war related theatre box of materials
Women's Theatre Camps Entertainments
Women's Theatre War Relief programme

Wellcome Library

British Women's Hospital Committee minute book/SANFN/A
British Women's Hospital correspondence

6

DEFENDING THE BODY, DEFENDING THE SELF

Women performers and the law in the 'long' Edwardian period[1]

Viv Gardner

Royal Court Theatre, 9 April 1907:

> A woman is arrested by a man, brought before a man judge, condemned by men, taken to prison by a man, and by a man she's hanged! Where in all this were *her* 'peers'? Why did men so long ago insist on trial by 'a jury of their peers'? So that justice shouldn't miscarry. A man's peers would best understand his circumstances … (Edith Wynn Matthison as Vida Levering in Elizabeth Robins's *Votes for Women*, Act 2)[2]

Central Criminal Court (The Old Bailey), 4 June 1918:

> Gentlemen … First of all, you should ask yourselves: is this a libel on Miss Maud Allan? Now you have heard what the 'Cult of the Clitoris' means. Is it a libel upon Miss Maud Allan? I have told you it is a libel if it is written and published and if it tends to hold her up to dislike, in fact defames her character – and who can doubt that it did? But I cannot decide it, and therefore I will formally ask you, although all through this case everybody has assumed that there can be but one answer to that question … (Lord Justice Darling, summing up in *Crown* v. *Billing*)

As if to prove Elizabeth Robins's point, and despite the judge's direction, it took the special jury at the Old Bailey only an hour and twenty-five minutes to find maverick independent MP Noel Pemberton Billing 'not guilty' of the charge of malicious publication of a false defamatory and criminal libel against the dancer and actress Maud Allan (Kettle, 1977: 63). The gentlemen of the jury vindicated the assertions implicit in a boxed paragraph published in Billing's journal, *The Vigilante*, on 16 February 1918, under the headline 'The Cult of the Clitoris'; this paragraph advised readers that Scotland Yard had only to seize the list of members about to attend a private performance of Oscar Wilde's *Salome*, in which Allan was to play the lead, to uncover several of the names of the estimated 47,000 'followers of Wilde' at large among the British cultural and political elite. By its verdict, the jury publicly declared Allan 'a sadist, a lewd, unchaste and immoral woman', whose performance would encourage 'obscene and unnatural practices among women' (Hoare, 1997: 177). This was, perhaps, as much a verdict on Allan's career and public image as on the legal case under scrutiny. Salome was her 'signature' role; she had first produced her *Vision of Salomé* in England, with its notorious 'Dance of the Seven Veils', ten years earlier in 1908.

In some ways, however, this infamous, complex and much-discussed case marks a watershed in the history of women performers' attempts to use the law to defend their reputations against public attack. The gender historian Lucy Bland sees this trial as 'pivotal' in 'the drawing up of battle lines in relation to the construction of a new, post-war womanhood, setting the stage for the [sensational] trials' of socially and sexually transgressive women that were to follow in the 1920s (Bland, 2013: 9). With the partial enfranchisement of women in February 1918, the qualification of women as parliamentary candidates in November 1918 and the swearing-in of the first female jurors in July 1920, the political, social and legal landscape for all British women changed significantly at the end of the war.

However, Allan was not just a woman but also a performer. She was defending her reputation on two fronts. For several decades before 1918 female performers had been one of the very public faces of professionalised women while still, for many, socially and sexually marginal. Allan's male co-plaintiff, the radical theatrical producer J. T. Grein, was given much less prominence in contemporary – and most subsequent – commentaries on the case; the focus was on the dancer, and the names alleged to exist in Billing's notorious 'Black Book'.[3] The 'Cult of the Clitoris' was just one of a series of legal cases brought by female performers between 1882 – and the second Married Women's Property Act in 1893, which gave married women the same powers to sue and be sued as men and spinsters and widows – and the end of First World War. From 1903 onwards, they did so in the shadow of the militant suffragists who were using their court appearances with increasing passion and skill to challenge both the law and society's unequal treatment of women. Women performers also used the courts to argue for self-determination and control, particularly of their public image. These were not the litigious widows of Renaissance drama (Stretton, 2005: 57–63), but public women seeking justice through the limited civil structures now available to them. Gone were the veils and victimhood that characterised nineteenth-century images of women in court (Nead, 2002), to be replaced by photographs, 'real' pictures, of women – some very well known – in fashionable dress.

'A quagmire of meaningless and grotesque anomalies': the laws of defamation

This chapter explores a number of legal cases brought by women performers and the issues that these raise. Most, but not all, of the cases were libel trials that also involved issues of copyright in images. A study of the *Era* for the period 1900–18 appears to show that female performers used the civil law, particularly civil and criminal libel, more frequently than their male counterparts. Their cases were also more frequently reported in the mainstream press. Actresses were good business, and media reporting of the trials – including the rhetoric and conduct of the representatives of the law – played a crucial role in the public perception of both plaintiff and defendant, and in reinforcing or challenging the public image of the 'actress'.

In 1903 an American lawyer, Van Vechten Veeder, described the English laws of defamation as 'absurd in theory, and often mischievous in practical operations' (Veeder, 1903: 546). As a measure of a civilised society's 'culture, liberality and practical ability … to protect personal character and public institutions from destructive attacks, without sacrificing freedom of thought and the benefit of public discussion', he found Britain's laws of libel and slander wanting, a 'quagmire' of 'meaningless and grotesque anomalies' (Veeder, 1903: 546). The use, therefore, of Veeder's 'quagmire of grotesque anomalies' as a weapon for female litigants proved a double-edged sword. The defining criterion of defamation as 'an offence to personal character' was sufficiently ambiguous to allow many different types of prosecution, but the 'test' of defamation, that it should be an offence agreed by 'any reasonable person', was equally open to interpretation and bias – Justice Darling thought Billing's publication a libel; the jury of 'reasonable' men did not. In addition, Britain's case-law-based legal system means that the verdict in one case effectively creates law, by precedent, in any future case.[4]

The motives of the women in these cases might have been ambiguous – part personal, part professional and commercial – but the progress, conduct and outcomes of the libel cases were very much a 'measure of the culture, liberality, and practical ability' of the age, particularly as it related to women. The practical ability of the law to control women is demonstrated overtly in the Allan case. Allan stated that it was her 'ambition to be an actress as well as a dancer' (Bland, 2013: 33); in accepting the role of Salome in Wilde's play she was not repudiating her status as 'a modern classical dancer', but seeking to progress as she aged – she was 45 in 1918. Instead her professional life was all but destroyed by the outcome of the libel case, with its personal attack on her 'libidinous and obscene' performance (Hoare, 1997: 218–21).

Reputation and hierarchy were increasingly important in the theatre industry in the early twentieth century. The class status of women performers in particular had always been ambiguous, and the conflation of 'actress' and 'whore' remained an issue, particularly for dancers and chorus girls, or the more economically-vulnerable provincial and suburban players. The increased professionalisation and respectability of the stage as a career for men and women by the end of the nineteenth century paradoxically made 'reputation' an even more precious and precarious commodity for those who had it, and widened the gap between the reputable and disreputable in the profession. This was reinforced by an increased divide between the 'serious' and the popular stages. Women performers were almost always lumped together as 'actresses' whatever their professional expertise and area of employment (singer, dancer, comedienne, Shakespearean etc.), and 'serious' actresses increasingly sought to distance themselves from their singing and dancing lower-caste sisters (or former selves). These distinctions were in a state of flux, but important both personally and professionally, as many of these cases show.[5]

'What constitutes an actress?': *Thomas* v. *Frohman and A. and S. Gatti* (1905–06)

In 1905 Ethel Lucy Carrie Thomas, performing under the name of Ethel Karri, sued Charles Frohman and the Gatti brothers for damages for wrongful dismissal. Thomas had been engaged by actor-manager Seymour Hicks to play a Gibson Girl in *The Catch of the Season* at the Vaudeville Theatre. There had been no written contract, but this was not an unusual practice for an 'actress' or minor performer.[6] By the opening night her lines had been cut from three pages to two lines, then, after two weeks, Thomas was dismissed with a fortnight's notice. The reason given was that some of the original members of the company had returned and had to be placed. Hicks claimed in court that 'Miss Thomas, like other chorus girls, was subject to a fortnight's notice', and that 'nobody but a madman would engage a chorus girl in any other way'. Thomas sued Frohman and the Gattis on the grounds that she had been hired as an actress not an 'extra', chorus or a show girl. Luminaries – inevitably all male – from West End theatre managements were called for both sides. Hayden Coffin, Robert Courtneidge and Augustus Moore made appearances in court, and the debate was picked up in the newspapers under such headlines as 'What is an Actress?', with opinions from George Alexander, George Edwardes and Beerbohm Tree generating publicity about the case and its participants.[7] Thomas's two lines were, 'I am a perfect wonder at spotting winners, and I hardly ever lose at bridge', and 'Dear old Hyde Park'. Charles Wyndham in a written deposition said that 'he considered that a lady who had to speak such lines … must be intelligent'; 'the words', in his view, 'were so foolish that it required a lot of intelligence to give them life' and therefore Thomas must be an actress who could not be dismissed at a fortnight's notice like a 'show girl'. The dramatist Owen Hall supported Wyndham but went further, arguing that he would describe Thomas as 'a small-part principal'; he himself 'considered the term "show girl" offensive, and one that was not used in high-class theatres'.[8]

Wyndham's judgement might appear facetious but the eventual verdict did turn in part upon the 'intelligence' required to 'give character' to a line and therefore 'act'.[9] Important as this issue of 'taxonomy' was for the profession, facetiousness appeared to be the dominant mode of legal exchange in court as reported by the newspapers. The barristers, as well as established performers, tended to 'play to the gallery', and in the first trial even Justice Darling – who presided over many of these 'theatrical' trials – mindful of his reputation as a wit, frequently provoked 'loud laughter' with such faux-naive questions as whether 'the person who plays "Hamlet" [would be] engaged on the same terms as the person who says "The carriage waits"?'[10]

Thomas was awarded £50 damages after the second trial, but fought on. Finally, after three trials, the case was found for Thomas, who received £200 in damages – the equivalent of a good year's salary for her – with costs.[11] While it is impossible to say what motivated Thomas, she must have had the self-belief and financial means to persevere, though it is possible she also received support from the Actors' Association, whose secretary, Charles Cruickshank, spoke for her at all three trials. Above all, it was sufficiently important to 'Ethel Karri', both financially and personally, for her to fight for her right to be designated an actress, rather than a chorus or show girl, with all the connotations that these involved. She risked her future employment prospects by alienating possible employers by being so 'uppity' (as *Grahame* v. *Robertson* below shows), but equally she risked lower status and future levels of pay if she did not defend her professional standing.

Defending the body: *Studholme* v. *Foley* (1904); *Monckton* v. *Dunn* (1907)

Risk to professional reputation was at the heart of most theatrical libel trials. Some cases were relatively straightforward. The variety artist and actress Hettie Chattell was awarded by a jury the extraordinary sum of £2,500 in damages from the *Daily Mail* when the paper falsely named her as the mother of the Gaiety Girl Rosie Boote. Since Chattell was only 28 at the time, and single, the case for defamation was hard to deny.[12] Since Chattell had only asked for £1,000 in damages in the first instance, she appears to have accepted this lower sum after the case went to appeal in December, and the Master of the Rolls agreed that although the libel had been 'of a very grave character', he deemed the jury's award 'excessive and out of all proportion to the injury the lady had suffered'.[13]

However, other libel cases were more complex and the defence not simply one of reputation. A significant factor that emerges from these legal disputes was the problem of the copyright ownership of images in the early twentieth century; this became critical with the increased visibility of women performers through changes in print culture. Developments in paper production had reduced the cost of paper exponentially, but it was the invention of the rotary press that truly revolutionised the print industries. The old steam newspaper presses were 'gradually replaced by rotary presses capable of mass production [and] the railways transformed the process of getting the paper to readers anywhere in the country' (Engel, 1996: 56–7). It was not simply newspapers that accelerated the 'celebrity culture' of the 1900s. The rotary press and advances in the mass reproduction of photographs, using lithography as opposed to intaglio engraving, line drawings and woodcuts, enabled not just photographic newspapers – the first was the *Daily [Illustrated] Mirror* in January 1904 – and populist theatrical magazines such as *Play Pictorial* (1902–39), but also the photographic postcard industry which became enormously important in the commodification and mass circulation of performers' images (Gardner, 2004a). The law, however, was struggling to keep up with these advances. While Britain was a signatory to the 1886 Berlin Convention, which first recognised copyrights among sovereign nations, and the 1891 International Copyright Treaty, it implemented regulation selectively, largely through case law. In the early part of the twentieth century the law relating to ownership of photographic images (by the subject, the photographer or the photographic company) was still in a state of development.[14]

The women who went to law to protect their reputation when it was 'traduced' through the dissemination of an undesirable image were therefore safer using the laws of libel rather than copyright, although to all intents and purposes it was the ownership of their image that was in dispute. Many cases centred on representations of part or the whole of the performer's body. Given the increasing prominence of 'real' images of women in the period through photographic newspapers, magazines and postcards, the negotiation and control of how, how much and for/to whom the body was exposed became critical for the ordinary as well as the celebrity performer.

The musical comedy star Marie Studholme was renowned for her 'bewitching smile' that graced many a 'fancy stationer's window'.[15] Many of the numerous postcard pictures of her focused on 'her wonderful smile' (Jupp, 1923: 69), and perfect dentition. Like many performers, she had capitalised on her 'assets' by allowing her image to be used in advertising.[16] In an advertisement for Sozodont dentifrice in the 1890s she testified that '[t]o an actress nowadays a pretty set of teeth is a necessity. In burlesque, especially, a smile is as good as a song. And a smile is enhanced if the teeth are pretty, for pretty teeth are an actress' stock in trade' (Figure 11).

When the West End dentist Edward Foley was looking for a 'suitable head to work upon' for a brochure advertising his cosmetic dental practice, he unsurprisingly bought a picture postcard of Marie Studholme. Her teeth, according to the account in the *Morning Bulletin*, 'were touched up by artists, and a photograph was taken from it, representing "with good teeth." Then several teeth were blacked out, and another photograph was made to indicate "without good teeth."'[17] Half-a-million booklets using the 'before and after' photographs were printed, but Studholme, on hearing about the publication, sued Foley for libel. The matter was settled out of court, but all the booklets were destroyed and Foley was forced to pay damages with costs. He also had to make a 'sincere apology', printed in newspapers designated by Studholme, in which he admitted that having used her portrait 'in a manner calculated to induce persons to erroneously believe that certain of her front teeth

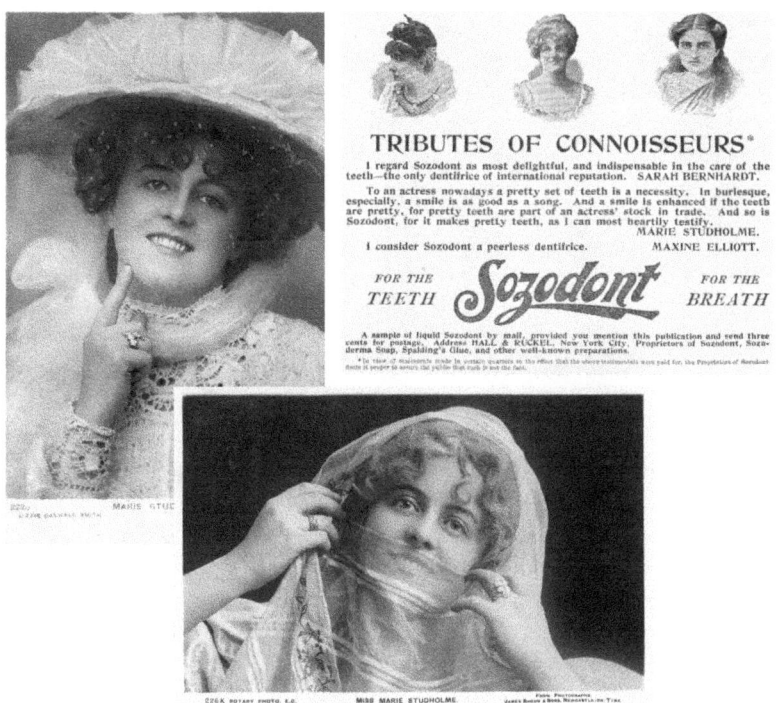

11 Marie Studholme and her bewitching smile.

are missing, and have been replaced with false ones' constituted a libel. 'That particular penny post card involved its purchaser in an outlay of about £200' the *Morning Bulletin* quipped.

It is doubtful whether the £50 damages awarded to Studholme, then at the height of her career, was her motive in suing Foley. Like other celebrity women performers from the period, Studholme was very careful of her public image. Despite humble origins in Bradford, she was marketed as the epitome of female beauty in romantic picture hats, fashionable dresses and stage costumes. Though not named at the trial, there were others who had interests in maintaining Studholme's reputation as the perfect romantic beauty. From about 1900 almost all postcards of Studholme were produced by the Rotary Photographic Company from photographs by Frank Foulsham (or the duo Foulsham and Banfield). In the same period she worked almost exclusively for George Edwardes at the Gaiety Theatre. These men's commercial interests were also at stake if

12 Gertie Millar in three pirated postcards by Ralph Dunn (l to r): in a nightdress, as 'La Source', *The Orchid*.

Studholme's reputation was 'tainted', or if they lost control of the circulation of her image. It is, perhaps, no coincidence that this 'triumvirate' were all represented at a later trial for libel brought by another Gaiety star, Gertie Millar.

In 1907 Millar sued a small postcard publisher, Dunn and Co., for the libel implicit in adding her head to images of other women's bodies on three pirated postcards. The first card showed Millar in a nightgown with a candle in her hand. The second 'was taken from a well-known picture called La Source [in which] the figure was draped in a peculiar way'; counsel for the plaintiff pointed out that 'the attraction of the picture [consisted] in the insufficiency and apparent insecurity of the costume' (Figure 12). The third picture was described as merely 'vulgar and ridiculous' and showed Millar crawling out of an eggshell.[18]

The commercial imperative gradually emerged in the reporting of the case. In court Millar was accompanied by her husband, the composer Lionel Monckton; Foulsham, who was not only photographer for, but also director of, the Rotary Photographic Company; and George Edwardes, who was reported to be 'smiling genially' throughout much of the proceedings. Millar had consulted Foulsham before bringing the action and he introduced her to the solicitor, a fellow director of the Rotary Photographic Company, who went on to represent her in court.[19] One of the points of dispute in the Millar case was the price at which Ralph Dunn was selling the pirated cards. A Millar card by Rotary, Tuck,

Philco or Valentine cost 2d, or 3d coloured; Dunn was selling his cards for one penny. Justice Darling, spotting an economic agenda, observed: 'I have been thinking for some time' that this was 'Mr Foulsham's action and not this lady's'; and the defence barrister also expressed the belief that the case had been brought to 'boycott' his client. Replying to these charges, Millar, perhaps disingenuously, pleaded ignorance of any conspiracy by 'the publishers of 2d postcards to prevent the publishers of penny cards getting photos from the photographers'.[20]

As in the Studholme case, tellingly, it was not the photographer and/or the photographic company that sued Dunn under copyright law for the flagrant theft of an image, but the performer making use of the libel laws. In a peculiar twist in the Millar case, it emerged that she, and presumably Rotary, had allowed a pirated image of herself in *The Orchid* to be published by Dunn a year or so earlier, in which an original photograph of Millar admonishing a spider had been replaced by one with a 'piccanniny' in striped trousers (Figure 12). This fact, however, was not included in the judge's summing-up, as it was a libel not a copyright case. Had a copyright case been brought, presumably this previous lack of action would have undermined the plaintiff's (whether Millar, Foulsham or Rotary) case.

Like Studholme, Millar was at the height of her popularity in 1907, and like Studholme and other stars, her body was repeatedly photographed and commodified, but the image that was projected was highly controlled. She was photographed in role, in pictures that perpetuated images of middle-class domesticity and occasionally in fantastic mock-ups with her emerging from a cracker for Christmas, or (ironically) an egg at Easter, but always fully and fashionably clothed. She was saucy without being sexual. These photographs were frequently sold as 'real pictures', a fantasy that would have pleased but not fooled her fans. To the modern eye, the pirated pictures are extremely anodyne; in the Edwardian context, however, the sinuously posed 'La Source' image in its 'insufficient' and 'insecure' clothing is suggestive, and while the nightdressed figure is well covered, the tilt of the head lacks only a 'Marie Lloyd' wink to turn it into an invitation. The postcards are of poor quality both pictorially and materially; not the sort of charming, professional image Millar et al. wished to see in circulation. Importantly, they lack the lively, performative quality to be found in a Foulsham or a Bassano photographic card.[21]

The intrinsic performance element in the cards was influential in the final judgment, as was the conduct of the trial. As so often in these cases, the papers reported the courtroom scenes as an extension of the plaintiff's onstage performance. The judge, Justice Darling again, became a fellow protagonist, setting up Millar's 'act', and frequently interrupting Dunn's defence to support the actress; the whole affair was repeatedly punctuated by 'loud laughter' from the body of the court. Millar's actual demeanour in court is difficult to determine. The *Daily Mirror* described her as 'favour[ing] the Court with her most charming smile', sweeping 'gracefully ... into the witness-box', and reported how '[h]er eyes brightened with indignation as counsel called her attention to the pictures'. She is cast as the 'heroine', one who treats the defence counsel's questions 'in the manner with which she addresses stage villains ... with a contemptuous curl of her fair lip'. Counsel on this occasion had need to 'muster up courage' to respond to her before 'getting bolder' and going on to admit that 'it was [his] misfortune never to have seen [her] at the Gaiety'. At which point the feisty heroine transformed into a flirt as a 'roguish smile [came] over Miss Millar's face, "You have missed a treat," she [said]', and counsel gave out 'a sigh over lost opportunities'.[22]

In what was undoubtedly an attempt to appeal to their female readership, the popular press paid significant attention to Millar's in-court 'costume'. On the first day, the *Mirror* described Millar as 'being snugly stowed away in a very ample, though perfectly fitting, fur jacket. On her head was the most piquant of fur toques. Her beauty shone demurely through a dainty veil.'[23] The *Daily Express* records her as 'dressed tastefully in velvet, with white headdress, collar and cuffs' on day two,[24] which for the *Mirror* was 'even more entrancing than her first [outfit] ... Her ermine-trimmed toque made every woman in the court envious.' The *Mirror* justified its interest in Millar's costume, arguing that the 'staidest lawyer could be pardoned for paying close attention to the fair plaintiff's toilet for', it argued tellingly, 'it was on the question of dress that the issue of the case turned'. The *Mirror* reporter felt that the power of this 'fascinating woman ... looking at her very best' would have swayed the 'ungallant' jury to find in her favour – had she stayed in court for the summing-up.[25]

Whatever her appeal to her public, and the all-male jury, Millar lost the case. It is possible that Millar's 'exceptionality', her stellar 'performance' in court, her perceived theatrical charisma and her clothes-as-costume worked against her interests. The jury found for Dunn, strongly guided by the judge whose summing-up was predicated on the difference between the actress and the 'ordinary woman' and the ownership she therefore had of images of her body. Darling advised the jury that they 'must act impartially in the matter and must not be affected by the fact that on one side they had got a commonplace man carrying on business and on the other a lady of exceptional charm, exceptional ability and exceptional attractiveness'. He continued:

> Mrs Monckton got her living as an actress, and was constantly before the public. She allowed people to photograph her and she took money for it. She also allowed her photograph to appear in fancy costumes. It might well be that if you wished to take a person who lived retired from the world and published a photograph of her in fancy costume, it might be libellous. Supposing, for instance you were to publish a photograph of the vicar's wife as La Source. She would have reason to be annoyed. But that is not quite the same as publishing the picture of a lady, who had often been photographed in fancy costumes, in another fancy costume.[26]

The judge's steer to the jury was clear; to a 'reasonable person', there was a difference between an actress and an 'ordinary', private woman, and therefore a difference between their rights to control the ways in which their bodies were disseminated.

Defending the (professional) self: *Grahame* v. *Robertson* (1900); *Wood* v. *Sandow, Sandow Limited & the Dover Street Studios* (1914)

Millar was protected from damage to her career by her popularity and the fact that she had her management on her side; if anything the conduct and reporting of the case, as well as the verdict, reinforced her 'exceptionality'. This was not true for the majority of performers; it is rare to come across a case, like Ethel Thomas's, where a non-celebrity performer challenged the powers that controlled their livelihoods through the courts. However, there are examples. In 1898 a provincial actress, Gracie Grahame, was overheard by the manager's wife complaining about backstage conditions in the theatre at Yarrow. Later the manager, H. Robertson, wrote to a fellow manager saying that he would only take up his play 'on the understanding that Mrs. Grahame will not be connected with this show in any shape or form, playing a part or otherwise ... as she made herself objectionable to the audience and everyone about the place when she was last here'. Grahame sued Robertson for libel, and while a York jury found in her favour the verdict was successfully challenged on appeal in London.[27]

13 Jane Wood in an advertisement for Sandow Corsets, and arriving at court, 1914.

A more high-profile case was that of Vera Jane Wood, who sued physical culture proselytiser and entrepreneur Eugen Sandow and the Dover Street Studios for libel and infringement of copyright in a photographic image. Wood, a rising young actress, visited the highly reputable Dover Street photographic studios in March 1914. Having relatively recently begun on the stage and achieved some success, she wanted photographs taken and offered to the fashionable papers such as *Tatler* and *The Sketch*, which regularly published 'classy' images of musical comedy performers. She received four pictures for her own use, which she paid for, but shortly afterwards she saw her picture being used in a half-page advertisement for Sandow Corsets (Figure 13).

In 1910 Sandow had produced a 'revolutionary' 'Patent Health and Perfect Figure Corset' that was endorsed by celebrity female performers as diverse as Sarah Bernhardt and Irene Vanbrugh, and musical comedy stars Phyllis Dare and Gertie Millar. An album of pictures featuring a 'celebrity' model was available to visitors to his corset salon, or by mail order in a private 'exchange' between corsetière and customer. Wood's mother had seen her daughter's photograph in a newspaper, and it had 'annoyed her'. Asked in court, 'Why did it annoy you?' Miss Wood's mother replied, '"The cheap publicity! I wrote at once to my daughter."

The witness added that she regarded the appearance of this photograph as derogatory to her daughter.' Wood sued on the grounds that she had not given permission for the reproduction of her image in an advertisement, intending her photograph to go to a fashion paper not a 'trade journal'; and secondly, that in so doing the defendants had 'defamed' her. Counsel for the plaintiff argued that the 'illustration suggested that the lady's figure was the result of wearing Sandow's corsets; but the lady had never worn those corsets'. Wood felt that the use of her image in this way 'did her a real injury among her friends'. Her employer, comedian George Graves, confirmed this, testifying that 'in his opinion it would do her no harm or good professionally; but in society he thought it would do harm'. Central to her case was her argument that, because she had not been identified in the advertisement as an actress (on a par with the well-known names in 'the book' and other advertisements), she 'had not been represented as a celebrity, but as a corset model. There was a great difference.' Much was made in court of her respectability – she was a married woman 'with good connections'; her mother confirmed that she had another daughter on the stage 'with her husband' and another 'married to a medical man'.[28]

According to the corset historian Valerie Steele, 'courtesans and actresses were the first to wear conspicuously erotic underwear' (Steele, 2001: 115), and contemporary onstage erotica resembling corsetry further elided differences between the actress and the courtesan. Reputation and representation was therefore still a carefully negotiated area for women performers. While Wood was happy to be identified as an actress – especially in the company of reputable and successful women such as Millar and Gladys Cooper – she was not happy to be identified as a corset model. She was also happy to be represented in fashionable gowns, but not 'in connection with stays' – even with clothes over them; the advertisement, by its very nature, invited the reader to 'imagine' the revolutionary corset underneath the dress.

Wood had none of Millar's support in court. Ranged against her were Sandow and one of the largest photographic businesses in London. Compared to the stars who had agreed to advertise Sandow's corsets, Wood was 'a nobody' with no economic or celebrity power. Despite this, the Wood case, like Millar's, was represented as a performance, with Wood very much 'The Actress'. She is reported to have to responded 'proudly' and to 'retort' when questioned. Her costume is described in detail – 'a blue costume with white collar and a black hat trimmed with white leaves'. The judge in the Wood case, Lord Justice Scrutton, was less supportive of Wood than Darling was of Millar, but like him invited levity in the court. He made jokes at the expense not only of Wood but her whole profession when he suggested ('to laughter') that, as an actor, George Graves might be qualified to offer an opinion on his profession but not on 'social [i.e. Society] matters'. He titillated the court when the 'book containing pictures of actresses wearing Sandow corsets' was handed to the jury: 'Ought I to have lady assessors here, or can I rely on the [gentlemen of the] jury?' he asked 'archly', continuing, 'It will distract them horribly if you let them see it.' When counsel was proceeding before all the jurymen had a chance to look at the book, the judge stopped him – 'you are shutting the back row out!' and 'a pause followed while the back row's claims [to see the book] were satisfied'.[29]

In his summing-up, Scrutton, like Darling before him, distinguished between the rights of an actress and of an 'ordinary' woman, saying that if the lady sat as an ordinary customer, the negative was her property. But if she was an actress and wanted to do what other actors and actresses wanted – to have a complimentary sitting so that the photograph should be published by the illustrated papers – then the photograph belonged to the photographer.[30]

There was, therefore, no case to answer. The image as contained in the negative was judged to belong to the subject, not the photographer or the studio, unless that person was an actress. However, like the 'ordinary' sitter, Wood had actually paid for her photographs, not asked for a complimentary sitting, though she had left the negative with the photographer to promote her professional self in the 'fashionable' papers. The studio's use of the photographs, though legal under copyright law, abused the sitter/photographer agreement and exemplified the legal vulnerability of the actress as a public as opposed to private person.

Defending the (private) self: *Crown* v. *Frederick Henry Woofries* (1906); *Dillon* v. *Charing Cross Kinematograph Theatre and Barnett* (1916)

The Millar and Wood libel cases show how difficult it was to enforce the boundary between the professional/public self and the private individual in the case of the performer. The celebrity industry had grown exponentially with the 'massification' of the print industries. The private lives of theatre stars were marketed though self-promoting publications such as memoirs, magazine interviews and photo opportunities for newspapers, magazines and postcard images. Gossip circulated freely,

 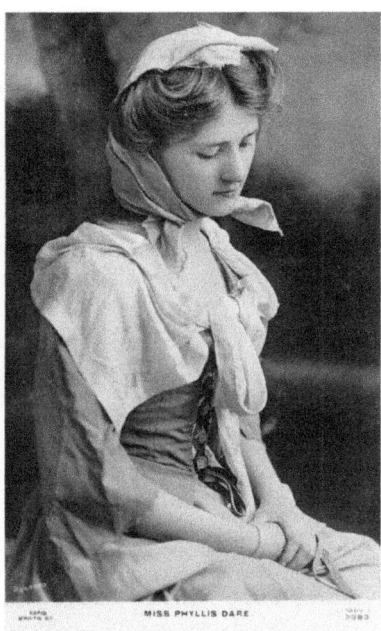

14 Seymour Hicks and 'his nice wife', Ellaline Terris, in *The Catch of the Season*, 1905; Phyllis Dare in *Cinderella*, 1905.

constrained only by Britain's imperfect laws of defamation, but rumours often found their way into English-language newspapers overseas. Well-known figures were particularly at risk for, as the counsel in a libel case involving Phyllis Dare and Seymour Hicks opined in court, 'It might be thought that these atrocious libels would not be believed, but there [are] ignorant people who would believe anything of a libellous nature.' In his view there were people who, 'hearing an appalling story of this kind connected with the theatrical profession', would be more inclined to believe it, expressing 'unctuous horror that such depravity would be possible'.³¹

The 'dastardly accusations circulated by male and female blackguards' (Dare, 1907: 104) about Dare and Hicks were that the 15-year-old Dare, instead of being at a convent school in Brussels completing her education, was 'in trouble in Paris; in fact, expecting to become a mother' (see Maggie B. Gale's chapter in this volume). The culprit was said to be 'no less a person than Mr Seymour Hicks, a man with a nice wife and child', who had drugged 'the poor girl ... by something put in some sweets or fruit, and [then] politely told her he does not intend to help her' (Figure 14).[32] Both Hicks and Phyllis Dare's family had heard the story in London, and Hicks had 'received verbal communications and a considerable number of anonymous letters', causing both families 'the greatest annoyance ... and great unhappiness'. Despite attempts to trace the origins of the scandal, it was not until an employee of Hicks visited a bar in Lime Street, Liverpool, 'much frequented by people connected with the theatrical profession', that the source was found. The story had apparently originated with a young engineer, Frederick Henry Woolfries, who in seeking to hide a criminal past had assumed the name Frederick Vernon Dare and passed himself off as Zena and Phyllis Dare's brother. He spoke 'from time to time of writing to them, gave his landlady their photographs, and left letters addressed to them about his room, so as to give colour to his claim'.[33] Critically he had written about his 'sister's' plight in four cliché-ridden letters to his 'fiancée', a barmaid at the hotel, in which he talked of being 'absolutely heartbroken' and how 'horsewhipping' was too good for Hicks.[34] He had created 'a fairy story' in a 'silly attempt at self-glorification, also an endeavour to obtain fictitious importance in the eyes of the girl he loved'.[35] Woolfries pleaded guilty to the charge of unlawfully and maliciously publishing defamatory libels of Hicks and Dare and was sentenced to eight months' hard labour.

In his summing-up, the judge warned of the dangers of 'untrue statements ... made in such a place' as Liverpool, 'an important theatrical centre', proliferating and travelling 'quickly through the country'.[36] The theatre network was itself seen as a contaminant and propagator of scandal. Dare, writing obliquely about her experience in her memoir the following year, fulminated about the stage being the 'happy hunting ground for busybodies and malicious, meddling gossipers, who aspire to "bring down" some luckless member of the profession about whom they think the story they propose to fabricate will be swallowed with avidity by the many to whom they relate the outcome of their imaginative brains'. She finds solace in the 'sweet sympathy [of] thousands of strangers' who realised that rumour had 'probably never before so wronged an actress in the whole history of the stage' (Dare, 1907: 95–9). Dare's response may be hyperbolic, but the attack had been personal.

Even more experienced artists were sensitive to real or imagined attacks on their reputation. In 1916 Marie Lloyd, under her married name of Dillon, sued the Charing Cross Kinematograph Theatre, alleging that she had been 'greatly injured in her reputation and credit, and had been held up to public ignominy' when, in August 1915, they had 'caused to be exhibited to passers-by in the Strand, in front of their premises, a large poster, containing a portrait, almost life-size' of herself, 'with the words in large letters at the top and bottom of the poster: White Slave Traffic'.[37] The exhibitors knew what they were doing in the juxtaposition of Lloyd's image with the title of the film they were showing alongside footage of Lloyd in performance. In 1913 she and her lover, Bernard Dillon, on arriving in New York, had been detained on Ellis Island and threatened with deportation for 'gross moral turpitude'. They had travelled to America on the liner *Olympic* as man and wife. Dillon was charged under the 1910 White Slave Act of attempting to take into the country a woman not his wife. Lloyd was charged with being a passive agent. Although the pair were eventually allowed to enter the country on a surety each of $300 and on condition they did not live together while in America, Lloyd's sister, Alice, claimed that 'the indignity ... went to Marie's heart in a way she never survived. She could not bear to talk of that awful twenty-four hours' (Gillies, 2001: 237–40).

Lloyd was very clear that the detention was an infringement of her privacy; she told the *New York Sun* that 'I have always supposed and considered that my private life was my own affair ... [this is] a personal matter, my own business – or', she goes on emphatically, 'it would be if I did not happen to be an actress ... when a drunken woman gets hauled into court she calls herself an actress, and you see the headlines to that effect in the newspapers in the morning'.[38] The Kinematograph Theatre admitted the libel and apologised, but Lloyd was not content to settle until the apology was repeated in court; a public offence required a public apology.[39]

Defending the body, defending the self: *Crown* v. *Billing* (1918)

The public vilification of Maud Allan was accompanied by 'deafening cheers and shouts [and] a storm of applause accompanied by the stamping of feet'. The pandemonium continued 'both in the court, in the hall of the Old Bailey and from a large crowd which had gathered outside'. In the scenes that followed Maud Allan was twice reported to have broken down and wept. A jubilant Billing was photographed 'waving his hat to the cheering crowd'.[40]

The prosecution 'submitted that it was not an accident that Miss Allan had been libelled',[41] and Billing himself admitted that 'it grieved [him] very much to cross-examine Miss Maud Allan at all' (Hoare,

1997: 170). He had provoked the prosecution to expose the corruption he saw at the heart of government and society; the 'victim' was almost incidental, but the Maud Allan case exemplifies many of the problems that women had faced in the earlier trials discussed in this chapter. She and Grein had originally brought the case of malicious libel to defend their professional and personal reputations. They had sought to separate the actor from the role. But during the trial, Allan was repeatedly questioned about aspects of her professional and personal life by Billing, who conducted his own defence, much of it irrelevant to the case. Her history as a performer was 'on trial'. Billing set out to prove that it wasn't just that she was a dancer/actress – after all he himself had spent four years on the professional stage – but that she was, through her performances, 'ministering to moral perverts'.[42] Allan's body was central to the defence's case (Figure 15). She was questioned closely about her costume as Salome, not only in the production, but also in her signature performance of the 'Dance of the Seven Veils'. '"Am I right in saying," asked Mr. Billing, "that at the Palace Theatre your dress was mainly composed of beads?" Miss Allan: "No, I had more dress than just beads."' Allan went on to describe the costume in detail,[43] and the critic for the *Morning News* testified that, in his view, her costume in Salome was 'very light, but not so light as I have seen worn by people of high position lately'. In his summing-up the judge asked the jury to say

15 Maud Allan as Salome in the 'Dance of the Seven Veils', and outside the Old Bailey, 1918.

whether 'Miss Maud Allan [was] a sadist, a lewd woman .... because she wore too indecent a costume, too light for the stage'. The jury's verdict said that she was (Kettle, 1977: 265).

Much of Billing's cross-examination of Allan turned upon the conflation of the performer, her self, with the role of Salome. Billing argued that if *Salome* was, as he believed, 'a grossly immoral play, and one which persons of a healthy mind and wishing to remain healthy would do well not to witness', then 'moral perverts, with their perversions lying dormant, might be led by seeing pantomimic acts of sadism [referring to Salome's sexual excitement as she bites the lips of the dead Jokanaan] to practice them themselves, and that in enacting this, Allan was "committing an act of sadism" herself'. Allan responded that she had not written the play. 'But', Billing went on, ' you are acting the play?' To which Allan retorted, in an echo of Charles Wyndham in 1905, 'Does that make me the part because I act it? Of course not ... I was not the play' (Kettle, 1977: 80–1). But, again, the final judgment said otherwise.

The Allan case may have been pivotal in 'drawing up the battle lines for twentieth century womanhood', but it was also the culmination of two decades in which women performers had begun the fight to control their public and private selves from abuses peculiar to their profession and sex. At the end of the Allan trial Lord Justice Darling observed that '[i]n a very short time women will be able to have their influence upon legislation'. It was another two years before Vida Levering's call for women, like men, to be tried by their peers was achieved. It is unlikely, however, that Darling's concern that women should use their new powers 'to see that much more purity is introduced in public representations than ... at present'[44] would be shared by many actresses. As the cases discussed here have demonstrated, they had been fighting in the courts for a different type of public representation, for reputation and respect, and a profession where public performance and display did not make them entirely 'public property'. Given Maud Allan's defeat, in 1918 the battle had hardly begun.

Notes

1 This chapter refers to UK law, most particularly English law; although UK law usually encompasses Ireland and Wales, Scottish law developed slightly differently in some areas. All the cases under consideration took place in England.

2 *Votes for Women* opened at the Royal Court in 1907; it was published as a

novel, *The Convert*, the same year and the play script was published by Mills and Boon in 1909.

3 The civil libel case was originally brought by Allan and Grein against Billing, but it became a criminal, hence Crown, case as an obscene and defamatory libel, an offence against public decency. A full analysis of the trial is beyond the scope of this chapter; however, for that, Grein's role, and more on the other public woman defamed by default in the case, Margot Asquith, see Bland (2013), Hoare (1997), Kettle (1977), Medd (2002).

4 As opposed to statutory or regulatory law – which is also used extensively, but not predominantly, in the UK – or the civil law systems that dominate in Europe, whereby 'past judgments are no more than loose guides'. http://www.economist.com/blogs/economist-explains/2013/07/economist-explains-10 (accessed 14 January 2016).

5 There is not space here to explore the complex and nuanced relationship between the personal and the professional for the actress, but a reading of the many memoirs and autobiographies from the period show how powerful the hierarchies were within the profession and how this impacted on performers' aspirations. See Davis (1991), Gardner (2004b), Richards (1993), Sanderson (1984).

6 *The Era*, 23 June 1906, p. 12.

7 *Daily Mail*, 3 February 1906, p. 5.

8 *The Era*, 23 June 1906, p. 12.

9 Ibid.

10 Ibid.

11 Thomas had been employed at £3 a week for the run of *The Catch of the Season*, and claimed a loss of the £150 which she would have earned for the whole run, minus the £32 she had earned from playing pantomime after her dismissal by Hicks. Thus £200 was a generous settlement. *The Era*, 23 June 1906, p. 12. Average annual nominal earnings in 1905 were £69.67 (£25,000 at 2015 values).

12 *St James's Gazette*, 13 December 1901, p. 14.

13 *The Era*, 14 December 1901, p. 23.

14 The history of copyright law is extremely complicated, but the 1911 Copyright Act which implemented the 1886 Berne Convention in part (it did not fully ratify the Berne Convention until 1988) effectively extended the notion of 'author' to all types of work, not just printed material. However, the issue of ownership of a work created in the course of employment, e.g. a photograph, remained problematic until the 1980s.

15 *Evening Express*, 20 January 1904, p. 2.

16 See Loeb (1994) and Rappaport (2000) for both specific reference to the use of actresses in advertising, and a more general overview of gender and consumer developments in the period. See also Hindson (2011) for an exemplary case study.

17 *Morning Bulletin*, 7 March 1904, p. 6. Subsequent quotations in this paragraph are from this source.
18 *The Times*, 29 January 1907, p. 15.
19 Ibid.
20 See *The Times*, 30 January 1907, p. 3; *Manchester Guardian*, 30 January 1907, p. 4.
21 The fashionable photographer Alexander Bassano also worked for Rotary. He opened a studio in 1850 in Regent Street, London, moving to Old Bond Street in 1876. Bassano retired in around 1903, but the premises were refurbished and relaunched as Bassano Ltd, Royal Photographers. http://www.npg.org.uk/collections/search/person/mp08062/bassano-ltd (accessed 8 November 2016).
22 *Daily Mirror*, 30 January 1907, p. 4.
23 *Daily Mirror*, 29 January 1907, p. 4.
24 *Daily Express*, 30 January 1907, p. 5.
25 *Daily Mirror*, 30 January 1907, p. 4.
26 *The Times*, 30 January 1907, p. 3.
27 *The Times*, 26 April 1900, p. 3; *The Era*, 28 April 1900, p. 8.
28 *The Times*, 27 June 1914, p. 4.
29 *Daily Mirror*, 27 June 1914, p. 4.
30 *The Times*, 30 June 1914, p. 4.
31 *Daily Mail*, 24 September 1906, p. 5.
32 *The Times*, 25 September 1906, p. 9.
33 *Auckland Star*, 10 November 1906, p. 13.
34 *The Times*, 25 September 1906, p. 9.
35 *Citizen*, 28 November 1906, p. 5.
36 *Daily Mail*, 28 November 1906, p. 5.
37 *Stage Year Book*, 1916, p. 194.
38 *New York Sun*, 4 October 1913, p. 3.
39 *The Times*, 15 April 1915, p. 3.
40 *Daily Mirror*, 5 June 1918, p. 3.
41 Ibid.
42 *Daily Mail*, 31 May 1918, p. 3.
43 *Daily Mirror*, 5 June 1918, p. 2.
44 *Daily Mirror*, 5 June 1918, p. 2.

References

Bland, Lucy (2013), *Modern Women on Trial: Sexual Transgression in the Age of the Flapper*, Manchester: Manchester University Press.
Dare, Phyllis (1907), *From School to Stage*, London: Collier.
Davis, Tracy C. (1991), *Actresses as Working Women*, London: Routledge.

Engel, Matthew (1996), *Tickle the Public: One Hundred Years of the Popular Press*, London: Victor Gollancz.
Gardner, Viv (2004a), 'Gertie Millar and the "Rules for Actresses and Vicars' Wives"', in Martin Banham and Jane Milling, eds, *Extraordinary Actors*, Exeter: Exeter University Press, pp. 97–119.
Gardner, Viv (2004b), 'The Three Nobodies: Autobiographical Strategies in the Work of Alma Ellerslie, Kitty Marion and Ina Rozant', in Maggie B. Gale and Viv Gardner, eds, *Auto/biography and Identity: Women, Theatre and Performance*, Manchester: Manchester University Press, pp. 10–38.
Gillan, Don, www.stagebeauty.net.
Gillies, Midge (2001), *Marie Lloyd: The One and Only*, London: Orion Books.
Hindson, Catherine (2011), '"Mrs Langtry seems to be on the way to a fortune": The Jersey Lily and Models of Nineteenth-century Fame', in Su Holmes and Diane Negra, eds, *The Limelight and Under the Microscope: Forms and Functions of Female Celebrity*, London: Continuum, pp. 17–36.
Hoare, Philip (1997), *Oscar Wilde's Last Stand*, New York: Arcade Publishing.
Jupp, James (1923), *The Gaiety Stage Door*, London: Jonathan Cape.
Kettle, Michael (1977), *Salome's Last Veil: The Libel Case of the Century*, London: Granada.
Loeb, Lori Anne (1994), *Consuming Angels: Advertising and Victorian Women*, Oxford: Oxford University Press.
Medd, Jodie (2002), '"The Cult of the Clitoris": Anatomy of a National Scandal', *Modernism/modernity*, 9.1, pp. 21–49.
Nead, Lynda (2002), 'Visual Cultures of the Courtroom: Reflections on History, Law and the Image', *Visual Culture in Britain*, 3.2, pp. 119–41.
Rappaport, Erika (2000), *Shopping for Pleasure: Women in the Making of London's West End*, Princeton, NJ: Princeton University Press.
Richards, Sandra (1993), *The Rise of the English Actress*, Basingstoke: Macmillan.
Robins, Elizabeth ([1909]), *Votes for Women*, London: Mills and Boon.
Sanderson, Michael (1984), *From Irving to Olivier: A Social History of the Acting Profession in England, 1890–1980*, London: St Martin's Press.
The Stage Year Book (1916), London: Carson and Cornerford.
Steele, Valerie (2001), *The Corset: A Cultural History*, New Haven, CT: Yale University Press.
Stretton, Tim (2005), *Women Waging Law in Elizabethan England*, Cambridge: Cambridge University Press.
Veeder, Van Vechten (1903), 'The History and Theory of the Law of Defamation. I', *Columbia Law Review*, 3.8, pp. 546–73, http://www.jstor.org/stable/1109121 (accessed 8 April 2016).

Part II

WOMEN AND POPULAR PERFORMANCE

7

EMOTIONAL AND NATURAL

The Australian and New Zealand repertoires and fortunes of North American performers Margaret Anglin, Katherine Grey and Muriel Starr

Veronica Kelly

It is difficult to assess the international careers of touring stage performers in the early twentieth century without considering the related categories of the transnational and technological biographies. Deacon, Russell and Woollacott state that situated and regional readings of global mobility have their value: 'we must abandon the search for the "whole subject" and allow that fragments of identity are produced in specific times and places' (Deacon, Russell and Woollacott, 2010: 9). Australia and New Zealand from 1908 to 1930 provide a site from which a diagnostic perspective may be constructed and articulated concerning the careers of touring theatre stars during a crucial phase of globalised mediated entertainments. As Platt, Becker and Linton demonstrate in the case of the dominant genre of musical theatre, the early-century transfers and translation of scripts, scores, business cultures and performers between Berlin and London operated 'across centres competing for authority', even during periods of intense conflict (Platt, Becker and Linton, 2014: 3). The Australasian fortunes of the stage actors Margaret Anglin, Katherine Grey and Muriel Starr indicate that dealings with the technological 'centres of authority' of cinema and – to some extent– radio could be as significant to overall careers as eminence in their native theatrical discipline. These dealings may involve direct engagement with cinema, or – as here – mainly rejection, but both imply their necessary situational relations with mediated entertainment. Sometimes, as was the case with Muriel Starr, global technological and financial revolutions, their consequences reaching even to, say, the tiny Victorian Alpine town of Tumut, could remorselessly strike down the career of a genuinely popular stage favourite.

In a real sense, a completely non-international twentieth-century actor is a rare being. Newspaper saturation, accompanied by the international penetration of performers via the related intermedial forms of radio and film, ensured that in Tumut, no less than in neon-lit metropolitan theatrical centres, touring performers were enveloped by the colourful discursive aura of the varied industries of global entertainment. Thus, for audiences, the 'vicarious experience' (Iriye and Mitter, 2010: xi) of the transnational operates as a dynamically textured, if partial, reception context. As they travelled Australasia, Anglin, Grey and Starr were ghosted by the discursive presences of those mostly North American stage actors who may have first created 'their' star parts abroad; by other theatrical performers in the Australian region who created or recreated their signature roles; and increasingly by the silvery phantoms of Hollywood actors performing 'their' stage successes on silent, and eventually talking, screens. Thus, the mediated presence of the movie stars Clara Kimball Young, Norma Talmadge, Loretta Young, Pola Negri, Norma Shearer and Pauline Frederick surround the Australian presence of Anglin, Grey and Starr, generating comparisons about their respective dramatic work. The distinguished American tragedienne Frederick was the only one of these luminaries to undertake stage work in Australia, and her signature film performance in *Madame X* (1920) for Goldwyn Pictures (de Groat, 2006) places her beside Starr in this local context, particularly as her 1925 visit coincided with Starr's third tour. In this transnational discourse, live presence initially trumped 'tinned theatre' in critical esteem. For example, cinematic roles that had been premiered as a Starr vehicle were 'introduced to Australia by Muriel Starr' and her performance held up as the gold standard: she was 'responsible for its Australian version', said a Tasmanian paper of Dorothy Mackaill's 1924 silent version of *The Man Who Came Back*.[1] But by this decade's end, Starr's popular dramatic vehicles were in a neck-and-neck race with the exhibition of their screen versions, with both frequently playing the same centre simultaneously, and the time gap becoming generally ever narrower.

As professional workers within global modernity, stage actors are significant coalmine canaries for mapping economic crises and disruptions, and revolutions in the generative practices of creation, mediation and distribution. In 1908 the popular and accomplished 'empire actor' George Titheradge (Kelly, 2009: 15), recruited to support Margaret Anglin on his third and her only Australian tour, declared his happiness at returning to Melbourne. After a twenty-year absence from the West End, he noted the effects of the long run in restricting opportunities for actor training, and the downplaying of performer versatility

Emotional and Natural 165

gained through touring experience in favour of copycat performances or mere 'personalities'.² Not all revolutions were managerial. Marlis Schweitzer's study of early-century transatlantic exchanges emphasises the materiality of the 'infrastructural elements and technological advances that supported the globalisation of popular entertainment': transatlantic liners, telegraph cables, typewriters, offices, newspapers and postcards (Schweitzer, 2015: 4). Such spaces, technologies and networks are all prone to mishap and failure as when, for example, war cuts the submarine cables or sinks the ocean liner. But war is a capricious agent, dispensing opportunity as well as disaster. Much of the Australian success of Muriel Starr, apart from her genuine popularity, was due to the opportunities created by the First World War. This interrupted the flow of European entertainers and caused entrepreneurs to seek North

16 Margaret Anglin in 1930, at the time of her NBC broadcast of *Iphigenia in Aulis*.

American performers who could sail from Vancouver and San Francisco on the safer Pacific routes. So, just as the Wall Street copper panics of late 1907 caused thousands of Broadway and provincial American actors to be stood down (Schweitzer, 2015: 28), so too were the international careers of Anglin, Grey and Starr subject to global contexts such as the First World War, the Great Depression, silent film, broadcast radio and eventually sound film. While live theatre accommodated the first two of these innovations in mostly happy coexistence, the rapid phasing-in of the talkies in the major city theatres in late 1928, simultaneous with the Depression, saw an increase in suicides, hunger, desperation and mass unemployment for stage musicians and actors, as indeed for their audiences.

'American' actresses, natural and emotional

Born in Ottawa, Margaret Anglin (1876–1958) was clearly identified in the land of her birth as Canadian, even while establishing herself as a major performer in the USA. As Cecilia Morgan demonstrates, she flexibly claimed Canadian and American identity, together with social and cultural identifiers such as Irish or Catholic, enabling her to '[appeal] to a variety of class, gender, ethnic, national and imperial audiences' (Morgan, 2010: 152). While Anglin was always advertised as American by her Australian management, socially she was happy to be interpellated as variously Canadian, a 'loyal Britisher', American or Irish, and she attracted an unusual amount of favourable coverage in the Australian Catholic press.[3] The stage life of Montreal-born Muriel McIver (1888–1950), who took the stage name Muriel Starr, commenced in childhood. Although she was also professionally identified with American experience, in her case provincial touring in melodrama and musical comedy, in Australia Starr was also pointedly hailed as Canadian. No such ambiguities were applied to the San Francisco-born actor Katherine Grey (1873–1950), born Katherine Best, whose American origin and training was used in Australia as a selling point when realistic American social problem plays were dominating a significant sector of Australian dramatic production. The showcasing of this repertoire by the 'Firm' of J. C. Williamson Ltd put at a discount the high-romantic zest of American actors such as Grey who were well capable of producing it; and – in Anglin's case – determined to do so.

Vocally, these performers would have sounded somewhat familiar to Australian and New Zealand ears. Each employed the dramatic *lingua franca* of the 'English' accent, as Anglin did in her 1908 Shakespeare premieres in Adelaide and Sydney, where her German-American co-star Henry Kolker incurred disapproval for using his native accent in contemporary and classical plays alike. Except for American pieces, where Starr, a New Yorker from the age of six, produced a ringing Broadway vernacular, she too cultivated the voice beautiful with musicality and low tones: 'no excruciating accent spoils the sweet melody of her voice'.[4] In 1910 a New Zealand interviewer detected in Katherine Grey's rich tones 'now and then just the faintest suspicion of the American accent'.[5] Throughout the roughly three decades of silent film, a beautiful and thrilling voice remained a stage actress's major asset, filling the house and reducing audiences to jelly. Starr, whose voice, she insisted, is 'quite English, you know', found the part of Domini in Robert Hichens' desert melodrama *The Garden of Allah*, which headlined her third Australasian tour, 'difficult and thankless' since she was required to listen in silence to her co-star's lengthy monologues. This was not, she observes, how audiences wanted to experience their leading ladies.[6] Hence, the advent of talkies also compromised this unique and valued advantage of the stage 'emotional actress'.

The category of 'naturalness' in performance remains ever relative and slippery. The 'natural' performance is to an extent place-bound but more essentially time-bound, as a culture's social modes of self-presentation evolve and mutate alongside its theatrical codes of mimetic representation, locked in a reciprocal dance whose conventionality is largely obscured from contemporaries, though more evident to the view of subsequent or foreign audiences. In the context of Australia before the First World War, Dennis Carroll judges that North American performers such as Muriel Starr were 'powerful and real' in contrast to 'the bombast and large effects common with English performers' (Carroll, 1995: 48). While reports of Australasian performances by Anglin, Grey and Starr certainly attest to their ability to produce the 'natural' effect, their performances belie any simple apportioning of distinctive performance styles to national origin. In Australasia, little was perceived as natural in the 'emotional' American star Minnie Tittell Brune's performances, while such English performers as Florence Trevelyan (Mrs Brough) or George Titheradge produced fine examples of elegant precision. It is more useful to consider actors as perfecting their own range according to their repertoires and working apprenticeships with established players, and seeking genres and roles to showcase their lines of work or challenge their distinctive abilities. The multi-regional genealogies of training, experience and lineage are more revealing than classifying performance styles according to national origin.

While these three performers were all praised in Australia for their 'natural' acting, they were simultaneously hailed as 'emotional actresses'. Sited in the then-dominant tradition of Bernhardt, Stella Campbell, Olga Nethersole or Nance O'Neil, the 'emotional actress' was the default interpreter of dramatic melodrama and some classical work well into the 1920s, bearing major responsibility for audience engagement and connection. Only in the genres of musical comedy, farce or light comedy did she not dominate her stage. A fascinating yet graceful kinetic style and thrilling vocal tones were her major assets. Her characters embodied a maternal yet sexy kind of mature femininity, drawing from the conflated roles of saintly magdalene, redemptive heroine or sacrificial mother. These transgressors educe a morally transfigured validation beyond mere social laws, and the task of the emotional actress was to ensure this effect in performance. Anglin was first tagged as an emotional actress when she performed in *Mrs Dane's Defence* in New York in December 1900, where she subverted the play's rigid sexual morality by winning sympathy for its erring and prevaricating heroine (Le Vay, 1989: 53–5). A standard press question to performers was whether the actress 'really' felt the emotions she portrayed. Anglin's response to the riddle of 'emotionalism' was a cryptic 'Where would I have been without it?',[7] and upon her arrival in Australia she gracefully fielded the inevitable query: her emotional roles were not reflected in the offstage life of an actress, any more than light, frivolous or saintly ones were.[8] Even Grey, whose forté was George Bernard Shaw and social problem dramas critiquing the ills of America's urban capitalism and legal system, was nonetheless hailed as America's 'chiefest interpreter of the emotional drama'.[9]

As for any male equivalents of the 'emotional actress', few are identified as such. Indeed, the skin-part specialist Ernest Hendrie, in Australia to play the Dog in *The Blue Bird*, joked that since there was currently no emotional display perceivable in the West End, the 'emotional actors and actresses' would have to play animals.[10] A search of Australasian newspapers between 1890 and 1930 reveals scant examples of the phrase 'emotional actor'. It was awarded to the great Italian tenor Fiorelli Giraud in *I Pagliacci* (1901) in Melbourne[11] and to the Dutch cellist August van Biene, who performed in his own playlet *The Broken Melody* over four thousand times.[12] As the 1920s proceed, the sole local occurrences of the phrase are found in the country press, and applied only to such film actors as Sessue Hayakawa, 'the famous Japanese emotional actor' (*The*

17 Katherine Grey, commercial postcard.

Call of the East), Henry B. Walthall (*Birth of a Nation*) and Tom Mix (*The Coming of the Law*). In the meantime, on the silent screen of the 1920s there reigned countless 'emotional actresses', confirming that a highly coded gendered physicality no less than voice was a vehicle of their emotional impact. Starr particularly endeared herself to Australian and New Zealand audiences on her first tour (1913–14) as 'the brilliant young emotional actress' (Black Kitten), her roles being the falsely accused shop girl Mary Turner in *Within the Law*, and the criminal but sacrificial mother Jacqueline Floriot in *Madame X*. On her two subsequent tours (1918–20 and 1924–30) the 'Firm' of J. C. Williamson showcased Starr in the arty Orientalist spectacles *The Bird of Paradise* and *The Garden of Allah*, which played only the capital cities.

Yet when subsequently touring with her own stock company, Starr preferred quick-turnover repertoires based on the 1920s craze for comedy-thrillers and mystery-thrillers. The Firm, now in partnership with her, purchased their Australasian rights in order to feed her repertoire. These vernacular dramas contrast urban American plutocracy with its slums, featuring poor women under financial or moral pressure, drug fiends, slang-speaking Broadway molls, capitalist tycoons and the inevitable detective: variously tough or gentlemanly, genuine or imposter. The thrillers feature eerie séances, locked-room mysteries, terrified flappers, masked murderers and death by telephone, evoking fearful suspense and dispelling it through laughter. Playing into the audience fandom of these campy self-conscious genres, dramatists ingeniously combined their stock characters and generic features into startling innovations. In *Cornered* (1920) by Dodson Mitchell, premiered in Melbourne in May 1927, Starr played the dual roles of the crooked shop girl and the society lady. Max Marcin's *Cheating Cheaters* (1916) was filmed in 1919 starring Clara Kimball Young, and again as a Universal silent in late 1927. In this, the chief (female) crook turns out to be an intrepid detective working sting operations on two rival gangs simultaneously. When Starr's production premiered in Adelaide on 7 December 1927 it had just been preceded in that city by Kimball's movie, while the MGM talkie of *Madame X* with Ruth Chatterton (successor to Frederick's silent version) was shown in Australia in August 1929: portents of the revolution in stage actors' professional environment. Even though by 1929 Starr had been playing in this vigorous repertoire in most of Australia and New Zealand, the national sensation caused by her 1913 performances in *Madame X* and *Within the Law* had solidified her identification with her early 'emotional' roles, re-demanded by tenacious audiences as must-see epochal landmarks right up to her departure.[13]

Actors, roles and managers

Artistic validation by association with great writers, major theatrical stars or managerial moguls was important to the reputations of Anglin and Grey; less so to the adventurous born-in-a-suitcase trouper Muriel Starr. The Greek tragedians and Shakespeare (in a minor way) were significant

MURIEL STARR

LAST AMERICAN APPEARANCE — LEAD IN "JOHN HAWTHORNE" THE-
ATRE GUILD N. Y. **STARRED FOR THE PAST SEVEN YEARS** — ENGLAND,
AFRICA AND AUSTRALIA IN "SECRETS"—"EAST OF SUEZ"—"THE LETTER"
"THE ENEMY"—"DE CLASSE"—"BILL OF DIVORCEMENT"
AND "THE PELICAN"

EXCLUSIVE MANAGEMENT MAC QUARRIE AGENCY
Phone GLadstone 2200

18 Muriel Starr seeks work in the USA, from *Standing Cast Directory*, Hollywood, July 1931.

in securing Anglin's prestige as a public-minded classical actor, while in her early American career Grey was an apostle of Bernard Shaw and of modernism generally. Anglin's Shakespearean ventures commenced in Australia, though their remote origins lay in youthful school dramatic recitations as preparation for a lady-like career of drawing-room reader. In her early work with the American melodramatic touring star James O'Neill, he proclaimed 'Mary, you must do Shakespeare, you have the Irish Sea in your voice' (Le Vay, 1989: 41). Allegedly because of expensive Australasian performing rights, Anglin was debarred from starring in her recent American success, William Vaughan Moody's *The Great*

Divide (1906). This play's Australian premiere was actually performed by Muriel Starr on her second tour in 1919, when the theatres reopened subsequent to the Spanish Influenza outbreak.[14] Hence, Anglin's tour was rather muted in its impact compared with the popular sensations caused by Grey and Starr. Part of this was due to such external events as weather and strikes, some to her management's response to national events, and also to her rather undazzling repertoire before she resolved to produce her own Shakespearean comedies on the Firm's dime. Its publicity agent Claude McKay said of the Anglin tour that '[t]he theatre was comfortably filled throughout the season, but we were not turning crowds away' (McKay, 1961: 110).

Anglin's group sailed to Australia from Vancouver on 23 May 1908 on the *Aorangi*, which was crammed with many other American performers. Aboard were the companies of the musical comedies *The Red Mill* and *The Prince of Pilsen*, plus fellow Irishwoman Ada Dwyer and other cast members of the rural comedy *Mrs Wiggs of the Cabbage Patch*. The *Aorangi* was not the only vessel of importance then upon the Pacific. The 'Firm' of J. C. Williamson was ensuring that the naval visitors of Roosevelt's Great White Fleet, eagerly awaited in both newly federated Australasian nations, would be surrounded by American entertainers and generally made to feel 'at home'. In this fevered Americanophile moment, and given her prominent reputation, local interest in Anglin's visit was strong. Yet initially her partner George Titheradge was hailed as the season's real star and Anglin as his leading lady, recruited because her style was perceived as similar to that of his famed co-star Mrs Robert Brough.

Anglin premiered in Sydney on 27 June 1908 in *The Thief*, a translation of Henri Bernstein's *Le voleur* (1906), which had appeared on Broadway in September 1907 and was also running at the St James Theatre in London with Irene Vanbrugh. It was Anglin's debut in this role, bought and imperiously bestowed upon her by J. C. Williamson himself. In nine days she undertook the tasks of rapid study, version-making and production: multiple roles in which she was well practised. Williamson was pleased with the result: 'She has won hands down. I knew she would!'[15] Anglin was acclaimed as compelling in a way not seen since Ristori and Bernhardt.[16] Her performance was 'so amazingly natural that, till one sees her, one doesn't realise what stage naturalness may mean', but the play was considered shallow and unworthy.[17] *Zira*, adapted with a South African setting from the venerable Wilkie Collins stalwart *The New Magdalen*, gained little impact. Nor did Clyde Fitch's comedy *The Truth* fare much better. Thanks to heavy rainfall plus a transport strike, it lasted in Sydney for only ten nights, though 'the thoroughness of this actress's methods and resulting technical perfection' was again commended.[18]

On 20 August 1908 tens of thousands of Sydneysiders walked or strap-hung on trams to South Head to see the Fleet enter the harbour. Anglin also snatched a few hours from rehearsals to witness the spectacle, which she cheekily 'reviewed' for the press.[19] The next day she was despatched to Melbourne while *Mrs Wiggs* took her place at Her Majesty's, which had been too large a venue for Anglin's intimate repertoire. Melbourne appreciated Anglin: 'She [stands] right outside the character she portrays, so that she may rack the emotions of her auditors without straining her own.'[20] Then, over her manager's protests, she began rehearsals for *The Taming of the Shrew*, generating critical enthusiasm at the prospect of a full version of a play usually seen in Australia as the Garrick farce *Katherine and Petruchio*. Unlike Oscar Asche and Lily Brayton, who finally performed the full version in Australia to huge success the following year, Anglin omitted the Induction and most of Bianca's scenes. *Twelfth Night*, the next premiere, was dressed with the lovely scenery designed for George Musgrove's 1903 production (Kelly, 2009: 39–91). *The Shrew* was also played in Adelaide and Ballarat before a more successful Sydney farewell season. A thoroughly fatigued Anglin sailed for Europe on the *Mongolia* on 19 December 1908, and Ola Humphrey, with Kolker and Titheradge, was assigned for a New Zealand tour of the 'Anglin' plays. Cicely Hamilton's feminist shop-girl drama *Diana of Dobson's* (1908), which Williamson originally secured for Anglin, was subsequently premiered by Minnie Tittell Brune (Kelly, 2009: 139–40).

Anglin, something of a cultural missionary, returned to Shakespeare on an extensive North American tour commencing in late 1913, again leading with *The Shrew* followed by *Twelfth Night*, then *As You Like It* and *Antony and Cleopatra*. Le Vay (1989: 253–6) notes a subsequent 1928 Lady Macbeth at the University of California with a design by Edward Gordon Craig, but overall the Shakespearean impetus begun in Australia was not sustained. In order to support such choices, many pot-boilers and hit plays had to be performed and exhausting national tours undertaken. Anglin's determined commitment to Greek drama, however, secured her a measure of patronage from well-funded and prestigious institutions. Commencing with *Electra* in 1913 (Le Vay, 1989: 142), the outdoor Berkeley Theatre at the University of California became her

19 Katherine Grey in costume drama, *c.* 1894.

venue for summer arena spectacles using huge casts of extras, dancers, musicians and choirs. In 1915 were added *Medea* and *Iphigenia in Aulis*, with original music by a fifty-piece orchestra, five hundred extras and chariots (Le Vay, 1989: 161–9). Others followed sporadically during the 1920s, financed by her arduous commercial tours and performed in such diverse sites as opera houses, parks and on radio. While the prestige and impact of these ambitious classical spectacles were considerable, they were never going to be career-sustaining money-earners. Anglin's plans to permanently institutionalise the Greek summer events at Berkeley failed for want of a sufficient initial money guarantee (Le Vay, 1989: 248). Later in her career she turned to production: 'I like to create, I like to see things grow and happen ... An actress cannot do this' (Le Vay, 1989: 179).

Katherine Grey's vehicles in Australia and New Zealand included Charles Klein's *The Third Degree* (1908), Shaw's *Arms and the Man*, Fitch's *The Truth*, Edward Sheldon's *Salvation Nell* (1908) and Eugene Walter's *Paid in Full* (1908), which Muriel Starr later toured extensively in Australia. Her American apprenticeship displays wide experience in popular theatre undertaken with major managements, which soon flowered into enthusiasm for modern plays and the classics. Grey began in Augustin Daly's New York company, whose female star was Ada Rehan, and then joined one of Charles Frohman's companies supporting another superstar, Maude Adams. Kyrle Bellew, Nat Goodwin and Charles Coghlan were her later co-stars, implying a performer of some achievement. Her first great success (and Starr's first stage appearance) were in productions of James A. Herne's sentimental *Shore Acres* (1893), but Grey also succeeded as the tropically emotional heroine in Hall Caine's *The Christian*: a cat-tearing role which sustained many a touring actor. Like Anglin, she made an impression in Jones's *Mrs Dane's Defence*, which prompted Amy Leslie of the *Chicago News* to venture comparisons. Grey was

> a sensitively emotional and delicately artistic actress [...] and without in the least attempting to compare two players so totally different in method and personality as Miss Margaret Anglin and Miss Grey, it must be admitted that Miss Grey is both sweeter and more tenderly womanly than the robust Canadian, and equals her in strength and fire.[21]

Grey's New York training suited her for touring as lead in contemporary plays interspersed with classics and poetic drama. In 1894 she played in the first American performance of *Arms and the Man* at Herald Square Theatre, produced by its Bluntschli, the great Shakespearean, Savoyard and Shavian Richard Mansfield. However, Grey was no stranger to romantic costume parts, and in a commercial partnership with Mansfield she performed Roxane in *Cyrano de Bergerac* and Belasco's *Sweet Kitty Bellairs*. Producing these dramas along with Shaw and Molière, she and Mansfield lost their savings. Undaunted, Mansfield went on to premiere an epic *Peer Gynt*: his last great role, whose New York season at the New Amsterdam Theatre was cut short by his death on 23 March 1907. During this run, for her own repertory company at the nearby Berkeley Lyceum, Grey also performed her early signature role of Christine Dehring in Arthur Schnitzler's comedy *The Reckoning*. *Candida* and *The Man of Destiny* were included in this season. In 1909 she formed her own company, playing San Francisco and Denver in a modern repertoire of Shaw, Fitch's *The Truth* and Ibsen's *A Doll's House*.[22] Hence at the time of her Australasian tour the slight-figured Grey was an established American performer and independent producer with a distinctively modern dramatic taste and very credible enterprises and achievements.

Grey's work in Australia and New Zealand proved something of an unexpected local sensation – not, as she might have wished, in the plays of her beloved Shaw, Ibsen and Rostand, but in the topical American dramas which agitated for labour equity and critiqued the police and justice systems. Her Sydney debut in January 1910 was as the new leading lady for the Firm's major romantic costume star Julius Knight, in Charles Klein's 1905 social drama *The Lion and the Mouse*. As Shirley Rossmore, the 'mouse' who overcomes the economic and gendered power of the 'lion', the multi-millionaire tycoon John Burkett Ryder, Grey's first entrance was greeted with a burst of prolonged applause. She struggled to conceal a severe cold, but as the performance proceeded and the newcomer showed her determination to earn her reputation, conventional star-worship became genuine appreciation with outbursts of cheering and repeated calls. What Grey was doing – and more importantly, not doing – was to play an 'emotional' role without overt foregroundings of emotionality. Vocally she used a 'conversational style', and her strengths were her 'absolute naturalness and her wonderful power of restraint'.[23]

Her 'dowdy' costumes for *The Lion and the Mouse* simulated the off-the-peg garb of the American female urban worker. The contrast with the newly arrived Lily Brayton's lavish and artistic stage dresses was pronounced. Grey's costumes were of intense interest to those Australian working women seeking low-cost but smartly fashionable and durable clothing. *Table Talk* noted the straight severe cuts with their new clean collarless style and V-necks: '[s]he looks just as if she stepped from a picture in one of the American fashion magazines'.[24] Other observers missed the full-flounced signifiers of sensuous femininity: her Shirley Rossmore 'would be a thing of joy to suffragettes, feminine candidates for Parliament, and other champions of the sex'.[25] However, the *Bulletin* objected to her work being praised as 'untheatrical', citing the stagecraft that built up her first entrance as Shirley: Margaret Anglin, it

20 Grey as Louka in *Arms and the Man* in Chicago, from *The Stage*, July 1895.

averred, would have cut such effect-making business. Few knew Anglin had entered onstage in *The Thief* until she actually spoke: she was 'the genuine article in the art line', unlike Brayton, 'that beautiful but essentially stagey young woman'.[26]

In the Australian *Arms and the Man* premiere Grey played Raina to Julius Knight's Bluntschli, though she preferred the part of Louka which she had created for America. 'I think I was in every Bernard Shaw piece produced in America', she told an Adelaide interviewer. 'I would love to play Ibsen. I know Mr Williamson wishes I didn't.' Thereupon she 'fell back and her chair and laughed merrily'.[27] This exchange alludes to the strong possibility of prior discussions between actor and manager in which the prospect of Grey playing in Ibsen had been raised and firmly vetoed. Whereas Anglin had imperiously over-ridden Williamson in devising her own Shakespeare productions, Grey's position was unlike that of (say) Nance O'Neil, who performed *Hedda Gabler* in Australia in 1900. While also sponsored by Williamson's organisation, O'Neil brought her own dramatic company, and so could do much as she pleased. Upon Knight's return to England, Grey took over as costume heroine with her dashing new co-star William Desmond. New Zealand also found her success 'absolutely reliant on her splendid art': in *The Lion and the Mouse* she performed with 'wonderful naturalness' and a 'quiet, placid, adroitness'.[28] Since many successful American pre-war plays during these decades were social protest pieces, gun-wielding crook plays or raucously colloquial comedies, Williamson was inclined to secure American casts for these. Grey accordingly performed Edward Sheldon's tear-jerking slums and sweatshops drama *Salvation Nell* throughout New Zealand.

Muriel Starr: stage and picture-shows

If Grey and Anglin were appreciated for their artistry, in the anxious years before the First World War Muriel Starr became both a popular national craze, with audiences mobbing theatres with almost hysterical enthusiasm, and an admired personality adopted into the local community for her displays of grit and commitment against the economic odds. She was less of a glamorous 'star' in the mould of Anglin, Lily Brayton or even Grey in her earlier career, but rather a character actor who ran her own touring troupes, for preference in interesting far-flung regions. When Bayard Veiller's Broadway play *Within the Law* (1912) opened in the Melbourne Theatre Royal on 24 May 1913, Starr led an all-American company.[29] The press declared that she

> helps to confirm the impression already formed by a study of the acting of her American sisters, Miss Anglin and Miss Katherine Grey, who, in the portrayal of the emotions and actions of real people stand almost alone. Miss Starr acts quietly and naturally – her voice is like her acting – quiet and harmonious but full of colour and expression where needed.[30]

Other cast members were also commended for what are usually seen as the cardinal 'English' virtues of subtlety and restraint, though the play itself, a drama dealing with American social and economic conditions, cannot really be said to exemplify either of these virtues.

Like many of Tittell Brune's vehicles, *Within the Law* appeals to the 'shop girl' thematic, so scorned by critics of a feminised modernity yet so keenly appreciated by Australasian young women (Kelly, 2006). Mary Turner is wrongly accused of theft by her employer Gilder and serves three years in gaol. She protests that even the standard wage for workers such as she cannot sustain the necessities of life. Upon her release Mary sets out upon an elaborate revenge, marrying Gilder's son and masterminding a variety of lucrative rackets which, like the shop-girl's standard wage, are only just 'within the law'. Third-degree police interrogations, stool pigeons and murders by silenced revolvers fill out the action. Theatres displayed testimonials from Theodore Roosevelt: 'Six of the biggest department stores in New York raised the wages of their shop girls through WITHIN THE LAW!'[31] The production played Broken Hill during a strike by shop employees. Cheering workers thronged the

21 A publicity postcard of Muriel Starr as Mary Turner in 'the great American Drama', *Within the Law*: 'The most absorbingly interesting drama of human nature ever produced in Australia.'

theatre and Starr was showered with letters and given a vote of thanks by unionists.[32] The lives of shop girls did not, as their detractors claimed, revolve merely around escapism and 'gush', but involved them in serious economic struggles.

At the Melbourne Theatre Royal in April 1914 Starr took the lead in an American version of Alexandre Bisson's 1908 *Madame X*, a maternal melodrama that had been played by Bernhardt.[33] The play's scheduled two weeks were extended to six and a similar long run followed in Sydney. The *Bulletin* considered it the dampest weepie ever, a curious vehicle in which to impress through 'natural' playing, yet Starr triumphed in this mingling of registers.[34] Jacqueline Floriot deserts her husband and child for her lover, and upon her penitent return she is discarded by her husband. Twenty years of drink, hard drugs and low living ensue for Jacqueline until she shoots her current protector to protect her family's honour. Terminally ill, she stands trial as 'Madame X'. Her husband sits on the bench, but the defence counsel is the son she deserted, who, fired by obscure sympathy for the degraded yet charismatic stranger, secures a verdict of not guilty. As she dies, a mutual recognition occurs between mother and son. Accompanied by 'multitudinous sniffs from the darkness', Starr's performance '[touched] the heights of genius'.[35]

As the world moved towards war, the Firm urgently needed to retain its popular contracted actors. Starr's salary increased from £40 to £50 and her contract was now for 52 weeks rather than the Firm's usual cautious 26-week hires. Her next role was the tough-talking Nora O'Brien in *The Chorus Lady* (1906), written by Canadian-American James Forbes, in which the eponymous heroine saves her wilful sister from a moneyed sexual predator, with slangy repartee and generally hard-boiled goings-on. Starr showed her flair for comedy and also her dramatic 'magnetism'. She was thoroughly back in her 'emotional' territory in the controversial play *The Yellow Ticket* by Michael Morton, which opened at the Criterion in September 1914, one week after the declaration of war. This American script, premiered in New York in January of that year, treated in high sensational style the restrictions on residence and occupations inflicted upon Jews in Tsarist Russia. Starr as heroine opts to obtain the prostitute's 'yellow ticket' as affording her more civil rights than those which Jews enjoyed. Despite its scandalous prostitute thematic, wartime governmental panics about venereal disease among the troops ensured the play lively attention and even official endorsement.

Starr preferred the 'gypsy life' of constant global touring in flexible repertoire, for which reason she had agreed to the Firm's engagement in

Emotional and natural 181

"THE CHORUS LADY."
Muriel Starr as Pat. In the dressing room.

22 Hal Gye sketch of Muriel Starr in *The Chorus Lady*, from the *Bulletin* [Sydney], 24 December 1914.

the first place, but instead her popularity had forced her into long runs. Touring was in her blood, she told one Wellington paper.[36] 'I like to be on the move. When I came to Australia I looked for travel all the time.' Privately, her managers were worried about their actor's endurance. The Firm's managing director George Tallis wrote to his partner Hugh Ward on 31 August 1914 that her tour to Western Australia cost her two stone in weight and that her health was 'awful'. This was inconvenient, since they had secured for her the two American vehicles *The Yellow Ticket* and George Broadhurst's *Bought and Paid For*. Her first Australasian engagement had stretched to two and half years, and upon leaving in August 1915 she was contracted to appear the following year in Firm theatres in South Africa.[37]

Starr returned to Australasia as a headliner, partnered by the distinguished Anglo-Australian actor and later screenwriter Frank Harvey (Vagg, 2006). In the USA, she had been playing Chicago and San Francisco for Oliver Morosco in Richard Walton Tully's spectacle drama *The Bird of Paradise* (1911), which opened her reappearance at Melbourne in December 1917. Typical of interrupted wartime patterns of theatrical circulation, this play was premiered in Australia twenty-one months before its London showing. Described as 'a mixture of orientalism, colonialism, and a particularly American variation of the Pacific imaginary' (Balme, 2015: 1), it saw Starr in blackface amid fiery volcanoes, swaying Hawaiian dancers and plangent steel guitars: these latter forming the play's major attractions. Further vehicles included more of the American moral-regeneration dramas which now spoke anew to post-war trauma and upheavals in sexual mores: Eugene Walter's *The Easiest Way* (1909), *The Man Who Came Back* (1916) by Jules Eckert Goodman, and George Broadhurst's *Bought and Paid For* (1911). During the Sydney run Starr took an afternoon off to marry William Hartwell Johnston, the Chicago-born Sydney representative of Wrigley's Spearmint chewing gum. A New Zealand tour was undertaken in late 1919, followed by three years of domesticity in Chicago.

Meanwhile silent screen versions of Starr's vehicles made in the second decade of the century, plus the more glamorous 1920s silent remakes, had been, or would shortly be, exhibited in Australia. Starr's career and the output of Hollywood were now meshing in what was initially a collaborative competition for the interest of popular audiences. At this juncture, the stage set the critical standard for emotional contact:

> It is always a big test for a cinematograph film to follow a successful play, and repeat that success ... [T]he great American drama, 'Within the Law', made its first local appearance on the screen and scored an instant triumph ... the magnetism of the living portrayal has been conveyed into the pictorial narrative, so that the crowded audiences ... were gripped by the intensity and appealing force of the human tragedy, just as they were affected in the legitimate drama.[38]

This refers to the 1917 Vitagraph version with Alice Joyce, but such was the material fragility of film stock and the short exhibition runs that, by 1919, the writer may have forgotten the Australian film made by the very actor who had first introduced this 'great American drama' to the country. During her first tour Starr had played in a four-reeler *Within the Law* directed by Monte Luke. As the war dried up overseas material and increased internal transport costs, the Firm entered the world of cinematic production, filming their recent successes such as Fred Niblo in *Officer 666* and *Get-Rich-Quick Wallingford* in order to reach country audiences cheaply. In late 1915 Starr filmed the feature *Within the Law* in between her stage rehearsals and performances (Pike and Cooper, 1980: 77). Hence, early one morning outside the Melbourne Law Courts, passers-by recognised their theatrical favourite being pursued and manacled by the police. A belligerent crowd quickly gathered, only dispersing when it was explained that she was being filmed for a 'picture' (Marsden, 2009a).

After an unsuccessful tour to a troubled South Africa, Starr arrived back in Australia in March 1924 with her troupe partner Harvey Adams, sharing the *Mongolia* with the Melba Opera Company. By now she was worth a weekly £80 to the Firm. The lugubrious *Garden of Allah* ensued, a show with a 'sheiky flavour'[39] employing Sweetie, the Firm's veteran stage camel, plus a host of donkeys, goats and sheep.[40] It showcased Frank Harvey's considerable acting abilities but did little for Starr. Melbourne's season opening in August 1924 continued the East-meets-West thematic with Starr as the treacherous Chinese 'half-caste' in Somerset Maugham's *East of Suez*, with the Pola Negri silent film released in January 1925 in hot pursuit. By April 1925 the stage version had played Brisbane and Adelaide and was dropped.

Then, after her contract expired at the beginning of 1926, Starr's third tour radically altered in character. She had saved £600 and the lure of the road called again. She formed her own company with Harvey Adams, who also directed her productions for the strenuous touring. Starr believed there was room in Australia for a good stock company, despite the 'pessimists [who] tried to dissuade her, telling her that musical comedy and the pictures had knocked the bottom out of drama'.[41] But she had weathered plenty of gruelling back-roads travel and non-appearing salaries, and remained optimistic.

> My idea was to take a small company out, and do the small towns, so that I could visit parts of Australia and New Zealand that in all my time here I have never had a chance of seeing. I was most anxious to see Northern Queensland, for instance, and I had never seen Rotorua. Then everyone wanted me to take 'Within the Law.' This meant a larger company, so I thought that as I had the company I might us well have a few other plays, and so the venture grew.[42]

Leasing the Firm's theatres and dramatic properties, she began an exhausting series of stock visits to regional cities and towns. As the world slid into the Great Depression, this venture became more and more desperate, her finances drained completely, and the rural centres became ever smaller.

At first, the touring was successful financially as well as dramatically, with *Within the Law* securing steady income. She played Tasmania

184　　　　　　　　Women and popular performance

for eight weeks and twenty in New Zealand. Sustained seasons were generally lucrative with a varied repertoire of thrillers, crook plays and comedies. In Adelaide in 1927 the company sustained 100 performances of a weekly-change repertoire. Major capitals were revisited towards the end of 1928, when the omens of the coming catastrophe became clearer. In Hobart the Musicians' Union walked out of Starr's season premiere in protest at being replaced by 'tinned music' via the panatrope.[43] It was not only 'tinned music' but tinned performances which in a few short months would also turn the actors out of their theatres.

"SWEENEY TODD." THE DEMON BARBER OF FLEET-STREET.

Top: Sweeney Todd (Scott Alexander), who murders his customers and, with an eye to economy, drops them through his shop floor to a bakehouse. . . . Bottom Left: Susan Lovatt (Muriel Starr), in charge of Todd's pie shop, supervises the making of the victims into pies. . . Bottom Right: Doctor Lupin (Edward Landor), one of the shop's customers, who is delighted with the excellence of the pies.

23　Harry Julius sketch of the cast of *Sweeney Todd* at the Sydney Savoy, from the *Sydney Mail*, 17 July 1929.

Starr's last Australian year, 1929, shows her battling gallantly against the odds, increasingly so as the Depression destroyed her audience base. The Firm's metropolitan Melba and Pavlova tours were fairly quarantined, but their expensive productions of Noël Coward's revue *This Year of Grace* and of *Show Boat* – the latter playing to disadvantage alongside Universal's hybrid silent-sound version (1929) – bore the brunt of the collapse. The Firm then sent Starr to a series of small outback towns for the sole events still guaranteed to attract potential audiences: the annual agricultural shows. In Sydney in July, she appeared at the Savoy as Mrs Lovett the pie-shop keeper in *Sweeney Todd*: an early example of the popular pro-am *grand guignol* productions whose gruesomeness and ingenious stage tricks would sustain local actors through the 1930s. After October 1929 Sydney's stage productions decreased from eight to two, and the Firm wired its major urban houses for sound. Since the innumerable country picture theatres were slower to adopt this expensive innovation, the regions became the major territory for stage performers not working in musicals in the remaining urban theatres. The Australian comedy star Yvonne Banvard lamented the crowds who preferred the 'shadow shows' to their long-time stage favourites.[44] By February 1930 Starr could not pay her actors and went into voluntary sequestration with debts of over £3,400. Utterly bereft of cash, she was sustained in Sydney by a 'mysterious friend' who left her food parcels anonymously, telling the landlady 'she deserves it, after all I know she has done for others when she had it'.[45] After the Firm gave her a farewell benefit matinee, Starr sailed for San Francisco on 7 June 1930.

Although Australians may have hoped to see her in future Hollywood talkies, the wartime *Within the Law* (now lost) remains Starr's only film venture, and Anglin and Grey also survived the 1930s without recourse to film. Anglin briefly formed a Picture Corporation in 1916, but neither then nor later did she seriously seek a film career (Le Vay, 1989: 180). Grey appeared in four Broadway shows after 1929 before her death on 21 March 1950, mostly cast as older women in short-run plays in small theatres, the last being in 1940 when she was 67.[46] Like most ageing actors during the Depression, she gained income by occasional radio talks and live broadcasts. Starr toured widely in India, China and Japan, returning to America in 1935. Between 1937 and 1950 she did five Broadway plays, none particularly distinguished. Some Federal Theatre Projects were undertaken in 1938, plus understudy work, radio and television. On 19 April 1950, one month after Grey's death, Starr died of a heart attack in her New York dressing room after the first act of *The Velvet Glove*.[47]

Australia and New Zealand audiences thus, in fact, got the best that Starr had to offer, and in these regions her work was widely seen and made considerable impact.

These three 'emotional' and 'natural' North American actors initially, and logically, saw Australia and New Zealand as a profitable career site within the English-speaking world, even if a lot of that 'English' consisted of dialogue in a lower-class American argot. Validation by artistic status and modernity, variously wielding the banners of Shakespeare or Shaw, was significant in building a credible track record but was not necessarily central to their Australasian repertoires. These were framed managerially by the commercial Firm of J. C. Williamson, which, while not fundamentally averse to 'art', was sceptical about its economic viability. This chapter indicates that, while major metropolitan theatre centres in Australasia or elsewhere might offer some protection and career prospects, the early-century economic and geopolitical revolutions – wars, depressions and cinema – worked to complicate the supremacy enjoyed by the transnational nineteenth-century 'theatrical trade routes' travelled by touring performers (Balme and Leonhardt, 2016: 1). By 1930 those who circulated globally on ocean liners and trains were less likely to be solely the adventuring theatre tourists such as Starr, nor even prestigious showcased actors such as Anglin and Grey. Mobile stage performers everywhere were now complemented and rivalled by the 'tins' of talking film that conveyed the gendered thrills of feminine 'nature' and 'emotion' to popular audiences in Toronto, Melbourne and Tumut alike.

Notes

1 'Princess Theatre', *Daily Telegraph* [Launceston], 26 January 1925, p. 8.
2 'Mr G. S. Titheradge, Coming to Sydney. His Impressions and Experiences', *Evening News* [Sydney], 12 June 1908, p. 6.
3 'Loyal Britisher', in 'Theatrical Enterprise. Arrival of Leading American Actress. Miss Margaret Anglin. Interesting Interview', *Brisbane Courier*, 15 June 1908, p. 5. The Australian Catholic newspapers which interested themselves in theatre and boosted Anglin were *The Referee* (Sydney), *The Catholic Press* (Sydney) and *The Freeman's Journal* (Sydney).
4 Oberon, 'Vivacity and Smiles. Miss Muriel Starr Talks. New York Shop Girls', *Daily Herald* [Adelaide], 19 August 1913, p. 2.
5 Orpheus, 'Mimes and Music', *Evening Post* [Wellington, NZ], 5 February 1910, p. 11.
6 'Miss Muriel Starr Discusses Plays and Parts', *Port Adelaide News*, 24 April 1925, p. 3.

7   Francis John, 'Emotional Acting Briefly Considered. Peculiar Question Gives Food for Speculation', *Winner* [Melbourne], 4 August 1915, p. 10.
8   'Acting and the Emotions. Miss Anglin's View', *Sunday Times* [Sydney], 21 June 1908, p. 2, and 'Emotionalism on the Stage. A Chat with Miss Margaret Anglin', *Age* [Melbourne], 22 August 1908, p. 14.
9   'A Visiting "Star". Miss Katherine Grey. Leading Lady in Two Years. Plays Moral and Unmoral', *Evening Post* [Otago], 18 January 1911, p. 8.
10 *Table Talk* [Melbourne], 18 April 1912, p. 24.
11 'Amusements. Italian Opera at Her Majesty's. *I Pagliacci* and *Cavalleria Rusticana*', *Age* [Melbourne], 1 July 1901, p. 9.
12 'Theatre Royal. Mr Geo. Musgrove's London Dramatic Company. "The Broken Melody"', *West Australian* [Perth], 20 July 1905, p. 5.
13 'Sob Stuff', *Sunday Times* [Sydney], 20 May 1928, p. 19.
14 'Stage Notes', *Critic* [Adelaide], 19 February 1919, p. 11.
15 The Don, 'Sydney Shows', *Punch* [Melbourne], 9 July 1908, p. 37.
16 'Theatres &c', *Australasian* [Melbourne], 29 August 1908, p. 27.
17 *Bulletin* [Sydney], 9 July 1908, p. 8.
18 *Bulletin* [Sydney], 13 August 1908, p. 8.
19 'Miss Margaret Anglin, the great American actress, thinks that the arrival of the Fleet and its welcome were decorous and dignified; that the pageant was splendid, the scenery, so to speak, beautiful and artistic, but that the stage management was bad.' 'A Theatrical Opinion. Good First Act. Bad Stage Management', *National Advocate* [Bathurst], 24 August 1908, p. 2.
20 'Her Majesty's', *Table Talk* [Melbourne], 24 September 1908, p. 17.
21 Cited by 'Orpheus', *Evening Post* [Wellington], 15 January 1910, p. 11.
22 Grey's lengthy professional relationship with Mansfield, creator of the stage role of Dr Jekyll and Mr Hyde, had its fractious and litigious moments (*Evening Post* [Wellington], 9 June 1900, p. 3). For an assessment of Mansfield's career, see Turney (2016).
23 Orpheus, 'Mimes and Music', *Evening Post* [Wellington], 5 February 1910, p. 11.
24 'Ladies Letter', *Table Talk* [Melbourne], 10 March 1910, p. 28.
25 *Age* [Melbourne], 7 March 1910, p. 8.
26 *Bulletin* [Sydney], 31 March 1910, p. 9.
27 '"Shirley Rossmore". Miss Katherine Grey Interviewed', *Advertiser* [Adelaide], 31 March 1910, p. 10.
28 'Entertainments. Katherine Grey Dramatic Season. "The Lion and the Mouse"', *Evening Post* [Wellington], 19 January 1911, p. 2.
29 Starr's contract in the Williamson 'Contract File' at the Performing Arts Centre (Melbourne) shows that she was contracted by Clyde Meynell in New York in March 1913 to 'play as cast' for £40 for six months, and *Within the Law* is stipulated as one of the productions.
30 'Entertainments. "Within the Law"', *Evening Post* [Wellington], 20 December 1913, p. 3.

31 See e.g. *Evening Post* [Wellington], 23 December 1913, p. 2.
32 'Amusements. The Drama &c', *Leader* [Melbourne], 14 November 1914, p. 36.
33 Bisson's play gained international exposure through translation, novelisation (McConaughy, 1910) and numerous screen versions.
34 *Bulletin* [Sydney], 9 July 1914, p. 8.
35 'The Criterion. "Madame X"', *Sydney Sportsman*, 15 July 1914, p. 3.
36 *Evening Post* [Wellington], 4 October 1913, p. 11.
37 *Evening Post* [Wellington], 21 August 1915, p. 11.
38 '"Within the Law". A Notable Attraction at West's', *Register* [Adelaide], 18 November 1919, p. 9.
39 'Atmospherics. "Garden of Allah"'. Muriel Starr's Return', *Sun* [Sydney], 13 April 1924, p. 2.
40 'Sandstorms and the Camel', *Truth* [Sydney], 30 March 1924, p. 4.
41 'Stock Drama. Miss Muriel Starr's Record', *Register* [Adelaide] 3 November 1927, p. 10.
42 'Her Great Adventure. Muriel Starr's Philosophy', *Table Talk* [Melbourne], 5 May 1927, p. 27.
43 'Trouble at Theatre. Unionists Walk Out. Objection to Gramophone. Pickets Distribute Bills', *Mercury* [Hobart], 28 December 1928, p. 6.
44 'Get Out! Actress' Advice', *Mail* [Adelaide], 15 February 1930, p. 1.
45 'The Mysterious Friend. Parcels of Groceries Sent to Muriel Starr. Remains Unknown', *Evening News* [Rockhampton], 20 May 1930, p. 10.
46 'Katherine Grey, Stage Actress, 77. Noted Trouper Appeared With Mansfield, Sotherns and Drew – Dies in Orleans, Mass', *New York Times*, 22 March 1950, p. 26.
47 'Muriel Starr Dies A Veteran Actress', *New York Times*, 20 April 1950, p. 29.

References

Balme, Christopher (2015), 'Selling the Bird: Richard Walton Tully's *The Bird of Paradise* and the Dynamics of Theatrical Commodification', *Theatre Journal*, 57.1, pp. 1–20.

Balme Christopher, and Nic Leonhardt (2016), 'Introduction: Theatrical Trade Routes', *Journal of Global Theatre History*, 1.1, pp. 1–9.

Capern, Alwyn (1995), 'Muriel Starr', in Phillip Parsons and Victoria Chance, eds, *The Currency Companion to Theatre in Australia*, Sydney: Currency House, p. 555.

Carroll, Dennis (1995), 'American Influences', in Phillip Parsons and Victoria Chance, eds, *The Currency Companion to Theatre in Australia*, Sydney: Currency House, p. 48.

Deacon, Desley, Penny Russell and Angela Woollacott, eds (2010), *Transnational Lives: Biographies of Global Modernity, 1700–Present*, Basingstoke: Palgrave Macmillan.

De Groat, Greta (2006), 'Pauline Frederick, Tragedienne of the Silent Screen', *The Pauline Frederick Website*, http://web.stanford.edu/~gdegroat/PF/Essay.htm (accessed 1 May 2016).

Iriye, Akira, and Rana Mitter (2010), 'Foreword', in Desley Deacon, Penny Russell and Angela Woollacott, eds, *Transnational Lives: Biographies of Global Modernity, 1700–Present*, Basingstoke: Palgrave Macmillan, pp. xi–xii.

Kelly, Veronica (2006), 'An Australian Idol of Modernist Consumerism: Minnie Tittell Brune and the Gallery Girls', *Theatre Research International*, 31.1, pp. 17–36.

Kelly, Veronica (2009), *The Empire Actors: Stars of Australasian Costume Drama 1880s–1920s*, Sydney: Currency House.

Kelly, Veronica (2010), 'North Star and Southern Cross: Shakespeare's Comedies in Australia, 1903–1904', *New Theatre Quarterly*, 26.4, pp. 383–94.

Le Vay, John (1989), *Margaret Anglin, A Stage Life*, Toronto: Simon and Pierre.

Marsden, Ralph (2009a), 'Melbourne's Forgotten Movie Studio', *On Stage*, 10.2, pp. 1–6.

Marsden, Ralph (2009b), 'Melbourne Stage-by-Stage', *On Stage*, 10.3, p. 18.

McConaughy, J. W. (1910), *Madame X: A Story of Mother-Love. From the Play of the Same Name by Alexandre Bisson*, New York: H. K. Fly.

McKay, Claude (1961), *This is the Life: The Autobiography of a Newspaperman*, Sydney: Angus and Robertson.

Morgan, Cecilia (2010), '"That Will Allow Me to be My Own Woman": Margaret Anglin, Modernity and Transnational Stages, 1890s-1940s', in Desley Deacon, Penny Russell and Angela Woollacott, eds, *Transnational Lives: Biographies of Global Modernity, 1700–Present*, Basingstoke: Palgrave Macmillan, pp. 144–55.

Morgan, Cecilia (2014), '"A Sweet Canadian Girl": English-Canadian Actresses' Transatlantic and Transnational Careers through the Lenses of Canadian Magazines, 1890s–1940s', *International Journal of Canadian Studies*, 48, pp. 119–35.

Parsons, Phillip, and Victoria Chance, eds (1995), *The Currency Companion to Theatre in Australia*, Sydney: Currency House.

Pike, Andrew, and Ross Cooper (1980), *Australian Film 1900–1977: A Guide to Feature Film Production*, Melbourne: Oxford University Press.

Platt, Len, Tobias Becker and David Linton, eds (2014), *Popular Musical Theatre in Berlin and London 1890–1939*, Cambridge: Cambridge University Press.

Schweitzer, Marlis (2015), *Transatlantic Broadway: Infrastructural Politics of Global Performance*, Basingstoke: Palgrave Macmillan.

Turney, Wayne S. (2016), 'Richard Mansfield (1857–1907)', http://www.wayneturney.20m.com/mansfieldrichard.htm (accessed 8 May 2016).

Vagg, Stephen (2006), 'Frank Harvey: Australian Screen-Writing Pioneer', *Australasian Drama Studies*, 48, pp. 79–98.

Archives

National Library of Australia, Canberra

Sir George Tallis Papers (1889–1948), NLA MS 9522/3, Correspondence and Business Records

Victorian Arts Centre, Melbourne

J. C. Williamson Collection, Royalty and Production Agreement Contracts. Performing Arts Collection

8

LILY BRAYTON

A theatre maker in every sense

Brian Singleton

Lily Brayton (1876–1953) is barely remembered today, overshadowed in historical accounts of British theatre history by her Australian-born husband, Oscar Asche, who penned the most commercially successful production on the London stage in the first half of the twentieth century (*Chu Chin Chow*, His Majesty's Theatre, 1916–21). Brayton was lead actress in most of the productions directed by Asche, and was generally regarded by contemporary critics as one of the best Shakespearean actresses of the early twentieth century. Despite her prominence in a succession of syndicated managements of His Majesty's Theatre from 1907 to 1922 with Asche, the in-built bias against women in the commercial and theatrical worlds in Edwardian England and afterwards meant that the visibility of her work in theatre production was masked by that of her husband. Onstage she may well have been known as actress Lily Brayton, but offstage and to the public, she performed the role of Mrs Oscar Asche.

Asche and Brayton followed in the footsteps of theatrical couples from the late Victorian period who became reputable actor-managers, and had to negotiate their marriage and their business in the context of what Tracy C. Davis refers to as 'gentlemanly capitalism' (Davis, 2000: 286). For Brayton this was even more precarious than was experienced by her Australian husband, as she had to perform her private role in the marriage in the very public realm of theatre both on and off the stage; as such, according to Davis, we might recognise actor-manageresses such as Brayton as 'iconoclasts or subalterns: publicly oriented women who claim the right to make representations – this is what theatre does, after all – yet who nevertheless in representations of them cannot be separated from either their marital state or their particular marriage

24 Lily Brayton and Oscar Asche offstage.

partners' (2000: 286). This negotiation of self-presentation is also one of the reasons why Brayton is largely absent from history. While onstage she may have presented images of strong and clever women, and much of the time played those women opposite her husband, offstage it was Asche who spoke publicly on her behalf.[1] As Veronica Kelly admits, 'Distinguishing Brayton's own input and achievements thus faces the problem of self-presentations produced by these stars as part of their successful public personae' (Kelly, 2006: 1). Further, the success of Brayton's onstage success, renowned and remembered as she was for her 'beauty',[2] also overshadows her contribution to the financing, management and production of theatre, for which her husband publicly took the credit. This essay follows on from Kelly's reclamation of Brayton as a theatre 'artist' while on the company's two tours to Australia (1909–10, 1912), by reading between her self-presentation on and off the British stage, and the evidence pertaining to the full extent of her 'labour' in the theatre.

Lily Brayton was born Elizabeth Brayton in 1876, the youngest of four daughters of Margaret Brayton, housewife, and John Grindall Brayton, physician and surgeon, in the burgeoning mill and coal-mining town of Hindley, near Wigan in Lancashire.[3] In such an environment and at such a time, acting as a profession for a doctor's daughter from the North of England would not have been considered suitable or respectable. However, like many other young women, Brayton took elocution lessons with Miss Morden Gray in Manchester, though less as a social attribute and more with an eye to a career.[4] After her father's death in 1892, she defied her parents' wishes to keep her off the stage, and wrote to the notable Shakespearean actor-manager Frank Benson.[5] Benson not only wrote back to her, but also granted her an interview while on tour to the Theatre Royal Manchester in 1896, and immediately hired her (Fletcher, 2004: 11). Margaret Brayton's dismay at Lily's chosen career was compounded when her younger daughter Agnes followed Lily into the profession.[6] It was in F. R. Benson's Shakespearean Company that Lily learned her craft, graduating over the tours of Britain and Ireland to larger roles, and playing twenty-one Shakespearean women in fourteen plays over four seasons (from 1897) in Stratford alone. In Benson's company she met Oscar Asche. Almost six years her senior,[7] with his athletic build and booming voice Asche was a rising star in Benson's company. Despite protests from her mother, Lily married Oscar in her family church of St Peter's in Hindley on 22 June 1898, one day shy of her 22nd birthday, with her sister Mary as bridesmaid and Oscar's friend and actor Harry Hignett as best man.[8] After a honeymoon in Stratford-upon-Avon, they returned to Benson's company, to hone their skills and rise through the ranks to more significant roles. Oscar's weekly wage at this time was three times more than Lily's, but that was to change considerably over time as their marriage facilitated their development as a theatrical duo and a partnership brand that turned them into actor-managers of renown, celebrity and considerable wealth.

The 1900 season of Benson's company at London's Lyceum Theatre propelled both their careers to unexpected heights. Lily played Helena in *A Midsummer Night's Dream* and Olivia in *Twelfth Night* to very favourable reception,[9] leading to an invitation from Herbert Beerbohm Tree to play Viola in *Twelfth Night* in 1901. Viola, disguised as Cesario, helped to define Brayton as an actress. Her performance both conformed to and defied the gender expectations of the time, and captured critical attention. A long section of the unattributed opening night review, for instance, in the *Illustrated London News* was devoted purely to Brayton:

> Unheralded and unsung, the young lady, who filled a subsidiary position in "Henry V." at the Lyceum twelve months ago, at one bound came forward and carried the house along with her. We do not say that Viola is a part which tries an actress to the full. It would be almost a cruelty for so young and graceful a lady as Miss Brayton to be handicapped on her first appearance by demands which can only justly be made on a full-blown tragedy queen. But the sympathy, the tenderness, the womanliness, the charm of a soft and gracious personality, added to beautifully clear-cut elocution, made the new-comer "safe" in the first five minutes. Of no commanding physique, yet endowed with convincing earnestness and simplicity of method, Miss Brayton made Viola what she rarely is – plausible both as girl and boy. Every word she uttered reached the furthermost corner of the theatre, and what lent chief charm to her work was the avoidance of point-making and the conventional simpering, overdone artificialities by which heroines masquerading in male clothes frequently make themselves ridiculous. The value of this performance cannot well be exaggerated. It lends to "Twelfth Night" a sustained and continued ray of brightness. At the risk of appearing to praise too highly – it is never kind to do that, because the limits of an actress's possible achievement cannot be set out so early in her career – we would express extreme pleasure at so delightful a piece of acting, studied, natural, and independent of all artifice. The calls for this lady at curtain-fall were generous and general.[10]

Although the reviewer tempers his description of the audience reaction to Brayton, and cautions about this being a performance of an actress early in her career, most of the review is taken up with analysis of her acting skills, her interpretation of the role and her impact on the contemporary stage. It also focuses on her playing with gender. Production photographs of her costume reveal a bi-gendered image, with swathes of flowing fabric in the form of a white linen shirt, lavender tunic, crimson silk hose, cap and sash replete with dagger. Although a replica of her brother Sebastian's costume, Viola's costume differed significantly from those worn by men (doublet, hose and stiff cuffs). Reading between the imagery and this extended description in the review, Brayton refrained from playing a man, in exaggeration or caricature, but truthfully played a woman with masculine attributes and designs. With her contralto voice, she was able to attenuate her femininity vocally as well, and command the stage and the house with a voice that gave her character the power

25 Lily Brayton in profile, date unknown.

and presence of woman as man, recognisably bi-gendered, but readable as woman for all that.

The *Illustrated London News* was the paper of choice for the Victorian middle classes. As Jemima Kiss reports, the woodcut imagery and later photographs (by the time of Brayton's arrival on the London stage) that accompanied the text increased the consumption of news of political, social and cultural events: "'It was the multimedia of its day," according to Seth Cayley: "In one sense, people didn't know before then what the rest of the world really looked like. *ILN* was the strongest paper of its sort and helped shape the middle class.'"[11] It also put faces to names for the first time for a general readership of approximately 300,000 at its height, again acting as a conduit for further consumption beyond its pages, and exciting a desire to experience the real. Such a glowing review for Lily Brayton would thus easily have caught the attention of the theatregoing public in London. The reviewer continues with a description of the impact that Brayton's performance had and was to have on *ILN* readers and future spectators:

> Here in the finest playhouse of London, before a crowded and discriminating audience, this graceful girl, with the musical voice, made a hit – a palpable hit. Is it any marvel that the theatre casts such a glamour over the imaginative and emotional aspirant; is it any marvel that hundreds of Miss Brayton's age and sex will turn with envious admiration to this clever little woman who with no "friends at court," has come and conquered?[12]

Eliding actress with character, the reviewer finally and unequivocally announces the new star of the London stage.

Asche joined Beerbohm Tree's company a year later and the couple grew in skill and fame, in equal measure. Mutual recognition of each other's creativity and their matching popularity propelled both their careers into theatre production. With a lease taken out on the Adelphi Theatre by fellow Bensonian Otho Stuart, and joined by other fellow Bensonians, the 'Oscar Asche–Lily Brayton Company'[13] was launched in September 1904 with a repertoire of Shakespeare and contemporary poetical drama. During the three-year lease, nine productions were mounted in repertory. The first of their Shakespeare productions, *The Taming of the Shrew*, would be revived no fewer than five times during the lifetime of the company and it became their second most popular production of all time. Asche believed they played it more than 1,500 times (Asche, 1929: 112). There is little doubt that the success of the production lay in the pairing of husband and wife producers, Oscar and Lily, as Petruchio and Katharina, in an onstage duel for gender supremacy. Historically the production is remembered for the inclusion of the twenty-minute Induction scene[14] in which Asche played Christopher Sly, a character that would act as a template for his many orientalist characterisations to come. The popularity of the production lay in the style in which they chose to perform. As Asche gleefully admitted, 'We played it as a jolly farce and it always went with a scream' (Asche, 1929: 112).

Contemporary critics and historians confirm the approach and its popular success. The review in the *Illustrated London News* focused on Asche's masculinity (for which he had already made a name in the West End): 'Mr Asche's reading of the shrew-tamer is one that lays stress on brutal, masculine force, which is no mask with him – scarcely even policy, but first instinct; and with the actor's robust physique and sonorous voice such a Petruchio proves irresistible.'[15] If Asche's masculinity was to prove irresistible, then it was, according to Veronica Kelly, framed as the drunkard Sly's fantasy, in which he rendered 'feats of woman-taming unlikely outside the brilliant play world of Renaissance Italy' (Kelly, 2006: 43) and thus the transformation of Katharina highly unlikely. Hesketh Pearson remembered how Brayton was credited as much as her husband for the production's success:

> Lily Brayton was incomparably the best Katharina of her time, and both of them jumped at a bound to the front of their profession. It was a breathless, knockabout, rampageous show, played on broadly farcical lines, and the audiences rocked with laughter. Wherever it was performed it raised the roof [...] (Pearson, 1950: 66)

Looking back on the production, Claude McKay wrote of how 'the pair took London by storm', and noted Brayton's performance as being equally memorable.[16] They were both lauded for their voice and movement skills, a success that was due in no small part to Brayton being the first British actress to use the technique of F. M. Alexander who had arrived in London just before the play opened. Having been cured of laryngitis, she would return to Alexander numerous times during the season at the Adelphi, and credited him with improving her technique and stamina as an actor. She and Oscar were such enthusiasts of the technique that they introduced their friends to Alexander and were primarily responsible for the huge influence of the 'Alexander technique' on British theatre training that persists today.[17]

Brayton's Katharina was also renowned for her five costumes, challenging gender norms visually to match her physicalised performance. Veronica Kelly describes the first – a green hunting dress conveying 'a cross-gender vestimentary repertoire of leather and masculine fabrics pierced by slashes and cross lacings, topped by a piratical scarf and masculine hat, the whole adorned with buckled belt, daggers horns and glinting spiked metal' (Kelly, 2006: 44–5). Every detail of the costume suggested a woman of action, equal in every way to Petruchio. On their first Australian tour in 1909–10 they were presented with a pair of greyhounds as a gift, a nod to Asche's hobby of dog-breeding and racing, but it was Brayton as Katharina who appeared on stage with the dogs, and would do so in subsequent revivals of the production back in London. Audiences who followed the by-now celebrity couple's relationship in the weekly magazines and papers would well know that the dogs were primarily Asche's passion, and the sight of Brayton with the dogs on stage, and not Asche, would have caused much amusement. Audiences would also have read this usurpation of her husband's hobby as another sign and layer of Katharina's gender battle on stage. The *Illustrated London News* review of the production was very clear as to who won the battles of the sexes:

> Principal honours, without a doubt, fall to Miss Lily Brayton, whose Katharina is an even finer piece of work than her Viola [...] Mr. Asche gives the impression of 'how to tame a shrew,' yet the manner of his taming is likely to win the sympathy of the audience for the shrew herself.[18]

The playing together of the two performances, brute strength and spiritedness, as a husband and wife team resonated with the already popular battles of the sexes in musical comedies. As the revivals mounted up in the ensuing years against a background of suffragism in England and anxieties about Empire and the threat of war, this production provided a vehicle for a not too political nod to the realities of gender inequality. Lily Brayton did not go as far as to represent the 'New Woman' in the theatre, and offstage she declined politely any association with the Actresses' Franchise League.[19] However, as we shall see, she found a way of playing her gender in both English and Orientalised contexts as Veronica Kelly describes, 'according to the contemporary understanding of the "womanly" heroines of Shakespeare who variously projected fortitude, shrewd enterprise, good sense, and moral charisma' (Kelly, 2006: 46). This was precisely the role she played offstage, too, deferring to her husband in public, while taking more of a lead as producer and in the conscious presentation of self onstage. For the next three decades the company title gave equal billing to both Lily and Oscar, though his name almost always came first. However, as we shall see, with all the qualities Kelly describes regarding her onstage persona, Lily's shrewdness in the business of theatre would come to the fore, and eventually the order of the names would be swapped in the billing as the power dynamics of the celebrity couple shifted.

If Shakespeare's heroines were to make her name and reputation, it was Brayton's many roles as the 'oriental woman' that were to bring her unprecedented fame, further agency in the production process, a directly executive role in the management of the Asche–Brayton Company, and ultimately wealth and security in the precarious West End business of theatre in a decade of war and its aftermath. Brayton made her first appearance as an 'oriental woman' in Beerbohm Tree's touring version of his production of David Belasco's play *The Darling of the Gods* which had its London premiere in 1903. Asche describes in his autobiography his first encounter with his wife as an 'oriental woman': 'I remember arriving home very late one night, or morning, after a long rehearsal. I went into the bedroom, and there on the bed, sound asleep, with a wonderful headdress, a Japanese girl. It was Lil' (Asche, 1929: 105–6). Orientalism on the London stage by that time was extremely fashionable, particularly in musical comedy from the late 1880s onwards. It reached its apogee in the Edwardian period, with its excuse for an exoticism particularly in costume design, stage spectacle and plots of English woes and travails mapped on to 'oriental' characterisations and situations. The Orient of Edwardian theatrical orientalism was a halfway place sited between the exoticism of a desire for an imaginary Other (in terms of sex, religion and culture) and a profound anxiety, provoked by the reality of an aggressive late-Victorian New Imperialism, and fear of the Other (in terms of war, death and civilisation). While British melodrama of the late nineteenth century played out the fears and anxieties of the home nation, the stages of musical comedy and pantomime were filled with charming plots, recognisable characters thinly disguised as foreign, and imaginative decoration to delight the senses.

In the first seven years of the Asche–Brayton Company, oriental characters did not feature at all. It was upon their return from the company's first Australian tour (1909–10) that everything changed. Although Asche acknowledged direct experience of other cultures on their journeys back and forth to Australia as being a source of influence for the change of direction, it was primarily the vogue for orientalism in the theatre at the time that should be credited. Two examples of contemporary European theatre had the most influence on the company's change of direction, as they both moved the vogue of orientalism higher up the cultural scale. First was the visit of Diaghilev's Ballets Russes to the London Coliseum in 1910 dancing Rimsky-Korsakov's *Scheherazade*, designed by Léon Bakst and choreographed by Michel Fokine. It was most memorable for an orgiastic Bacchanale scene, which, along with its choreographer, would feature ultimately on the Asche–Brayton stage. The second production that set the critics alight was the Berlin Deutsches Theater's production of *Sumurun*, a modernist and orientalist dumb-show (or pantomime as it was described at the time) directed by Max Reinhardt that also played at the Coliseum in 1911.[20]

Asche jumped on the trend and set to work immediately obtaining the English and Australian rights to Edward Knoblauch's play *Kismet* (formerly 'Hajj's Hour'), and crafted for it a dramaturgy that he knew well from his version of *The Taming of the Shrew*. He set himself up as the Sly figure Hajj, whose vision of the Orient appeared, introducing a bazaar scene for spectacle and a harem bathing scene similar to that of the Ballets Russes. In terms of production, Asche was experimenting with lighting to an even greater degree than is evidenced in the prompt books of his earlier Shakespeare productions. Brayton meanwhile, adjusted to the new vogue, as well as to the possibilities of Asche's lighting effects, with fabrics that created 'dazzling, glamorous magic'.[21] She played the role of Marsinah, daughter to Asche's less than noble beggar Hajj, who was in a secret relationship with the Caliph, but whom Hajj wished to sell to the Wazir. Wrenched from one suitor to another by her father, audiences would not have failed to see the comedy of the couple as father and daughter rather than as husband and wife. Though Hajj was punished for his deeds at the end, Marsinah achieved a social elevation marked by a clothing change, a fact that would not be lost on a contemporary audience.

Though an 'Arabian Nights' morality tale, *Kismet* spoke clearly of the English class system, thereby allowing Brayton's second 'oriental woman' to climb socially, and transgress the stereotype of the veiled virgin to become a woman of agency in a strict gender hierarchy and ultimately a woman of substance. But there is evidence, too, of the fashion icon that Brayton had become, as her costumes liberated her from strict English conventions and permitted the revealing of more flesh. Costumiers B. J. Simmons & Co., who realised Percy Anderson's designs under the supervision of Brayton, made similar costumes available to hire to the public subsequently, for the fancy-dress balls that were all the rage at the time in middle-class society: 'Since "Sumurun" and "Kismet" first showed the dancing world the picturesqueness and freedom of the Persian dress, ladies of the harem, sheiks and caliphs have littered the floor of every fancy-dress ball. All Suburbia has a yashmak...'[22] In fashion writer Mrs Aria's costume handbook of 1906, there is a clear indication that the veiled woman of the Orient acted as signifier of an imagined, unveiled one.[23] Thus the costume designs for Brayton and the many dancers in the production veiled the flesh in flowing fabrics that Asche's lighting effects then unmasked.

Between the success of *Kismet* in 1911 and the defining period of the Asche–Brayton Company from 1916 to 1922, Lily Brayton was to portray three further characters of different nationalities in similar manner: the eponymous heroine in Shakespeare's *Antony and Cleopatra*, in a production that opened in Melbourne's Theatre Royal in 1913; upon their return to London from Australia via a stopover tour of South Africa, a Zulu princess in the eponymous *Mameena*, an adaptation by Asche of Henry Rider Haggard's recently published novel *Child of Storm* (Globe, 1914); and finally a Spanish Juanita in a pirate play *The Spanish Main* (Apollo, 1915) penned by Asche under a pseudonym.[24]

Although Brayton's name was in the original registered company title (the Asche–Brayton Syndicate Limited) which was set up for their first season at His Majesty's in 1907, she did not start off as an investor or director.[25] However, her succession of leading roles and her offstage performances with her husband in acting, sporting, charity and royal circles would suggest that she played a major role in the success of the brand, if not the company at the time. However, a number of interviews with Australian journalists while on tour, as Veronica Kelly has revealed, point to Brayton's active role in the decision-making processes of theatrical production, particularly in terms of design. While her husband continued to experiment with lighting, as evidenced in the extant prompt books to his Shakespeare productions and in his autobiography, Lily Brayton began to reveal her role in the dressing and re-dressing of the productions, notably with an eye to the signification of clothes in terms of how they were read socially, but also significantly how they operated as part of an organic scenographic process.

The Melbourne weekly *Table Talk*, an illustrated magazine with an interest in public figures and their fashion and social engagements, was the perfect vehicle for Brayton to reveal the signification of her work and relationship with clothes both on and off the stage. During the first two Australian tours on which Brayton accompanied Asche, *Table Talk* conducted a series of interviews that specifically referred to her design role in the productions, though this was not credited in any advertising, playbills or theatre programmes. In a 1910 interview, prior to the opening of *Kismet* and the beginning of the fantasy orientalist design spree by the company, Brayton revealed: 'Nowadays not only are the dresses for our productions made under my direction, but I took premises in London where the bulk of them were made, and staffed it so that the workers were directly responsible to me.'[26] She also reveals a hand in design:

> The great difficulty I find in dressing our plays in the character of the period is in getting the colors. In several instances we have been quite unable to get just the shade that was required, and I have had to get the cloth specially woven, after a great deal of experimenting with dyes. This was done with the 'rainbow' dress in 'Othello'.

But she also reveals that dresses are not her only interest in terms of stage design:

> I work morning, noon and night, in the theatre, always pottering about at the dresses, the furniture, or something. Of course, my interest in our productions does not begin and end with studying my part and playing it. I look upon the wardrobes as my own special department, and supervised the re-dressing of the plays produced in Australia[…].[27]

And specifically in terms of stage design she recalls an anecdote of finding by accident the table for the design of *Count Hannibal* (1910). In a later interview with the same magazine, she specifically details her precise role in the design process: 'Yes, I design some of the dresses, and always supervise them, the color harmonies and blendings, and that kind of thing, but usually we have an expert to design, to have them historically correct.'[28]

The interviews she gave in Australia, as Veronica Kelly has noted (Kelly, 2006: 39–59), provide details of Lily Brayton's views on fashion as well as her knowledge of the production processes of theatre. Here Brayton revealed how she worked together with her husband, articulating and situating her own contribution within their productions. Her taste for the medieval in terms of the shape of dresses indicates how her costumes, which do not specifically reveal the shape of her body, have been read as bi- or transgendered. Yet her talk of the possibilities of modern colour in terms of dyes, of brightness and illumination, and of

26 Lily Brayton and Oscar Asche in *Hannibal*, 1910.

how fabrics both absorb and reflect light are completely of an equal to her husband's knowledge of and experimentation with stage perspective and lighting.

Moving from purely acting to the design processes of theatrical production was a natural step for the actor-manager that Brayton had become in the pre-war period. But her role as investor in her own productions occurred during the most unlikely of times, the First World War and after. The production in question was *Chu Chin Chow*, an 'Arabian Nights'- inspired tale based on *Ali Baba and the Forty Thieves*, penned by Asche. Generically it fell between several stools; pantomime was at its base, much of it was in the style of musical comedy, but its tales

27 Lily Brayton in *Kismet*, 1911.

of revenge and plot twists, and occasional patriotic jingoism, steered it into the territory of melodrama. Not only did it have the Shrew-like characterisations of *Kismet*, it also presented an extravagant though thinly disguised Orient that spoke to the anxieties and desires of a nation at war. Further, it responded to the course of the war with scene revisions, additional songs and regular re-dressings to entice a home audience, and the soldiers on leave, to return to see the show on more than one occasion.

At the outset no theatre was interested in *Chu*; producers of musical theatre, among them George Dance and Robert Evett, turned it down, even though Asche and Brayton had assembled around them key artistic personnel from previous successful productions (scene designer Joseph Harker, costume designer Percy Anderson and composer Frederic Norton). Asche specifically created a lead character for Brayton as an inducement for her financial investment in the production. And so Brayton invested £3,000 of her own money, to match the sum Henry Dana, the manager of His Majesty's Theatre, invested on Herbert Beerbohm Tree's behalf, in a syndicate called Eastale Limited (Asche, 1929: 161). The syndicate, according to Asche, was made up of only two shareholders, Brayton and Beerbohm Tree, who held 50 per cent of the share capital each. Further, Asche signed over 50 per cent of the author's royalties to his composer Norton, while the remaining 50 per cent were assigned to Brayton, in return for a personal loan of £500. The contractual arrangements point to how Asche was already indebted financially to Brayton, both in personal and professional capacities. Given that no production had ever matched the financial targets for the pay-out of royalties on the London stage, Asche, unlike Brayton, was prepared to work in the show, for up to ten performances a week, for a simple actor's fee. Nevertheless, Asche earned a considerable sum from this contract (over £200,000), despite his lack of finances at the beginning. Meanwhile, Brayton was contracted to earn one of the largest returns on an investment in British theatre. The new syndicate was not credited on any publicity and the theatre advertising for *Chu* heralded the 'Oscar Asche Lily Brayton Season', thus continuing the brand of the celebrity couple, and masking the contractual inequity between the two. But at the beginning of the most successful period in the couple's career, only Brayton had the financial capital to show for her celebrity as an actor, as Asche had already begun to squander his earnings on lavish parties and gambling. The dynamics of the duo were shifting through their differing attitudes to money. *Chu Chin Chow* opened in His Majesty's Theatre on 31 August

1916 and ran for five years, 2,238 performances and a record box office income of nearly three and a half million pounds. Unlike Brayton, Asche spent the money as fast as he earned it.[29]

Throughout the long run, Brayton's name continued to remain uncredited for her work on the production, apart from her acting role. However, *Chu Chin Chow* saw the culmination of the pair's experimentation with fabric and colour to the point where it became the most talked-about show of its generation, principally because of its exotic and highly revealing dresses, which were overhauled every six months. Photos of the dressing and re-dressings appeared in society magazines such as *Tatler*, to whet the appetite for audiences to return. Lucinda Gosling points out the complicity between the society magazine editors and the production: '"Very suitable for the sultry climate of Baghdad", reported *Tatler* in September 1917, with a palpable leer when it featured six photos of the latest designs' (Gosling, 2014: 202–3).

Like those society magazines, *Chu Chin Chow* offered escapism from the war, while barely disguising the scenes of Old Baghdad in the fight for justice against a common enemy. Popular songs in the show became emblematic of the war effort, particularly 'The Robbers' March', ironically repositioning the forty thieves to reflect the heroics of the British Army. But it was the celebrations of Armistice Day, 11 November 1918, that were to conjoin the production unashamedly with the nation's war effort. A new scene called 'The Allies and the Dominions' was included, featuring a procession of the chorus personifying Britain's allies and dominions, to the tune of 'Rule Britannia'. The procession fanned out on to the stage and the performers took up positions around a gap. That gap was to be filled by none other than Lily Brayton, dressed up as the female personification of the nation, Britannia, letting fly a white dove to complete the picture. Audiences were ecstatic, and were spurred on by the appearance of Asche as John Bull who made a victory speech to cement in everyone's mind the production's patriotism. This imagery of an assumptive pseudo-royal couple lived on in the production for six months after the Armistice, providing for audiences a repeatedly clear image of Brayton as the very embodiment of nation. Offstage she compounded the image with highly publicised charity work as a direct contribution to the war effort. National sentiment was at its highest, and so too was the popular acclaim of the actress, whose Britannia costume, replacing the scanty clothes of old Baghdad, reminded audiences that this production was a British representation of an Orient of Empire, though one of the often licentious imagination. But it was also a production that had earned the right to mark and celebrate a national military triumph with the nation's iconic female figurehead at the helm.

His Majesty's Theatre's publicity machine made much of the long-running success of *Chu Chin Chow*, especially when the final performances were announced in 1921, increasing demand for tickets to an unprecedented level, such was the extent of the myth and lore surrounding the production in the public imagination, particularly its role in defending and celebrating nation both before and after the Armistice. Asche had meanwhile penned a new musical, entitled *Mecca*, scheduled to take over from *Chu* at His Majesty's, a musical more spectacular and more controversial. It had been produced by Morris Gest and had been a hit in New York in 1920.[30] However, in London the production was threatened with censorship by the Lord Chamberlain's Office, which had to respond to *Daily Mail* readers' letters and conservative Christians objecting to the increasing state of undress of the actors on Asche's stage in *Chu*. Further, a Muslim cleric, Mustapha Khan, objected to the Lord Chamberlain's office's licensing of the play on the grounds of religious offence.[31] With a compromise solution of a name change, and some minor amendments to the script, the newly titled *Cairo* replaced *Chu* on the stage on 15 October 1921.

By this time, with huge income from the American rights for *Mecca*, the American and Australian stage rights for *Chu*, and indeed its film rights, as well as having directed two highly successful musicals at Daly's Theatre in London,[32] Asche's finances had never been healthier. He had already purchased a country retreat, Sugley Farm in Gloucestershire, a purchase that would become associated with his financial and personal demise. So after a long hiatus in which Brayton's wealth had superseded his own, Asche was ready to invest once more in theatre. The Asche-Brayton couple re-emerged with *Cairo* in a new syndicate and an investment of £5,000 and 25 per cent shares each, with the other half of the finance put up by His Majesty's Theatre's new lessees, George Grossmith and J. A. E. Malone.[33] But this time there were also a number of notable changes in the credits that alert us to Lily Brayton's position both in the syndicate and the production process, which was revealed for the first time in the English press. In the *Play Pictorial* the credits run as follows:

> Mime by Oscar Asche. Music by Percy Fletcher.
> The Play Produced by Oscar Asche.
> General scheme of Decoration under the personal supervision of LILY BRAYTON
> LILY BRAYTON and OSCAR ASCHE's Season.[34]

Note how Brayton is credited separately from Asche as producer, and her credit with supervising the 'decoration' confirms what Brayton had been saying to Australian journalists over a decade earlier. Note, too, that Lily's name comes before Oscar's for the first time. There is no evidence to indicate why this came to pass, though the *Play Pictorial* makes mention of the precise role that Brayton played in the 'decoration', or, rather, the acknowledgement that Asche's all-encompassing role as producer was being unravelled: 'It is true Mr. Asche has had the assistance of able experts in their respective spheres of occupation. Miss Lily Brayton with her womanly sense of decorative appropriateness.'[35] This was not necessarily news to readers; nevertheless the placing of Brayton's name before Asche's in terms of the 'season' at His Majesty's must have been striking. Until now they had always worked under the umbrella title of the Oscar Asche–Lily Brayton Company, until *Chu* when the syndicate without Asche was referred to as 'The Oscar Asche Lily Brayton Season'. Since the Asche–Brayton theatrical partnership by this time had become a successful brand name, it points to a tectonic shift in their relationship that was reflected in Asche's fewer appearances onstage in *Cairo*, his increasing weight through a lavish lifestyle, his financial losses at his newly acquired farm and rumours of extra-marital affairs.

After 267 performances *Cairo* was taken off the stage unexpectedly on 2 June 1922, though box office returns were reported to be good, and Asche said the production made a profit of £12,000 (Asche, 1929: 174). Asche set off to his native Australia on a tour hastily arranged by His Majesty's theatre manager and fellow former-Bensonian Carl Leyel, without Brayton for the first time. The sudden departure of Asche and the disappearance of Brayton from both British theatre and public life was unexplained and inexplicable. Their separation was to be permanent, and the couple would have no further impact on the London stage.

Pre-empting the number one question of Brayton's absence when he reached Australia, Asche was not shy in informing journalists of the reason,[36] and even had tour producer J. C. Williamson point out the absence in the souvenir programme that accompanied *Cairo*: 'but for the urgent necessity of Lily Brayton taking a long rest from the strenuous work of several years in "Chu Chin Chow" and "Cairo", the latter piece would probably have still been running in London, and Oscar Asche would not now be with us again'.[37] Apart from a reference to Brayton suffering a nervous breakdown, as reported in Melbourne's *Argus*,[38] the precise details of the demise of the production and the celebrity couple were never fully exposed. Later at his bankruptcy trial in October 1926, when questioned by two barristers, Asche revealed that he had been having an affair with a chorus girl, Marguerite Martini, from approximately March 1921.[39] When Lily discovered the affair in May 1922, she refused to act with him onstage and threatened to name the chorus girl, who was half his age, as co-respondent in a very public divorce. He confirmed newspaper reports that Lily had suffered a nervous breakdown because of the revelation. He also claimed to have signed over his Gloucestershire farm to Martini, a fact that, if true, surely should have ended the marriage for good. But he kept that to himself at the time, and departed with some of the costume stock from the show, and some of the actors, having removed his effects from Brayton's house.

Brayton politely had Martini removed from Sugley Farm shortly afterwards, and Martini followed Asche to Australia a few months later, joined Williamson's company while on tour and appeared in minor acting roles. Two years later she returned to England with Asche on the same ship. The new couple moved back to Sugley Farm, had a child[40] and ran up even more debts. Two years further on, in 1926, with hardly any income during that time, Asche was declared bankrupt. He managed to hold on to the farm, despite bankruptcy, by suspiciously producing two unverified documents at his hearing; one dated two days before his departure signing over the farm to Martini, and the second, typed by the chorus girls in Australia, leasing the farm back from Martini to Asche for £5 per week. Asche and Martini set up a company, the Oscar Asche Greyhound Association, retained the house and grounds, rented out the land, but only filed accounts for 1928 and 1929. Thereafter the company ceased trading and Lloyds Bank called in the mortgage.[41]

But before all this, and though they remained estranged in marriage, Brayton reconciled with Asche to form a new syndicate, Asche Brayton Productions Ltd, to present *The Good Old Days* at the Gaiety Theatre in 1925.[42] Brayton invested £1,500 of her own money out of £10,000 raised. However, she lost the entire sum, as the production only lasted for thirty-seven performances. According to Asche's autobiography, an organised protest by disgruntled Gaiety chorus members who had not been hired for the production disrupted the opening night. Reviews generally were favourable, but the timing of the production was unfortunate, opening the week before Remembrance Day, and followed by the death of Queen Alexandra. Although this was the only play produced by the company, the pair continued their professional relationship. Brayton also co-produced her husband's last orientalist spectacle, *Kong*, at the Cambridge Theatre in 1931, but this only lasted for twenty performances, so unfashionable was the form by then. Why did Brayton continue the professional relationship with Asche, given his profligacy and infidelity? It is highly probable that Brayton knew nothing of the details of Asche's defence in the bankruptcy hearing or of the precise details of his affair and its duplicitous legal machinations, given her personal investment in their post-separation productions. Asche's 1929 autobiography revealed none of this. As a woman of considerable means in her own right, and separate bank accounts and property, Brayton never filed for divorce, and she remained on good terms with her husband in his final years.

Brayton did return to the stage one final time, ten years after she left it, to reprise her role as Portia in Shakespeare's *Julius Caesar* at His Majesty's in 1932, again under the Asche–Brayton brand, though Asche was no longer leading man material and played Casca. While critics praised Brayton's return to the stage and indeed her performance, the production was generally criticised for being nostalgic and outmoded, and signalled how out of touch Asche and Brayton as producers had become. Yet, as evidenced in the souvenir programme for the production, this revival was a clear attempt by both of them to salvage their reputation for posterity, as it featured single-page and separate acting profiles of the two actors, with their Shakespearean roles only as credits; nowhere in the official material is any mention of the orientalist roles and productions through which they had become hugely popular and financially successful. With only sixty-four performances, the impact of this reputation-saving device was negligible, and Brayton retired finally to the country.

Although Asche continued to have a sporadic career in the theatres of others, dabbled in cinema, and wrote novels and an autobiography, his career was finally over in 1934. Apart from the two years he spent in Australia (1922–24), Brayton never estranged herself from Asche, despite his many personal failings. Determined to keep in close contact with him, she rented for him a cottage called Endways, appropriately named for his last days, beside her new home in Bisham, near Marlow. While Brayton lived in The Thatched Cottage with her long-time dresser and companion Emily Mabel Davis, Asche divided his time between Endways, even becoming a member of the Marlow Operatic Society, and Marguerite Martini and their daughter in Maida Vale.[43] Asche died alone in Endways in 1936 at the age of 65, leaving a total of £20 16s 4d. The filed recipient was Rose Marguerite Martin (a.k.a Martini).[44]

Lily Brayton remarried two years later, to Douglas Chalmers Watson, a Scottish doctor, with whom she lived for the next ten years. After his death in 1948 she bought a house in Dawlish in Devon and lived there with her former dresser, along with her sister Agnes and family. She died in 1953, a very rich widow twice over;[45] notably, however, she willed her ashes be buried in the same grave as Oscar in Bisham, reuniting the duo who had taken London by storm fifty years earlier. The epitaph under her name on the headstone quotes Shakespeare's sonnet 18: 'thy eternal summer shall not fade', and her name is recorded there for posterity as Asche's 'wife', though the marriage had broken down some thirty years earlier. However, their theatrical legacy as a couple did not survive beyond the grave.

Just as her career abruptly stopped, so, too, did her reputation as an actress, and if she was remembered at all in published reminiscences and histories, it was mostly for being married to an actor whose life imploded professionally, financially and personally. But Brayton ought to be remembered not only for her many positive and successful images of women on both classical and popular stages, but also as a creative producer whom the times and social conventions regarding gender in the theatre nearly erased from view. Historically, Asche is barely remembered, primarily because of his drift to populist entertainment and his sudden fall from grace, but he still earns a place because of his visible trace as author of the longest-running musical on the London stage, a record that lasted until 1956.[46] He is also remembered because he made sure that he was, by penning an autobiography in his later fallow years. But Lily Brayton remained only in the imagination of the generation who knew her with popular affection in her roles from Katharina to Britannia. Never associated with modernism in theatre or the 'New Woman' in drama, Brayton's contribution to twentieth-century British theatre has been consigned historically to that of the 'subaltern'. However, the shift in power dynamics from Asche to Brayton, signified by the change of name and the records of their company for their last major success (*Cairo*), and corroborated by them both in their self-presentation off-stage, indicates that Lily Brayton was far more than a stage 'beauty' of populist entertainment, or even a 'marriage partner'; she was a highly skilled and both critically and commercially successful actor, scenographer, producer, investor and manager – a theatre maker in every sense.

Notes

1 Asche, however, consistently acknowledged throughout their partnership the prominent role Brayton played in their productions beyond what was visible on stage.

2 http://www.npg.org.uk/collections/search/person/mp00544/lily-brayton (accessed 1 July 2016).
3 In Stoney Lane Brayton's neighbours included not only a retired grocer and a schoolmistress, but also a coal miner, laundress, church keeper, calico weaver, factory operative and a colliery carpenter. 1891 Census for the Administrative County of Lancaster, Parish of Hindley, Ecclesiastical Parish of St Peter's.
4 'A Chat with Miss Lily Brayton', *Wigan Observer*, 27 November 1901.
5 'The Interviewer: Miss Lily Brayton in Private Life', *Table Talk*, 12 August 1909, p. 17.
6 They remained close throughout Brayton's career. Agnes lived with Brayton and Asche in London for a time, and later, when Brayton had twice been widowed, Agnes and her family moved in with Lily in Devon in her final years.
7 There are conflicting reports of the birth date of her husband Oscar, a conflict deriving from subsequent submissions of his age in the 1901 and 1911 censuses that indicate a lesser gap. In fact, he reduced both their ages on both census forms. On the headstone of their grave, Oscar's birth year is 1872. His birth certificate, however, states 24 July 1871.
8 Marriage Records of St Peter's Church, in the Parish of Hindley, in the County of Lancashire, No. 298.
9 She was described as 'a star of the future' for her performance as Helena in a review of *A Midsummer Night's Dream* in the *Standard*, 23 February 1900.
10 Unattributed review of *Twelfth Night*, *Illustrated London News*, 6 February 1901.
11 Jemima Kiss, 'Illustrated London News Goes Online', *Guardian*, 15 April 2010, https://www.theguardian.com/media/2010/apr/15/illustrated-london-news-archive-online (accessed 20 June 2016).
12 *Illustrated London News*, 6 February 1901.
13 This was the beginning of the Asche–Brayton brand. At this stage neither invested in their own productions.
14 According to the prompt book, the scene began at 8.20 pm and finished at 8.40 pm. Shakespeare Centre Library, Stratford-upon-Avon.
15 *Illustrated London News*, 10 December 1904, p. 854.
16 Claude McKay, 'How Oscar Asche Spent a Fortune', *Sun-Herald* [Sydney], 19 October 1952.
17 Letter from Lily Brayton to F. M. Alexander, 26 January 1906 (cited in Bloch, 2004: 56. See also 52, 58.)
18 *Illustrated London News*, undated press cutting, V&A production file.
19 Invited by fellow actress (and activist) Winifred Mayo to participate in a conference of the Actresses' Franchise League at Memorial Hall in London on 14 February 1914, and to join a demonstration in Trafalgar Square, Lily Brayton was unavailable. See letter from Winifred Mayo to fellow actress and activist

Maud Arncliffe Sennett, London, 23 January 1914, in 'A Collection of press cuttings, pamphlets, leaflets and letters mainly relating to the movement for women's suffrage in England, formed and annotated by M. Arncliffe Sennett', Vol. 25, No. 96, British Library, C.121.g.1 (cited in Hirshfield, 1985: 140). See also Naomi Paxton's chapter in this volume.
20 A contemporary reading of both productions and their effects can be found in Huntly (1912).
21 Claude McKay, 'How Oscar Asche Spent a Fortune', *Sun-Herald* [Sydney], 19 October 1952.
22 Unidentified press cutting, *Kismet* production file, Harry Ransom Humanities Research Center, University of Texas at Austin.
23 See Aria (1906: 102). For a further analysis of how this double signifier worked in *Kismet*, see Singleton (2004: 81–3).
24 Vasco Marenas.
25 Asche Brayton Syndicate Ltd, National Archives, Company No. 94235. The syndicate was initially intended to be called The Dramatic Enterprise Ltd, but this was struck off and replaced with the star actors' names at the last minute before registration. Its initial capital was £12,000, and no annual financial returns for the company are extant, suggesting that it was created in order to take over the running, though not the lease, of His Majesty's Theatre in 1907. It was eventually dissolved in 1917, without having traded for many years.
26 '"How I Dress Our Plays": Miss Lily Brayton and Stage Dress', *Table Talk*, 13 January 1910, p. 16.
27 Ibid.
28 'The Interviewer: Miss Lily Brayton in Private Life', *Table Talk*, 12 August 1909, p. 17.
29 At his bankruptcy hearing he divulged earning approximately £200,000 from *Chu Chin Chow* alone, apart from his royalties from *Kismet* and earnings from his other productions. Brayton's earnings must have been even greater, given that she was a 50 per cent shareholder in the syndicate.
30 Opened on 4 October 1920 at Century Theatre, transferring to the Boston Opera House in September the following year, for a month.
31 For a full description of the attempted censorship of the production, see Singleton (2010: 351–77).
32 *The Maid of the Mountains* (1917) and *A Southern Maid* (1920).
33 Asche referred in his bankruptcy hearing to two syndicates being set up, one called Mecca Productions (Asche and Brayton) and the other by the lessees called Grossmith and Laudrillard Ltd. However, neither company is listed in the Companies' Office.
34 *Play Pictorial*, xxxix.237, 1921, p. 116.
35 Ibid.
36 'Mr Oscar Asche: Australian Season of Plays', *Argus*, 25 August 1922, p. 6.
37 Phil Finkelstein, 'Souvenir Edition of Oscar Asche and his Complete London

Production of Cairo', p. 57, *Cairo* production file, B. J. Simmons Collection, Harry Ransom Humanities Research Center, University of Texas at Austin.
38 *Argus*, 25 August 1922, p. 6.
39 Rose Marguerite Martin.
40 Marguerite Asche, born 1926, Paddington, London. Mother's maiden name: Martin.
41 The Oscar Asche Greyhound Association Ltd was registered as a company, with Asche having only one share in it, but Marguerite Martini holding 80 preferential and 3,000 ordinary shares, making her the biggest shareholder. It was formally dissolved in 1932. Company No. 226808. National Archives, BT31/30070/226808.
42 Company No. 208684, incorporated 1925. National Archives, BT31/29 253/208684.
43 In the National Probate Calendar (Index of Wills and Administrations) she was listed both as Asche and Martin, living in Bexley, Kent; she died on 18 September 1978, leaving the not inconsiderable sum of £24,196.
44 https://probatesearch.service.gov.uk (1936, p. 102).
45 Her estate was worth £49,336 and 13 shillings (equivalent to approximately 1 million pounds at 2016 values). https://probatesearch.service.gov.uk/Cal endar?surname=watson&yearOfDeath=1953&page=6#calendar (accessed 3 September 2018).
46 It was overtaken by *Salad Days* at the Vaudeville Theatre in 1956.

References

Aria [Eliza (David)], Mrs (1906), *Costume, Fanciful, Historical, and Theatrical. Compiled by Mrs. Aria. Illustrated by Percy Anderson*, London: Macmillan.
Asche, Oscar (1929), *His Life, By Himself*, London: Hurst and Blackett.
Bloch, Michael (2004), *F. M.: The Life of Frederick Matthias Alexander: Founder of the Alexander Technique*, London, Hachette.
Carter, Huntly (1912), *The New Spirit in Drama & Art*, London: Frank Palmer.
Davis, Tracy C. (2000), *The Economics of the British Stage, 1800–1914*, Cambridge: Cambridge University Press.
Fletcher, Chrissy (2004), *A Theatrical Life: The Many Faces of Oscar Asche 1871–1936*, New South Wales: Burradoo.
Gosling, Lucinda (2014), *Great War Britain: The First World War at Home*, Stroud: The History Press.
Hirshfield, Claire (1985), 'The Actresses' Franchise League and the Campaign for Women's Suffrage 1908–1914', *Theatre Research International*, 10.2, pp. 129–53.
Kelly, Veronica (2006), 'Australia's Lily Brayton: Performer and Theatre Artist', *Nineteenth Century Theatre & Film*, 33.1, pp. 39–59.
Pearson, Hesketh (1950), *The Last Actor-Managers*, London: Methuen.

Singleton, Brian (2004), *Oscar Asche, Orientalism, and British Musical Comedy*, Westport, CT: Praeger.
Singleton, Brian (2010), 'Narratives of Nostalgia: Oriental Evasions about the London Stage', in Charlotte M. Canning and Thomas Postlewait, eds, *Representing the Past: Essays in Performance Historiography*, Iowa City: University of Iowa Press, pp. 351–77.

9

AERIAL STAR

Lillian Leitzel's celebrity, agency and her performed femininity

Kate Holmes

Circus was one of the largest mass live entertainments of the early twentieth century and was an industry that secured its popularity through a number of female stars. These women's careers were not only established by the highest-profile circuses but also contributed to their success. Although circus has been the focus of numerous memoirs or popular histories, few recent layered historical analyses of this complex entertainment form exist. As such, the female performers who played such an important part in its mass popularity have largely faded from view.[1] In this chapter I explore and evaluate the work of the pre-eminent circus celebrity of the early twentieth century, Lillian Leitzel (1892–1931). Circus stars were household names who entertained international audiences, and as an aerialist Leitzel excelled in one of the two most popular disciplines in the circus, the other being equestrianism. As an industry, circus has always capitalised on women's labour, placing them in prominent positions, whether as members of troupes or as soloists, but in the 1920s female soloists featured in a number of international circuses as their highest-profile stars. These solo aerialists were distinguished from their colleagues within mixed gender troupes because they performed independent feats of bodily control, at a time when women were claiming a more active role for themselves more generally. While stage representations of women and the flesh they exposed were constrained by censorship,[2] female solo aerialists' performances were predicated on openly demonstrating their physical capability and their physical freedom.

The 1920s was a particularly interesting time in circus history in the USA and England because of the popularity of circus and changes in the industry. In America, the Ringling Bros and Barnum & Bailey Combined Show was touring the country with a Big Top tent capable of holding over 16,500 audience members for twice-daily performances. The American Big Top may have reached its peak capacity in the 1920s (Dahlinger Jr, 2008: 224; Davis, 2002: 293), but this was not to last, as the economic downturn that created the American Depression in the early 1930s would become a key factor in the demise of huge tenting circuses – those that display under canvas. By contrast, UK circus was entering a period of reinvigoration that continued until the 1960s, spearheaded by Bertram Mills Circus. Temporarily occupying London Olympia, this most significant of British 1920s circuses was capable of finding audiences of approximately 6,000 people, again twice daily during a Christmas season.[3] The most popular UK and American circuses were therefore large-scale enterprises that entertained mass audiences. Performers who appeared in circuses owned by Ringling and Mills benefited from significant levels of publicity and exposure that was central to the fashioning of their public images. This enabled the most popular performers to gain year-round employment by using the prestige gained in circus to secure seasonal and short-term contracts in related professional contexts: entertainments such as American vaudeville and European variety during the circus off-seasons. The interwar period was significant not just in terms of the popularity of circus, but also because it was arguably the last era when circus celebrities could globally draw upon such powerfully coordinated circus publicity to inspire the popular imagination.

'Queen of the Circus'

Perhaps the most surprising early twentieth-century circus star to have been forgotten by all but the most informed circus fans is the solo aerialist Lillian Leitzel, who earned the title 'Queen of the Circus'.[4] From 1915 until her death in 1931 Leitzel secured bookings with the most prestigious American circuses owned by the Ringling family.[5] Born Leopoldina Alitza Pelikan in Breslau, Germany in 1892, she used the German and Bohemian childlike diminutive of Alice, 'Leitzel', as her solo stage surname.[6] The choice of surname points to a facet of her performance style that combined dainty and girlish appearance with a modern assertive expression of femininity that included sexual agency. Throughout the 1920s Leitzel performed annually in America's largest circus, Ringling Bros and Barnum & Bailey Combined Show, as its premier performer. This engagement formed the spine around which she, and other premier Ringling–Barnum performers, secured international contracts that ensured continuous employment throughout the year. During her lifetime she gained preferential treatment from Ringling management backstage as well as in press and publicity, where her image and name were used heavily. She had a special clause in her contracts that secured her space, privacy and comfort when travelling across America with the circus, while her image was reproduced in souvenir programmes more frequently than that of any other performer.[7] Leitzel died at the height of her popularity as a result of an injury sustained in performance on 13 February 1931.[8] While her death gave her star image a notoriety that ensured that she is still remembered by some circus fans today, she was undoubtedly the most prominent circus artist of the 1920s.

What is particularly interesting about this diminutive performer is that her stardom derived from an endurance act that required considerable strength, at a time when demonstrations of female strength might conventionally be considered remarkable. Leitzel was among the first aerial stars to be heavily promoted for her endurance and athleticism at a time when sport and sports participation was becoming popular. What set her apart from her fellow female aerialists was her expert showmanship, which relied on a complex performance of femininity and balanced risk with skill to create the pleasurable *frisson* of excitement for audience members.[9] In this chapter, I focus on her expert performance of gender, because she challenged both nineteenth- and emerging early twentieth-century stereotypes of femininity, while gaining widespread popularity across the mainstream entertainments of circus, American vaudeville and European variety. Circus memoirs often centre her popularity on her crowd-pleasing feat of endurance – one that simultaneously emphasised her weightlessness and strength – but it was Leitzel's almost contradictory performance of her gender that was responsible for her success. Her star image is fascinating because not only did it represent her as the 'Queen' within the circus, but her international engagements were predicated on publicly presenting her as having control over her professional career.

Public autonomy

The pattern of engagements that female performers secured had significance for the fashioning of their public images. The largest circuses in both America and England were run by male impresarios: John and Charles Ringling (up until the latter's death in 1926) and Bertram Wagstaff Mills. Both chose to use marketing strategies that linked their identities to their circus and made them celebrities. The appearance of John Ringling at a European or American circus indicated that he was scouting for performers (North and Hatch, 2008: 122), while Bertram Mills Circus is said to have obtained its reputation from the fact that a member of the Mills family had personally vetted every act (Williamson, 1938: 10). On both sides of the Atlantic, these prestigious circuses were represented as deriving their quality standards from the personal curation of either John Ringling or Bertram Mills (and sons). The visible relationship between the male impresario's professional identity and the circus provides a wider structure through which female soloists' performances must be read. The very mobility that performers demonstrated by appearing across a range of international venue types complicates the manner in which female soloists were represented in male-managed circuses.

Leitzel's visible mobility confuses the subordinate relationship of the female performer to the male impresario, because audiences were not restricted to viewing their empowered acts of female strength in just the circus venue, but could also enjoy them in variety and vaudeville venues – the most illustrious of which were the London Palladium or the Palace in New York. Although these permanent venues were also managed by men, it is the fact that female acts appeared across such venues and across international locations that allows the perception that the most popular performers had some autonomy over their own careers: they were demonstrating their choice over where and when they performed.

Questions of female agency within male-managed entertainments are further complicated when the female star's celebrity is significant enough to claim a different or dominant position for her professional identity, as was the case for Lillian Leitzel. Leitzel may have been most closely associated with the Ringling Bros and Barnum & Bailey Combined Show because she appeared annually with them, and played only a single season with Bertram Mills Circus; however, there is a similarity in how Leitzel was depicted on both sides of the Atlantic. At Olympia in January 1922 the business manager Captain Pickering presented Bertram Mills with 'an illuminated address ... And a gold mounted, inscribed reading glass, and Miss LILLIAN LEITZEL, on behalf of the artists, presented Mrs Mills with a bouquet of mauve and pink tulips'.[10] This was probably a role she had been performing for the Ringling–Barnum circus in America for some time. Pasted into American circus fan Lorabel Laughlin Richardson's scrapbook is a cutting that describes an occasion when the Iowa Circus Fans Association hosted the Ringling–Barnum 'circus performers and executives'.[11] What is particularly interesting is that the scrapbook clipping outlines all of the individuals who spoke at the event. The article lists the representatives of the Circus Fans Association before the three members of Ringling staff who spoke at the event: John Ringling, Fred Bradna (Equestrian Director) and Lillian Leitzel. Here Leitzel's role as premier artist puts her in the position of performer-spokesperson with a public status that places her alongside the circus owner and management. In both situations it is Leitzel's job to speak or act on behalf of the performers alongside their management. Her celebrity status as 'Queen of the Circus' positioned her as more than simply a hired performer. Unlike film stars, she was not shackled to a particular studio system in a particular country. In professional terms, Leitzel's pre-eminent international popularity meant that she could publicly demonstrate both her star status and her mastery over her own career.

Despite being the most successful circus celebrity of her generation, as evidenced in her roles as performer representative, the primary sources left to enable us to reconstruct and describe Leitzel's act are fragmentary. This is partly because circus programmes were so packed that to provide full coverage of every act would have required unreasonably long newspaper reports, but more significantly perhaps, it is due to the difficulty of describing such embodied practices with language alone. In reconstructing Leitzel's performances, her extraordinary popularity has at least meant that snatches of publicity and press reports, photographs, costumes, film and memoir have survived to describe elements of her act. Although fragmentary, these sources can be used to historically reimagine her act with the benefit, here, of my own embodied experience as an amateur aerialist.

A remarkable act

Flanked by a maid and footman, Leitzel enters the tent to begin the first section of her act, described by memoir writers as an 'exquisite gymnastic turn' in which Leitzel demonstrated her 'artistry' (Pond, 1948: 124; North and Hatch, 2008: 184; Manning-Sanders, 1952: 242). As the circus band plays 'The Crimson Petal' waltz by Fred A. Jewell, which became closely associated with her act (Studwell et al., 1999: 9), she takes premier position centre ring. At less than five feet tall she appears small in comparison to her six-foot-tall footman. Her petite stature combined with her short frilled dress makes her appear dainty and exposes her body

28 Photograph of Lillian Leitzel hanging from Roman rings, 1925, edit of CWi 873 glass plate negative. Circus World Museum, Baraboo, WI, Harry Atwell.

– opening it up to a desiring gaze (Kline, 2008: 60–1; Bradna and Spence, 1953: 148). Her maid and footman assist her in removing the cloak or long transparent train that covers her shoulders, while she kicks off the high-heeled mules that protect her performance shoes from the ring (Bradna and Spence, 1953: 149; Taylor, 1956: 221).[12] Reaching for the rope, she flicks it seductively, holding it high with one hand and throwing the tail with the other to display her moving body. Leitzel then reaches high to grip the rope and pull her body up, curving her back over her hand. Reaching higher again, she kicks up and curves her body over again, propelling herself upwards. She continues to use this climbing technique, more usually associated with male performers due to the strength it required (Croft-Cooke and Meadmore, 1946: 65; Bradna and Spence, 1953: 149), until she reaches her Roman rings. Here she blows kisses to the crowd before reaching across to the first ring and then the second, until she is grasping both (O'Brien, 1959: 124).[13]

Hanging from her rings she begins the first main section of her act in earnest, using a combination of momentum, strength and deliberately graceful poses. She kicks her legs up and hooks them into the rings, pulling herself up to sit and look out at her audience. She hangs from one ring, kicking her feet up and curving her back over her hanging arm, stretching the free arm over her head to assist her balance. Pausing for a second she releases her body, letting it fall downwards before using the momentum at the bottom of the swing to kick up again – simultaneously appearing weightless while hinting at the strength required. The movements fit with the rise and fall of the waltz's music and rhythm. Hanging by one ring she extends one leg and points the other in a position reminiscent of the *retiré* in ballet, using momentum to spin her body and the swivel rigged into the equipment (Figure 28). Grasping both rings, she kicks her legs back and forth to propel her body over her head. She first performs a handstand made more difficult by the instability of using the rings as a base. She adds embellishment to her muscular control by kicking her feet together as she holds her body, inverted and parallel – obscuring the effort through this elaborately feminised display. Sometimes she drops from this position to begin her revolutions between her shoulders, and at other times she kicks her legs back and forth, driving her legs over her head to create the required momentum. Moving from her rings she reaches for her rope. Gripping it under her armpit she reaches downwards for the rope, gripping and releasing so that she appears to spin towards the earth until her toes reach the ground.[14]

The crowd wait expectantly as they anticipate the endurance feat that is said to have made her famous and that is at times denigrated by memoir writers as crowd-pleasing or 'common stunting' (Manning-Sanders, 1952: 242; North and Hatch, 2008: 184). While her maid arranges her hair and clothing and Leitzel pauses to look at the audience, the announcer frames her act, emphasising the 'test of endurance' (Pond, 1948: 124) and concluding with 'Miss Lillian Leitzel, the only living person to perform this feat!' (Kline, 2008: 209). As he finishes speaking she slips her wrist into the loop at the bottom of the planche rope required to perform her spectacular finale and swiftly travels upwards with elegantly pointed toes as property men haul on the free end of the rope.[15] As the pulley hits the plunger her body jerks and she begins to kick and scissor her feet back and forth. Simultaneously she pushes down on the rope, pushes her hips upwards and her head back, to begin the first planche turn revolution of her body around her wrist.[16]

For this finale the musical accompaniment changed to emphasise the spectacular nature of each turn. Towards the beginning of her career her planche turns were accompanied by Rimsky-Korsakov's *The Flight of the Bumblebee*, which added a sense of frenetic tension to the performance. From around 1925 this changed to a special arrangement by Ringling Bros and Barnum & Bailey bandmaster Merle Evans to the staccato 'The Dance of the Hours' from *La Gioconda* by Amilcare Ponchinelli (Bradna and Spence, 1953: 150). Heightening anticipation further, each revolution is accompanied by a strike of the bass drum and the announcer who encourages the audience to join together in counting Leitzel's progress through a movement that is far from smooth (O'Brien, 1959: 125). Her body slows as her head comes underneath it and her legs reach the apex at the top of the swing, forcing the rope to jerk. This jerkiness, in combination with continuous revolutions, is perhaps what led some to describe Leitzel's planche turns as 'violent' while also making her body 'whirl' (Taylor, 1956: 220).[17] Yet what is most engaging about her performance is the wide smile that accompanies a body that appears subject to jerky movements while whirling weightlessly free.[18]

One or two of these revolutions around the wrist would be considered extraordinary, but Leitzel performed around one hundred towards the beginning and sixty towards the end of her career, twice daily. The feat requires considerable core, arm and shoulder strength alongside the engagement of leg muscles. Part of the excitement of watching Leitzel derived from seeing how many of these planche turns she could or would perform in that particular performance. As she progressed through her many revolutions, the force of her movement was emphasised as her hair slowly unravelled and whirled with her body (Bradna and Spence, 1953: 150; Taylor, 1956: 220). Once she had completed her revolutions, the property men released her to the ground, slowing as she reached the earth so that her elegantly pointed toes could skim the sawdust before she alighted. Her choice to slowly alight, rather than speed towards the ground with force, diminished the apparent risk she demonstrated to audiences while it self-consciously emphasised her balletic appearance.

Performing femininity

Although much of the act itself might appear remarkable for its aerial virtuosity, what strongly emerges is Leitzel's complicated performance of her muscular acts within the frame of the 'feminine'. While the performance incorporates traditional markers of femininity, it is also built around the display of strength and an assertive modern expression. For Leitzel: 'Strength is not a matter of sex [...] It is purely a matter of power [...] It is a matter of nerves and muscles, irrespective of whether you are masculine or feminine.'[19] Such a statement indicates that Leitzel was aware of how she performed and of how she might negotiate gender.

What makes her performance of femininity particularly significant is that she was performing in the context of changing stereotypes of femininity. The 1920s was often presented in the popular press and through advertising as the era of the 'modern girl', known as the flapper in the UK and USA, but by the terms *garçonnes*, *moga*, *modeng*, *xiaojie*, schoolgirls, *kallege ladki*, vamps and *neue Frauen* in other national contexts (Barlow et al., 2005: 245). This remarkably widespread phenomenon extended, Søland suggests, 'across class lines, post-war female youths did in fact seem to understand and define themselves as a generation' (Søland, 2000: 13). The assertive modern girl was an evocative icon of the period who claimed a different femininity for herself across global and class boundaries – even if the precise expression varied according to these parameters (Søland, 2000: 17; Barlow et al., 2005; Kingsley Kent, 2009: 39–40; Melman, 1988). Examining Leitzel's performance of femininity in light of the idea of the 'modern girl' reveals striking similarities, but also differences that point to Leitzel's act pushing beyond the boundaries of this challenging new popular stereotype of modern femininity. Her performed femininity incorporated both older and modern expressions, allowing a radically muscular representation of femininity to appear within the mainstream.

Film stars such as Clara Bow and Louise Brooks epitomised the modern girl stereotype, embodying fun, physical activity and agency. These women speed, for example, through narratives that 'concern the flapper's pursuit of modern life – independent from parental and other authoritarian control – and a modern romance in which her defiant actions, unruly behavior, and daring dress are either obstacles or catalysts, or both' (Landay, 2002: 224). They have a role in defining their own futures, which to some extent reflects their status as being the first generation of women to have easier access to an independent income because of expanding work opportunities (Søland, 2000: 6; Kingsley Kent, 2009: 152). Wearing the latest fashions, they are frequently filmed laughing and enjoying themselves in energetic activities such as dancing. The active personas they present take advantage of one of the film star's biggest assets, the eyes, to challenge any simple designation of the film star as objectified. Lori Landay argues that their eyes demonstrate the ludic potential of comedy to disrupt objectification and, in Clara Bow's case, a powerful 'desiring female gaze that is so active we can see it reach across the frame' (Landay, 2002: 240). Not every woman would be prepared to risk the danger of being associated with such an uninhibited expression of the active modern girl as demonstrated by film stars, but many did aspire to this stereotype, self-fashioning an expression of it that made them feel 'modern'.

Although the modern girl was fashionable, her femininity was problematic for the older generation. Susan Kingsley Kent paints an evocative description of the 'problem':

> young women of virtually every class – called, derisively, 'flappers' – dressed in boyish fashions, cut their hair short, smoked cigarettes, drove cars, and generally pursued an active, adventurous lifestyle [...] Boyish women and effeminate men dominated the fashion pages of newspapers and magazines, representing the carefree, youth-orientated, pleasure-seeking, even hedonistic nature of the post-war generation sick and tired of a devastating war to which they had been unable to make a contribution; for others they constituted proof that society was in a complete state of disorder – disorder represented in gendered and sexualized terms. (Kingsley Kent, 2009: 39–40)

In striking contrast to the Victorian ideal of the 'Angel in the House' – representing the attributes of submissiveness, passivity or devotion to the men in their lives – these women were assertively claiming their right to enjoyment on whatever terms they could. This enjoyment included control over their own physically active bodies, with participation in exercise figuring as an essential part of women's engagement in modernity and the ideal of a fun-loving, vibrant modern girl (Søland, 2000: 48; Skillen, 2012: 752; Zweiniger-Bargielowska, 2011; Skillen, 2013). Fashions associated with this stereotype also hinted at an interest in sex through the exposure of arms and legs. These modern girls symbolised the proposition that a host of young women were beginning to take more control of their own lives than they ever had before.

Analysing Leitzel's performance in the context of such changing attitudes to femininity provides answers to some of the apparently contradictory expressions of femininity that appear within her act. There are plenty of examples of her assertiveness in returning the audience's gaze and demonstrating bodily control, but there are also examples of her drawing upon older ideals. Leitzel cleverly included enough conservative allusions within her expressions of femininity to be popular in the mainstream, while pushing at the boundaries of being acceptably modern.

Although what Leitzel was doing was a particularly complex performance of femininity, it should be noted that aerial performance as a form also suggests the sort of gender blurring that was causing some levels of social anxiety. This is because aerial action relies on both grace and strength, traditionally attributed as feminine and masculine respectively. The description of Leitzel's act above highlights the strength required to perform the planche turns and her handstand in the rings, but all aerial action requires the upper body to hold, push or pull the body into position. However, aerial movements do not just rely on strength, they are also made easier through the use of good technique that appears graceful by requiring tensed, extended and elongated muscles and the use of momentum created by movement. This has led Peta Tait to describe the aerialist's body as where 'double-gendering' occurs (Tait, 2005: 31). The combination of strength and movements that suggest extension contribute to aerial action appearing weightlessly graceful. Against the context of anxiety around blurring the boundaries of the sexes in both the USA and UK in the 1920s, this combination was instead a negotiation of gender that is, most usefully, seen as part of the wider cultural 'reframing' of femininity.

The relationship between grace and femininity in the 1920s is an interesting one because it evoked both modern and conservative femininity. Ballet is traditionally considered both graceful and feminine, primarily because technique gives the impression of 'weightless femininity' (Newey, 2013: 111). Some of the gestures, such as pointed toes and extended hands, are shared by ballet and aerial performance. Leitzel deliberately chose to emphasise these gestures and to reference ballet by adopting positions that were directly comparable: thus, when she spun beneath her rings, her choice of alighting on pointed toes, and her costume (described in detail below). Not only that, but the form itself implies weightlessness through the use of momentum to achieve positions. Weight is pushed outwards in one direction and slows as gravity and momentum equalise, giving the impression of a brief pause. The most extreme example of this in Leitzel's act was the planche turn, during which her body appeared to both instigate actions and to be subject to jerky movements beyond her control. At the same time as she was described by the announcer as the only person capable of performing the feat, she was also considered by her contemporaries to 'whirl' free of effort. Although Søland primarily describes the Norwegian articulation of the modern girl, her identification of three key elements of a modern physical style is relevant for Anglo-American contexts: 'physical self-confidence, a graceful feminine body language, and a certain "natural" ease' (Søland, 2000: 56). Grace might initially be identified as a traditional attribute of femininity in the 1920s for its allusions to weightless femininity, but it instead holds a dual position that spoke to both modern and conservative audiences in slightly different ways.

What is interesting is that this reframing strategy was being used to some extent by young women of the day in order to make their challenging fashions more acceptable. For example, short bobbed haircuts risked censure for appearing masculine or mannish, but young women who aspired to be modern girls allayed these claims by reframing such fashions as *different* expressions of femininity. In the case of short hair, this was reinscribed as feminine by adopting wavy hairstyles that meant the style could be distanced from masculine short hair. It was the

> clear stylistic differences between short hair for men and short hair for women [that] soothed critics, and gradually their opposition faded. With their confidence in the stability of sexual difference restored, some of the harshest opponents were even able to admit a few years later that they actually found short hair quite charming and attractive. (Søland, 2000: 40)

Read against this context, Leitzel's mixing of older and more modern expressions of femininity represents a similar negotiation of gender to that which young women were performing more widely. However, in Leitzel's case it allowed her to incorporate strength into her embodiment of femininity.

Leitzel's choice of being pulled into place by the property men is another example of reframing the modern as acceptable through elements considered traditional. This choice for her finale was a deliberate decision, because she had previously climbed up independently to reach her permanently rigged Roman rings. During the matinee performances when the tent was filled with light, these property men were visible and complicated her appearance of autonomy. At one moment she appeared subject to their action, yet at the same time these men would have appeared as no more than incidental subordinates carrying out a risky requirement of her act. It is interesting in the circus setting that the most conservative reading of this moment in her act was available during the matinee performances, while during the evening performances these men would probably have been invisible in the darkness. Even when a more modern reading is possible, where the property men are her subordinates, this is complicated by her 'regal' performance, making unusual use of her maid and footman and of publicity that designated her as circus 'aristocracy'. Analysing this further, a more 'modern' interpretation that allows for female agency and situates these men as her subordinates draws upon the authority of traditional social hierarchies to establish Leitzel's dominance within the circus.

Leitzel's choice to alight briefly before beginning the planche turns is a notable framing, as it demonstrates her modern self-confidence. In none of the reports of her contemporaries is there evidence of any other performer choosing to break up their short act (probably of around eight to ten minutes) into two such distinctive parts. Today this would also be an unusual choice in either traditional or corporate circus, where short acts are still performed as the norm.[20] Rather than being concerned that she might disrupt the pace of her act, Leitzel was sufficiently self-assured to consider that as the premier aerialist of her generation this would build anticipation for her signature trick. It also provided another opportunity to demonstrate her weightlessness as she sped towards the tent roof.

Such a modern attitude can also be seen in Leitzel's performance of enjoyment during the planche turns. Her performance style was very different to that of many of her contemporaries and to many aerialists working today. The experience of aerial performance is one where the convention is to hide pain as steel bars bruise limbs and ropes burn flesh. Feature articles devoted to Leitzel frequently emphasise the physical cost of her work, which included 'calluses … water blisters', 'Rope burns' and 'raw … hand[s]'.[21] Memoir writers describe a constant sore created by the friction of the planche rope cuff against her skin (Kline, 2008: 208; Bradna and Spence, 1953: 150; Taylor, 1956: 218–19). Rather than masking the pain of her aerial movement with a blank face or slightly disconcerting fixed smile, Leitzel's wide smile instead demonstrated her pleasure in her body's aerial action. This contributed to the illusory sense that Leitzel was weightless through her hiding of the true effort and pain of her aerial action, but more importantly, it demonstrated her enjoyment in her body's movements – much as the modern girl reportedly demonstrated her fun-loving attitude when undertaking more moderate exercise.

There was, however, also something inescapably sexual about the visible effects of the planche turns on Leitzel's body that hints at her sexual agency. Fred Bradna considered Leitzel to have deliberately unpinned her hair for effect during her feat (Bradna and Spence, 1953: 150). Hair is frequently conflated with female sexuality, and Leitzel's unravelling locks during the planche turns emphasised her femininity. Leitzel's performance relied on her athletic ability and stamina. Her physical activity caused her heart rate and body temperature to rise and her breathing to become more pronounced. On alighting from the rope she had loose hair, she was breathing hard and she would have appeared flushed to those watching from the seats closest to the ring or stage. Not only did her appearance open her up to a reading of sexualisation through comparisons to a body that had orgasmed, it also demonstrated Leitzel appearing precisely in control of her own sexual(ised) physique. Audience members with a clear sight of Leitzel could arguably not have missed the sexual connotations and possible comparisons to a post-coital female body. The descriptions of Clara Bow and Louise Brooks above suggest that in film women were increasingly being represented as being in control of selecting their partner, while Barlow et al. consider women at large to have been claiming more control over when and if they married (Barlow et al., 2005: 288). It is likely that some members of the audience would have sexualised Leitzel's body without acknowledging her active role in the encounter, but I consider her performance to have deliberately emphasised her enjoyment of her aerial movements, whether they left her open to being sexualised or not.

Dainty yet sexy costume

The complex performance of femininity is also apparent in Leitzel's costume choices. Two very different costumes remain in the Tegge Circus Archives, and their survival dates them to the end of her career: the first appears similar – although not identical – to those Leitzel was photographed wearing for circus publicity, while the second is startlingly different. These two costumes indicate that Leitzel made very specific choices about how to expose her body in different performance settings. The way in which Leitzel managed her bodily exposure demonstrates how important presenting her gendered femininity was within her performance register.

Photographs depicting Leitzel from around 1925[22] and the circus costume (Figure 29) demonstrate how she combined her apparently contradictory daintiness with sexualised display. Her costume in 1925 highlights her female form: her breasts, the prime signifiers of the female body, are covered by two large triangles of fabric that stretch over her

29 Lillian Leitzel's pink circus costume, *c.* 1925. From the collection of Timothy Noel Tegge/Tegge Circus Archives, Baraboo, WI, Timothy Tegge.

shoulders; her small waist is accentuated by a band that encircles it and includes the traditional feminine accessory of a flower; the skirt evokes a ballet tutu as light, chiffon-like fabric cascades and pleats over her hips; the shortness of the skirt exposes short trunks that elongate the apparent length of legs clothed in silk stockings; her feet are covered by shoes that also bear comparison to ballet shoes. Examination of both earlier and later photographs of Leitzel and the circus costume in the archive indicate that Leitzel's ballet-like skirt emerged around 1920 and remained a feature of her costume until her death in 1931.[23] This was a costume that sought to draw upon more conservative ideals of femininity through the references to ballet, the flower accessory and her choice of wearing long hair rather than cutting it fashionably short. It is these conservative elements that give an impression of daintiness, and even make the diminutive Leitzel appear almost doll-like. Yet there is clearly something modern in exposing arms and dressing legs in fashionable silk stockings. Like the act itself, her costume negotiated gender in a complex manner, presenting her body as conventionally dainty at the same time as it was sexualised by exposure.

Although the overriding impression of Leitzel's costume may have been one of girlishness, there is a sexualised tension related to the amount of flesh exposed. The shortness of Leitzel's skirt sexualised her body, exposing more leg than even the modern girl may have considered acceptable. The later circus costume demonstrates how Leitzel managed and developed this exposure throughout her career (Figure 29). This light pink costume is made of two parts linked at the back by faded and degraded elastic: the top half is formed of two triangles that would have covered her breasts but exposed her midriff; and again the bottom half is a combination of short trunks covered by a skirt which is this time much briefer. Sequins are sewn into both top and bottom, but most densely congregate around the waistband and the triangles that cover the breasts. The sides of the skirt are made of light fabric, but the central panel and the trunks underneath it are made of lace-like material that hints at exposing the body. Costume is separate from everyday wear and is acceptable provided that exposure fits within the conventions of the particular performance space. It was a safety requirement for aerialists to wear clothing that closely fitted arms and legs, or else exposed them. However, Leitzel went far beyond the normal conventions of circus costuming, and by the end of the 1920s was pioneering in the exposure of her midriff: her circus costume is designed to expose, as much as clothe, her body.

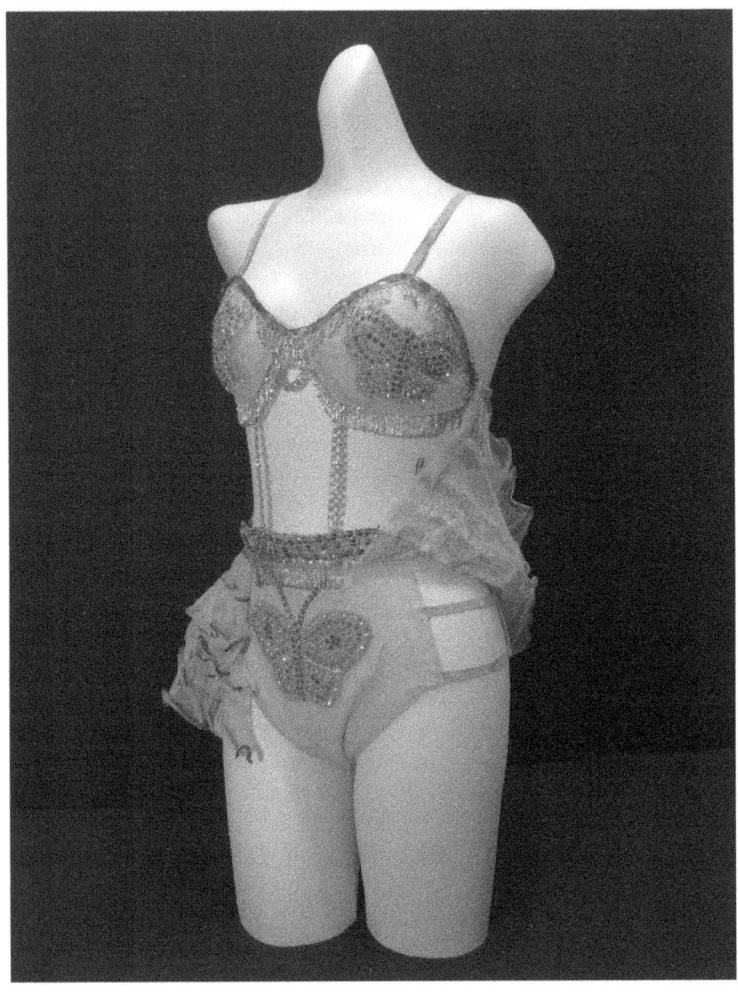

30 Lillian Leitzel's vaudeville costume, late 1920s. From the collection of Timothy Noel Tegge/Tegge Circus Archives, Baraboo, WI, Timothy Tegge.

The circus was not the only performance space in which Leitzel exposed most of her strong body. The second costume in the archive is strikingly brief and unlike any that I have seen her photographed wearing: it resembles less a short dress and more a bikini (Figure 30). Even if age has degraded the elastic that holds the top in place, it still does not seem strong enough for the costume to have retained its position during her violent planche turns, suggesting that a body stocking must have been worn underneath. Regardless, Leitzel's body would have been startlingly on display, with her sex emphasised due to the positioning of the glittering butterflies over breasts and in the proximity of the crotch. The slight ruffles of fabric at the hips evoke the circus ballet skirt but were designed to expose bare hips when her body was inverted. This is clearly a costume that sells sex more overtly within another performance context. The most likely answer is that this costume was one Leitzel used in vaudeville or variety spaces where she would have appeared alongside the 1920s showgirls and chorus girls who exposed more of their bodies than in the circus (Latham, 2000: 109). In the context of vaudeville's more significant exposure, Leitzel made the decision to make her body appear closer to nudity in order to succeed.

What makes this exposure unusual is the body that was exposed and presented as desirable. Aerial practices such as Leitzel's require a strong upper body that leads to increased muscle mass. Although Leitzel was always described as feminine, her developed upper body was compared to that of a 'middle-weight boxer' or 'professional wrestler' (Verney, 1978: 202; Butler, quoted in Taylor, 1956: 219). Not only does this depict her body as muscular, it also indicates that such muscularity was associated with masculinity, as boxers and wrestlers were almost exclusively male professionals in the 1920s. Here the tension regarding sex, exposure and agency becomes apparent: Leitzel deliberately positioned her body as a sexual object in order to perform sexual agency – much in the same way that modern girls were exposing their limbs in fashion-wear as well as claiming more sexual choice for themselves. What is radical here, perhaps, is that this woman enjoyed her strength and muscularity and deliberately chose to sexualise her body via its unusual muscle mass. Leitzel's significant bodily exposure was a matter of pride; she gloried in her muscle in the moment of performance rather than hiding it from view – positioning a muscular female body as desirable within a mainstream popular entertainment.

Agency and performance style

It may seem quite a bold statement to claim that Leitzel was positioning herself as having sexual agency through her bodily exposure, when a simplistic reading would position her as a passive sexualised object under the control of a desiring gaze. However, Leitzel's performance of femininity was always a series of contradictions: she presented herself as conservative yet challengingly modern, dainty yet unabashedly sexual. As with so much surrounding Leitzel, the key to understanding the paradox is to consider how the act was framed or performed. In performing the public face and unconventional body of Lillian Leitzel, she performed herself as being in control. Not only was she in control of the sexualised encounter, her control had the power to disrupt the circus itself, without Leitzel suffering any future consequences other than an increase in popularity.

The fullest written accounts of Leitzel's act appear in memoirs, and when subjected to analysis these inevitably highlight these contradictions in her performance persona. Robert Lewis Taylor's description of the opening moments of her act highlights how daintiness and sexual *and* professional power coexisted within her sophisticated performance of femininity. It is worth quoting at length here.

> The house lights faded, a single spot played over the arena, then caught her up, as if by surprise, at the entrance. When she walked or was carried into the center ring, the snare drums accompanied her in a long roll and a cymbal crashed as she finally bowed, very slightly, as royalty might incline the head. The star herself was usually costumed in a sequined brassière, with a bare midriff, and over them a short, sheer skirt. Altogether, Miss [Jennie] Rooney [an aerial colleague of Leitzel's] says, the effect was sexy … It was at this point of entrance that Miss Leitzel was supposed to throw off an ankle-length cape she wore in, kick aside a pair of gold-colored mules, and buckle down to work. But she seldom did, and therein lay a rub, for a circus performance runs on a kind of rail-road-tight schedule. She savored and tasted her power. She stood at ease and looked around, establishing the wonderfully electric connection between herself and her audience. She would giggle slightly, and people would break into roars of sympathetic laughter. With an arch look that seemed to mean, Miss Rooney felt, 'I've noticed *you* in particular; anything can happen,' she would kick-off her mules slowly, as if in a prelude to something intensely personal, and men, quite literally, often started down out of the stands. (Taylor, 1956: 221)

Taylor's writing style is somewhat extravagant, but what is particularly fascinating about this excerpt is the way in which 'girlish' attributes, sexualised display and sexual power are all identified. Leitzel giggles girlishly and is sometimes carried into the ring; the effect of her bodily exposure is sexual, but she is in control of the sexualised encounter because she chooses her mate. In fact, Jennie Rooney's statement that Leitzel's look meant 'anything can happen' suggests that she expected to be a key instigator rather than a subordinate in any sexual activity. Replace Leitzel for a moment with Louise Brooks or Clara Bow and the sexual assertiveness and choosing of a partner would perhaps be appropriate. Leitzel may have appeared dainty, but her performed assertive sexual agency cannot be in doubt.

It is also interesting that Taylor remarks on Leitzel's power and that he identifies this as related to sexual agency, her electric connection to her audience and her ability to disrupt the circus schedule. This performance of femininity included within it strong elements of modern self-assurance, which might also be considered an attribute of good performance technique, and is precisely what allowed her to represent herself as being in control of the circus. The American Ringling Bros and Barnum & Bailey management themselves had accorded Leitzel the prestige and honour of having action stopped in all other rings and on all other stages during her performance. This allowed her performance of control to appear unchallenged by any other action. Taylor reports moments, other than during her entry, when Leitzel would deliberately extend the duration of her act, describing how she would 'rock gently back and forth for several minutes, smiling, [and] waving [at the top of the rope she used to climb up to her rings] ... The audience was delighted and encouraged her to disrupt the show as long as she pleased' (Taylor, 1956: 216). By performing the assertive role of diva, Leitzel demonstrated the agency that her glamorous celebrity conferred. The Ringling–Barnum circus emphasised the logistics required to transport a circus of its scale in publicity, and a few extra minutes of performance would have delayed the striking of the Big Top and movement on to the next city. Against this context, Leitzel's disruptive power is significant and evidences the ways in which she could publicly disrupt the entire circus logistics itself. The fact that Taylor treats this as commonplace indicates that there were no adverse consequences for Leitzel. This performance of female power was central to her success – as circus 'royalty' Leitzel could do what she pleased, provided her audience were 'delighted' by the disruption.

Leitzel's act and the way in which she performed her femininity was remarkable. The planche turns performed as an endurance act, in particular, were an extreme feat of strength with or without any gendered framing. The way in which Leitzel performed her femininity by reference to its various expressions designated her personality as feminine, reframing the planche turn finale as a remarkable feminine demonstration of strength. The planche turns may have represented an exhibition of 'masculine' strength and endurance, but Leitzel also performed her complex femininity *through* them – challenging a reading that gendered them as purely masculine. This argument explains how Leitzel turned an act of strength into part of the female repertoire, with women famously copying Leitzel's trademark planche turns in the latter years of her career and soon after her death – Mickey King, Irma Ward and Janet May (Kline, 2008: 213).

Leitzel was, however, the only performer who could, and did, choose to challenge circus management through her refusal to consider circus logistics before the success of her own act. The paradox was that in order to get away with such disruptive acts she needed to be the most popular circus star, yet her popularity relied on such performances of power. In the moment of performance Leitzel positioned herself as having choice over whether to disrupt the entire Ringling–Barnum circus. Lillian Leitzel was the Queen of the Circus in part because she performed such complex representations of femininity. Her success and that of her female soloist colleagues relied on the balancing act they performed between reflecting progressive modern stereotypes of femininity, while including just enough conservative allusions that modern and traditionalist readings could coexist and, in some cases, even be challenged. Through her extraordinary physical abilities, Leitzel's dainty yet agency-infused performances of female sexuality were cultural contradictions on which her success relied – her act expressing and reflecting cultural anxieties surrounding changing stereotypes of femininity, as well as feeding on a public fascination with physical feats. Solo female aerialists as a whole were performing similar acts of gender negotiation as those of modern girls within wider society, by presenting muscular bodies as feminine and glamorous. Female aerial soloists were public figures who popularised strong and active female bodies within mainstream culture. Today we may have some reservations about Leitzel's decision to use the tool of sexual desirability within a patriarchal system. However, through this strategy she claimed a more dominant role for herself by performing female agency at a time when this was still controversial, and by her publicised control over her professional career. Not only that, by appearing as a sexually desirable *and* muscular woman in the mainstream entertainments of circus, vaudeville and variety, she almost certainly contributed to physical strength becoming more acceptable as a form of performed femininity.

Notes

1. Those notable exceptions who designate aerialists as stars, such as Helen Stoddart (2000: 56–7) and Peta Tait (2005, 2007), do not, however, explore issues of stardom.
2. For a detailed discussion of how representations of women were restricted by censorship in the early twentieth century, see de Jongh (2001: 35–81).
3. Alfredo Codona, correspondence with Billy Adolph, 4 January 1926, Codona Family Collection, Tegge Circus Archives, p. 1.
4. The origin of this title is hard to ascertain, as 'Queen' is used by performers and management alike to describe Leitzel in their memoirs, as well as in press and publicity placed by the Ringling–Barnum circus, obscuring the origin of the accolade (Kline, 2008: 208; North and Hatch, 2008; 'Circus Has Own Aristocracy – Marriage of Lillian Leitzel and Clyde Ingalls Reveals Rigid Rules in the Sawdust Ring Profession', 7 February 1920, T-CLP Leitzel, Lillian, Billy Rose Collection, New York Public Library).
5. Robert L. Parkinson, research note, 1971, CWM Small Collections, Leitzel, Lillian – letters and other documents, Circus World Museum, Baraboo, Wisconsin.
6. Alfred Pelikan, correspondence with Karl Kae Knecht, 20 February 1931, CWM Small Collections, Leitzel, Lillian – letters and other documents, Circus World Museum, Baraboo, Wisconsin.
7. Ringling Brothers, Artists's Contract and Release with Lillian Leitzel, 11 October 1916, CW Employment Contracts, Ringling Brothers Small Collections Box 2; Ringling Bros and Barnum & Bailey, *Ringling Bros and Barnum and Bailey Combined Shows The Greatest Show on Earth Daily Review Magazine*, 1927, tenting/road edition, CWM Mss3, Circus World Museum, Baraboo, Wisconsin.
8. Leitzel fell at the Valencia Music Hall in Copenhagen when one of the swivels of her Roman rings snapped as she was coming out of a handstand. She died in hospital a few days later, on 15 February 1931. Maud Clemings, correspondence with Fred and Melba Pelikan, 15 February 1931, CWM Small Collections, Leitzel, Lillian – letters and other documents, Circus World Museum, Baraboo, Wisconsin.
9. For more on my argument about how risk and skill contributed to aerial celebrity and were gendered in the 1920s and early 1930s, see Holmes (2016: 124–54).
10. 'Olympia Circus – Presentation to Captain Bertram Mills', *The Times*, 20 January 1922, p. 7.
11. 'Governor Sips Punch with Performers and Other Dignitaries', no date, Lorabel Laughlin Richardson's scrapbook, Tegge Circus Archives.
12. See film of Lillian Leitzel's act, no date, Codona home videos, Tegge Circus Archives.

13   Ibid.
14   Dan DeBaugh, *Dan DeBaugh Presents The World's Largest Circus in Action: Ringling Bros and Barnum & Bailey in the Nineteen-Twenties*, 1928–33, and film of Lillian Leitzel's act, no date, Codona home videos, Tegge Circus Archives.
15   Planche refers to a whole series of moves that rely on the body appearing straight despite the effort of gravity – it means 'board' in French. The climbs described earlier as mainly performed by men are actually a type of planche climb. The planche rope is a type of rope that allows the planche turns to be completed and is only used for this trick. People performing this trick today would probably only do one or two as part of a wider act on rope or straps.
16   P. H. Paulinetti, 'The World's Greatest Gymnast', *Strength – The Magazine of Good Health*, April 1923, p. 41, Tegge Circus Archives; DeBaugh, *Dan DeBaugh Presents The World's Largest Circus in Action*; and film of Lillian Leitzel's act, no date, Codona home videos, Tegge Circus Archives.
17   'The Star Act', *Harrisburg Patriot*, 27 June 1911, p. 10.
18   See the photograph by Harry Atwell of Lillian Leitzel performing a one-arm planche, CWi 1031, glass plate negative, 1930, Circus World Museum, Baraboo, Wisconsin.
19   C. E. Williams, 'Strength is Life Says Lillian Leitzel, Circus Queen', *Physical Culture*, July 1923, p. 92, Steve Wennestrom Collection, SW-Bx6F52, HJ Lutcher Stark Center for Physical Culture and Sports.
20   This is not true of contemporary circus because performances are generally longer in duration. Rather than existing as separate acts, contemporary circus seeks to unify the performance through a theme or narrative. It might best be imagined as a combination of traditional circus and physical theatre and less frequently, live art.
21   Basil Queed, 'How'd You Like To Be In My Place? Leitzel, the Circus Queen, Tells Why She Longs to Be a Typist', *Liberty*, 5 June 1926, p. 51, CWM Small Collections, Leitzel, Lillian, clippings, Circus World Museum, Baraboo, Wisconsin.
22   Although listed as taken in 1928 by Circus World Museum, I date these images to around 1925 (including Figure 28). The series of black-and-white images taken by Harry Atwell show Leitzel in the same white or light-coloured costume, suggesting that they were taken during the same shoot. One of the images appears edited in the 1925 New York *Ringling Bros and Barnum and Bailey Combined Shows The Greatest Show on Earth Daily Review Magazine*.
23   See also Daguerre, photograph of Lillian Leitzel telling off a doll, 1920, Lillian Leitzel portraits 8 x 10, CWM Small Collections, Circus World Museum, Baraboo, Wisconsin.

References

Barlow, Tani E., Madeleine Yue Dong, Uta G. Poiger, Priti Ramamurthy, Lynn M. Thomas and Eve Alys Weinbaum (2005), 'The Modern Girl around the World: A Research Agenda and Preliminary Findings', *Gender and History*, 17.2, pp. 245–94.

Bradna, Fred, and Hartzell Spence (1953), *The Big Top: My Forty Years with the Greatest Show on Earth*, London: Hamish Hamilton.

Croft-Cooke, Rupert, and W. S. Meadmore (1946), *The Sawdust Ring*, Watford: Odhams Press.

Dahlinger Jr, Fred (2008), 'Afterword', in Henry Ringling North and Arlen Hatch, *The Circus Kings – Our Ringling Family Story*, Gainesville, FL: University Press of Florida, pp. 384–400.

Davis, Janet M. (2002), *Circus Age: Culture and Society under the American Big Top*, Chapel Hill, NC: University of North Carolina Press.

De Jongh, Nicholas (2001), *Politics, Prudery and Perversions – The Censoring of the English Stage 1901–1968*, London: Methuen.

Holmes, C. J. (2016), 'Aerial Stars: Femininity, Celebrity and Glamour in the Representations of Female Aerialists in the UK and USA in the 1920s and Early 1930s', PhD thesis, University of Exeter.

Kingsley Kent, Susan (2009), *Aftershocks. Politics and Trauma in Britain, 1918–1931*, Basingstoke: Palgrave Macmillan.

Kline, Tiny (2008), *Circus Queen & Tinker Bell – the Memoir of Tiny Kline*, ed. Janet M. Davis, Urbana, IL: University of Illinois Press.

Landay, Lori (2002), 'The Flapper Film: Comedy, Dance, and Jazz Age Kinaesthetics', in Diane Negra and Jennifer M. Bean, eds, *A Feminist Reader in Early Cinema*, Durham, NC: Duke University Press, pp. 221–48.

Latham, Angela J. (2000), *Posing a Threat: Flappers, Chorus Girls, and Other Brazen Performers of the American 1920s*, Middletown, CT: Wesleyan University Press.

Manning-Sanders, Ruth (1952), *The English Circus*, London: T. Werner Laurie.

Melman, Billie (1988), *Women and the Popular Imagination in the Twenties: Flappers and Nymphs*, Basingstoke: Palgrave Macmillan.

Newey, Katherine (2013), 'Fairies and Sylphs: Femininity, Technology and Technique', in Kara Reilly, ed., *Theatre, Performance and Analogue Technology*, Basingstoke: Palgrave Macmillan, pp. 97–116.

North, Henry Ringling, and Arlen Hatch (2008), *The Circus Kings – Our Ringling Family Story*, Gainesville, FL: University Press of Florida.

O'Brien, Esse Forrester (1959), *Circus Cinders to Sawdust*, San Antonio, TX: The Naylor Company.

Pond, Irving K. (1948), 'The Lovely Leitzel', in Rupert Croft-Cooke, ed., *The Circus Book*, London: Sampson Low, pp. 123–5.

Skillen, Fiona (2012), '"Woman and the Sport Fetish": Modernity, Consumerism and Sports Participation in Inter-war Britain', *The International Journal of the History of Sport*, 29.5, pp. 750–65, http://dx.doi.org/10.1080/09523367.2012.67 5206.

Skillen, Fiona (2013), *Women, Sport and Modernity in Interwar Britain*, Bern: Peter Lang.

Søland, Brigitte (2000), *Becoming Modern: Young Women and the the Reconstruction of Womanhood in the 1920s*, Princeton, NJ: Princeton University Press.

Stoddart, Helen (2000), *Rings of Desire: Circus History and Representation*, Manchester: Manchester University Press.

Studwell, William Emmett, Charles P. Conrad and Bruce R. Schueneman (1999), *Circus Songs: An Annotated Anthology*, London: Haworth Press.

Tait, Peta (2005), *Circus Bodies: Cultural Identity in Aerial Performance*, London: Routledge.

Tait, Peta (2007), 'Circus Performers as Action Hero: Codona and Leitzel', in Robert Sugarman, ed., *The Many Worlds of Circus*, Newcastle: Cambridge Scholars Publishing, pp. 37–45.

Taylor, Robert Lewis (1956), *Center Ring: The People of the Circus*, New York: Doubleday.

Verney, Peter (1978), *Here Comes the Circus*, London: Paddington Press.

Williamson, A. Stanley (1938), *On the Road with Bertram Mills*, London: Chatto and Windus.

Zweiniger-Bargielowska, I. (2011), 'The Making of a Modern Female Body: Beauty, Health and Fitness in Interwar Britain', *Women's History Review*, 20.2, pp. 299–317.

Archives

Circus World Museum, Baraboo, Wisconsin

Harry Atwell, Lillian Leitzel performing a one-arm planche, CWi 1031, glass plate negative, 1930

Maud Clemings, correspondence with Fred and Melba Pelikan, 15 February 1931, CWM Small Collections, Leitzel, Lillian – letters and other documents

Daguerre, photograph of Lillian Leitzel telling off a doll, 1920, Lillian Leitzel portraits 8 x 10, CWM Small Collections

Robert L. Parkinson, research note, 1971, CWM Small Collections, Leitzel, Lillian – letters and other documents

Alfred Pelikan, correspondence with Karl Kae Knecht, 20 February 1931, CWM Small Collections, Leitzel, Lillian – letters and other documents

Basil Queed, 'How'd You Like To Be In My Place? Leitzel, the Circus Queen, Tells Why She Longs to Be a Typist', *Liberty*, 5 June 1926, pp. 49–52, CWM Small Collections, Leitzel, Lillian, clippings

Ringling Brothers, Artists's Contract and Release with Lillian Leitzel, 11

AERIAL STAR 241

October 1916, CW Employment Contracts, Ringling Brothers Small Collections Box 2

Ringling Bros and Barnum & Bailey, *Ringling Bros and Barnum and Bailey Combined Shows The Greatest Show on Earth Daily Review Magazine*, 1925, New York (Madison Square Garden) edition, CWM Mss3

Ringling Bros and Barnum & Bailey, *Ringling Bros and Barnum and Bailey Combined Shows The Greatest Show on Earth Daily Review Magazine*, 1927, tenting/road edition, CWM Mss3

HJ Lutcher Stark Center for Physical Culture and Sports, University of Texas, Austin

C. E. Williams, 'Strength is Life Says Lillian Leitzel, Circus Queen', *Physical Culture*, July 1923, pp. 29–32, 92–3, Steve Wennestrom Collection, SW-Bx6F52

New York Public Library

'Circus Has Own Aristocracy – Marriage of Lillian Leitzel and Clyde Ingalls Reveals Rigid Rules in the Sawdust Ring Profession', 7 February 1920, T-CLP Leitzel, Lillian, Billy Rose Collection

Tegge Circus Archives, Baraboo, Wisconsin, http://www.teggecircusarchives.org

Alfredo Codona, correspondence with Billy Adolph, 4 January 1926, Codona Family Collection

DeBaugh, Dan, *Dan DeBaugh Presents The World's Largest Circus in Action: Ringling Bros and Barnum & Bailey in the Nineteen-Twenties*, 1928–33, film

Film of Lillian Leitzel's act and behind the scenes, no date, Codona home videos

'Governor Sips Punch with Performers and Other Dignitaries', no date, Lorabel Laughlin Richardson's scrapbook

P. H. Paulinetti, 'The World's Greatest Gymnast', *Strength – The Magazine of Good Health*, April 1923, front cover and pp. 30, 37–42, 74

10

Ellen Terry

The art of performance and her work in film

Katharine Cockin

The reputation of Ellen Terry (1847–1928) as an actor is associated with her stage performances at the Lyceum Theatre, London from 1878 to 1902, and in Shakespearean roles, notably Beatrice, Portia and Lady Macbeth. However, in 1916 she ventured into popular cultural performances in film and music hall. It is her film acting at the time of the rise of the film industry in the 1920s in particular which is considered here as a new dimension to the historiography of Terry's career. Nina Auerbach's portrayal of Terry as a 'player in her time' (1987) is further complicated because that 'time' coincided with the new era of film. Terry was more than the sum of her stage roles and she was fully aware of the value of her reputation in the commercial international market of theatrical tours and related merchandising. She privately mocked the publicity photograph depicting her as feminine subordinate under Henry Irving's dominant leadership by annotating it 'Naughty girl!' and her amusement was justified, given her discrete financial involvement in Irving's Lyceum Theatre and the power this vested in her.[1]

Ellen Terry's film appearances offer new insights into her performance work. They demonstrate her motivation to diversify from theatre into film, her willingness to adapt creatively and explore a new medium and reach a new audience. This chapter explores some of the contacts Terry made in the new film industry and how that industry used the Ellen Terry brand and its associated cultural prestige to enhance the potential circulation of films in a post-war period of reconstruction in which Englishness had a transatlantic value. Much of Ellen Terry's paid work in her later years has been interpreted as an attempt by mother and daughter to sustain the extended family income (Steen, 1962: 336). Terry's correspondence reveals indeed that the opportunities presented by the wide appeal of film promised greater commercial success (see Cockin, 2010–15). Although financially unable to retire, Terry was not solely concerned with the much-needed income her film roles brought. She was interested in new technologies generally and specifically in the aesthetic potential of the new medium of film.

With her devoted following and international reputation, Terry was well placed to move into film. Like other stage actors of her generation, she obtained film roles on the basis of her earlier successes in theatre, but she was slower to get involved than Sarah Bernhardt, for instance, who had played Hamlet in a short film as early as 1900 (Gottlieb, 2010). Terry was sceptical about plans to experiment with theatrical productions which were neither financially sound nor informed by a thorough understanding of the likely audience served by the particular theatre venue.[2] Her private correspondence has revealed extensive evidence of a thoughtful and sustained approach to her acting roles, the extent to which she researched and responded to advice and her involvement in the overall aesthetic design of the production. This thoughtfulness also applied to her professional film work.

As one of the performers associated with the 'crossover between theatre and cinema' (Gledhill, 2003: 11), Ellen Terry also brought a reputation as a 'pictorial' performer, exemplifying 'a pictorial style of acting [in which performers made] of themselves living pictures' (Booth, 1986: 83). With reference to Graham Robertson's recollection of Terry's appeal, Michael R. Booth notes the tendency of critics to respond to Terry's performance in the context of artwork, especially that of the Pre-Raphaelite movement. These self-presentations were neither entirely self-directed nor homogeneous. The pictorial mode lent itself to the conceptualisation of performance in a series of frozen moments or tableaux amenable to the aesthetic of film.[3] These pictorial associations also tended to be conventional in gender terms and proved to be a commercial success with the audiences that were drawn to the lavish productions at the Lyceum Theatre. However, there is agency in this feast for the eyes: Terry was prepared to serve herself up for the audience's gaze. Her popularity in conventionally feminine roles did not deter others from identifying her as a role model for female emancipation. The 'Womanly Woman' stage role contrasted with the life she lived offstage; in many ways the one paid for the other. She was also associated for some with the latest figures of female independence and transgression: the New Woman and the Freewoman.[4] Although Terry was financially independent, her economic circumstances fluctuated and she had many dependants. So she had good reason to be cautious about the commercial success of her ventures and could not afford to court a reputation for the vulgar or controversial. As long as it was appropriate for the typical audiences of the theatre she was working for, she was always willing to embrace experimentation.

It is therefore perhaps not surprising that, at a later stage of her career, she was more open-minded than many of her contemporaries as to the viability and aesthetic potential of the new medium of moving pictures. The popularity of film and the consequent development of this new sector of the entertainment industry created new opportunities for work, but posed a threat to some established stage actors who associated it with a popular, commercial rather than artistic medium. In this regard, for instance, Ellen Terry was of a different opinion than her contemporary Madge Kendal, as recalled by George Bernard Shaw:

> [Kendal] talked so well and so continually that she never listened, and consequently never learnt anything except her stage parts, with the result that to the day of her quite recent death she spoke of Irving as a ridiculous young pretender, and of the cinema as a vulgar penny gaff with which no self-respecting player could possibly be connected.[5]

Shaw implied that Terry (unlike Kendal) was prepared to listen, learn and adapt herself to new performance challenges. His respect for Terry's breadth of knowledge of the theatrical arts is demonstrated by his extensive consultation with her on the potential difficulties of staging his own plays. Nevertheless, for many actors there were uncertainties about the extent to which the transition from one medium to the other might be achieved successfully. In film the actor's relationship with the audience was fundamentally changed, and new interactions were required as entrepreneurial roles emerged in the expanding fields of film production and marketing.

Actors adapted their acting style for film, and when stage plays were adapted for film significant changes, even additional characters, were sometimes introduced. For instance, in 1916 the film adaptation of A. W. Pinero's *The Second Mrs Tanqueray* included a prequel, involving the first Mrs Tanqueray, in a new introductory scene. The programme provides a detailed description of these alterations, apparently made with the agreement of the author.[6] It seems that cinema audiences were presumed to need more prefatory or contextual information with a clear and coherent sequence of determining events in order to make sense of the plot. One such addition, in 1920, was Terry's role as 'the Widow Bernick' in the film adaptation of Ibsen's *The Pillars of Society*.⁷

Ellen Terry's third husband, James Carew, had found little opportunity for acting in British theatres, but after a number of silent features he became a regular in films directed by Cecil Hepworth and Fred Paul.⁸ Carew was so successful in the film industry that by July 1920 Terry was confident that he had relevant networks to use in order to promote the sale of her jewellery. She wrote: 'If you know where Douglas Fairbanks is to be found, do get him to go to the sale of my few Jewels at Christie's & buy something for his Mary & do ask <u>any other</u> <u>very rich</u> people you are acquainted with, to go & do likewise'.⁹ In this letter to Carew, Terry mentioned the suitability of specific items based on her own knowledge of other film actors' work:

> Did you see Gertrude E. in "The Eyes of Youth" – She was <u>extraordinarily</u> good in it – now <u>one</u> of my things which are to be sold, is a wonderful snake necklace Indian work – enamel & gold – Just the thing # for Gertrude in that Play! – When she acts the <u>wicked singer</u> – (or Actress) I'll let you know when the Sale is to come off at Christie's = & send you 2 or 3 Catalogues ---
> The young Americans love pretty things, & are, most of them, very well off – Is <u>Miss Laurette Taylor</u> wealthy? – if so do send to her – I don't know her personally – but I love her <u>on the Stage</u> as "Peg o'my Heart" she was just a delight = Do your best <u>please</u> Jim to make some of your friends buy <u>something</u> "that once belonged to Ellen Terry" = <u>Look up the Fairbanks if you can</u> = Sale in about 3 weeks = (or 2 may be – !) It is lovely down here – I hope you are well – Love from Nell
> Perhaps they will buy The Farm!!¹⁰

At the time of her letter, Terry's financial circumstances had reached a critical point where she was obliged to sell her possessions. Four years earlier, when she made her first film performance, Terry was particularly driven by financial problems to seek whatever employment opportunities were available:

> I shd not have done this hard work in my old age, but <u>I</u> <u>had</u> <u>to</u> – !!! to meet my responsibilities – & I thank God I found work to do – it was <u>really</u> <u>Providential</u> in coming my way = & I hope before long to get more employment of the same kind =
> Now if only Queen Alexandra wd Command a performance of it – it <u>might</u> make me a rich woman – – Even now = Of course I've very little time now to look forward to, & I <u>must</u> <u>work</u> to the end = .¹¹

Having accepted that retirement was out of the question, Terry was fully aware of her role in sustaining the livelihood of her family and their dependants. So Terry's film performances were self-consciously designed for commercial consumption and the related financial benefits this would bring.

From *Her Greatest Performance* to wartime work on screen

Terry's first film role was auspiciously entitled *Her Greatest Performance* (1916). Terry's nephew, Denis Neilson-Terry, and her daughter, Edith Craig, appeared with her in this film. It was produced by Fred Paul for the Ideal Film Company, whose managers, Harry and Simon Rowson, were described by Terry as 'delightful chaps – kind – & keen'.[12] From the outset, Terry was working with the British leaders of the new industry. Over the next decade, Simon Rowson was to become a highly influential expert on the film industry.[13] The extant footage from *Her Greatest Performance* gives an insight into the serious approach of the film-maker to social commentary. It shows a scene of squalid circumstances, where Edith Craig as the dresser to the famous actress is seen wretchedly moving about in a state of restless anguish.

Her Greatest Performance was marketed by the New York company Cosmofotofilm, together with three other British films, *The Lyons Mail*, *The Vicar of Wakefield* and *Lady Windermere's Fan*, guaranteeing 'handsome distribution profits' based on the 'stars and plays whose names are household words wherever the English language is spoken' (quoted in Slide, 2005: 10). In this illustrious list, which included Sir John Hare, Irene Rooke and H. B. Irving, Ellen Terry's name appears in confirmation that her brand had continued to hold its value in the international marketing of film distribution. Anthony Slide notes that it was on the basis of these five stars that *The Bohemian Girl* (1922), directed by Harley Knoles, was also marketed by the American Releasing Corporation, and that it had 'reputation values and drawing power over millions of Americans' (Slide, 2005: 10). Terry's film work therefore successfully reached a transatlantic audience at a time when competition was extremely fierce.

For Terry, *Her Greatest Performance* was one job in a very busy schedule:

> I have been overworking myself frightfully – First in acting here, there & everywhere for the dear Imperial Troops, & then in accepting an engagement to act for the Cinema – which by the way proved very interesting

to me = Edy acted with me – & my brother <u>Fred's</u> boy Dennis Neilson Terry – & for a month we "<u>went at it</u> hammer & tongs –" & it's a success they say.¹⁴

The acting techniques in *Her Greatest Performance* were different from customary stage conventions. Terry was surprised to find film acting technically easier since she was not required to use her always vulnerable voice. The experience of film acting constituted a different order of reality for her: 'Altho' after the *<u>real</u>* acting <u>on the stage</u> where the only <u>real</u> difficulty *<u>begins</u>* <u>with</u> <u>the</u> *<u>Voice</u>*, it seemed to me mere childs [*sic*] play = & not <u>acting</u> at all.'¹⁵ In practical terms, she was overwhelmed by the intensity of the long hours and the oppressiveness of the studio environment:

> All the same it was precious fatigueing [*sic*] – The light was blinding, & gave me sever [*sic*] headaches nearly all the time – & every scrap of air was shut out of the Studio – then for one month the hours were from 10 until 6 in the evening – altho' there were pauses for luncheon & a delicious Tea = A few days we were lucky enough to have the scene laid out o' doors – in the gardens of some various friends of mine – & of the Company = of course that was delightful, & we were treated & honoured splendidly – .¹⁶

Terry's account does not merely express her bemusement. It also acknowledges this existential moment, watching her own image on screen and the audience's reaction to it: 'Everyone who saw the Private Show given for me to see, <u>loved it</u>, & cheered & applauded all the time as if it were <u>really me</u> acting – most amusing – & gratifying ='.¹⁷ This seems to have been Terry's first encounter with the mediatised world of film. She acknowledged the difference in value – whether aesthetic or representational – between the moving and the static image: 'I must send you a few of the photographs – but remember they don't *<u>Count</u>* by the side of the moving pictures ='.¹⁸ This particular letter marks Terry's experience of a historical turning point, visualised as stage meets screen in her gaze. The emphasis in her description of the experience is on a perception of the audience's interaction with her screen image and her profound sense of recognition of herself in a representation. The subjunctive tense ('as if it were <u>really me</u> acting') highlights Terry's sense of alienation.

Ellen Terry appeared in the wartime film *Victory and Peace* (1918), directed by Herbert Brenon for the National War Aims Committee and Ministry of Information. In a tragic scene, she features as the mother receiving a telegram informing her of the fate of one of her sons. The action draws on familiar iconography from Bamforth & Co. picture postcards which showed the impact of war casualties on the family, notably on the mother. The scene in *Victory and Peace* shows Terry, like the mothers in the postcards, in the act of reading the official news of death or missing in action. Terry's own family were not exempt from wartime fears; her grandson Philip was on military service and her son was in Italy. Terry played her part in 'acting for the tender Imperial troops'[19] and became embedded in the popular imagination of London's wartime audiences from her performances at the Coliseum, run by Oswald Stoll. In June 1920, when Vesta Tilley retired, a farewell event was held at the Coliseum, with reminders of wartime performances as Terry provided the feminine gravitas to contrast with Tilley's famous cross-dressed performance in military uniform.[20]

At the same venue, Terry was a regular at charity events, often in scenes from Shakespeare, especially those of Portia in *The Merchant of Venice*.[21] These were predictably successful with audiences who would be glad to pay to see her appear on the stage at all, and they arguably served to raise the tone of the Coliseum's programme. Terry's popularity with the Coliseum audience was demonstrated in 1918 by the presentation of a wreath from 'Admirers of Shakespeare at the Coliseum' to mark her birthday.[22] As part of the wartime charity and fundraising entertainments, Ellen Terry's performances in scenes and recitations at this time have hitherto been regarded in terms of the diminished capacities of an ageing performer motivated by commercial gain. A few lines constituted all she could manage and reflected the exploitation of a frail older woman beyond the point where sustained employment was feasible. By contrast, Terry's brief accounts of her film work in this period demonstrate that she continued to take performance seriously. She approached it with an aesthetic appreciation of the medium and contemplated potential innovations.

The Bohemian Girl

The circumstances of post-war reconstruction appear to have influenced the films in which Ellen Terry appealed to a sense of nostalgia, and evoked a suffering femininity as a vehicle of service to home and nation. In this context, Terry's final film role as a minor but pivotal character in *The Bohemian Girl* (1922) has wider international cultural and political implications in the post-war period when the film was made. Audiences familiar with the opera of the same name, first performed at

Drury Lane in 1843, would recognise the plot concerning a child's abduction by gypsies and subsequent reunion with her aristocratic family.[23] Richard Schoch has noted the 'diverse positions occupied by Bohemia in Victorian theatrical culture' including the burlesques of *The Bohemian Girl* opera in the 1860s and 1870s (Schoch, 2003: 10). The 1922 film had a special resonance for its post-war audience. It spends considerable time on the individuation of various gypsy characters and on establishing their resistance to injustice as well as the prejudice meted out to them. It engages with cultural diversity, prejudice and conflict but ultimately privileges a liberal optimism in the resolution to the plot and reiterates racist stereotypes of Romany people.

The minor role of the elderly nurse Buda seems entirely suitable to Terry's abilities at this time. As Buda, Terry conveys the burden of awareness of her own diminishing competence. It is when Buda falls asleep that the child Arline is abducted by Devilshoof, leader of the gypsies, played by C. Aubrey Smith. Devilshoof has stealthily entered the upstairs room and charmed Arline with the promise of a visit to the gypsy camp. He thereby secures the child's silent complicity in the abduction. Other scenes, such as when the abducted child, who becomes 'the Bohemian girl', is endangered by a bear in the forest, are designed to elicit sensational thrill. It would have resonance with audiences used to early film 'serial-queen melodramas' which often incorporated the term 'girl' in their titles and featured plots concerning 'contradictory extremes of female prowess and distress, empowerment and imperilment' (Singer, 2001: 222).

Terry imbues the role of Buda with her earnest expression of emotional intensity, conveying mood and reaction as she interacts with the other performers. She appears self-consciously to position herself with furrowed brow and mournful gaze for the close-ups (Figure 31). These gestures would have been informed by her experience of posing for photographs or portraits and performing in melodrama at the Lyceum Theatre. The role of Buda exploits associations with a suffering femininity and a discourse of service which was particularly meaningful for Terry.[24] In her film roles later in life, Terry performed archetypal older women – the widow, the grieving mother, the nurse – who were reminiscent of her earlier stage roles in such plays as *The Good Hope* (1903), *The Merry Wives of Windsor* (1902) and *Alice-Sit-By-The-Fire* (1905). The casting of Terry in these sorts of roles played on the familiar, generating a meta-theatrical significance in connection with her former roles.

31 Ellen Terry in costume as Buda (seated), surrounded by cast in costume on the set of *The Bohemian Girl*, 1922. From left: Constance Collier as the Gypsy Queen; Henry Vibart as Count Arnheim; Harley Knoles, the film's co-director; Gladys Cooper as Arlene Arnheim; C. Aubrey Smith as Devilshoof; and Ivor Novello as Thaddeus.

Buda conveys the reassuringly familiar aspects of loyalty and commitment but also an increasing unreliability. She is of questionable competence in her childcare role. Numerous scenes focus on her tiredness. She appears physically incapable of keeping up with the energetic Arline. Buda's vulnerability therefore means she is easily duped by Devilshoof, the 'king of the gypsies'. In this respect, Buda functions as a device to facilitate the plot, which exploits racist anxieties about the Romany community as a mobile and predatory force.[25] As Jodie Matthews has established, the cultural stereotype of gypsies and 'the preponderance of abduction narratives demonstrates a latent cultural anxiety about this coherence [of the family] and the associated ideological impact on the power relations organised around race, class and gender' (Matthews, 2010: 144). These fears are also at work in the awkwardness conveyed by Ivor Novello as Thaddeus in response to Arline's developing romantic feelings for him. As the romance is initiated by the innocent young woman, it is presented as somehow elevated from any suspicions of abuse, but the differences between Thaddeus and Arline in age and cultural background are emphasised. Thaddeus is the Polish exile disguised as a gypsy and hiding in Bohemia. He is shown in conflict: concerned to preserve his anonymity and aware of his duties as unofficial guardian of the abducted child. His reticence is also presented as evidence of his advanced education (emphasised in the film's text cards) and sets him apart from the Romany community. In the post-war period, fears about change and risk were topical. In this film they highlight the new dangers facing children and the family and the phenomena of migration and exile. These prejudices and fears are to a certain extent questioned by Ivor Novello's character, as an unjustly treated Polish refugee protected by the Romany community, which is shown to be generally mistrusted and falsely accused.

When Terry appeared in this film, her co-stars Gladys Cooper and Constance Collier already had significant stage profiles and Ivor Novello was a rising star.[26] It is striking that Terry is the only protagonist to appear in the film without being announced first by a descriptive storyboard. The audience was expected to be already familiar with the great actress. The film was a great success in America. Kenton Bamford locates *The Bohemian Girl* not just at a significant moment in Novello's career but also in the development of D. W. Griffith's film company:

> Ivor Novello in *The Call of the Blood* (1920) 'his first professional acting assignment of any kind' and 'With Harley Knoles directing, Novello made *Carnival* (1921) and *The Bohemian Girl* (1922)'. American reviews of *The Bohemian Girl* were ecstatic; the *New York Evening Mail* assured its readers that 'Ivor Novello gives every indication of becoming another Valentino'; he was described as 'a Greek God who is both handsome and an intelligent actor', and his performance was admired for its 'admirable dignity and restraint'. Novello was contracted to D. W. Griffith at the time and with Griffith's company maximizing the attention being paid him, *The Bohemian Girl* became one of the most popular foreign movies shown in America. (Bamford, 1999: 57–8)

Novello's style of acting was similar to that of Terry's performance in the film. It also drew on the conventions of melodrama and historical drama. The incidents of villainous acts, child abduction and family reunion in the film typify the conventions of Hollywood melodrama for 'strong pathos' and 'heightened emotionality' (Singer, 2001: 290). Devilshoof, in particular, uses melodramatic, villainous gestures, stance and facial expressions to convey thoughtful contemplation, determination and the potential for violence. These performance features are consistent with melodrama and visually reinforce the familiar racist stereotypes.

Bamford's comparison between the 'pictorial sense' of Hepworth and the work of the Pre-Raphaelites (Bamford, 1999: 114) is relevant for *The Bohemian Girl* too. In Harley Knoles's *The Bohemian Girl*, Ellen Terry provides a direct link not only to the Pre-Raphaelites, with acting memories of Edward Burne-Jones's design for *King Arthur* (1895), but also to the theatrical cultural capital of Henry Irving's Lyceum Theatre. Terry lends a unique blend of gravitas, enhancing the pictorial splendour of the setting in Leeds Castle. In the early scenes of the film she is on the battlements of the castle, keeping a supervisory eye on Arline, her young charge, who is playing dangerously near the edge of the moat. It seems clear that this is the film to which Terry referred in a letter to a friend: 'I am "doing a Film" nearby at Leeds Castle a lovely little Castle with a Moat around it & I drive over each day from here & back again in the evening ='.[27] Novello's deployment in his performances of sensitivity and emotionally intense physicality engendered a powerfully unstable force.[28]

Bamford notes that 'in the battle for screen time the British film industry employed a nationalist offensive, pitting itself, its values and its product against the invasion of foreign films and the values displayed in those films' (Bamford, 1999: xi). Films by Hepworth and Knoles typically exploited the geographical location, architectural features and generally visually appealing features of the setting. These spatial forms were exploited in a particular ideological formulation aligned with Englishness, similar to the reinforcement of the hegemonic effects in period drama and aspects of the heritage industry later in the century.[29] Bamford quotes Hepworth's strategic approach:

> 'It was always in the back of my mind from the very beginning that I was to make English pictures, with all the English countryside for background and with English atmosphere and English idiom throughout.'
> If the cinema was sometimes known as the theatre of dreams, then Hepworth must be seen as one of the principal purveyors of a dream of English which was 'essentially rural and essentially unchanging'.
> (Bamford, 1999: 11)

Simon Rowson, the owner of the company that produced *The Bohemian Girl*, emphasised the political implications of film production and the significance of geographical setting for the promotion of Englishness:

> Producers should be urged to specialise in the production of films which have specially English settings. Too many of our films are produced in a neutral background in which there is little that is specifically English except the language in which the actors express themselves. Why has no one yet produced an important British film set in our ship-building yards, or the Sheffield steel trade, or the British agricultural industry, or indirectly demonstrating our police and judicial and municipal systems, or our school and university systems? All these have yielded backgrounds for many worthy stage productions in the past and can be equally well utilised for film purposes. (Rowson, 1933)[30]

The Leeds Castle location of *The Bohemian Girl* reinforced a sense of Englishness even though the story was supposed to be set in Eastern Europe. Given Rowson's commitment to promoting the English landscape on screen, this recognisably English setting seems to have been a strategic choice rather than an expedient measure.

Terry's appearance in film occurred at a time when the film industry was still developing and yet, in Britain, was vulnerable because of the influx of films from America. A move into film acting was generally considered to be a dubious choice for an actor; as Matheson Lang noted, it was 'considered a little "infra dig" for a leading actor to play in a film and I had been one of the first actor managers to do so' (quoted in Bamford, 1999: 55). Terry's image was associated with enduring youthfulness and vitality (Bloodworth, 2011). *The Bohemian Girl* benefited from the prestigious Terry brand, the commercial potential of her co-stars Cooper, Collier and Novello, as well as the attractive heritage setting in an English castle. The film achieved success in America as well as Britain. It had the ingredients to appeal to the developing capitalist cultures of both nations, and the inclusion of Ellen Terry provided a nostalgic reference point to nineteenth-century transatlantic cultural exchanges during the heyday of the Lyceum Theatre's tours of America and Canada.

Ellen Terry: inspirations for film

Ellen Terry became an inspiration and a role model when film critics looked back to successful stage performance in order to calibrate present-day film performance. It was in this context that Terry arguably provided the gold standard: thus according to Kenton Bamford, 'Joan Morgan – daughter of the director Sidney Morgan – was praised as an "embryonic Ellen Terry"' (Bamford, 1999: 45). Morgan had appeared with Terry in *Her Greatest Performance*. A general concern about standards of film acting features in the controversy regarding the female performers' failure to use facial expression to convey emotion. This was perceived by St John Ervine as a 'craze' of the younger generation, in contrast to 'the vivacity of Ellen Terry and Marie Tempest' (Ervine, quoted in Gledhill, 2003: 66).[31] Terry was an inspiration for individuals in the film industry, and years after her death she was to feature as a character in a Disney film. Her childhood association with Charles Dodgson captured the imagination of Aldous Huxley, whose mother, Julia Arnold, was one of the children photographed by Dodgson. Terry features in Huxley's film script as a character trusted by Dodgson with a draft of *Alice in Wonderland*. In conversation with Alice, Terry acts protectively by warning Alice about Dodgson's 'secret':

> [She] describes Mr. Carroll's peculiarities. Ellen laughs. 'So you know why you can never see Mr. Carroll?' she asks and, when Alice says no, she whispers something in her ear. 'You mean that Mr. Dodgson . . .?' says Alice. 'Sh-sh,' says Ellen. 'It's a great secret. If you told anyone, the queen might say, "Off with his head."' (Higdon and Lehrmann, 1992: 72)

Huxley's adaptation of *Alice in Wonderland* for an animated Disney film was unfortunately never realised.[32]

It is widely known that Ellen Terry regretted that she had never had the opportunity to play the part of Rosalind in *As You Like It* (see Terry, 1932: 97). However, it transpires that Terry had also wanted to extend her Shakespearean performances from stage into film. In a letter to her daughter she mentions having developed an idea and wanting to try it out, confidentially, to get feedback on it:

> I've an idea about the Cinema that I'll not speak of except to you which I think might be very good – & that you & I could do it together = It is concerning Shakespeare, who as he stands at present in relation to a Film is only made absurd & altogether uninteresting – my idea (!) came of something you lately said to me about your remembering the words of the trial scene M of V only the words Henry & I spoke & the dreadful inefficiency of the other players! – I long to hear if you will think my Idea (!) of no use now no prejudice, but I'll see if I can impress you in the performance of it – On trial (in a tiny way) all to myself I'm rather impressed myself !!! – but it may be nothing – & if you don't give me a little encouragement when you hear it, it certainly will be – nothing = .[33]

It is likely that the idea of a film performance of scenes from *The Merchant of Venice* had emerged from a combination of Terry's recent experiences on tour in brief recitals and scenes and her own experiences of film acting.[34]

Ellen Terry's repertoire in stage and screen performance

In *The Bohemian Girl* Ellen Terry represented an enduring but vulnerable maternal force, signifying home and status quo. She is a largely static vehicle for an anguished emotional response to the abduction of the child. The gypsy encampment is presented as a subversive mobile force, potentially disruptive, and, for the purposes of the plot, it provides a means of protecting Thaddeus from the intransigent oppressors. The film presents opposing views and values in a post-war context and their resolution. The revelation of the noble status of Thaddeus proves that aristocratic ties are those that bind most strongly, and a return to the status quo appears inevitable rather than a genuine openness to diversity. The harnessing of such powerful and conflicting forces seems to have made it a transatlantic success and cemented Ellen Terry's reputation in film.

32   Ellen Terry as Buda with Gladys Cooper as Arlene Arnheim and Henry Vibart as Count Arnheim (seated), in costume on the set of *The Bohemian Girl*, 1922.

The post-war reconstruction era locates *The Bohemian Girl* in long-standing fears related to gypsy abduction narratives in a particularly unstable historical period when concerns about the resilience of the family and social hierarchies were well founded, given the unprecedented social changes brought about by the First World War. The casting of Terry in the pivotal role of the nurse, Buda, as failed protector of the child signalled the end of an era: hitherto reliable and stable cultural reference points were receding. In 1920 Terry and the stalwarts of wartime fundraising and recruitment efforts were brought together one last time at Vesta Tilley's retirement performance. The reference by the press to Terry's role as Juliet's nurse demonstrates the associations that her Coliseum performances had with the care of others.[35] Terry became a signifier for the guardianship of home and family, but her advanced age has an added poignancy. Terry's style of performance in *The Bohemian Girl* provides an additional dimension to this sense of vulnerability in her repertoire.[36] As Buda, Terry's tired and distracted demeanour conveys not just an inability to control the child in her care, but a sense of generally diminished capacity.

At the time of this great success in film, Ellen Terry's stage career was in decline. In 1922, with *Potter's Clay* and *The Bohemian Girl*, Terry made her final appearances on screen. Her enduring brand was exploited in the marketing of the films and she was cited as a stable reference point to a passing era of stage performance. In this sense she was a strategic draw for that sector of the audience familiar with celebrities of the stage but unacquainted with the newly developing medium of film. For those viewers who had missed Terry at the peak of her stage career, these films introduced them to her renowned skills. For someone at the end of her career and moving into this new field, she showed remarkable enthusiasm and thoughtfulness in her approach to film. She appreciated the opportunity of employment, but rather than a financially expedient swansong, Terry's film work demonstrated her enduring attention to the artistic potential of performance.

Notes

1 For further discussion of this photograph and Terry's financial circumstances, see Cockin (2011).
2 Terry understood the theatrical market and it was for this reason that she arranged to perform *Nance Oldfield* as a curtain-raiser to guarantee an audience and some ticket sales for her son's production of *Dido and Aeneas* at the

Coronet Theatre; see *The Collected Letters of Ellen Terry* (Cockin, 2010–15) (hereafter *CLET*) 4: 1142.

3 David Mayer identifies the formal transition from the technology of lantern slide lectures to silent film in the use of 'ballad melodrama' material (Mayer, 1996: 225).

4 When Sydney Grundy's play *The New Woman* came out at the Comedy Theatre on 1 September 1894, Terry was bemused by the reaction; *CLET* 3: 583. In 1911 in the first issue *of The Freewoman*, Terry alone is named in the editorial as an example of 'the freewoman'.

5 Shaw wrote to Edith Craig an account to be read out at the Ellen Terry memorial performance on 21 July 1940 (Laurence, 1988: 568–72; transcript held at THM 384/9/10, V&A Theatre Collection) in which he quotes Terry's view of Kendal confided to him in a letter of 31 October 1896; *CLET* 3: 756.

6 The programme for *The Second Mrs Tanqueray* is annotated in what appears to be Ellen Terry's handwriting, 'trade rehearsal March 7 1916 at the Cinema Theatre' [Grand Ideal Picture]; ET-D841, National Trust's Ellen Terry and Edith Craig Archive, British Library (hereafter ETEC). Ellen Terry and her family were fascinated by film, both commercial and artistic. A large collection of programmes from the Film Society (1926–38) in ETEC demonstrates that filmgoing and visits to the New Gallery Kinema, Regent Street, London, where the Film Society screenings were shown, was a regular event for members of their household. The Film Society was founded in 1925 to screen on a Sunday afternoon films that were not commercially orientated. It influenced the film societies, festivals and activities which were later led by the British Film Institute.

7 An extant photo shows Terry and Norman McKinnell in *The Pillars of Society*; NT/SMA/PH.2641, ETEC. Terry was invited to the private showing at the London Pavilion, Piccadilly Circus, London on 23 September 1922; ET-D417, ETEC. I am grateful to Joan Templeton for her comments on Terry's role in this film.

8 James Carew appeared in several films by Cecil Hepworth, 'the leading British film producer of the time' (Bamford, 1999: 6). Hepworth described Carew as a stalwart acting member of his film crew (Hepworth, 1951). Carew appeared mostly in supporting roles in films which, like *The Forest on the Hill*, were set on location in atmospheric places.

9 Douglas Fairbanks had married Mary Pickford in 1920 and, the previous year, Fairbanks, Pickford, Charlie Chaplin and D. W. Griffith took the strategic decision to form their own company, United Artists, to control the production, quality, sale and distribution of films. Carew had annotated Terry's envelope 'Sale of Jewelry, Rich people. Douglas Fairbanks. Maxine Elliott. Gertrude Elliott. Laurette Taylor'; July 4 [1920]; *CLET* 6: 1880.

10 Ibid.

11 7 September 1916; *CLET* 6: 1825.

12 *CLET* 6: 1824
13 Simon Rowson became managing director of Gaumont-British Picture Corporation Ltd as well as managing director of Ideal Films Ltd and Member of the Advisory Committee to the Board of Trade under the Cinematograph Films Act (1927).
14 To Rosey, 7 September 1916; *CLET* 6: 1825.
15 Ibid.
16 Ibid.
17 Ibid.
18 Ibid.
19 Ibid.
20 The newspaper coverage of Vesta Tilley's farewell at the Coliseum on 5 June 1920 highlighted the appearance of Ellen Terry; see, for instance, *The Stage*, 27 May 1920, p. 12; *The Era*, 6 July 1921, p. 12.
21 Terry appeared as Beatrice in scenes from *Much Ado About Nothing* in a charity matinee for the British Red Cross at Middle Temple Hall and Gardens on 13 July 1916, and helped at the summer fair party in aid of the wounded at Kensington War Hospital Supply Depots on 21 July 1916 (letter, 11 July 1916; *CLET* 6: 1823). In the autumn of 1917 she appeared as Mistress Page with Edith Evans as Mistress Ford in scenes from *The Merry Wives of Windsor* at the London Coliseum.
22 *CLET* 6: 1855.
23 The film was based on the familiar plot derived from Cervantes' *La Gitanella* (1613) and adapted for Michael William Balfe's Drury Lane opera of 1843. The opera's international success inspired burlesque adaptations in the 1860s and 1870s (Schoch, 2003). In 1936 the film was remade and substantially altered with Laurel and Hardy replacing some aspects of the character of Thaddeus.
24 It is reminiscent of her role as the washerwoman in *Madame Sans Gene* but also features in a playful letter to George Bernard Shaw in which she fantasises for herself a Cinderella role in serving Shaw and his new wife (14 September 1897, *CLET* 3: 851; Cockin, 2017: 35–6).
25 See Bardi (2007) and Matthews (2010).
26 Novello and Terry had already appeared together on stage in London as, respectively, Bingley and Mrs Long in Edith Craig's production of *Pride and Prejudice* at the Palace Theatre in aid of the Bedford College for Women, London on 24 March 1922 (play programme, ET-D414, ETEC).
27 *CLET* 6: 1945.
28 Novello's gypsy performance in the film invites a wider queer application of Kirstie Blair's argument for the 'gypsy' signification of lesbian desire (2004). Terry's daughter was notably compared by Vita Sackville-West with 'the old Romany matriarch' and her lesbian household designated a gypsy 'encampment' (Sackville-West, 1949: 118).
29 In the same period, the English rural novel positioned the countryside in a

nostalgic light. One of these, Constance Holme's *Beautiful End* (1918), was dramatised as *The Home of Vision* and directed by Edith Craig in 1919 for the Pioneer Players theatre society, of which Ellen Terry was president.

30 The year of Rowson's talk saw the founding of the GPO film unit, led by John Grierson. This was renowned for its documentary film-making, exemplified by *Night Mail* (1936), which carried out the plans Rowson had outlined, in this case showing the transportation of the post by train at night. In 1930 Edith Craig directed the first play produced for the Masses' Stage & Film Guild, an organisation which controversially promoted the screening in Britain of Russian films, to the extent that it provoked a change in legislation to control Sunday-night entertainments (Cockin, 2017: 217–19). Rowson's papers presented to the Royal Empire Society and the Royal Statistical Society have become valuable sources (Hanson, 2007: 81).

31 Christine Gledhill quotes St John Ervine's article 'English Actresses and the Film: The Craze of Immobility' (1926).

32 The transcript of Huxley's 14-page synopsis, held in the Walt Disney Studio Archive, is reproduced as an appendix by Higdon and Lehrman (1992). It highlights the positioning of Terry as an object of Dodgson's desire in order to avoid what Disney referred to as a 'queer' representation of Dodgson. Disney had wanted to produce a film version of *Alice* since 1922; he was actively discussing possible approaches to the project in 1933, but it was not until 1945 that he hired Huxley to work on the script for a film involving animation and live action. In 1937 Edith Craig, Val Gielgud and Helen Terry featured in an educational film on the 'Effects of Heredity' for the Eugenics Society, whose president was Sir Julian Huxley, Aldous Huxley's brother (*Gloucester Citizen*, 15 June 1937; press cutting, EC-G100, ETEC).

33 1921; *CLET* 6: 1900.

34 These Shakespearean films are unspecified, but she may be alluding to those produced with Frank Benson and Herbert Beerbohm Tree (Burrows, 2002).

35 'Vesta Tilley's Farewell Tears', *Daily Mail*, 7 June 1920.

36 Tracy C. Davis's formulation of 'durable meanings' is relevant for considering the significance of care and service, empathy and endurance in Terry's screen performances and their intelligibility for audiences as constituents of Terry's repertoire on stage and latterly also on screen (Davis, 2009: 7).

References

Auerbach, Nina (1987), *Ellen Terry: Player in Her Time*, London: Phoenix.
Bamford, Kenton (1999), *Distorted Images: British National Identity and Film in the 1920s*, London: I.B. Tauris.
Bardi, Abby (2007), '"In Company of a Gipsy": The "Gypsy" as Trope in Woolf and Brontë', *Critical Survey*, 19.1, pp. 40–50.

Blair, Kirstie (2004), 'Gypsies and Lesbian Desire: Vita Sackville-West, Violet Trefusis, and Virginia Woolf', *Twentieth-Century Literature*, 50.2, pp. 141–66.

Bloodworth, Jenny (2011), 'The Burden of Eternal Youth: Ellen Terry and *The Mistress of the Robes*', in Katharine Cockin, ed., *Ellen Terry, Spheres of Influence*, London: Pickering and Chatto, pp. 49–64.

Booth, Michael R. (1986), 'Pictorial Acting and Ellen Terry', in Richard Foulkes, ed., *Shakespeare and the Victorian Stage*, Cambridge: Cambridge University Press, pp. 78–86.

Burrows, John (2002), '"It would be a mistake to strive for subtlety of effect": *Richard II* and Populist, Pantomime Shakespeare in the 1910s', in Andrew Higson, ed., *Young and Innocent: The Cinema in Britain 1896–1930*, Exeter: Exeter University Press, pp. 78–96.

Cockin, Katharine, ed. (2010–15), *The Collected Letters of Ellen Terry*, Volumes 1–6, London: Pickering and Chatto.

Cockin, Katharine (2011), 'Ellen Terry Creating the Brand', in Katharine Cockin, ed., *Ellen Terry, Spheres of Influence*, London: Pickering and Chatto, pp. 133–49.

Cockin, Katharine (2017), *Edith Craig and the Theatres of Art*, London: Bloomsbury Methuen Drama.

Davis, Tracy C. (2009), 'Nineteenth-Century Repertoire', *Nineteenth Century Theatre and Film*, 36.2, pp. 6–28.

Gledhill, Christine (2003), *Reframing British Cinema 1918–28: Between Restraint and Passion*, London: British Film Institute.

Gottlieb, Robert (2010), *Sarah: The Life of Sarah Bernhardt*, New Haven, CT: Yale University Press.

Hanson, Stuart (2007), *From Silent Screen to Multi-screen: A History of Cinema Exhibition in Britain since 1896*, Manchester: Manchester University Press.

Hepworth, Cecil M. (1951), *Came the Dawn: Memories of a Film Pioneer*, London: Phoenix House.

Higdon, David Leon, and Phill Lehrman (1992), 'Huxley's "Deep Jam" and the Adaptation of *Alice in Wonderland*', *The Review of English Studies*, 43.169, pp. 57–74.

Higson, Andrew (2002), 'Cecil Hepworth, *Alice in Wonderland* and the Development of the Narrative Film', in Andrew Higson, ed., *Young and Innocent: The Cinema in Britain 1896–1930*, Exeter: Exeter University Press, pp. 42–64.

Higson, Andrew, and Richard Maltby, eds (1999), *"Film Europe" and "Film America": Cinema, Commerce and Cultural Exchange 1920–1939*, Exeter: Exeter University Press.

Laurence, Dan H., ed. (1988), *Bernard Shaw, Collected Letters 1926–1950, Vol. 4*, London: Max Reinhardt.

Matthews, Jodie (2010), 'Back Where They Belong: Gypsies, Kidnapping and Assimilation in Victorian Children's Literature', *Romani Studies*, 20.2, pp. 137–59.

Mayer, David (1996), 'Parlour and Platform Melodrama', in Michael Hays and Anastasia Nikolopoulou, eds, *Melodrama: The Cultural Emergence of a Genre*, New York: St Martin's Press, pp. 211–34.

Rowson, Simon (1933), 'A British Influence through Films', address to Royal Empire Society, 20 March 1933, pamphlet, British Library, UIN: BLL01003178717.

Rowson, Simon (1936), 'A Statistical Survey of the Cinema Industry in Great Britain in 1934', reprinted from the *Journal of the Royal Statistical Society*, pamphlet, British Library, UIN: BLL01003178718.

Sackville-West, Vita (1949), 'Triptych', in Eleanor Adlard, ed., *Edy: Recollections of Edith Craig*, London: Frederick Muller, pp. 118–25.

Schoch, Richard (2003), 'Performing Bohemia', *Nineteenth-Century Theatre & Film*, 30.2, pp. 1–13.

Singer, Ben (2001), *Melodrama and Modernity: Early Sensational Cinema and Its Contexts*, New York: Columbia University Press.

Slide, Anthony (2005), *Silent Topics: Essays on Undocumented Areas of Silent Film*, Lanham, MD: Scarecrow Press.

Steen, Marguerite (1962), *A Pride of Terrys: Family Sage*, London: Longmans.

Terry, Ellen (1932), 'Triumphant Women', in Christopher St John, ed., *Four Lectures on Shakespeare*, New York: Benjamin Blom, pp. 79–124.

Films

Her Greatest Performance (1916), dir. Fred Paul, British Film Institute, http://www.bfi.org.uk/films-tv-people/4ce2b7258d1d2 (accessed 30 August 2018).

Denny From Ireland (1918), dir. William H. Clifford, USA, W. H. Clifford Photoplay Co., British Film Institute, BFI identifier 765672.

Victory and Peace (1918), dir. Herbert Brenon (also known as *The National Film* and *The Invasion of Britain*), National War Aims Committee and Ministry of Information, British Film Institute, BFI identifier 55774.

Pillars of Society (1920), dir. Rex Wilson, RW Syndicate; British Film Institute, http://www.bfi.org.uk/films-tv-people/4ce2b7d8c541d (accessed 30 August 2018).

The Bohemian Girl (1922), dir. Harley Knoles and Josef von Sternberg, Alliance Film Company; British Film Institute, http://www.bfi.org.uk/films-tv-people/4ce2b6a5f3a8d (accessed 30 August 2018).

Potter's Clay (1923), dir. H. Grenville-Taylor and Douglas Payne, http://www.bfi.org.uk/films-tv-people/4ce2b6b35897f (accessed 30 August 2018).

Newsreel footage

Ellen Terry at St Andrew's University with Sir James Barrie on the occasion of her honorary degree, 1922, http://www.britishpathe.com/video/stills/sir-james-barrie (accessed 22 May 2017).

Walton-on-Thames newsreel, 1925, British Film Institute, http://www.bfi.org.uk/films-tv-people/4ce2b6a1cc3ff (accessed 30 August 2018).

11

Mabel Constanduros

Different voices, voicing difference

Gilli Bush-Bailey

On 3 October 1929, *The Stage* published its weekly column on 'The Variety Stage', beginning with a review of the current entertainment on offer at Oswald Stoll's 'people's palace of entertainment', the London Coliseum:

> Making her first appearance in variety here this week is Mabel Constanduros, an artist who has achieved considerable fame in broadcasting and has added thereto with appearances at concert centres. Miss Constanduros has made the study of the cockney woman and girl her particular work, and whether she is suggesting the poor little child-mother looking after her youngest sister and selling lavender to keep the home fires burning, the prim marm who directs a children's concert and makes eyes at the curate, or the mixture of hard work, good temper, and complaint that goes to the making of *Mrs Buggins*, she is always true to life in her character drawing. Monday afternoon found her suffering somewhat from nervousness in her new environment, but her greeting was sincere, and it was clear that Miss Constanduros has many admirers already and will add greatly to their number.[1]

As the voice of BBC Radio's *The Buggins Family*, Mabel Constanduros was among a new generation of performers to make her name on the 'wireless' in the safety of the studio broadcast, where her audience was imagined but unseen. Broadcasting fame soon led to the demand for live stage appearances where, at the London Coliseum, her very visible audience were arranged over three vast tiers of seating and could number anything up to 2,500 people. The 'nervousness in her new environment', picked up here by the *Stage* reviewer, is hardly surprising. The moment, as depicted by Constanduros in her 1946 autobiography *Shreds and*

Patches, is more elaborately described, emotionally heightened and culturally complex:

> I was engaged to top the bill at the Coliseum [...] and I felt no triumph at all. I was just terror-stricken. This was a job of which I knew nothing. If I had been engaged to act in a play, I should at least have known how to set about it but I had no idea how to cope with a variety audience and felt secretly that my work was unsuitable for the variety stage. (Constanduros, 1946: 49)

It had been only four years since Mabel had successfully auditioned for the BBC. In that time she had become a familiar voice to the growing number of households buying their own wireless set and listening in to the BBC's National or Regional service where *The Buggins Family* had quickly become a firm favourite.[2] Writing and performing the voices for at least six of the characters in the everyday stories of her London 'cockney' family, Constanduros's creation of the cantankerous, but always comical, Grandma Buggins was particularly well loved. So, was this sudden rise to 'stardom' the reason why Constanduros writes of being 'paralysed with fright' as she waited in her 'lovely dressing room, the star room', reduced to a state of 'shaking and feeling extremely sick' (Constanduros, 1946: 50)? Although Constanduros's place at the top of the bill demonstrates the power of broadcast fame to provide a shortcut from the more usual repertory stage apprenticeship of the day, she was not a stranger to live performance. In fact, it was as a result of someone seeing her perform one of her monologues on the amateur stage that she had been invited to audition for the BBC in 1925. So the issue here perhaps was less the fear of a live audience, but rather more a fear of the cultural and social context of that audience:

> At that time – it will hardly be believed – I had never been inside a variety theatre. In my youth they were considered most unsuitable for young ladies [...] I should have jumped at an offer to go on the legitimate stage, but the prospect of being a variety artist did not allure me at all. (Constanduros, 1946: 49)

Shreds and Patches returns again and again to her felt conflict between legitimate and illegitimate entertainment, the still active divide between high and low art. The popularity she gained in the emerging industry of radio entertainment gave her access to the legitimate theatre she identified with, but the tension of social place, and placing herself professionally, is a recurring element in her writing, particularly in the reflective tone of her autobiography: 'Because I was relegated to that section of radio called Variety I was known as a variety artist, though I think of myself first as a writer and secondly as a straight actress' (Constanduros, 1946: 64).

Variety theatres, for all that had been done to expel the rackety inheritance of the nineteenth-century music halls and transform them into respectable places of popular entertainment, were simply outside the frame of the 'legitimate' stage profession that Constanduros envisaged for herself. As a broadcast performer at pains to express her liking and respect for her variety colleagues and their 'extreme competence', nonetheless Constanduros still saw her working world as separate and superior to theirs. Her initial contract for appearances over a period of eight weeks included dates in variety theatres in London, Leicester, Bristol and Manchester; the last she found particularly 'terrifying', as her northern audience were 'far less easily moved to laughter'. She speaks in self-deprecating terms of her 'ignorance', of the 'stroke of luck' that took her to the 'coveted position' at the top of the bill, and her sense of being an 'imposter' in that branch of the profession. She also counters these expressions of admiration for the variety world with a story of a particularly rough Saturday night when 'hardly anyone in the theatre seemed to be sober'. She nicely concludes that 'it was too lonely a life and the strain on [her] nerves too great' to accept any further contracts for venues where being heard was the main criterion for success (Constanduros, 1946: 52–3).

The explanation that Constanduros gives for initially overcoming her palpable revulsion for the 'feverish brightness one associates with Variety' is the familiar reason that many use to negotiate the gaps between the social milieu of their upbringing, the ambition for self determination and their immediate needs – money.

> Still, the salary they offered seemed to me then enormous. I had my son to educate, and I have always had an irresistible urge to try my hand at any new job which offered itself, just to see if I could do it, so I signed the contract, hastily put together an act and bought some dresses. (Constanduros, 1946: 50)

The pressing financial need is, of course, accounted for in the seemingly unavoidable expenditure for a middle-class parent – the fees for her son's schooling at preparatory and public school. There is also though the hint of a characteristic, sometimes reckless, spirit of adventure in Constanduros's acceptance of the challenge, followed swiftly by the apparently haphazard, almost off-hand approach to preparing performance materials and buying suitable clothes. There are conflicting energies at work here, of seriousness and an almost careless concern, that speak to the twenty-first-century reader of the precariousness of the times; the structure of feeling that was the cultural backdrop of interwar Britain. This was a culture in which the majority would soon gain the vote, and in which a new generation of middle-class women would work to reform their class identity and renew their certainties as they pursued new aspirations. Mabel Constanduros's writing uses many voices to work out her own place in the positions that women were negotiating in both private and public spheres. Her autobiography, her many published plays and monologues, *The Buggins Family* and a wide range of other materials for radio offer an opportunity to explore a particular cultural moment. It was a time of reviewing, making and remaking the norms of middle-class life, transmitted to ever-growing numbers of listeners across Britain and abroad through the monopoly on stability and authority held by the BBC. Broadcasting grew swiftly from its infant days at the BBC's London headquarters in Savoy Hill, and Mabel Constanduros was among its many forgotten female pioneers, carving out a professional practice and personal agency that is sometimes unselfconsciously revealed and, at others, deliberately veiled.

This chapter focuses on the different voices, tones and modes of address that Constanduros used in her public writing and professional correspondence. Her autobiography, written while her now-married son was in India on active service, continually returns to the depiction of herself as the successful artist but reluctant working mother, torn between economic need and her much-loved boy, Michael, from whom she 'hated being away' (Constanduros, 1946: 53). It considers her attitude to professionalism, particularly within the emerging industry of radio entertainment, and its alliance with and appropriation for the project of middle-class respectability. Juxtaposing the voice in her autobiographical writing, newspaper interviews, contracts and correspondence preserved in the BBC's written archives, this chapter attends to the shifting register of her voice as the wronged writer negotiating a better fee or doggedly chasing up her copyright. In her many letters to the Authors' Society (held by the British Library), she asks for legal advice and representation against unscrupulous publishers, while simultaneously attempting to get around paying fees for membership of the organisation that she wishes to act on her behalf. As a co-writer, sometimes fighting for joint rights or choosing to shelter behind the man she is working with – and it does always seem to have been a man – Constanduros can be found insisting on proper credit and fees according to her greater professional experience. As a performer of her own material, she argues for the right to perform outside the BBC, claiming copyright for the commercial exploitation of her most enduring character creation, Grandma Buggins.

Recordings of Constanduros's broadcasts, particularly *The Buggins Family*, sound strange to the modern listener, not least in their representation of 'cockney' voices and attitudes.[3] Even though films from the period can do much to acclimatise the modern ear, there is still much work to be done in exploring the aural conception and reception of performance practices in that period of relatively near-history. But it would be foolish to underestimate the power of the radio voice and the part that Constanduros's broadcast work played in delivering the greater task to 'inform, educate and entertain': the vision for the BBC that John Reith inscribed and that has been maintained by successive generations serving in that 'temple of the arts and muses' (Higgins, 2015: 39).

The BBC was not the only place for voices interested in capturing the attention of women up and down the country. 1928 saw fifteen million women gain the right to vote on equal terms with men, and there was much to negotiate across the shifting ground for women in the domestic sphere and beyond in the aftermath of the First World War, and the seemingly brief pause before a second. Alison Light draws attention to E. M. Delafield's *Diary of a Provincial Lady*, published weekly in the left-leaning, modernist magazine *Time and Tide* (1929),[4] followed, a little later, by Jan Struther's 'Mrs Miniver', published in *The Times* (1937–39).[5] Both offer humorous takes on society through the eyes of the central female character, a wife and mother struggling, but managing, of course, to maintain a fitting lifestyle in the ever-changing picture of upper-middle-class family life. As Light notes, for the 'upper' and increasingly just the 'middle' class, the burning question in the immediate aftermath of the First World War was where domestic servants might be found and how to avoid losing them (Light, 1991: 119–20). The troublesome cook, the emotional governess, the string of defecting housemaids that worried Delafield's 'provincial lady' were still relevant to many households reliant on the labour of 'other' women. But 'living-in' servants give way to the 'daily help', and the cheerful 'charlady' who 'came in and did' for Mrs Miniver became an increasingly familiar figure as an object of 'affectionate' fun and bemusement to her employer.

The working-class wife and mother is central to the families in which Constanduros's 'cockney' characters are situated. In some ways such characters simply reinscribe conservative class values, but do they also work to disturb and re-evaluate the old categories of 'them' and 'us' that preoccupy the middle class in the ongoing project of establishing class position and defining the all-important hegemonic 'we'? In Grandma Buggins Constanduros established a redoubtable, resolute 'cockney' grandmother on the airwaves (Figure 33), later visualised, in the minds of the public at

33 Unattributed sketch of Mabel Constanduros as Grandma Buggins, 1937.

least, by Giles in the *Express* newspaper comic strip cartoon and, arguably, reaching forward to the twenty-first-century in British comedy actress Catherine Tate's television character, Nan.[6] These are not rosy-cheeked grandmothers of the middling sort or wide-aproned nannies of the upper-middle-class nursery. Constanduros's 'Grandma' was a cussed old matriarch[7] who was popular enough to be used to broadcast recipes during the food shortages of the Second World War, and on film being shown the latest in post-war kitchen design.[8] How Mabel Constanduros came to find her own 'voice' through giving voice to her cockney characters, how she established her professional practice and from it voiced agency as script writer, performer and author, is at the heart of the present enquiry. It is also interesting to explore how her writing maps across the larger project of quieting middle-class anxiety, reassuring and adapting in the face of the rapid changes that the interwar years brought to both public and private expressions of British domestic life.

Finding her voice

Mabel Tilling was born in 1880 into a comfortable middle-class London family, her father being the managing director of a successful bus company built up by his father, Thomas Tilling.[9] Mabel was educated at Mary Datchelor School in Camberwell. As her autobiography records, the strain of early success there took its toll: 'my health broke down – for I was only fourteen when I got into the sixth form and was working with girls three years my senior – so I was sent to school at the seaside' (Constanduros, 1946: 28). Mabel thought little of the finishing school she was later sent to, considering that 'the fees were extremely high, the standard of education was incredibly low. I said so and was not popular' (1946: 30). After this, her father offered to pay for her to have a university education at Cambridge's Girton College, but her mother wanted her to stay at home. Constanduros's autobiography effortlessly elides stories from her past with reflections on the present – the 1940s – touching only lightly on moments in the twenty-five or more years between her leaving school and being offered a place 'in the first Radio Repertory Company' (1946: 40). By 1925 Constanduros was 45 years old, a wife, and mother of an 8-year-old son when her professional life began.

A clue to the almost complete absence from her narratives of her husband, from whom she derived her professional name, might be found in a small moment of reflection on her parents' refusal to consider her request to go to a drama school:

> My parents decided that my wish to go on the stage was only a craze – so many girls had it, but forgot all about it when the Right Man came along. Did they ever reflect how much less likely one would be to say 'Yes' to the wrong man if one had work in which one was passionately interested? (Constanduros, 1946: 31)

Exactly why Athanasius (Ath) Constanduros was 'the wrong man' is far from clear, but in one of the few remarks made against the otherwise 'pleasant life' of 'wonderful holidays twice a year' and no 'worry about money' that Mabel enjoyed with her parents is the observation that her life was too 'sheltered', and that, like so many other generations of young women, she had been led to believe that being married was all that was needed for a woman to 'live happily ever after'. Mabel and her 'beloved sister Norah' married the Constanduros brothers in 1907 when Mabel was 27. They 'lived side by side, eventually in Sutton', a suburb on the Surrey side of London, 'upon small incomes' and a great deal of determination it seems (1946: 31–2). Athanasius was an insurance broker who continued to live in Sutton until his death in July 1937, by which time Mabel had not only rented a flat in central London but also owned her own cottage in West Sussex. It is not clear exactly when she moved from the marital home, but the briefest of references to circumstances that may have contributed to their unrecorded separation – there is no evidence of a divorce – tells of the loss of two children:

> I had a little boy called Tony to whom I was entirely devoted, and he died when he was four years old. Even today I cannot write about it. Michael was my third and only surviving child, and I daresay I was an over-anxious mother. (1946: 33)[10]

Michael was born in 1917, by which time Mabel was 37 years old.

While living with Ath in Sutton there is nothing to suggest that Mabel had any work in which to be 'passionately interested' prior to her employment with the BBC. There is evidence, however, of her considerable involvement in amateur dramatics, an interest shared with her husband and moving beyond the local amateur company in Sutton.[11] In January 1923 *The Times* reviewed a popular comedy, *French Leave*, performed by Lloyds Dramatic Society. Mrs Constanduros and Mr A. Constanduros are listed, and Mabel is picked out for her performance as 'the voluble landlady of the Brigade billet'.[12] Around or just before this time, Mabel sought opportunities for dramatic training. Marion Cole, a student with Elsie Fogerty at Central School of Speech and Drama, describes a Thursday afternoon diction class held at rooms in the Albert Hall:

> There was a little woman, married, who struggled with lovely lyrics, which her strangely husky voice just did not suit; but it was clear that she loved poetry and Fogie was always encouraging to her. One day she spoke a charming poem which nobody knew, her whole voice changed. Fogie looked up with her special smile and said 'Dear, it's come! Your breathing – control – everything. Now you are free! You wrote that … Yes – I think you will be able to write too. Bring me something quite different next time, dear, please … I'm so very glad: I knew you could do it.' Next week, 'something quite different' was a sparkling cockney sketch, also original, which had us helpless with laughter: but this great little artiste, once in command of her own voice, could reduce us to tears just as easily. Her name was Mabel Constanduros. (Cole, 1967: 88)

Through the unavoidable elaborations of a moment recalled after a gap of forty-five years, the sense of a liberating change being recognised by those in that upper room of the Albert Hall is inescapable, and chimes all too clearly with Constanduros's own recollections of

> Miss Fogerty [who] was the greatest help and encouragement to me. She used to make me write more and more monologues, and it was her appreciation that perhaps gave me courage to go through the door of Broadcasting House on that February morning in 1925 – the door that led to a new life. (Constanduros, 1946: 38)

The BBC's Written Archive Centre (BBC WAC) reveals the strength of Constanduros's business voice, especially when she is writing to negotiate fees for the many characters she created for radio.

As a writer, Constanduros's first contract appears to have been signed on 19 January 1926, when a fee of ten guineas was agreed for the play *Devoted Elsie* and the '[n]ame of author to be b'cast [broadcast] as author'.[13] Billed as a 'radio comedy', it was broadcast in February of that year with Constanduros as the eponymous Elsie, working in the kitchen with the cook, where, 'to help pass the time away whilst hard at work, they discuss with vital interest Mr. 'Arold. Elsie's admiration of Mr. 'Arold is beyond description.'[14] This was not, however, the first time that she had performed her own material. The first record of a 'comedy sketch by Mabel Constanduros' is dated 14 September 1925, but 'A Day in the Country' by Mabel Constanduros was broadcast earlier on 18 July, and she is named as an individual performer/entertainer on 29 June. Her first featured broadcast appears in records for 1 May,[15] which coincides with her own account:

> I was offered my first solo broadcast in the spring of 1925. I went to see Kenneth Wright, who said they were prepared to pay me two guineas for a five minute's broadcast, provided that the material was original and that the B.B.C. would not have to pay any copyright for it [...] soon after this my friend K.H. Wright sent for me again and told me that he thought I was not being paid enough and that they proposed to raise my fee to three guineas. A few weeks later still they sent for me again and told me they proposed to make me a star (which meant five guineas). (Constanduros, 1946: 42–3)

This marked Constanduros's sense of the move across 'the dividing line' between being an amateur and a professional: 'A professional writer or performer may never fall below a certain level of achievement, though her work may be above that level often' (1946: 43). As a professional writer she quickly developed a series of characters for herself as a professional BBC performer. Her understanding of the burgeoning industry she had entered, the demand for new entertainment product in a format that was familiar and instantly recognisable to her listening audience, is remarkable at this early point in broadcasting history:

> One voice is apt to become tiresome on the air if it goes on for a long time, so I invented my cockney family – Mrs Buggins, the good natured, much tried housewife; Grandma (an old tartar if there ever was one); and two children. Occasionally I added neighbours, and Aunt Maria who came from the North. I think seven voices was the greatest number I ever attempted in one broadcast, but being several people at once enabled me to do sketches, which I think more entertaining than monologues. (1946: 43)

'Mrs Buggins Chooses a Hat' went out on 29 August 1925, with 'The Buggins Family Out for the Day' broadcast on 2LO (London) on 1 September, at 8 o'clock in the evening. The BBC copyright files are very thin for the decade between 1925 and 1935, and her 'artist's file' doesn't begin until 1935, but it is worth noting that in a letter dated 6 December 1927 she writes to enquire about 'how to proceed' in relation to a song of hers that has been broadcast without her permission. Mr Howgill replied for the BBC, stating that the singer did not include it in the programme that she had submitted before broadcast, and he asks Constanduros to go and see him, at which point, one must assume, an apology, and possibly a fee, was accepted. In the 900 entries for Mabel Constanduros gathered together in the BBC Genome project, she is referred to as an 'entertainer' performing 'selections from her Repertoire'. Sketches 'written' by her and issues of copyright and overseas broadcast relating to longer pieces are evidently of concern where she is formally identified as the 'author'. What is clear is that from the very start of her career Constanduros was a determined negotiator, and little seems to have stood in the way of her rapid professional progress; least of all, her husband.

Male company

Jennifer Purcell's interviews with Mabel Constanduros's family, particularly her nephew and later co-writer Denis Constanduros, confirm that Athanasius was a cautious, quiet, 'latter-day Mr Pooter' (Purcell, 2014: 7–8). Mabel's brief reference to his concern that their neighbours might hear her typing her sketches and articles – 'to his mind such an occupation was beneath my dignity' (Constanduros, 1946: 65) – led me to wonder why there seemed to be no evidence of the expected resistance to her pursuing her new-found professional life. But then I looked again at the early BBC contracts and began to question his signature as witness. I have no proof of forgery but merely note that the two signatures, Mabel's and her husband's, are surprisingly similar. From 'ten-shilling articles' for magazines and two-guinea sketches for the BBC in 1925, Constanduros received six guineas for a sketch on 2 January 1928, followed two months later by twelve guineas for a play, *The Strutham Amateurs Rehearse Dick Whittington*, which was broadcast on 9 April of that same year. Constanduros is credited as author and also appears in the cast list alongside Michael Hogan, with whom she began a significant performing and writing partnership.

Constanduros records that the first Radio Repertory Company consisted of eight to ten people, only two of whom were women. Phyllis Panting had even less acting experience than Constanduros, being a fashion journalist and editor for a women's magazine (later *Woman's Own*)[16] but, like Constanduros, she quickly settled into writing and performing for radio. At the end of 1925 Constanduros reported that a new actor had joined the Radio Rep: 'I was struck at once by his excellent cockney accent and the charm of his speaking voice in straight parts. His name was Michael Hogan' (Constanduros, 1946: 41). The almost coy understatement of this introduction to Hogan in her autobiography is followed by a reported verbal exchange which seems at odds with other representations of her vocal independence and self-confidence.

> One day, as he and I were snatching a hasty meal at Lyons' between a rehearsal and transmission, we were talking about the poor material we were given sometimes to put over.
> 'Why shouldn't we write a play?' he asked. 'Not a one-act play; a long one.'
> 'But Michael, I couldn't,' I said.
> 'We could together,' he insisted. 'I'll go and see R. E. Jeffrey and get him to commission it.' He did, and we wrote it. (1946: 41)

The Survivor, 'A mystery in three acts by Michael Hogan and Mabel Constanduros', was broadcast simultaneously on 29 May 1928 on three of the regional stations, including 2LO (London), at 9.40 in the evening.[17] Although he was not without professional experience, it is surprising to find Hogan billed first, before his more established collaborator. A month later, on 12 June and 26 June, Michael Hogan witnessed Constanduros's signature for two contracts (worth £25 and £20 respectively) relating to a 'Mrs Buggins' revue.[18] In another contrasting narrative voice, Constanduros reported that '[s]oon after I met Michael Hogan, I asked him to join the Buggins family as "Father", and for seven years we wrote broadcast material together and travelled all over the country doing concert work' (1946: 46). In 1927 Constanduros and Hogan created a spin-off from the Buggins, *Ag and Bert*, for which they are both credited as writers for the 31 August broadcast.[19] *Ag and Bert* is also listed as appearing on Sunday performances at the Arts Theatre, London, in December 1928,[20] and the IMDB lists a 1929 film (sketch) of *Ag and Bert* in which both Constanduros and Hogan appear, but here Constanduros alone has the writing credit. There is no contract evidence of their joint work until 1936, when Constanduros writes on 1 May to question the £25 fee they have been offered, stating that previously they had each received £50 'for the last two similar shows we wrote. If this one is going to be done twice that's all right, but I don't think £25 is enough.'[21] A reply dated 4 May informs her that the work is not scheduled for repeat broadcasting and offers 35 guineas and an agreement for a further 15 guineas if there is a repeat transmission. It is clear that Constanduros's voice led the negotiations for this successful partnership.

In the winter of that year she suddenly dropped out of a planned Buggins Christmas broadcast and boarded a ship for America with her friend, the actress Grizelda Hervey. Hogan did not go with her but appears on the passenger list of the same ship, the *Normandie*, three years later. The IMDB has writing credits for him on three Hollywood films, beginning with *Rebecca* (Alfred Hitchcock, 1940). Constanduros is notably silent, making no reference to their decision to go their separate ways, professionally or personally, and no further reference to him appears. Her contractual wranglings now concern her work with two other writing partners: her nephew, Denis, and Howard Agg. These two collaborators alone were included by Val Gielgud (head of Radio Drama, BBC) in Mabel Constanduros's obituary in 1957, with no mention of Hogan.[22]

Constanduros returned to England in spring 1937 as she was increasingly concerned about her son. Buried in a chapter largely voicing maternal concern for Michael, his health, his lack of settled employment and his hopes of marrying Constanduros's former secretary, is the briefest of references to the death of her husband.[23] A more distracted voice on the impact of Ath's death can be heard in her letter of 14 July 1937, but only as an aside to the main purpose of her correspondence with the BBC, in which Constanduros is, once again, fee wrangling. She begs forgiveness for

> not having answered before your letter of July 9th but the sudden death of my husband on that date has thrown all my affairs into confusion. I consent to the terms set out in that letter concerning the musical play Horti-mania on behalf of my nephew and myself.[24]

Denis and she were a successful writing partnership, creating another popular radio series, *The English Family Robinson* and later having a play, *Acacia Avenue* (1943), running in the West End, also adapted as *29 Acacia Avenue* for release as a film. There is no doubt that Constanduros did much to open doors for Denis, who was to become a highly respected radio and television writer in his own right, but she was also sure to make it clear that she was the senior and more experienced writer in the partnership, and she expected recognition of that fact, as seen in a letter dated 2 September 1937:

> Dear Mr Hamilton Marr
> If you consult your files you will find that you paid me fifteen pounds – or guineas – for both my Conversations in the Train. It was my nephew, Denis, who got twelve pounds. I am quite willing to accept the same fee as I had before for this one.[25]

Later correspondence with Hamilton Marr, dated 11 May 1939, continues in similar tone, reinforcing her clear sense of the commercial competition to the BBC monopoly and the opportunities emerging for creative artists, insisting on fair dealing, and throwing in a personal appeal for good measure:

> I'd be awfully glad if you could see your way to paying a little more than fifteen guineas for our Play ... It does seem very little, especially if it is to include a relay to Empire, because now I can generally sell my things separately to Australia and Canada. Of course I know it sometimes can't be managed, but, as I have said before, original work seems to be paid so much less adequately than adaptation. I cannot understand it. Do your best for us, won't you?[26]

In this instance she was refused and accepted the lower fee.

Constanduros continued to be the leading negotiator in her writing partnership with Howard Agg, at least initially. He is introduced in her autobiography on the last few pages, although they began writing together in 1937, and it is only in this last partnership that she speaks of the difficulty of having to consciously develop a method of working collaboratively. Their main interest was in plays for amateurs, a flourishing market, with Samuel French's editions leading the field. Constanduros had first-hand experience of amateur companies, and her successful commercial exploitation of that market in sketches, monologues and duologues has resulted in at least two of her pieces remaining on French's lists today. Agg already had a section of that market in mind:

> So we talked out a plot for an all-women play, since Howard had always specialized in these [...] It was a hopeless business. Our minds worked in different directions; we could not pull together at all [...] We were fired with the idea of making a volume of six plays for women, and we did eventually achieve this with some difficulty for he was employed during the day at other things and so was I. (Constanduros, 1946: 129)

Agg appears to have been on the staff of the BBC, but it is not clear what his 'day job' was or if it started before or after he began writing with Constanduros.[27]

As well as maintaining her performance and writing career for radio, Constanduros was working in film, writing songs, and had several successful stage appearances. She devotes a chapter of her autobiography to theatrical touring, and particularly theatrical landladies (1946: 79–87). She stopped touring when war was declared in 1939, returning to her radio broadcasts and writing:

> Writing with Howard was a great solace during the war. From plays for amateurs we turned our attention to writing for broadcasting. From the autumn of 1940 to the autumn of 1943 I think we wrote fifty that were accepted. (1946: 130)

The gently insistent tones of Constanduros's negotiating voice give way to Agg's sometimes 'flip' and certainly arrogant voice as he takes over negotiations with the BBC, accepting and signing contracts on their behalf from the summer of 1940. He requests a fee of 35, not 30 guineas, for their play *The Lady From Abroad*, adding that 'if you cannot do this, of course, we shall quite understand'.[28] The issue for the BBC appeared to be the length of the piece, and it was pointed out that accurate timing of pieces had to be clear so that fees would be consistent. On 24 October of that year, Val Gielgud wrote a memo requesting that the copyright office negotiate with Constanduros and Agg for *The Man from the Sea*, adding 'perhaps at the same time you would note Mr Agg's change of address'. Subsequent letters to Agg are addressed to him at Constanduros's cottage, Prattenden's, in Bury, West Sussex. On 1 November Agg returned the signed contract, again from Prattenden's, adding: 'incidently [sic], would you please instruct whoever is responsible to make payment out to me when it comes due, as I am looking after this side of our partnership'.[29] This was apparently carried out, with no evidence to suggest that Constanduros had agreed. She seems to have been silent on the matter.

Constanduros refers to having decided to let her cottage for the duration of the war and writes from 9 Wetherby Gardens in London, until she speaks of moving back to Sussex 'when the flying bombs came over' (Constanduros, 1946: 76). Agg also writes from 9 Wetherby Gardens from 1942, and from New Cottage, West Burton (the neighbouring village to Bury) in 1945.[30] Agg and Constanduros produced a great deal of radio broadcast material, so much so that in December 1940 they asked that their adaptation of a novel for radio be credited to 'Peter Peveril', as their names had 'appeared against a good many plays lately'.[31] The extent of Constanduros's abdication from matters of money in their joint work did not extend to the work itself, which in the later 1940s included adaptations of Dickens's major novels. Constanduros's creative voice sounds clearly and most delightfully in *Mr and Mrs Sparkes*, a situation comedy which is a funny, yet toe-curlingly painful representation of the 'quiet, domesticated couple living in a small suburban house near London'. If there was a voice missing from Constanduros's married life in Sutton, it might be said to have been found here in the Sparkes' 'neat bright, soulless-looking room [...] quite pleasant and comfortable but, like hundreds of its kind, entirely without character' (Constanduros and Agg, 1941: Introduction. See Figure 34.)[32] Working with Agg did not stop Constanduros from continuing to write with Denis, nor does Agg's negotiating stance drown out her own voice in the pursuit of royalties.

34 *Mr & Mrs Sparkes: Six One Act Plays*, 1941, by Mabel Constaduros and Howard Agg.

In 1943 she sought the support of the Society of Authors in her battle against a publisher who was refusing to give proper sales accounts or return the plays he held so that she could hand them to the more reliable management of Samuel French. The Society of Authors pointed out that, first, she had failed to renew her membership for the previous two years and, secondly, some of the rights issues she was complaining about would be solved if she joined the League of British Dramatists, which would act as agents for such sales. The subsequent exchange demonstrates the often indignant edge that Constanduros's professional voice could reveal:

> Dear Mr Kilham Roberts,
> I hadn't heard of the League of British Dramatists before. Do I understand that it is an affiliated society to that of the Society of Authors, and that it undertakes to act as author's agent?
> In this case, does it undertake to offer material and has it the staff to offer it in foreign serial and other markets?
> Does it undertake to offer the material of all its members? This would seem to me to be a dangerous policy as many utterly incompetent people might join simply in order to have their goods marketed. Also, what commission does the society charge for acting as author's agent? Surely the membership fee doesn't include that?[33]

She received a swift reply dated 25 May 1943, giving her the required information, but by the end of that year she had written to say that she no longer wished to continue membership – though it is unclear whether she ever in fact held it.

Voicing difference

Mabel Constanduros placed a great deal of emphasis on the voice as the conveyor of truth. For her, the voice, not the eye, is the window to the soul: 'I find voices a great indication of character, especially if one's ear has a clear field to judge them and is not distracted by the impression the eye is sending at the same time to one's brain' (Constanduros, 1946: 129). She celebrates the freedom that radio gives her to be 'whatever character you choose, since your appearance can neither help nor hinder', but warns that the freedoms of apparently limitless artifice are constrained: '[t]he microphone is merciless, though, to affectation and insincerity. The moment you cease to mean what you say, listeners will find you out' (1946: 39). The 'listeners' are the unseen, all-important recipients of information, entertainment and instruction, enjoyed in an unlimited collective experience within Reith's paternalistic vision of cultural, if not social, equality:

> [B]ecause everyone can have as much as they like of it, broadcasting, at least as delivered by the fledgling BBC, is no respector [sic] of persons; it is the same for everyone: 'Most of the good things of this world are badly distributed and most people have to go without them. Wireless is a good thing, but it may be shared by all alike, for the same outlay, and to the same extent ... The genius and the fool, the wealthy and the poor listen simultaneously ... there is no first and third class.' Broadcasting, said Reith, had the effect of 'making the nation as one man'. (Higgins, 2015: 9, citing Reith, 1924)

This was also an essentially conservative project, and to pick up Alison Light's argument, radio was part of a 'contradictory process of a modernizing conservatism [...] central to the period [the interwar years] and to its formation, or reformation, of Englishness' (Light, 1991: 215).

Reith's democratising vision for the BBC might also be critiqued for its patriarchal assumptions about class and gender difference, an instance of the careless masculinity that has made and continues to make histories that marginalise or simply forget women, and here forgets their role in laying the foundations of today's broadcasting. Hilda Matheson, the first director of 'talks', programmed 'an extraordinarily mixed bag of subject-matter [...] from theatre criticism to economics from foreign affairs to tips for housewives' (Higgins, 2015: 17). While she broadcast the voices of women writers such as Vita Sackville-West, who gave a talk on 'the modern woman', Constanduros was writing and performing a new 'Buggins' sketch. Later in her 'afterword', Light speaks of the influence of the wireless among the other new media, and the 'buried chapter' in her book; one that would have focused on the 'significance of the absurd accents, pealing voices and clipped tones [...] which were once the new and distinctive sounds of class between the wars' (Light, 1991: 215). As she notes, the life and work of the pioneering women we want to reclaim in feminist histories are all too often full of awkward and often uncomfortable contradictions. In their bid for personal freedom, 'what began as a ventriloquy of masculinity and an attempt to emancipate themselves from earlier erotic codes of femininity, locked women into a paralyzing and potentially infinite series of social demarcations against their own kind' (Light, 1991: 215).

If Constanduros's discovery of her 'cockney voice' set her free, in the terms Elsie Fogerty first recognised in her diction classes, it also worked to reform and reinforce the conservative values of family and class disturbed so radically in the interwar years, and further, laid the foundations for the much-vaunted idea of the stoicism of the working classes, and particularly Londoners, on which so much wartime propaganda was to rest. A column-length article in the *Lancashire Evening Post* on 19 April 1937 led with a photograph of Constanduros, who was appearing in *No Sleep for the Wicked* at the Blackpool Opera House. The headline reads: 'A Voice and A Smile You All Know / Mabel Constanduros to Meet Housewives.' Constanduros is then quoted as follows:

> The English working-man's wife is the salt of the earth. I try with Mrs. Buggins to give a faithful picture of how good these people are; how they manage so marvelously in adverse circumstances. They are more important than any other class of beings in England.[34]

The journalist, Sylvia Heath, goes on to comment on the 'sincerity' of Constanduros's voice: she is 'small, quiet-voiced, and sincere. A social worker, who is looking forward to a time when her duties as broadcaster, actress and authoress will allow her to devote herself to the working families.' But her heart is always in Sussex with her '21-year-old son, Michael who is the apple of my eye', she tells the journalist. She then speaks of her nerves when performing, especially before a Lancashire audience who 'are supposed to be difficult', but reminds her audience that 'Aunt Maria of the Buggins family is a Lancashire woman'. The journalist closes with an assurance that 'deep sincerity, a quick wit and a true womanly understanding of others' troubles will make the real person as popular as the voice which has become that of a friend'.

What is so striking here is the mode by which the representation of the 'other' is portrayed as an act of do-gooding, part of a greater social work for 'others'. The Bugginses are not Constanduros or her kind/class/caste, but they are part of the fabric of nationhood that she is instrumental in making. And the Bugginses are 'good', 'important', and so she 'does good' for them. There is, of course, no acknowledgement of the good the Bugginses did for her in providing her with a living. Constanduros also plays the local card in her own favour, reminding the journalist and the readers of her affectionate and respectful depiction of the Northern woman in 'Aunt Maria'. The Buggins family, the suburban Mr and Mrs Sparkes and the later Robinson family all have their own corners of the local to convey, the specificities of different voices, voicing difference;

the 'us' and 'them' on which the success of domestic comedy stands and which Constanduros created so well in early radio.

There is one other voice running through Constanduros's autobiography that deserves attention. It is the voice of the constant, live-in, domestic help without whom little of Constanduros's work could have been carried out. She is mentioned throughout, but halfway through the book Constanduros reinforces her place as 'one of us' when she points out that 'Bina, my housekeeper, must certainly have a chapter to herself, because without her I could not have a home' (Constanduros, 1946: 75). Albina M. Smith came to work for Constanduros when 'Michael was about six', at which point they were still living in Sutton with Athanasius.

> She had not been in the house a week before I knew what a treasure had been sent to me. She is a beautiful cook, can sew and wash, mend a wireless set or a burnt fuse, make clothes, trim hats, and turn her hand to anything. We have lived together now for more than twenty-four years in great contentment and understanding. She has nursed me with skill and kindness through many illnesses. There is no difficulty that she cannot surmount, no task that she will not tackle; you never see her out of temper or in a muddle. (1946: 75)

This is the stuff of middle-class fiction, or at least envy, for a class increasingly left to its own devices by the diminishing ranks of women prepared to take on domestic work. This 'sturdy', 'dark-eyed' Welsh woman 'with a smile which is lovely because it is so kind' leads Constanduros to admit that '[w]hen I am away from Bina I miss her as a child would its nurse' (1946: 75–6). Constanduros heaps four pages of sunny praise on the woman, who also has 'a free and rather Rabelaisian tongue' and no hesitation in wielding a poker in defence of her mistress late at night, when an inebriated man refuses to leave the house having been told that Constanduros does not wish to see him again. 'She is a wonderful friend to have because she is discreet' is the only clue Constanduros gives to there being anything in her domestic life that requires discretion.

Mabel Constanduros's professional success, her life lived separately from her marital home, was made possible by the presence of another woman taking the weight of the domestic duties. This is not to say that Constanduros was not the devoted mother that she portrays in her autobiography, but that the domestic pleasure she enjoyed, in both her London and Sussex homes, was made possible by the domestic stability provided for her and her son by Bina. She also employed personal secretaries (Hilda later becoming her daughter-in-law) and gardeners in her Sussex homes.[35]

Constanduros forged a particular kind of freedom for herself during a period that gave unprecedented opportunities to middle-class women in the interwar years. Having found her voice(s), she is revealed as a hard bargainer, a determined professional, an engaging, generous friend and affectionate employer. As a writer and entertainer she has a remarkable grasp of the new medium:

> Here is a new kind of entertainment immensely important because it is within reach of everybody, which needs a special technique in writing. It would seem a better policy to encourage authors who understand it to write new radio material, which should be acted by people who understand radio. (Constanduros, 1946: 128)

As she reflects on her long and successful career, her autobiographical voice echoes something of the ambitions expressed by the first director of the BBC. But Constanduros's history of her broadcasting career voices the ambition of an uncompromising professional and a passionate working mother, determined to capture the hearts and minds of her diverse, but essentially middle-class, audience – from whom she is not so very separate.

Notes

1 *The Stage*, 3 October 1929, p. 4, https://archive.thestage.co.uk (accessed 30 November 2016).
2 *The Buggins Family* began its regular run in 1928, but the first sketch to be broadcast, 'The Buggins Family Out for the Day', went out on 1 September 1925 at 8 p.m. Records of broadcast details have been sourced via the work in progress of the BBC Genome project, http://genome.ch.bbc.co.uk, which draws information from the BBC publication *Radio Times* 1923–2009, specifically http://genome.ch.bbc.co.uk/schedules/2lo/1925-09-01 (accessed 30 November 2016).
3 Clark (2009) provides thirteen sketches first recorded between 1927 and 1932. Scott Jeffs (2016) examines the structure of a Buggins sketch as published for live performance by Samuel French and as captured via transcripts of performance scripts.
4 *Time and Tide* was a weekly review, first published in 1920.
5 Mrs Miniver became even better known through the 1942 William Wyler film of the same name, focusing on the pluck of the English housewife in

wartime and credited with influencing the American public's sympathy to US involvement in the Second World War.

6   For more on the legacy of Mabel Constanduros's cockney characters and her modern counterpart in Catherine Tate's 'Nan', see Bush-Bailey (2012).
7   Barry Took in *The Oxford Dictionary of National Biography* refers to Grandma as 'a crusty, cantankerous old biddy', http://www.oxforddnb.com/index/101060317/Mabel-Constanduros (accessed 30 November 2016).
8   'Dream Kitchen', British Pathé, 1945, https://www.youtube.com/watch?v=Y9DHu3YlCdg (accessed 30 November 2016).
9   For more detail on Mabel's family life and possible early subjects for her 'cockney' creations, see Purcell (2014). My thanks to Jennifer Purcell for her generosity in sharing materials she has accessed through contacts with the Constanduros families. Although living on separate continents, we have shared research findings and ideas about Mabel via email, skype and in our now annual meetings. Jennifer Purcell is currently preparing an extended biography of Mabel and Denis Constanduros.
10 Constanduros's autobiography is dedicated to the memory of her mother 'and Tony'. The third child is not named and possibly did not reach full term.
11 Constanduros is always enthusiastic about her amateur dramatic experience, citing the many professional performers and writers who started their careers in amateur dramatic companies (Constanduros, 1946: 36–7).
12 'Lloyds Dramatic Society', *The Times*, 10 January 1923, p. 12, http://www.thetimes.co.uk/tto/archive (accessed 27 January 2016).
13 The contracts and correspondence between the BBC and Mabel Constanduros and her collaborators are used with kind permission of the BBC Written Archives Centre (hereinafter referred to as BBC WAC). Mabel Constanduros, File 1A, 1926–1938.
14 BBC Genome. *Devoted Elsie* was broadcast on the Regional Programme, appearing first on 5 February 1926, 5WA Cardiff; 12 February, 5SC Glasgow; 15 February, 2BE Belfast; and 26 February, 6BM Bournemouth. There does not appear to be a record for 2LO, which identifies a London broadcast. Although the Regional Programme broadcasts were local transmissions, they all came under the BBC's broadcast monopoly. At the outbreak of war in 1939, they were merged under the umbrella of the Home Service, which then broadcast simultaneously across Britain.
15 BBC Genome.
16 Phyllis Panting is also credited with placing Mabel's articles and short stories in the press (Constanduros, 1946: 63).
17 BBC Genome.
18 BBC WAC, copyright, file 1A, 1926–1938.
19 BBC Genome.
20 *The Times*, 10 December 1928, p. 12.
21 BBC WAC, copyright file, 1A, 1926–1938.

22 *The Times*, 9 February 1957, p. 1. Hogan's apparently sudden disappearance from Constanduros's professional and personal life in 1936 is complicated further by West Sussex local histories, which suggest that Hogan once occupied a cottage in the village of Bury, where Constanduros still owned and occupied her house, Prattenden's.
23 Athanasius's 'sudden death' at his home in Sutton was noted in several local newspapers, always with reference to his relationship to the 'radio star Mabel Constanduros' (*Gloucester Citizen*, 10 July 1937, p. 1); '"Mrs Buggins" Widowed', *Western Gazette*, 16 July 1937, p. 13. If there had been early money troubles – and Mabel refers to Ath's ongoing pessimism about the future of insurance broking – he was recorded as leaving the net sum of £7,554 5s 9d, and his will directed that if his son, Michael, did not wish to take over the business, it was to pass to his two clerks (*Gloucestershire Echo*, 7 September 1937, p. 1). Michael did take over the business and ran it successfully (Constanduros, 1946: 105).
24 BBC WAC, copyright, file 1A, 1926–1938.
25 Ibid.
26 BBC WAC, copyright, file 1B, 1939–1940.
27 BBC WAC, copyright, file 2A 1941–1942, contract for 40 guineas fee for Constanduros and Agg's *Laughing Mirror*, dated 31 October 1941, and signed by Agg includes a note stating that he was able to secure higher fees when co-writing with Constanduros, otherwise he should receive staff fees. A separate file under Agg's name, identified as Agreements file 1942–1950, makes reference to Agg's BBC office (Room 431, Aeolian Hall) with reference to Constanduros and Agg's radio adaptation of Dickens's *Bleak House* (the last of thirteen episodes was broadcast on Sunday 7 January 1945) assigning all rights to the BBC for the considerable sum of 200 guineas.
28 BBC WAC, copyright, file 1B, 1939–1940, Agg/Candler letters, 30 August, 10 and 13 September 1940.
29 BBC WAC. The affirmative response is dated 4 November.
30 BBC WAC, Agg's contract agreement files 1942–1950.
31 BBC WAC, copyright, file 1B, 1939–1940, contract letters regarding *Yellow Streak*, 17 November–18 December.
32 The six one-act plays for three or four characters are introduced with a note that they first appeared on BBC Radio. Richard Goolden played Nelson Sparkes (Ducksie) and Mabel, Mrs Sparkes (Mummie). There were no little Sparkes.
33 British Library, Add MSS 63220, 1939–49, Society of Authors, letter dated 21 May 1943.
34 *Lancashire Evening Post*, 19 April 1937, p. 5.
35 My thanks to Jennifer Purcell who provided me with information from the Constanduros family scrapbook in which an obituary notice in the *Yorkshire Evening News* (n.d.) states that Mabel left Miss Albina Smith (Bina) £150 per annum, and £50 per annum to her gardener, Fred Ansett.

References

Bush-Bailey, Gilli (2012), 'Women Like Us', *Comedy Studies*, 3.2, pp. 151–9.

Clark, William J. (2009), 'Mabel Constanduros, The Buggins Family', recording, Windyridge Variety Series, http://www.musichallcds.co.uk (accessed 11 September 2018).

Cole, Marion (1967), *Fogie: The Life of Elsie Fogerty, Pioneer of Speech-training for the Theatre and Everyday Life*, London: Peter Davies.

Constanduros, Mabel (1927), 'Cheering Up Maria', in Maggie B. Gale and Gilli Bush-Bailey, eds, *Plays and Performance Texts by Women 1880–1930: An Anthology of Plays by British and American Women from the Modernist Period*, Manchester; Manchester University Press, pp. 636–41.

Constanduros, Mabel (1946), *Shreds and Patches*, London: Lawson and Dunn.

Constanduros, Mabel, and Howard Agg (1941), *Mr and Mrs Sparkes*, London: Samuel French.

Higgins, Charlotte (2015), *The New Noise*, London: Guardian Books.

Light, Alison (1991), *Forever England*, London: Routledge.

Purcell, Jennifer (2014), '"Behind the blessed shelter of the microphone": Managing Celebrity and Career on the Early BBC - Mabel Constanduros, 1925-1957', *Women's History Review*, 24.3, pp. 372–88, DOI: 10.1080/09612025.2014.964068 (accessed 11 September 2018).

Reith, John (1924), *Broadcast Over Britain*, London: Hodder and Stoughton.

Scott Jeffs, Carolyn (2016), 'Voice, Personality and Grandma: Mabel Constanduros and the Buggins Family', *Comedy Studies*, 7.2, pp. 124–36.

Took, Barry (2016), 'Constanduros, Mabel (1880–1957)', *Oxford Dictionary of National Biography*, Oxford: Oxford University Press, http://www.oxforddnb.com/view/10.1093/ref:odnb/9780198614128.001.0001/odnb-9780198614128-e-60317 (accessed 30 November 2016).

12

The odd woman

Margaret Rutherford

John Stokes

Although Margaret Rutherford's (1892–1972) presence became familiar to an enormous public, she remained in her performances the odd woman out: at times 'difficult', yet irrepressible; peculiar in dress, mannerism, speech, yet invariably to the fore. With their predilection for physical detail, at best careless, at worst cruel, all too commonplace at the time, critics liked to make fun of her features: her trembling chins, pursed lips, popping eyes, her mobile eyebrows. She was certainly physically memorable. Her whole body seemed to invite comment, especially when on the move: clasped hands, large strides interspersed with sudden darts, a bustling and, at the same time, purposive gait. Over the years her costumes and props became standardised: umbrella, beads, spectacles (alternating with lorgnette, monocle, even binoculars), a capacious shawl (or shapeless cape) and, always to top it off, floral hats that seemed to lead a horticultural life of their own. Throughout her career reviewers turned to animal epithets to describe her, but they were strangely mixed: porpoise, dragon, moth. It's as if the journalists were competing not only among themselves but with the actress herself in their attempts to capture her presence in a single stroke.

Rutherford's origins were unusual. A significant number of the actresses who achieved prominence in the early twentieth century came from a theatrical background – a vocational advantage that had often led to early starts as a child performer. The father of Fay Compton (1894–1978), for instance, was the actor Edward Compton, and she was acting professionally by 1911; Nina Boucicault (1867–1950) was a member of a long-standing theatrical dynasty; Joyce Carey (1898–1952) was the daughter of the actors Gerald Lawrence and Lilian Braithwaite. Rutherford, by contrast, was born into a quite untheatrical family with a troubled

35 Margaret Rutherford as Aunt Dolly in *I'm All Right Jack*, 1959.

history – her father William, who worked as a journalist, suffered from a severely depressive illness that erupted at times into extreme violence. In 1883 he was found guilty of the murder of his father and incarcerated in an insane asylum until 1890. Two or three years after his release his wife, Florence, attempted to rebuild their lives in India, taking with them their baby daughter Margaret, who had been born in London in 1892. This period ended tragically when Florence killed herself. Margaret was not to learn the details of a doubly sad story until some time later. In the meantime, she was brought up in south-west London by an aunt and other relatives, attending first Wimbledon High School and then a boarding establishment on the south coast. Although the record of her appearances in school productions shows that she already displayed an interest in acting, her musical abilities were considered more suited to a respectable career and so as a young woman she became a piano teacher around Wimbledon. The desire to perform, however, would not be appeased: she trained as an elocutionist and took part in amateur productions. Eventually she persuaded Lilian Baylis to take her on as a trainee at the Old Vic, beginning with a string of non-speaking parts in the 1925/6 season. Let go by Baylis, she returned to the amateurs but managed to find employment – including the role of Madame Vinard in *Trilby* – at a number of repertory theatres in outer London and in Oxford.

When Rutherford finally began to attract attention, several actresses born within a very few years of her were already well established. Fay Compton had made her name in J. M. Barrie's *Mary Rose* in 1920; Gladys Cooper (1888–1971) had been a Gaiety Girl in the early 1900s and later did well in revivals ranging from Pinero's *The Second Mrs Tanqueray* to *Peter Pan*; Edith Evans, born in 1888, was by the 1920s combining Shakespeare with major roles in Shaw and Congreve. For these women the main opportunities, apart from Shakespeare and the occasional classic, came from Coward, Maugham, Novello, Barrie and Shaw, major dramatists of the first three decades of the new century. Rutherford's progression would be rather different.

In one of her earliest West End appearances, *Hervey House*, a light comedy about an aristocratic *ménage à trois* at Her Majesty's directed by Tyrone Guthrie in 1935, Rutherford offered 'a most lively sketch of a troublesome aunt' (Avery, 1935: 15). The run was short but Rutherford's interpretation attracted some positive attention. Being older than the average newcomer made her an eligible candidate for such roles and in this case she replaced the more established Athene Seyler (1889–1990). In the same year, in a play by Robert Morley entitled *Short Story*, Rutherford confirmed her ability to represent the awkward element by giving 'a brilliant performance as the Gorgon of the village institute' (Brown, 1935: 22). By now she was 43 years old and several female performers significantly younger than her were already succeeding in the classical repertoire – women such as Peggy Ashcroft (1907–91), Flora Robson (1902–84) and Celia Johnson (1908–82). Formal training had become much more available with the setting up of the Central School of Speech and Drama and the Royal Academy of Dramatic Art (Sutherland, 2007): Johnson and Robson trained at RADA; Ashcroft was a product of Central. In 1932–33 alone Ashcroft played six Shakespearean roles together with major parts in *She Stoops to Conquer* and *The School for Scandal*. By the mid-1930s she was Juliet to the alternating Romeos of Gielgud and Olivier, and participating in the increased interest in Chekhov with *The Seagull*. Johnson began with a role in *Major Barbara* in 1928 and took on Ophelia in 1929. Having first been directed by Tyrone Guthrie in Cambridge, Robson continued with serious roles in Shakespeare, Chekhov, Pirandello and, above all, Ibsen.

However one configures dates and careers, Rutherford's professional experience looks out of kilter with that of these, her peers. It was too late for her to be considered for youthful heroines, including Shakespearean heroines. When it came to casting, she belonged, if anything, with a handful of actresses older than herself, stylish women who had made their names before the First World War but who were available to take on mature roles which, more often than not, carried traces of a lively past. Lilian Braithwaite (1873–1948) made a name for herself as the hysterical mother in Coward's sensational *The Vortex* in 1924; Marie Tempest (1864–1942) starred in Coward's *Hay Fever* (1925) as an actress worried about her fading looks. The remarkable Mrs Patrick Campbell (1865–1940) played Mrs Alving in Ibsen's *Ghosts* in 1928; Irene Vanbrugh (1872–1949) played Shakespeare's Gertrude in 1931. Significantly enough, these tended to be maternal roles, passionate women burdened with difficult children. Rutherford's unglamorous style, coupled with her late start, would oblige her to establish herself as a 'type' outside the immediate family circle and yet omnipresent within the modern world. It would be, in every sense, a creative challenge.

When, much later on in her career in 1960, Rutherford appeared in a not very well-regarded play, *Farewell, Farewell, Eugene,* the *Observer* critic wrote of her ability to convey 'illumination through extravagance'.

> Miss Rutherford – it's time to say it – is not only a great comic but a great actress. I know that she acts in a highly personal manner. Yet what we see is not Margaret Rutherford, the actress, but a woman of the Margaret Rutherford type, and in real life there are women we can only describe by referring to her. If acting can be called creative here surely is a high example. (Jones, 1959: 22)

Unlike a good deal of critical commentary, this is actually very helpful, because it encourages us to consider the ways in which a unique type might enable us to comprehend 'real life'. Of course, when thinking of a 'type' we shouldn't expect absolute consistency, since roles are chosen by agents, producers, directors, who will sometimes simply aim for repetition of known ability, but at other times will opt for more nuanced casting, playing games with established characteristics and occasionally deliberately casting against them. Not that there was anything passive about Margaret Rutherford, nor about the roles that she chose to play. For all her recognisability, at no point did she simply become the creation of manipulative producers, directors or, on occasion, writers. Her biographers all suggest that she was an active force in selecting parts and, crucially, in deciding what to do with them. There are clear signs from very early on that, whenever she could, she opted for roles in which the woman was comically, even harshly, represented, at least on the surface, and then looked for an explanation. She was funny – sometimes sublimely so – because she always seemed to know why her character behaved as she did.

What, though, was the 'type' that Margaret Rutherford's performances made real? One answer takes us away from the theatre altogether, away from comedy, and to a quite different meaning of 'odd' that originated in the nineteenth century amid an increasing fear that women were now outnumbered by men, leading to a numerically 'odd' number of unmarried, and probably unmarriageable, females. The presence of these 'odd' women, sometimes referred to as a 'surplus', was explained as the result of an imbalance within the population as a whole: around the turn of the century statistics based on the census suggested that there were simply not enough men to go around. Of course, there always had been unmarried women, but the degree of social concern was new – in 1893 George Gissing actually published a novel entitled *The Odd Women* – and it was to increase, partly on the basis of supposed evidence supplied by the official census, partly for reasons less easy to identify. In 1821 the ratio of men to women was 1,000 to 1,036; in 1901 it was 1,000 to 1,068 (Jeffreys, 1985: 88–9). In 1911, although the ratio remained constant, the number of single women over 25 increased. Another and quite overwhelming factor was soon to come into play – the loss of countless young male lives in the calamity of the First World War. Now to the number of the 'odd' had to be added young widows, bereaved fiancés and girlfriends. Following the 1921 Census the figures that appeared in the press varied enormously – anything between one and two million 'surplus' women (Nicholson, 2007: 22–3). Of particular import was the fact revealed by the 1931 Census that a significant proportion, some 50 per cent, of the women who had been aged between 25 and 29 and unmarried in 1921 were still single a decade later (Nicholson, 2007: 70–1). For these women, spinsterhood looked very much like a permanent state.

What the figures claimed to show was one thing; how they were interpreted was another. It was all too easy to assume, perhaps fuelled by male fears of female autonomy, that the spinster was doomed to loneliness, frustration and failure and that she was invariably in a situation not of her own choosing, ignoring the possibility that she might have sought, and indeed found, sexual and social fulfilment outside of heterosexual marriage or that she might have preferred to direct her energies away from the family into creative or professional activities. Many feminist battles have been, and continue to be, fought over just such issues. Nonetheless, it was in this highly charged and prejudicial interwar climate that Rutherford developed and sustained her own persona by taking key roles in plays, written by both men and women, in which the figure of the spinster had an apparently marginal but, in fact, importantly functional role to play.

As Maggie B. Gale suggests in her study of women playwrights between 1918 and 1962, 'in plays of the period, the spinster was often, though not always, virginal, naïve or simply judgmental, thus becoming a comic figure or ideological device' (Gale, 1996: 174). She continues:

> Thus what connects these various spinster types is the fact that they are often used as 'fill in' to the main plot for moments of comic relief or as a means of opposing one ideology with another. They share with many representations of single, working women, a defined series of characteristics, but are rarely the centre of narrative focus. (1996: 175)

This is true, but neither does the spinster disappear within the narrative altogether. Much of Rutherford's comedy depended on the paradoxical joke that although 'surplus', she was also somehow essential. Another way of indicating that paradox was to describe her as 'eccentric', a cliché that countless critics turned to throughout her life, that, indeed, she sometimes resorted to herself. Applied not merely to an unusual manner or lifestyle, 'eccentricity' can be invoked more precisely as an indication of the position of the 'odd woman', at a distance from the 'centre' as it was occupied by the conventional nuclear family. Time and again the social centre cannot hold without her supplementary, her 'eccentric' presence.

One figure above all, a female identity in which Rutherford, following on from that 'troublesome aunt' in *Hervey House*, might be said to have specialised, brought a necessary element of asymmetry and incompleteness to what might otherwise have appeared to be an entirely idealised view of domestic life. This was the spinster aunt. In a remarkable essay on the nineteenth-century novel from Jane Austen to Henry James, Colm Tóibín has noted how the frequent absence of mothers is matched by the vital presence of women who either are or who act like aunts, relating this to the need for heroines to escape their immediate biological ancestors if they are to achieve any degree of independence. This does not necessarily mean that these aunts are always welcome agents. As Tóibín also says, they can be 'both kind and mean, both well-intentioned and duplicitous, both rescuing and destroying' (Tóibín, 2011).

The full distinctiveness of Rutherford's qualifications as a stage aunt became apparent when she created Bijou Furze in *Spring Meeting* by M. J. Farrell and John Perry, which opened at the Ambassadors in the summer of 1938, directed by John Gielgud. 'M. J. Farrell' was the *nom de plume* of Molly Keane, an Anglo-Irishwoman who had already published some seven novels specialising in a kind of semi-comic Irish Gothic, set among families preoccupied with hunting and other country pursuits, worried about their financial state, but oblivious to the political world around them. *Spring Meeting* belongs with this branch of the so-called 'Big House' genre, but at the same time it relates to family comedies such Noël Coward's *Hay Fever* (1925) or Dodie Smith's *Dear Octopus* (August 1938). In *Spring Meeting* a cantankerous and excessively parsimonious landowner, a widower, has two unmarried daughters: Joan is dangerously old still to be single, although she is in love with a former stable boy who is unsuitable in terms of class and because of his Catholic background. Baby, the younger woman, is much more lively and already desperate to catch a man. Sir Richard also has a spinster sister – Bijou, the part that Rutherford made her own. Bijou is middle-aged, snobbish, selfish, indolent and puritanical, though an inveterate punter. She bullies the girls with visions of a future much like her own present: 'at your age you should be done with all ideas of marriage. Settled down to mind the house and garden, and help in the parish like your aunts before you.' Bijou's place in the family is continually played off not only against her two nieces but against a louche divorcee, an old flame of Sir Richard's, who is over from England together with her son, on whom Baby has her eye, At the conclusion – increasingly farcical and fast paced – not only are Bijou's nieces engaged to be married, but so too is Sir Richard. Joan and Michael must leave the Big House if they are to achieve independence, but the others will remain, prepared to take the risk despite the

36 Margaret Rutherford in *Spring Meeting*, 1938.

threat of penury. Bijou, too, will stay on, unmarried but linked to the family unit through a shared love of the turf.

Bijou Furze made a notable impact because Rutherford found depths – not always pleasant – in what remained in many ways a grotesque creation. For all that they readily invoked Chekhov, Synge and Shaw, few reviews failed to focus their attention on her performance, speaking of it as 'a study which is both hilarious and almost painful in its pathological exactitude' (Agate, 1938: 4) and noting 'the force and the pathos' (Brown, 1938: 11). Bijou, as the critics recognised and as Rutherford herself realised, is a social remnant, a member of the 'surplus' as pathetic as she is malevolent. Joan, the niece, recalls that after the war 'chaps were scarce'. James, the butler, remembers 'Miss Bijou when she was a young girl the same as yourself. I remember her as it were yesterday with a fine head of hair and a blue silk dress, and as light in her step as yourself. A lovely girl. And not a one to court her.' After all, if Bijou 'got a husband and family she wouldn't be the pitiful old lady she is to this day'.

Some said that when Rutherford came to play Miss Prism in Wilde's *The Importance of Being Earnest* the year after *Spring Meeting*, she brought to the role much the same quality of feeling as she had discovered in Bijou Furze. One critic wrote of 'the human, almost too hauntingly human Prism of Miss Rutherford' (Brown, 1939: 9). Rutherford herself later both denied and admitted the point, saying that although she never intended a similarity, it may have been that she saw in both characters 'a deep strain of loneliness, of withdrawal from the world', adding 'this I have always personally understood' (Rutherford and Robyns, 1972: 59).

The very fact that Rutherford is one of the few – Athene Seyler is another – to have played both Lady Bracknell and Miss Prism is some indication of her ability to match contraries. Bracknell is both aunt and mother; she is also a wife, although we hear very little about that side of her life. Prism would seem to be the quintessential spinster, although she does find romance at the end. Wilde plays havoc with our preconceptions, which made both parts ideal for Rutherford. Moreover both women are largely oblivious of the effect they are having on others – a tendency that is shared among several characters that Rutherford made her own in the 1930s. Solipsists all, they sail blithely ahead, pursuing their own goals.

There were three years between Bijou Furze and Madame Arcati, the highly 'eccentric' medium in Noël Coward's *Blithe Spirit*, which opened at the Piccadilly Theatre in 1941. This was in some ways a development

The Odd Woman

out of Rutherford's mid-1930s roles, which Coward must have seen. As has often been pointed out since, and was, in fact, remarked upon at the time, Coward's 'improbable farce' came at a time when death was in the air.

> Madame Arcati, as grotesquely gay an old party as ever gulped Martinis and fresh air in equal quantities, prior to materialising a tambourine. This part, superbly played by Miss Margaret Rutherford, is the saving of this farce about the dead because it keeps it away from fact and feeling, wildly ludicrous and so offering as Hamlet said of this own theatricals, 'no offence in the world'. (Brown, 1941: 7)

Such comments, though suited to 1941, are insufficient to account for the lasting appeal of Rutherford's performance as it is preserved in the film version released in 1945. The role of a spiritualist medium confirmed her unique ability to convey the ambiguities of what she herself called 'my usual dotty old lady stuff' (Rutherford and Robyns, 1972: 83). According to the *OED*, 'dottiness' originally referred to an uncertain way of walking, suggesting either feeble-mindedness or someone who was away from their normal environment. By the 1920s, or perhaps earlier, it had become noticeably gendered. The touchstone here is P. G. Wodehouse, creator of Jeeves and Wooster and a great connoisseur of aunts, who provides the first dictionary citation for 'dottiness' as meaning 'eccentricity'. Certainly very little of that original meaning remained in Rutherford's performance, since her customary walk by no means implied a lack of direction and was extremely determined. Although undoubtedly 'dotty' in the more modern sense because she believes in the supernatural, Arcati has absolute confidence in her own intellectual and physical abilities. A keen cyclist, she has a habit of placing her hands behind her hips, hauling up her shoulders so that she quite literally 'puts her back into it'. Her very language is active, a matter of re-energised cliché: 'Rome wasn't built in a day', 'Hungry as a hunter', 'Chin up', 'Great Scott', 'Good hunting'.

Apparently Rutherford was at first unwilling to take on the role, not wishing to make fun of spiritualism. Later on Coward was to complain of her actual performance as 'fussy' (Merriman, 2009: 71–2). However, one or two reviews and the evidence of the later film suggest that it was out of these tensions that Rutherford created the role. If Arcati is a fraud, she is giving nothing away, and Rutherford imbues her with great vitality and an unexpected lightness. James Agate's review suggests that he may have known something about initial differences between author and actress

– and comes down firmly on the side of the actress. 'Whether Miss Margaret Rutherford does or does not present the medium Mr Coward first imagined', wrote Agate, 'I neither know nor care.' He continued, 'nothing could be more wildly funny than this grotesque embodiment, now pursuing the humdrum of her craft as soberly as a monthly nurse, now orgulous and ecstatic in inspired flight, for which sofas and settees are made to serve as springboard – not metaphorically, but literally' (Agate, 1941: 2). This technical observation is borne out by many other Rutherford performances in which she rises from a sitting position, a technique she perfected as she got older. Indeed, it is revealing how often Rutherford was described as bird-like. The title of Coward's comedy may derive from Shelley's 'To a Skylark' ('Hail to thee, blithe Spirit!/ Bird thou never wert'), and may most obviously refer to the deceased but still flirtatious Elvira; in performance it could equally be applied to Rutherford's soaring presence.

In the films she made during and soon after the Second World War, Rutherford was almost invariably cast as a leader, a female equivalent of men in government or in the field. *The Demi-Paradise* (1943) has a flashback structure, from the wartime present to the immediately pre-war. A Russian engineer played by Laurence Olivier visits England to develop a revolutionary new ship's propeller, encounters the 'old' England, and watches it respond to desperate circumstance. Rutherford is a do-gooder, bossy and commanding, energetic but old fashioned, who collects for a children's charity and organises the town's annual historical pageant. At first the Russian accuses the English of 'living in the past' and being 'a bit sleepy', but eventually he discovers the solution to his propeller problem by gazing at a cup of English tea. The English throughout make the best of things. They don't give up, appreciate the value of a sense of humour, are warm and friendly beneath the surface and, above all, 'love freedom'. The first version of Rutherford's pageant features the Roman occupation of England, Elizabeth I, news of the Battle of Waterloo. The second version has all this plus a final march of international soldiers – Polish, Czech, Belgian etc. – with the Rutherford character exhorting her company: 'Forward March', 'Let Victory be Unveiled'. The obvious propaganda message is that it is in the interests of both the Russians and the English to become allies.

Russia features, too, in *The Yellow Canary* (1943), which opens in September 1940 somewhere in Russia, as a romantic Russian tells English sailors his story in flashback – it is essential to hark back to pre-war times in order to explain the present. Much of the remembered

37a–d Sequence of photographs taken in 1935: the costume in which Margaret Rutherford gave her audition for first West End appearance in *Hervey House*, 1935, at Her Majesty's Theatre.

action takes place on board a ship captured by the Germans. Rutherford is a noisy upper-class woman, a gossip with a taste for cliché who gets most things wrong, but is basically on the right side. When she deliberately trips up a German who calls her an 'old sow' (in German), she shows herself to be more courageous that her male companion, a veteran soldier. (In her autobiography Rutherford claims that the kick was her own invention: 'my own statement on how I felt about everything to do with the war' [Rutherford and Robyns, 1972: 83]). On her return, she commences selling her house in Berkeley Square and moving to Balham, so there's also an atmosphere of inter-class solidarity. Finally, *English without Tears* (1944), scripted by Terence Rattigan and Anatole de Grunwald, shifts from an unspecified pre-war date to 1940. Rutherford is Lady Cristobel Beauclerk, an aristocrat who campaigns for the protection of British migrating birds (though described as an 'old bird' herself). On a trip to the League of Nations to argue her case she finds herself confronted by international mayhem. Flash forward to 1940 and she is accommodating foreign refugees in her grand house – now known as 'The Sanctuary' – a lesson to the country as a whole.

A constant feature in these wartime films and plays, the eccentric woman became representative of the supposed British spirit, at times even Churchillian. In the films she made a little later on, Rutherford's leadership, although remaining endearing, was more open to mockery and yet more strongly feminised. When the eccentric woman meets an eccentric man in a battle for control, it is the eccentric woman who invariably wins. The opponent might be a theatre director who pours scorn on the play she has written (as in *Curtain Up*, 1952) or a headmaster who expects a headmistress to fall into line during a crisis. John Dighton's popular farce *The Happiest Days of Your Life*, which opened at the Apollo on 29 March 1948 and was later filmed, takes place in a boys' boarding school. The time is presumably the present but clearly harks back to the recent wartime past. A girls' school is billeted by an incompetent 'Ministry of Evacuation' on a boys' establishment; Rutherford, who is given top billing, is the headmistress, Miss Whitchurch, 'a formidable woman of about fifty, severely dressed in travelling clothes'. When her transplanted school is threatened by a visit from a group of parents, she has to conceal the fact that the sexes are living together in close proximity. At first at severe odds with her opposite number, the head of the boys' school which is undergoing an inspection, she eventually links up with him to outwit their common enemies with a series of lies and increasingly chaotic semi-military manoeuvres.

Much of this is in the tradition of Will Hay's schoolmaster sketches and Ian Hay's comedy *Housemaster* (1936, filmed in 1938). Indeed, as the critic J. C. Trewin said, one can confidently expect the boys to end up at St Olde's, the Oxford college in *Charley's Aunt* (Trewin, 1949: 10). Nevertheless, the play has its own distinct frame of reference. While

38 A montage of images from *The Happiest Days of Your Life*, 1948.

harking back to the wartime period of compulsory evacuation of children, it mocks the officious bureaucracy that for some marked the early years of the welfare state and the 'men from the ministry'. 'Muddling through' is, of course, the underlying motif. The film, released in 1950, makes the post-war environment much more explicit, with references to rationing, the black market, petrol coupons and nationalisation of the railways. The kitchen staff walk out, a reminder that this was also an age of strikes. When Rutherford takes the initiative, she is still like a military or political leader, either 'battle axe or Amazon' (a phrase that occurs), although capable of blackmail. In the film version the part of the headmaster was played by Alastair Sim, which pitted her masculine forcefulness, however manic, against his feminine dithering. At one point Sim actually becomes her secretary, taking down dictation. In this respect *Happiest Days* looked forward to the popular St Trinian's series and, in fact, its opening titles are by the cartoonist Ronald Searle. At the end of the film, very different from the play, Rutherford and Sim are romantically hand in hand. She mentions going to work on the 'ground-nuts scheme': the famously ill-fated project developed by the Labour government to grow peanuts on a massive scale in Africa. Their joint future, although a touching thought, seems less than assured.

Alastair Sim's wife, Naomi, recalls the comic partnership between Rutherford and her husband in this way:

> They matched each other perfectly during their scenes together when you felt that their mutual anger might cause them to ignite at any minute. I always felt that those two had a lot in common in that their playing of anything at all was so highly individual. You couldn't employ a Margaret Rutherford 'type' or an Alastair Sim 'type'. (Sim, 1987: 132)

Her point is astute. As an actress Rutherford almost always managed to take the lead by responding to others, acting alongside or sometimes against established male actors such as Sim and Robert Morley, as well as younger men, up-and-coming comedians such as Frankie Howerd and Norman Wisdom, who carried music-hall stereotypes over to radio, cinema and, at least for a while, television. An air of gender competition, though usually resolved, permeates the comedy at the level of performance.

Teachers and other authority figures often feature in these later films. In *Passport to Pimlico* (1949) Rutherford's Professor Hatton-Jones, Professor of History at London University, is an authoritative bluestocking obsessed with her subject, who is required to deliver a lecture which she does in fine declamatory style, making her both 'dotty' and brilliant at one and the same time. In *The Runaway Bus* (1954) Rutherford is an adherent of 'positive thought' who pronounces that 'negative thought can do nothing. Positive thought can do anything.' At the same time the roles became increasingly benevolent, sometimes downright philanthropic. In *Miss Robin Hood* (1952) Rutherford is a spinster schoolmistress, Heather Honey, who runs a school in Hampstead and wants to free children from boring teaching, and organises resistance against a wicked press baron determined to fire a popular children's writer who, like Honey, believes in a 'kind, sunshiny world'. What is perhaps the best example of the genre, *Aunt Clara* (1954), has a pre-credit sequence showing film of the Blitz, but turns out to be a version of the good angel myth. Aunt Clara (Rutherford) inherits the estate of her corrupt uncle Simon and sets about redistributing it among those who he had abused in life. The underlying joke is that as Clara investigates the shady world of his past, so she is obliged to appear less socially perceptive than she really is. In the end she manages to help some ill-treated racing greyhounds (Simon was a gambler) and a household of prostitutes (Simon was a regular patron). Terminally ill – a fact she has kept from others – Aunt Clara has a 'saintly' death, and in the closing sequence appears complete with angelic wings. Even in the Norman Wisdom vehicle *Just my Luck* (1957), Rutherford's character is Mrs Dooley, a rich Irish widow who lives with an ape and an elephant among other creatures, races her horse merely for exercise, not for money, and calls her pets her 'children'. By the end of the 1950s the war had begun to be presented not so much as a recent reality as an increasingly distant backdrop. *I'm All Right Jack* (1959), directed by John and Roy Boulting, a famous satire in its day, opens with documentary footage from 1945 featuring Churchill. Rutherford is the aunt of the upper-class ingénu who has found himself involved in a conflict between trades unionists and their bosses (both equally corrupt). Aunt Dolly hates the working class – 'all muscles and sweat' – as well as the 'horrid unions', but nevertheless bonds with the wife of the main union leader. Female common sense almost wins out, though not quite. 'What a nation we are when stirred!': Aunt Dolly's patriotic belief is not enough to counteract the concluding vision of national chaos.

Certain basic structural principles are at work throughout these films, constituents of a national self-image, which includes, of course, relationships between genders and classes. Invariably there is a romantic young couple, too young to have served in the war, bright, energetic and sincere, whose minor sub-plot carries on in tandem with a farcical main story. There is frequently a comic bureaucracy of some kind, a genial swipe at the red tape of the new welfare state, against which Rutherford is likely to be pitted. Nevertheless, it would be wrong to see her career as given over entirely to such engagingly 'dotty' and socially anarchic roles during this period. She participated in the fashion for contemporary French drama, Anouilh in particular, and doubled with Sybil Thorndike as the White Queen in a dramatisation of *Alice in Wonderland* in 1944. In 1945 she appeared in Ivor Novello's wildly romantic *Perchance to Dream*. As a film actress, she had by the 1960s achieved a level of international stardom that led to vignettes in major releases including *The V.I.P.s* (1963) for which she received an Academy Award for best supporting actress, and Chaplin's *The Countess from Hong Kong* (1967).

It was at this latish period in her career that Rutherford also took on stage roles, all of them unaccommodated women of one kind or another, associated with Restoration and eighteenth-century comedy. This was a repertoire that had steadily gained in respect and popularity in the course of the century. There were four roles in particular: Lady Wishfort in Congreve's *The Way of the World* (Lyric Hammersmith, 1953, and Saville, 1956); Mrs Candour in Sheridan's *The School for Scandal* (Haymarket, 1962); Mrs Heidelberg in *The Clandestine Marriage* by George Colman the Younger and David Garrick (Chichester, 1966); and Mrs Malaprop in Sheridan's *The Rivals* (Haymarket, 1966). Although comic, these women have it in common that they are either outside the family altogether or uncomfortably within it, the difference from her more recent film parts being that they all lack the element of generosity. This caused problems in reception and probably in Rutherford's actual performances as well.

Her Lady Wishfort of 1953 was generally praised, although it is clear from the reviews that she was dogged with a reputation as well as a physique. Kenneth Tynan's celebrated notice in the *Evening Standard* (Tynan, 1953: 11) carried the headline 'Miss Rutherford's Chin Steals the Show'. Time and again critical metaphors tell the same comic story, betraying an obsession with physical appearance above all else: 'like a marquee in a high wind' (Barber, 1953: 3), 'a Tenniel drawing of the Red Queen repeated in delectable sugar candy' (Anon., 1953: 2), 'a splendidly padded windmill' (Keown, 1953: 305). When she returned to the role in 1956, the pivotal year of *Look Back in Anger* and of the visit to London by Brecht's Berliner Ensemble, critics were now more wary of the mixture of scenic luxury and mildly camp innuendo favoured in the West End productions of H. M. Tennent. Along with other members of the company, Rutherford suffered in her turn. For Milton Shulman, never a great admirer, 'Miss Margaret Rutherford, looking like an abandoned stone quarry as Lady Wishfort, has some extremely comic moments but lacks a little of the healthy lasciviousness the part demands' (Shulman, 1956: 12). Even more damagingly, her film successes now threatened her integrity on stage. So, for instance, 'Margaret Rutherford, though quite unlike the scheming Lady Wishfort of Congreve's cruel imagining, cleverly substitutes in place of that greedy old fribble her own well-loved study of a hard-breathing headmistress' (Hope-Wallace, 1956: 5).

When she undertook the gossipy Mrs Candour in *The School for Scandal* in 1962 in yet another Tennent production directed by Gielgud, Tynan, unexpectedly tolerant of the show's typically 'spirited opulence', did manage to find darker depths in Rutherford's performance and chose a remarkably shocking simile to match the role's own *double entendres*: 'Margaret Rutherford as Mrs. Candour, warming to the task of character assassination like a midwife beneath whose benevolent exterior there beats an abortionist's heart' (Tynan, 1962: 28). So, for one critic at least, it does seem that on this occasion, and in this part, Rutherford did manage to achieve a level of malice – and bawdy – that she was rarely called upon to risk. (Interestingly, she had first attempted the part back in 1932 in a small off West End production.) Nevertheless, her final classic roles on stage were in general less fortuitous, a combination of ill-health, increasing age and antiquated production styles making her vulnerable to critical impatience. A rougher kind of realism was beginning to replace what Tynan called the 'high polite comedy' of the repertoire previously associated with the Restoration. The signal production was William Gaskill's *The Recruiting Officer* at the National Theatre in 1963. At Chichester in 1966, in her seventies, she played opposite Alastair Sim in *The Clandestine Marriage* by George Colman and David Garrick, which, although originating from 1766, has a good deal in common with Restoration comedy. Once again Rutherford played an aunt, the snobbish Mrs Heidelberg. But a perception of datedness pervades the critical appreciation

Just as there is no definitive performance, so there is no definitive response. Nonetheless, an overall atmosphere of irritation and disquiet begins to characterise these 1960s reviews. At a time when – thanks to the Royal Shakespeare Company and the new National Theatre – the idea of an integrated company was dominant, unashamedly star-based productions looked unbalanced. As styles and conditions changed, so new demands were made of the actor. No performer, however idiosyncratic, is ever immune to this cruel rule and, in a way, Rutherford became victim of her own eminence. She is even said to have curtsied to meet the applause at her first entrance, which was very old-fashioned behaviour indeed (Barker, 1966: 7). By contrast film critics tended to enjoy her presence quite separately from the narrative in which she was appearing. The

Miss Marple films of the early 1960s were very good box office, even if Agatha Christie is said to have been unhappy with the farcical element in Rutherford's interpretation.

To suggest that Margaret Rutherford in her prime belonged to her age, part as much as product, implies no disrespect, nor does it deny her capacity to entertain even today. Fortunately some of her most authentic work between, say, 1938 and 1959 remains preserved on film and in the words of her more discriminating critics. Hers was a unique, at times heroic, individual achievement and yet, in addition, in the roles for which she was best known, she left a record of changing social conditions as they affected single women in the mid-twentieth century. Initially a left-over, the much maligned yet unavoidable 'spinster' of the 1920s, in the 1940s she took on characters whose conduct was determined by the immediacy of conflict; in the aftermath, the 1950s, she came to stand for a form of moral intransigence. Although her voice had a class inflection – and class was at the heart of many of the comedies in which she appeared – it took its moral authority from female resilience. Often frustrated, her gestures were always exact.

References

Agate, James (1938), 'Irish Without Tears', *Sunday Times*, 5 June, p. 4.
Agate, James (1941), 'Mr. Coward's New Play', *Sunday Times*, 6 July, p. 2.
Anon. (1953), 'Lyric Theatre, Hammersmith', *The Times*, 20 February, p. 2.
Anon. (1956), 'Saville Theatre', *The Times*, 7 December, p. 3.
Avery, C. R. (1935), 'Hervey House', *Observer*, 19 May, p. 15.
Barber, John (1953), 'Pamela – Rogue in Gossamer', *Daily Express*, 20 February, p. 3.
Barker, Clive, and Maggie B. Gale, eds (2000), *British Theatre between the Wars, 1918–1939*, Cambridge: Cambridge University Press.
Barker, Felix (1953), 'At the Theatre. Fine Matters', *Observer*, 22 February, p. 11.
Barker, Felix (1966), 'The "News" Critics', *Evening News*, 2 June, p. 7.
Brown, Ivor (1935), 'Last Night's Play', *Observer*, 3 November, p. 22.
Brown, Ivor (1938), 'This Week's Theatres. Spring Meeting', *Observer*, 5 June, p. 11.
Brown, Ivor (1939), 'This Week's Theatre. The Importance of Being Earnest', *Observer*, 20 August, p. 9.
Brown, Ivor (1941), 'At the Play', *Observer*, 6 July, p. 7.
Bryden, Ronald (1966a), 'Bulls-eye at the Rag-bag Junction', *Observer*, 5 June, p. 25.
Bryden, Ronald (1966b), 'Villains of a Vicious Circus', *Observer*, 9 October, p. 24.

Darlington, W. A. (1956), 'Kay Hammond Unsuccessful as Millamant', *Daily Telegraph*, 7 December, p. 10.

Farrell, Molly J., and John Perry (1938), *Spring Meeting*, London: Collins.

Feigel, Lara (2010), *Literature, Cinema and Politics 1930–1945: Reading Between the Frames*, Edinburgh: Edinburgh University Press.

Gale, Maggie B. (1996), *West End Women: Women and the London Stage 1918–1962*, London: Routledge.

Hobson, Harold (1953), 'Player's Hurdle', *Sunday Times*, 22 February, p. 9.

Hope-Wallace, Philip (1953), '"The Way of the World". Revival by Gielgud', *Manchester Guardian*, 20 February, p. 5.

Hope-Wallace, Philip (1956), 'Congreve at the Saville', *Manchester Guardian*, 8 December, p. 5.

Hope-Wallace, Philip (1966), '*The Rivals* at the Haymarket', *Guardian*, 7 October.

Huggett, Richard (1989), *Binkie, Eminence Grise of the West End Theatre 1933–1973*, London: Hodder and Stoughton.

Jeffreys, Sheila (1985), *The Spinster and Her Enemies: Feminism and Sexuality 1880–1930*, London: Pandora.

Jones, Mervyn (1959), 'South American Casino', *Observer*, 7 June, p. 22.

Keown, Eric (1953), 'At the Play', *Punch*, 4 March, p. 305.

Keown, Eric (1956), *Margaret Rutherford*, London: Rockliff.

Kretzmer, Herbert (1966), 'Rutherford, Richardson ... a Must for the Devotees', *Daily Express*, 7 October, p. 4.

Macnab, Geoffrey (2000), *Searching for Stars: Rethinking British Cinema*, London: Cassell.

Merriman, Andy (2009), *Margaret Rutherford: Dreadnought with Good Manners*, London: Aurum Press.

Nicholson, Virginia (2007), *Singled Out: How Two Million Women Survived Without Men After the First World War*, London: Viking.

Rutherford, Margaret, and Gwen Robyns (1972), *Margaret Rutherford, An Autobiography as told to Gwen Robyns*, London: W.H. Allen.

Seyler, Athene, with Stephen Haggard (2013), *The Craft of Comedy. The 21st Century Edition*, ed. Robert Barton, London and New York: Routledge.

Shulman, Milton (1956), 'Mr Clements Loses his Touch', *Evening Standard*, 7 December, p. 12.

Sim, Naomi (1987), *Dance and Skylark: Fifty Years with Alastair Sim*, London: Bloomsbury.

Sutherland, Lucie (2007), 'The Actress and the Profession: Training in England in the Twentieth Century', in Maggie B. Gale and John Stokes, eds, *The Cambridge Companion to the Actress*, Cambridge: Cambridge University Press, pp. 95–115.

Tóibín, Colm (2011), 'The Importance of Aunts' (in the nineteenth-century novel), *London Review of Books*, 33.6, 17 March, pp. 13–19.

Trewin, J. C. (1949), *Plays of the Year, 1948–49*, London: Paul Elek.

Tynan, Kenneth (1953), 'Miss Rutherford's Chin Steals the Show', *Evening Standard*, 20 February, p. 11. Repr. in *Curtains: Selections from the Drama Criticism and Related Writings*, London: Longmans, 1961, pp. 38-9.

Tynan, Kenneth (1956), 'Second-Best Bed', *Observer*, 9 December, p. 11.

Tynan, Kenneth (1962), 'Turnout for the First Eleven', *Observer*, 8 April, p. 28.

Archives

Margaret Rutherford Biographical File, Victoria and Albert Museum, London

Powell, Dilys, et al., 'The Art of Margaret Rutherford', broadcast on Radio 3 on 10 December 1975. Sound recording available at Sound Archive, British Library NP2653

Index

actress 1, 4, 6, 7, 9–10, 13–14, 17–20, 22–9, 31–40, 42–3, 47–50, 62–4, 66–72, 74–5, 77–83, 87–91, 94–8, 100–16, 118, 121, 127–8, 130–3, 135–6, 138, 140–4, 148–52, 154–60, 166–9, 173, 175, 186–9, 191, 194–8, 206, 211–14, 245–6, 251, 259, 264, 268, 273–80, 286, 288–9, 295–6, 300, 302, 306
Actresses' Franchise League (AFL) 4, 6, 14, 15, 50–2, 103, 118–21, 126–7, 129–33, 135–6, 198, 212, 214
Alexander, George 2, 48, 53, 69, 74–5, 89–93, 142
   St James's Theatre 33, 69, 73–6, 82–3, 90, 92, 130, 172
Alexander Technique 197
Allan, Maud 106, 138, 152, 156–7
   Salome (Oscar Wilde) 138–9, 157
   A Vision of Salomé 139
Anglin, Margaret 164–8, 170–3, 175–8, 185–7, 189
archives and archiving 3, 10–12, 18, 21, 26, 29–31, 37, 44, 61, 98, 108, 229, 231–2, 237–8, 265, 270
Asche, Oscar 173, 191–3, 196–211
   Chu Chin Chow 191, 204–8
Ashwell, Lena 52, 71, 119–21
Australia 163–73, 175–9, 181–6, 191, 193, 198–202, 207–10, 275
autobiography 17–18, 20, 22–6, 28–9, 31–4, 37, 71, 199, 201, 209–11, 262–3, 265, 268, 272, 275, 281
   autobiographical 4, 10, 17–19, 28, 37, 70–1, 81, 265, 282

memoir 4, 34, 69–73, 75, 77, 79, 81–2, 152, 154, 216, 218, 220, 222, 228, 234

The Belle of Mayfair 23
Benson, Frank 79, 193
Bensusan, Inez 123–4, 134
biography 30, 34, 43, 65
Bourne, Adeline 52, 124–6, 132–3
Braithwaite, Lillian 106, 112, 120, 127, 286, 289
Bratton, Jacky 7, 11–13, 20–1, 47, 71
Brayton, Lily 9, 173, 176–8, 191–211
British Broadcasting Corporation (BBC) 262–3, 265–6, 269–72, 274–6, 279

Canada 253, 275
celebrity 1, 9, 17–19, 22, 24–6, 32, 69–70, 83, 100–1, 104, 107, 110–14, 119, 143–5, 149–52, 194, 198–9, 205–8, 216, 219, 220, 235
charity 10, 33, 86, 94–7, 100–4, 109–14, 129, 201, 206, 248, 296
   Actors' Benevolent Fund 52, 95, 119
   British Red Cross 42, 59, 129
cinema 8, 46, 163–4, 182, 186, 210, 243–4, 246–52, 254, 300
circus 228–36
Coffin, Hayden 142
Collier, Constance 120, 250–1, 253
comic performance 289, 291, 300–3
   monologues 120
   sketch 128
Constanduros, Mabel 2, 262–85
   The Buggins Family 262–3, 265–6, 273, 280

Constanduros, Mabel (*cont.*)
  Grandma Buggins 263, 266–7
  Mrs Buggins 262, 271, 273, 280
  Mr and Mrs Sparkes 276–7, 280
  Shreds and Patches 262–3
Cooper, Gladys 2, 24, 31–7, 127, 131, 151, 250–1, 253, 255, 288
copyright 140, 143–4, 147, 150, 152, 265–6, 271–2, 276
costume 25, 52, 95, 100, 145–9, 151, 156–7, 174–8, 195, 198–202, 205–6, 209, 220, 226, 229–34, 250, 286, 297
Courtneidge, Cicely 24, 106, 114
Coward, Noël 42–4, 46, 58, 185, 288–9, 292, 294–6
  Blithe Spirit 294
Craig, Edith 4, 6, 45, 47, 49–50, 58, 75, 246
Craig, Edward Gordon 45, 49, 58, 173

The Dairymaids (Robert Courtneidge) 24
Dare, Phyllis 23, 26, 32–3, 106, 108, 113, 150, 153–4
  From School to Stage 23
Dare, Zena 24
  The Sunshine Girl 24
Davis, Tracy C. 5, 7, 19, 36, 49, 191
Winifred Dolan 2, 69–88
domestic 2, 19, 20, 22, 26, 32, 111, 266, 268, 281, 292

Edwardian 1–2, 25, 81, 102, 109, 138, 147, 191, 199
Elliott, Gertrude 123–5, 128–9
employment 2–3, 7, 9, 10, 12, 23–4, 69–70, 72–4, 77, 82–3, 119–20, 141, 143, 166, 217–18, 245, 248, 274, 288
Enthoven, Gabrielle 4, 42, 44, 50, 52, 62
  Ellen Young 42, 55, 57

feminine 176, 186, 224, 226–7, 231, 233, 235–6, 242, 243, 248
femininity 168, 176, 195, 216–18, 224–7, 229, 231, 234–6, 248–9, 279
film 2–3, 9–10, 17–18, 22, 33, 57, 81, 111, 115, 164, 166–8, 170, 182–3, 185–6, 189, 207
First World War 1–2, 24, 31, 38, 42, 46, 96, 118, 124, 130, 165–7, 178, 204, 256, 266, 289–90
  refugees 133
  War Refugees Committee 58
Fogerty, Elsie 269–70, 280
Frohman, Charles 141–2, 175
fundraising 10, 94–6, 100–1, 113–16, 125, 127, 129, 131, 248, 256

Gaiety Girl 17, 24, 32, 107–8, 113, 143, 145–6, 148, 209, 288
Gale, Maggie B. 4, 10, 12, 71, 153, 291
Gardner, Viv 5, 10, 23, 28–9, 113, 130, 143
gender 5–6, 8–9, 11, 19, 21, 33, 73, 75, 97, 139, 166, 169, 176, 186, 194–8, 200, 202, 211, 216, 218, 224–7, 229, 231, 235–9, 243, 279, 295, 300–1
Gielgud, John 30, 289, 292, 303
Gielgud, Val 274, 276
Gledhill, Christine 8, 243, 254
Granville-Barker, Harley 26–31, 104, 108
Grey, Katherine 163, 166–9, 174–5, 178

Hall, Radclyffe 43, 46, 52
  Well of Loneliness 46
Hamilton, Cicely 4, 50, 52, 123–4, 173
  Diana of Dobsons 173
  How the Vote Was Won 132
  A Pageant of Great Women 50

Index

Harraden, Beatrice 51, 124
  Lady Geraldine's Speech 51
Hicks, Seymour 23, 141, 153

interwar 1, 46, 130, 217, 265, 268,
    279–80, 282, 291
Irving, Henry 43, 48, 73, 83, 242, 252

Kelly, Veronica 5, 9, 12, 193, 197–8,
    201, 202
Kendall, Madge 86, 131, 244
Kingston, Gertrude 52, 119, 127–8
Knoblauch (Knoblock), Edward 64,
    200

Labour 3, 5–10, 12, 18–23, 28–9, 34, 73,
    95–8, 100, 104, 121, 154, 176,
    193, 216, 266, 300
  strike 172–3, 179, 223, 299
law and legislation 2–3, 10, 30, 139–41,
    144, 147, 152–3, 168, 183
  Copyright Act 53
  Disqualification (Removal) Act
    1919 2, 31
  Education Acts (1870, 1902, 1918) 78
  Married Women's Property Act
    1893 139
  Representation of the People Act
    1918 1, 13
Leitzel, Lillian 2, 216–36
lesbian 45–6, 258
  'Cult of the Clitoris' 138–9
Lewis, Jane 2–3

Mander, Raymond and Joe
    Mitchenson 18, 108–9
  Mander and Mitchenson Collection
    6, 62, 108–9
masculinity 197, 233, 279
Mayo, Winifred 125, 131–2, 134, 212
McCarthy, Lillah 25–7, 30, 32, 36–7,
    43, 52, 107–8, 127
  Myself and My Friends 26, 29–31

Millar, Gertie 110, 146–52
Miller, Ruby 18–19, 32, 36, 131
Moore, Decima 119, 125, 131–2
Moore, Eva 119, 120–1, 125, 129, 131–2,
    134
musical comedy 17–18, 23–4, 32, 102,
    108, 110, 144, 150, 166, 168, 172,
    183, 185, 199, 204
music hall 18, 56–7, 107–8, 242, 264,
    300

Negri, Pola 17, 164, 183
networks 3–5, 42–9, 51–5, 73–4, 77,
    108, 131, 133, 245
nostalgia 18, 29, 109, 248
Novello, Ivor 24, 250–1, 302
  The Bohemian Girl 246, 248–53,
    255–6
  King's Rhapsody 24

Orientalism 182, 199–200
  Cairo 207–8, 211
  Chu Chin Chow 191, 204–8
  Kismet 200–2, 204–5, 213

Paxton, Naomi 3–4, 6, 9, 19, 50, 118
photograph 2–3, 11, 20, 25–6, 29,
    32–3, 44–5, 48, 61–2, 70,
    100, 103, 108–9, 113, 140,
    143–52, 154–5, 195–6, 220–1,
    229–32, 242, 247, 249, 254,
    280, 297
photographic 26, 32, 48, 109, 112,
    143–7, 150–1
photography 2
Pilcher, Velona 60–1
  The Searcher 60–1
Pioneer Players 50–1, 55–6
playwright/playwriting 6–7, 26, 32, 57,
    104, 120, 123, 291
postcard 3, 23, 25, 31–2, 108–9, 143–7,
    152, 165, 179, 248
Price, Nancy 47, 52, 55

professional 1–10, 12–14, 17–39, 42, 47, 49, 51, 54, 57, 69–75, 77–92, 94–5, 97–8, 102–4, 108, 110–12, 114, 118–19, 123, 133, 140–1, 143, 147, 149, 151–2, 156, 158, 164, 166, 170, 187, 205, 209–11, 218–20, 233–6, 243, 251, 265–6, 268, 271–4, 278, 281–4, 286, 289, 291

radio 2, 163–4, 166, 174, 185, 262–6, 268, 270, 272, 274–6, 278–9, 281–2, 300
Reeve, Ada 2, 17–19, 36–7
Robins, Elizabeth 4, 120, 123, 131, 138
Robins, Gertrude 98–9, 103, 107, 124
Rutherford, Margaret 286–306
  The Happiest Days of Your Life 298–300
  The VIPs 302

St John, Christopher 4, 47, 56
  How the Vote was Won 132
salary (wage) 19, 54, 142, 179, 180, 194, 264
Schweitzer, Marlis 14, 101, 165
Second World War 1, 36, 42, 58, 266, 268, 296
Sennett, Maud Arncliffe 126, 130, 133, 135, 137, 213
Shakespeare, William
  Antony and Cleopatra 173, 201
  As You Like It 173, 254
  Julius Caesar 210
  Macbeth 80, 83–4, 86, 173, 242
  The Merchant of Venice 248, 254
  The Merry Wives of Windsor 249
  A Midsummer Night's Dream 194
  The Taming of the Shrew 196
  Twelfth Night 194

Shaw, George Bernard 27–30, 45, 123, 168–71, 175–7, 186, 244, 288, 294
  Arms and the Man 175, 177
  Candida 176
  Fanny's First Play 28
  The Man of Destiny 176
  Mrs Warren's Profession 123
Six Point Group 13, 131
The Stage Society 52
Starr, Muriel 9, 163–72, 175, 178–86
  The Garden of Allah 167, 170, 183
Stokes, John 5, 10, 286
suffrage 6, 19, 28, 46, 51, 102, 118–22, 125–6, 130–3
  The Suffrage Girl 102
Suffragette 33, 119, 121, 176

Terry, Ellen 2, 4, 9, 42, 45–8, 63, 66, 73, 83, 242–61
  The Bohemian Girl 246, 248–53, 255–6
  Ellen Terry and Her Secret Self 45
  Her Greatest Performance 246–7, 253
  The Merchant of Venice 248–54
  Smallhythe 45, 50
  Victory and Peace 247–8
Theatrical Ladies' Guild 4, 54, 95, 119
Thorne, Sarah 49, 69
Theatre Royal, Margate 49, 69
Time and Tide magazine 4, 13, 266
tours and touring 9, 18, 23–7, 29, 31, 36, 38, 69, 76, 86, 106, 130, 163–7, 169–78, 180–6, 193, 198–9, 201–2, 208–9, 216, 242, 253, 255, 275
training 24, 27, 69, 74, 77, 79, 85, 88, 164, 166–7, 175, 197, 269, 288
  drama school 2, 69–72, 77–83, 88, 269, 288–9, 302
  Central School of Speech and Drama 79, 269
  (Royal) Academy of Dramatic Art 79, 289

Index

Tree, Herbert Beerbohm 48, 53, 79, 142, 194, 196, 199, 205
Trilby 288

Vanbrugh, Irene 37, 52, 83, 124, 128, 150, 172, 289
Vanbrugh, Violet 49, 52
Victoria and Albert Museum (V&A) 42–3, 45, 50–4, 70, 74
Victorian 2, 7, 47, 100, 109, 111, 163, 191, 196, 199, 225, 249

Webster, Margaret 125
West End (London) 2, 28, 47, 69–73, 77–9, 81–5, 88, 100, 108, 126, 130, 142, 144, 164, 168, 197, 199, 274, 297, 302–3
Whitty, May 124–5, 127, 129–32
Wilde, Oscar 42, 45–6, 48–9, 138–9, 141, 294
Women's Freedom League 122, 132
Women's Social and Political Union (WSPU) 118, 132

EU authorised representative for GPSR:
Easy Access System Europe, Mustamäe tee 50,
10621 Tallinn, Estonia
gpsr.requests@easproject.com

www.ingramcontent.com/pod-product-compliance
Ingram Content Group UK Ltd.
Pitfield, Milton Keynes, MK11 3LW, UK
UKHW032240100425
1771IPUK00001B/1